PRAISE FOR LIBBY F̶...

The Ellie Foreman Series

"A powerful tale... Foreman's pluck and grit married to Hellmann's solid storytelling should win a growing audience..."
—*Publishers Weekly*

"Libby Fischer Hellmann has already joined an elite club: Chicago mystery writers who not only inhabit the environment but also give it a unique flavor."
—*Chicago Tribune*

"A traditional mystery with a modern edge... the author's confidence shows from beginning to end... refreshing as soft serve ice cream on a hot summer night."
—*Crimespree Magazine*

The Georgia Davis Series

"There's a new no-nonsense female private detective in town: Georgia Davis, a former cop who is tough and smart enough to give even the legendary V.I. Warshawski a run for her money."
—*Chicago Tribune*

"Georgia Davis works the affluent suburbs north of Chicago, fertile territory for crime that's lain fallow far too long. Davis' arrival on the mean streets is long overdue."
—Sara Paretsky, author of the V.I. Warshawski Mysteries

Set the Night on Fire

"A top-rate standalone thriller that taps into the antiwar protests of the 1960s and 70s."
—*Publishers Weekly*

"Haunting... Rarely have history, mystery, and political philosophy blended so beautifully... could easily end up on the required reading list in college-level American History classes."
—*Mystery Scene Magazine*

A Bitter Veil

"The Iranian revolution provides the backdrop for this meticulously researched, fast-paced stand-alone... A significant departure from the author's Chicago-based Ellie Foreman and Georgia Davis mystery series, this political thriller will please established fans and newcomers alike."
—*Publishers Weekly*

"Hellmann crafts a tragically beautiful story... both subtle and vibrant... never sacrificing the quality of her storytelling. Instead, the message drives the psychological and emotional conflict painting a bleak and heart wrenching tale that will stick with the reader long after they finish the book."
—*Crimespree Magazine*

Havana Lost

"A riveting historical thriller... This multigenerational page-turner is packed with intrigue and shocking plot twists."
—*Booklist*

War, Spies, and Bobby Sox

"Libby Hellmann's prose is powerful. Every part of her WW II era yarns are methodically researched, taut, twist-filled and colorful with well developed supporting characters. A gripping performance."
—Charles J. Masters, author of *Gliderman of Neptune, The American D-Day Glider Attack*

A Bend in the River

"Gripping...Hellmann smoothly integrates into her harrowing narrative such aspects of the conflict as guerilla warfare, spying, Agent Orange, reeducation camps, and boat people. This passionate story of survival has staying power."
—*Publishers Weekly*

"Sisters Mai and Tam's very different paths to survival in war-torn Vietnam provide a compelling, page turning story. Hellmann brings history to visceral, tangible life by shining a light on torture from all sides of the conflict and shows the devastating effects on Vietnamese citizens. Questions of morality and justice are subtle in the point of view of each of the sisters who become different, yet equally sympathetic people in a trauma-filled world."
—Amy Alessio, *Book Reporter*

"Hellmann's simple but elegant prose conveys lush and colorful settings and makes us thirsty to see Vietnam with our own eyes...A Bend in the River is a thought-provoking read. It offers interesting nuance and added depth to a war we thought we knew but maybe did not entirely understand."
—*BookTrib*

A BEND IN THE RIVER

LIBBY FISCHER HELLMANN

THE RED HERRINGS PRESS
CHICAGO, IL

ALSO BY LIBBY FISCHER HELLMANN:

HISTORICAL STANDALONES

War, Spies and Bobby Sox

Havana Lost

A Bitter Veil

Set the Night on Fire

THE GEORGIA DAVIS SERIES

High Crimes

Nobody's Child

ToxiCity

Doubleback

Easy Innocence

THE ELLIE FOREMAN SERIES

Jump Cut

A Shot to Die For

An Image of Death

A Picture of Guilt

An Eye for Murder

NOVELLAS

The Incidental Spy

P.O.W.

The Last Page

Nice Girl Does Noir (short stories)

Chicago Blues (editor)

ISBN (Print): 978-1-938733-67-3
ISBN (Ebook): 978-1-938733-68-0
ISBN (Audiobook): 978-1-938733-69-7
Library of Congress Control Number: 2020912362

To Angela. Our finest adventures are yet to come.

MAP OF VIETNAM, CIRCA 1968

MAIN CHARACTERS

MAIN CHARACTERS		
Tâm	"dtum"	
Mai	my	
Quang	kwah-ng	Fisherman's father
Phong	fow-ng	Fisherman
Cô Cúc	koh cook (upward pitch)	Owner of the Saigon Café
Dr. Đường Châu Hằng	zuh-ng; chow; hah-ng	Doctor who enlists Tâm
Hạnh	hang (downward pitch)	Mai's roommate & coworker at the Stardust Lounge
Thạc	dack (downward pitch)	Owners of the Stardust Lounge
Biên	be-yen	Tâm's first Party name
Hiền	hee-yen (downward pitch)	One of Tâm's fellow trainees
Đắc	dah-ck (upward pitch)	Tâm's fellow truck driver
Diệp Hồng Bảo	dee-yep (downward pitch); how-ng (downward pitch); bow (mid-low pitch)	Tâm's lover
Đêm Nguyệt	day-em; witt (downward pitch)	Mai's son
Phan Trực Vinh	fahn; chuck (upward pitch); ving	Mai's lover
Linh	ling	Tâm's Party name when she goes to the Cao Đài
Yến	een (upward pitch)	Cao Đài temple desk girl
Đức	duuk (upward pitch)	Yến's cousin
Bà Thảo	bah (downward pitch); tow (mid-low pitch)	Tâm's landlady when she is with the Cao Đài
Dũng	Zuung (upward pitch)	Da Lat farm owner

PART I
VIETNAM, 1968

Tâm and Mai

CHAPTER 1

TÂM

Is there a warning the moment before life shatters into pieces? A minute shift in the light? The chirr of a monkey. Perhaps a heaviness in the air that tastes like disaster. For Trang Tâm and her sister, Linh Mai, washing their family's clothes in the river, the warning might have been a barely perceptible scent wafting toward them. Perfumed soap mixed with sweat. Unfamiliar. Foreign.

Or perhaps there was no warning at all. Absorbed in their task, the sisters squatted on a narrow strip of shore, scrubbing shirts with their brushes. They slapped heavier items against the rocks, then rinsed everything in the waters of the Mekong. The clothes would dry quickly. The hottest part of the year was approaching, and the combination of summer heat and the monsoons would produce an indolent lethargy that made even washing clothes a burden. Though it was only March, the sisters lifted their hair off their necks to catch the breeze.

Tâm, at seventeen, used her *nón lá* as a hamper for the clean clothes. At the moment it held only two pairs of tiny pants belonging to her little brother. Hùng Sáng, an unplanned surprise five years earlier, was now the prince of the family. According to their parents, no boy was as handsome, as talented, as lucky. With his arrival the girls' status declined. They had become afterthoughts, to be married off quickly. Sáng should not be burdened with his sisters' care. When he grew up, he would have enough to do for his own family and his parents.

Tâm wiped sweat from her brow. Mai, three years younger, nattered on, but Tâm only half listened. She was about to graduate from the Catholic school two villages away, and she was wondering how she would continue her studies. Where would she find the money to pay for university? What would her parents say when she confessed that was her goal?

"I'm sure you know him. Lanh Phúc. He's handsome. His is the wealthiest family in their village," Mai said. "Their home has a real roof. And windows. His father makes sampans . . ." Mai giggled. "I think he likes me, Chị Tâm. I hope Mama and Papa will agree to a match. I can already picture our wedding. Of course, we will honor the Rose Silk Thread God, but it will be modern too. We will have music to dance, and—"

Tâm cut in. "Mai, you can be a silly girl. Dreaming about weddings and dancing? This is a man you may live with the rest of your life. Have you ever shared a conversation? Talked to him about his future, *his* dreams?" She twisted water out her father's shirt and dropped it into the conical hat. "All I hear is that he is the son of a wealthy man and he is handsome."

Mai was the beauty of the family, delicate and tiny, with large black eyes, silky black hair, and soft skin that glowed white, even in shadow. Tâm had seen the longing on village boys' faces when she passed. Her parents would have no problem arranging a match for her. Tâm was taller, leaner, and while her face had the same classic features as Mai's, they were arranged differently. Her eyes did not appear to be as large; her nose more pronounced, her skin darker. She was attractive in her own way, but she wasn't a beauty. Although older, she wasn't waiting for an arranged marriage. She wasn't interested. She wanted to study plants: their growth, foliage, colors, blossoms, how they added to their environment or not. Her Catholic science teacher explained to her that what she wanted to study was "botany."

Mai, who usually deferred to her older sister, drew in a breath. "You're a fine one to talk. Do you have a suitor? You reject all the men our parents suggest."

Tâm sat back on her haunches. When had Mai developed such a sharp tongue? This churlish behavior was new. As Mai's *chị*, the older sister, Tâm should be treated with respect. She was about to say so when a wisp of smoke passed over them.

Tâm sniffed. The scent of the smoke was farm-like. Clean. The end of the dry season was approaching. A farmer was probably burning leftover corn husks or rotted fruit from his fields. Except that most farmers usually fed leftovers to their cattle or pigs. She frowned. Perhaps the smoke came from the dying embers of a campfire around the bend of the river. A fisherman or two cooking breakfast before a long day on the Mekong.

A second puff of smoke wafted over them. Stronger. This time it carried with it an acidic scent. Gasoline. Tâm's jaw tightened. She looked over at Mai, whose eyes grew round.

"Do you smell that?" Mai asked.

When the third gust of smoke reached them, even more intense, Tâm scrambled to her feet and beckoned to Mai. "Leave everything. We need to go home."

CHAPTER 2

TÂM

W hen the Japanese occupied Vietnam during World War II, a platoon of soldiers had seized the village. Those who stayed wanted easier access from the river. So they supervised the construction of a dock and steps leading from the river's edge up a hill. The steps ended at the dusty road leading into the village. Tâm and Mai's father had been conscripted to build the dock and steps in his teens, and his back bore the scars of beatings, an indispensable tool of Japanese brutality. Despite their harsh treatment, though, most of the villagers were pleased when the steps were finished. Outsiders could now be spotted as they approached, and villagers could determine whether they were friend or foe.

Yet it was still possible to climb the hill a dozen yards north of the dock. Under cover of cashew bushes, papaya, and jackfruit trees, one could secretly enter the village at its midpoint. Tâm and Mai took that route. As they hiked up the hill, a cacophony of sounds washed over them. Somewhere far above was a distant *thwup* of helicopter blades. On the ground, screams of terror. The occasional crack-spit of gunshots. The yelp of a dog that suddenly stopped. The squeal of a pig. Mechanical voices, as if someone was talking on a radio. And above it all, the thick, flat voices of men bellowing in what Tâm knew was English.

She froze. Americans. How had they found their tiny village? Not by water; Tâm and Mai would have seen them. But the land route was overgrown with dense forest and bush, impenetrable in some spots. Perhaps they came that way.

She worried about the helicopters. She'd heard how the U.S. dropped powerful bombs that erupted into fire, scorching everything on the ground. When the last flame was extinguished, the Vietnamese were left with barren fields and poisoned land unable to grow anything. The government said this was the only way to force the North and Viet Cong into the open, to halt their guerrilla war. She'd heard, too, that Americans liked to execute the VC they found, set fire to their villages, then force the inhabitants to relocate into squalid camps near Saigon. Tâm blinked fast, trying to suppress her rising fear.

Slowly, silently, she led Mai through the papaya trees. She stopped before they emerged from the bush and carefully pulled aside the fronds of a jackfruit tree. In front of her was the village square, an expanse of dirt studded with rocks where communal events, including weddings, births, and funerals, were celebrated.

Now, though, Tâm stared at chaos. There had to be more than twenty GIs in camouflage uniforms and helmets, rifles slung across their shoulders or in their hands. Some hoisted long, thick weapons much larger than rifles, but she didn't know what they were. Half a dozen soldiers moved from house to house, dragging villagers, their hands high in the air.

"Any VC in here? You VC?" they shouted in primitive Vietnamese. When the villagers frantically shook their heads, the GIs prodded them with their rifles toward the village square. "We heard there's a nest of enemy gooks in this hamlet," they replied in English. "Gotta make sure." Tâm didn't understand what they were saying, but she couldn't mistake their fury and vindictive tone.

Other soldiers poured gasoline on the thatched roofs of the now empty huts. Still others flicked their lighters and laughed when homes went up in flames.

Most of the villagers appeared to be terrified. The wife of a rice farmer planted herself at the entrance to her hut, shrieking and gesturing at the soldiers. She tried to explain that they had the wrong village. That they were simple farmers and fishermen with no interest in war. Of course, the Americans didn't understand, and barked orders in reply. When she refused to move, two soldiers dragged her to the square and shoved her to the ground.

About a dozen villagers, choking on the smoke, huddled in the square, heads between their knees, as if averting their faces would somehow mitigate the disaster. A soldier went back to the woman's hut, flipped his lighter, and touched the flame to her thatched roof. When it caught, he gestured to the villagers on the square, shouting "Lookie here. Roasted gook for lunch!" Some of the other soldiers guffawed. Again, Tâm didn't understand, but she watched flames devour the hut as if they were starving.

From their perch behind the trees, Tâm looked left and right. Smoke curled up in rolls. Soot darkened the sky. The air tasted acrid and sour, and the heat from the fires intensified. She counted five homes on fire, but their own home, thirty meters away, wasn't visible, and she couldn't tell if it was on fire.

The villagers on the square wailed as another house went up. Some choked on the smoke and the overpowering smell of gasoline. Others covered their faces with their hands. Tâm searched for their family. Mai was doing the same because she whispered, "I don't see Mama and Papa. Or Sáng. Where are they?"

"Maybe they escaped," Tâm whispered back.

Suddenly Mai grabbed Tâm's arm. "Look!" she said in a panicky whisper. She pointed past the square. Tâm followed her gaze.

Not far away was a mound of dead dogs, pigs, and even the calf born just two weeks ago. Their corpses, fresh and still bloody, dispensed a coppery, rancid smell that mixed with the gasoline. That was the source of the gunshots. The Americans were killing their animals. Flies were already swarming and settled on their hides. Tâm gagged, nausea rising in her throat. She swallowed to push it down.

Mai started to tremble. Tâm put an arm around her sister and let her lean against her for a moment, then straightened up. "We must be strong. We need to find Mama and Papa."

"How? We can't go home. They'll see us."

"Let me think."

Mai shook her head and pointed. "We can go around the path." A dirt path a few meters away ran along the back of a dozen huts, including theirs. But Mai wasn't as careful as Tâm. She would make noise or stumble, alerting the soldiers to her presence.

Tâm shook her head. "No. You stay here. I'll go."

Mai clutched her sister. "Don't leave me alone. Please, Chị Tâm!"

Tâm bit her lip. "Go back into the bush. You'll be safe there. Stay there until I come back."

"But I—I'm frightened. Stay with me, Chị Tâm."

"Be brave. I will be back. I swear it."

Tears filled Mai's eyes. "I don't . . . I can't."

Tâm raised a finger to her lips. She pointed to a cashew bush. "Hide behind that. But don't cry. They may hear you."

CHAPTER 3

MAI

Tâm slipped into the bush and was quickly out of sight. Mai retreated to the cashew bush and squatted behind it. She wrapped her arms around her knees. She could no longer see the square, but she didn't want to. The sounds and smells, plus what she had already seen, were enough.

Rocking back and forth, she tried to think about something other than the unfolding nightmare. The family had bought a transistor radio and they quarreled over it, each wanting to listen to something different. Finally, their father had parceled out times. News for him; classical music for Mama. Mai liked the station from the army base, even though it was broadcast in English. American pop was unfamiliar at first, but the songs were simple, and the throbbing beat was sensual. In fact, the radio, regardless of what was broadcast, had opened up a new world for the entire family. No longer were they isolated farmers and fishermen on the Mekong River, doing what their ancestors had done for centuries. Now, even if they couldn't join it—there was an enormous world out there. A world full of cities, different cultures, people, and, of course, war.

At fourteen, in fact, Mai thought differently about boys. They'd ceased to be bothersome. They had become mysterious creatures whose attention she wanted. She cared for her hair, making sure it was always oiled and scented with jasmine. She wore her uniform to school and her *áo bà ba*, her button-down shirt with black pantaloons, in the fields, but at the end of the day she would change into one of the two skirts she and Mama had sewn. She begged Mama to let her borrow her lipstick and mascara, particularly when she thought she might run into the sampan maker's son. Was this how girls became women?

She wasn't sure, mostly because Tâm wasn't like that. Her sister's nose was always buried in a science book she'd borrowed from the school library. When Tâm wasn't reading, she talked with Papa about history, politics, and the war. Mai and Mama weren't interested, but Papa was angry about the American War and their so-called pacification, which, he said, was just another phrase for death and destruction. He wanted the infidels gone. Vietnam could solve its problems by itself.

"But, Papa, we did not reach an agreement with the Communists," Tâm said, clearly trying to maintain a respectful tone.

Papa shot her a stern look. "If the French and then the Americans had not invaded us, we could have worked it out," he said. "Bác Hồ is a reasonable man. More than Diệm. Communists love their children too."

Then, less than two months ago, during Tết, North Vietnam launched a surprise attack on dozens of South Vietnamese cities and American forces. The campaign was long and aggressive, but the North ultimately failed, and they were forced to retreat.

Tết had triggered harsh retaliation from the Americans. Mama worried that war would come to their village. Tâm and Papa assured her it wouldn't. Their village was small. There was nothing worth fighting over.

They had been wrong.

Now Mai rose and went back to the spot where they had pushed aside the jackfruit fronds. More people now occupied the square, many crying or silent with shock. The heat from the fires baked their faces, and several of the women had fans. Mai spotted her friend

Dung among them. They'd listened to the radio together when it was Mai's turn, and spent long hours spinning dreams of the rich young men who would court them.

Dung wanted to move to Saigon. Everyone was rich there, she declared. "Servants do the chores. The women shop, and their husbands buy them sweets every day."

Mai's dreams were more modest. A big house in the village would do. She didn't mind housework. And she wanted children of her own. Lots of them.

All at once, Mai sucked in a breath. Her mother had just appeared in the square. She was carrying her brother, Sáng. He was sobbing. He had to be confused and frightened by the fires, the noise, the invasion of strange white men. Her mother's lips were stretched tight, the way they did when she was angry and about to mete out a punishment for misbehaving. Behind her was a soldier, his rifle poking her in the back.

Mai hugged her arms across her chest. Craning her neck, she tried to spot Papa, but there was no sign of him. Maybe Tâm was right. Maybe he was hiding in the bush, waiting for the Americans to leave.

Mama sat down with Sáng in her lap and rocked him. That did nothing to soothe him, so she gathered him to her chest and rested his head against her shoulder. Mai could see her mother's lips move. She was probably crooning a lullaby. Mai's throat closed up, and a deep longing came over her. She wanted to be with them, wanted Mama to sing *her* a lullaby. She belonged with her mother. But who knew what the Americans were going to do? Tâm said they were better off in the bush.

When it happened, Mai didn't believe it. Three soldiers guarding the villagers in the square whipped around and trotted in the direction from which Mama had come. Someone yelled out in Vietnamese, and once she heard the voice, she knew whose it was.

Papa was shouting in English. "Yankees go home! Uncle Hô warn us. You evil!" The people in the square stirred, murmuring among themselves, some with fearful expressions, others in horror. Two women shook their heads. Where had Papa learned English? The radio? Meanwhile the three GIs ran toward him. A spray of gunshots crackled and spit. Her father's rant suddenly stopped.

A chorus of wails went up from the villagers. More soldiers rushed over, aiming their rifles at the crowd and screaming. "Hands up, you bastard gooks!" one soldier yelled. "Get your fucking hands up! Any more VC here? Better tell us now!" Mai didn't understand the words, but when he pantomimed throwing his arms above his head, she got the gist of it.

The soldiers who had left the square returned, dragging a body between them. Papa! His face was bent at an odd angle to his body. Which didn't matter much, because most of it was blown away. His gut oozed blood, and his lower parts . . . Mai watched in a daze, as though she was in the middle of a horrendous but riveting play and couldn't look away.

When Mama saw Papa, a cry of revulsion ripped from her throat. Her mother placed Sáng on a neighbor's lap, jumped up, and hurried toward her father. One of the soldiers aimed his rifle at her and told her to go back. But she either didn't understand or didn't care. The soldier yelled out one more warning. She was heading toward the soldiers, one arm waving, the other tucked in the folds of her pajamas. Mai saw her withdraw a knife. The GIs saw it too. There was another *rat-tat-tat* of bullets. Mama fell to the ground, blood flowing from her head and ears. Horrified, Mai clapped a hand over her mouth.

"Where's the kid?" a soldier yelled. The woman cuddling Sáng kept her mouth shut. Mai realized when the soldier's eyes focused on Sáng that the soldier meant her brother. She didn't know what to do. She should try to rescue him. But she was frozen, paralyzed by fear. Where was Chị Tâm? The soldier shouted again in a mix of English and Vietnamese, more urgent this time. "Where's the little VC bastard?"

One of the women in the square pointed Sáng out. Chi, the village gossip. No one liked her. The Americans grabbed Sáng, whose terror temporarily silenced him. The soldier took him away from the crowd, out of sight. Another shot rang out. Mai's heart cracked.

But the shooting wasn't over. Papa's outburst had released something in the crowd. They must have been fueled with sudden courage, because they got to their feet, raised their fists high, and shouted at the GIs. Some repeated what Papa had said. Others protested their treatment of Mama, Papa, Sáng, their presence in the village, the invasion of their country, their very existence. Joined together in one angry mass, the crowd swarmed toward the Americans. The soldiers were taken aback, and, for a moment, there was no reaction. But then one of them—their leader? Mai wondered—barked out something even she could understand.

"Fire!"

The soldiers raised their rifles, aimed at the villagers, and shot them all. Bodies fell where they were, fists half raised, expressions of anguish. A minute later it was silent.

The horror. The flies. The heat. Mai vomited on the floor of the jungle.

CHAPTER 4

TÂM

Tâm watched the massacre from the path behind her family's hut. When they shot her parents and Sáng, a violent rage swept through her. She understood what her mother had done and why. She would have done it too. Now she wanted to attack, maim, and kill every American soldier in the village. Slowly and painfully. Like a photograph from her father's camera, the deaths and destruction of her village would be imprinted in her memory forever. They would pay.

But Mai was still in the bush. She couldn't abandon her sister. The only family Tâm had left. But Tâm couldn't take the chance that a clumsy step or the snap of a twig might reveal her to the Americans. So she squatted on the path. She couldn't see, but she could hear. The soldiers' leader was talking, his tone harsh and defensive. Long silences followed his words. He must be on a two-way radio. Was he receiving orders?

At last he signed off and yelled to his men. More heat spilled over Tâm. She peeked out. The Americans were burning the bodies. The fires were so intense she had to retreat into the bush. Then she moved, knowing her movements would be muffled by the crackle and hiss of the flames. She hid behind a grove of coconut palms until two helicopters approached and hovered overhead, their blades roaring and whipping the air into eddies and currents of wind. The men aboard the chopper must have given the all clear because after they thundered off, the GIs packed up their gear and headed out on foot.

She returned to the path and looked out. There was nothing left of the village except the foundations of straw huts, still-burning bushes and trees, charred lumps that were once humans, and blackened earth. The odor of burned flesh, thickly sweet and nauseating, permeated the air. A crow cawed. The vultures would swoop down soon.

Tâm cautiously made her way back to the jackfruit trees, a grief as deep as the Mekong River mingling with, then surpassing her rage. She debated whether to find her family's bodies and cremate them. That was the Buddhist way. Then again, the Americans had already done that. She gazed at the scene in the clearing. *Find Mai*, she heard her father's voice say. *There will be time to mourn. Protect your sister.*

It was the hottest part of the day and the heat was oppressive. But she didn't allow herself to think about that. She tried to imagine what she could possibly say to her sister—she didn't know how much of the massacre Mai had seen. But when she reached the spot at which she'd left her, her sister was gone.

Had she run deeper into the forest? Had the soldiers found her and—Tâm swallowed—killed her too? She didn't know what to do. She couldn't stay here. She and Papa had shared many conversations, but how to survive in the bush wasn't one.

The Americans seemed to be gone, but she didn't think it was safe to call out, so she trudged in ever widening circles around their original hiding spot. She crept slowly, making as little sound as possible, on the alert for human footsteps, their scents, the swish of brush moved aside.

Nothing.

Tâm ran her hands up and down her arms, feeling desperate. The nearest village was several miles away. Easy to reach in a cart with oxen, but there were no oxen. Had Mai ducked deeper into the bush?

No. Mai was afraid of forest critters, especially ones that foraged at night. And night would fall in a few hours.

Tâm retraced the path to the river. To be safe, she climbed down the hill rather than the steps. She didn't want to risk being seen by a passerby in a sampan or boat. As she neared the shore, she heard tuneless humming. Discordant notes. Tâm shaded her eyes from the sun and looked up and down the shore. There! Protected from the sun, a slight figure squatted at the edge of the river, rinsing shirts in the water. Mai. Tâm broke into a jog and hurried toward her sister.

"Mai," she cried joyfully. "I've been searching for you! I'm so glad you're here. But we are too exposed. We must move back from the beach and hide."

When Tâm started talking, Mai made no sign of recognition. In fact, she scrambled to her feet and ran in the opposite direction.

"Dirty Rabbit!" Tâm chased after her sister, using the nickname their parents had given Mai. Many Vietnamese parents bestowed unflattering, practically insulting nicknames on their children. An ancient tradition, it was done to keep evil spirits away. When the spirits heard what parents called their children, they would not be tempted to injure or allow bad karma to fester on them. Mai was "Dirty Rabbit." Tâm was "Stinky Monkey."

But hearing her family nickname only made Mai run faster. They used to race when they were younger. Mai was small and nimble and often beat Tâm. Now, though, a haze of leftover soot and smoke lingered at the river's edge, making it hard to breathe. Why was Mai running? Where to?

Mai peered over her shoulder as she ran. Tâm waved. "It's me, Mai. Please. Stop!"

But Mai showed no sign she knew who Tâm was. Tâm started to close the distance between them. When Mai glanced over her shoulder again, Tâm saw panic on her face and began to understand. Mai was fragile, her emotions close to the surface. Right now, Mai's mind was not her own. The trauma of the day's events had been too much for her. In her mind, Tâm was the enemy, intent on capturing and killing her.

Tâm slowed down and coughed up phlegm. She squatted on the narrow strip of beach and worried her hands through her hair. Her mother, when she felt helpless or afraid, would go to the temple to give an offering to the monks. After the nightmare of today, Tâm's faith was stretched thin. But if a prayer would bring Mai to her senses, she would give Buddha ten.

She must have waited more than an hour. The sun was beginning to dip toward the horizon. The haze in the air created a perversely beautiful sunset. How could Buddha or whatever deity controlled the sun have the nerve to paint such a brilliant combination of reds, oranges, and gold? In this light the Mekong looked clear and clean. Tâm bowed her head and rocked. She tried to recall what prayer she was supposed to say.

In a corner of their hut on a shelf above their heads, her mother had created a small shrine to Buddha. She'd bought a small statuette of the god and placed a gold bowl and wood bell next to it, easily the most valuable objects they owned. It was there that her mother placed fresh-cut flowers, lit candles, and burned incense a few times a week. As Tâm prayed, watching the sun slowly sink, she felt her spirit loosen. The day was ending much like it had begun. Calm. At peace.

Tâm wasn't sure how long she prayed. Dusk settled, lengthening shadows and darkening the water of the Mekong. Eventually she felt a light tap on her shoulder. She turned around. "Mai!" Her cheeks were dirty and tear streaked. Tâm got to her feet and they embraced.

CHAPTER 5

TÂM

"I'm hungry," Mai croaked through her tears. Tâm knew the hunger was for more than food. It was a hunger that would never be completely sated.

"Let's find some fruit," Tâm said.

"No!" Mai cried. "I—I can't go back—there."

Tâm intended to explain that they'd have to. That she didn't want to leave Mai by herself and that they'd have to forage in the bush if they wanted to eat. Then she thought better of it and simply held out her hand. "We can do it together."

Mai squeezed her eyes shut and let out a sob. Reluctantly she put her hand in Tâm's, and they trudged up the steps back to the bush, looking in all directions to make sure they weren't followed. Thirty minutes later, their arms laden with ripe jackfruit, mangos, papaya, and lotus fruit, they returned to the beach and wolfed down their food.

By the time they finished eating it was dark, but the heat still hadn't lifted. They were hot and exhausted and smelled of gasoline, char, and fear. The only light came from a waxing moon that spilled across the water. It was enough.

"We're sleeping here?" Mai said.

Tâm nodded. "You finish the washing and spread our clothes out to dry. I'll gather some palm fronds to cover us."

Mai glanced around fearfully. "But—but what if they come back?" she whispered. "Or what if someone saw the smoke across the river? They could be waiting for dark to loot whatever is left."

Tâm tried to sound confident. "We'll be hidden under the fronds. But that's not going to happen." At least not tonight, she hoped. They had already lived through one hell. They wouldn't survive another. "I'm going to take a bath in the river. You should too. Then we'll wash the rest of our clothes."

Tâm woke before sunrise. She hadn't slept well; during the dark hours a horde of mosquitoes had feasted on her skin. Mai snuggled against her back, snoring softly. Tâm blinked her eyes open. Memories of the massacre flooded through her. The life that she'd known was over. The certainty that the sun would rise, that she would read and study, work in the rice fields, and help her parents, was gone.

Why did the Americans choose their village? Was it just a random attack? They'd claimed to be looking for VCs, Viet Cong fighters and their enablers, to retaliate for Tết. The truth was they could have found them in any village. During the day the South Vietnamese were hardworking farmers or craftsmen, doing their best to feed their families and survive. After nightfall, however, people would flip their pictures of President Thiệu. On the other side was a photo of Hô Chí Minh with a benevolent smile. They would don black-and-white-checkered scarves and prepare food and drink for the guerrillas who crept out of the bush. Although they weren't fighters themselves, these collaborators, including Tâm's father, put their lives at risk. And the Americans knew it. Unable to battle their enemy directly, the soldiers used villagers for target practice instead.

Mai must have sensed Tâm was awake, because she rolled over

and opened her eyes. Her sleepy expression gave way to fear when she realized where they were and why. Tâm attempted a reassuring smile, but they both knew it was just for show.

They dressed quickly and ate the mangos they'd saved, after which Tâm took a sheet and folded some of their now dry clothes in it, tied it up, and hoisted it on her shoulder. Tâm pointed. "Start walking."

"Where?" Mai asked.

"Toward Saigon. Stay back from the water, closer to the brush."

"Is it safe there?" The capital city of South Vietnam had been a key objective for North Vietnamese and Viet Cong forces during Tết. They'd even held the American embassy for a few hours and fought hand to hand with South Vietnamese forces in Cholon, the old Chinese section of Saigon. After the invasion failed, though, it provoked a massive retaliation from the Americans and the ARVN, the South Vietnamese army. Fighting still continued on the city's outskirts, and some sections of Cholon were damaged by mortar attacks.

"The U.S. soldiers who attacked us are headed inland. Toward Cambodia, not Saigon," Tâm said. "So we'll go the other way. To Saigon." She hoped Mai wouldn't realize she hadn't answered the question. Tâm didn't know if Saigon was safe.

The shadow of a smile flitted across Mai's face. "Dung would have liked that."

"Why?"

Mai told her. Had it been any other time, Tâm would have belittled Mai's friend Dung, and Mai, too, for such superficial dreams. Mai didn't know she couldn't afford those dreams anymore. But Tâm kept her mouth shut and pointed.

"Don't forget our *nón la*." Mai ran back to pick them up.

They'd walked about half a kilometer when Tâm squinted at something in the distance. As they grew closer, she jogged toward it. Beached on the sand ahead was a sampan. She approached it cautiously, but no one was nearby. She peeked into the sampan. Its oars were stowed on gunwales on each side. And a fishing pole lay in the bottom of the boat. Tâm smiled for the first time in twenty-four hours. Buddha had blessed her with his compassion.

CHAPTER 6

MAI

By sunrise, Mai and Tâm were on the river paddling the sampan, Tâm in the stern, Mai the bow. Tâm told her to row quickly at first in case anyone saw them steal the boat.

"What happens when the man who owns the boat finds it gone?" Mai said. "Isn't stealing wrong?"

Tâm didn't answer for a minute. Then: "Yes. It is wrong. But so was the massacre that destroyed our home and killed our family. Which is the greater evil?"

Mai pondered it. Could a sin be forgiven if it was committed in response to a bigger one? Yesterday she wouldn't have thought so. But today? Perhaps.

Twenty minutes later, Mai's hands and shoulders ached. She wasn't used to rigorous physical activity. "My hands are blistering," she said.

"We can slow down for now," Tâm said.

Grateful, Mai rolled her shoulders and wiggled her fingers. Had the massacre not occurred, it might have been a pleasant journey. But she was beginning to see the world through a new lens of caution and fear. Occasionally they passed other boats and people on the shore.

Yesterday she would have offered a friendly wave, but now she kept her head down. Chị Tâm said it was too risky to acknowledge them.

A few minutes later, several large black helicopters materialized overhead, hovering low. Mai's heart thumped in her chest. She twisted around to Chị Tâm.

"Are they coming for us?" Her voice spiked in fear.

Tâm studied them. "No. Look."

Mai looked up. The helicopters spewed trails of what looked like orange smoke from their bellies. As the smoke drifted toward the ground, it dissipated into mist. "What is that?" Panic tightened Mai's stomach.

Tâm's eyes flashed with anger, not fear. "It's poison. They call it Agent Orange. It destroys everything that grows on the land and contaminates it for years."

"Why?"

"Without the cover of brush, the enemy can find villages like ours more easily."

"But why do they want to find us?"

"Mai, do—did you never listen to Papa's radio when the news came on?"

Mai shook her head.

Tâm sighed. "There are many villagers in the South who hate this war and what the Americans are doing. So they secretly help the guerrillas fighting for the North by feeding them at night when they come out of the brush. And giving them weapons."

"You mean the Viet Cong?"

"So you do know."

"Dung told me her parents helped. She made me swear not to tell."

"Ah. I am sorry your friend was killed."

Mai tightened her lips.

Tâm went on. "I think that is why the Americans attacked. They were looking for Viet Cong and assumed we were."

"Are—were we?"

"Papa perhaps." She paused. "Yes, I would say so. Mama, no. She was not political. And yet she would prepare food for Papa to give them once you were asleep."

Mai looked up at the helicopters again. "What if they spot us? Will they poison us too?"

"We are just two peasant girls looking for a place to fish, right?" Tâm dug her oar into the water. "I see a cove over there. Let's head over."

As they beached the sampan, the hull crunched on the sand. Mai looked up. The helicopters had moved on. She breathed a sigh of relief.

Tâm pulled out the fishing rod. "Have you fished before?"

Mai shook her head. She didn't know a fishing line from a laundry line.

"Then today you're going to learn. Take this." She held out the rod. "Get us some catfish."

Mai peered at the rod as if it was a snake that would curl up at any second and bite her.

"Take it. It won't hurt you."

Mai stood still. "What should I do with it?"

"What do you think?" The exasperation that ignited whenever Tâm was displeased with Mai appeared. Tâm bent over the sampan. "Hold on."

She explored the bottom of the boat. A moment later she let out a grunt of satisfaction. "Here." She straightened up. In her hand was a fishhook. Mai had never seen one at close range before. It looked like part of a thin curved earring, with a tiny eye on top and a sharp point on the curved end. She took it from Tâm warily. Tâm found a hand-held net in the boat, which she also handed to Mai.

"You need to loop the line through the eye at the top of the fish-hook, then drop it into the water and wait." She pointed to a large flat rock that jutted out over the river. "Over there is a perfect spot. I'll find bugs you can use for bait."

Mai gazed at the rock, then back at Tâm. When she didn't move, Tâm repeated, "Go." Mai opened her mouth, about to say something, but stopped. Tâm wasn't going to change her mind. She trudged over to the rock with the pole. Tâm waited until Mai had climbed onto the rock, then disappeared into the brush.

Tâm returned a few minutes later with a couple of grasshoppers in her hand. The bugs lay on their backs, their revolting tiny tentacles waving in all directions. Mai jerked back.

Tâm ignored her distress. "I will show you how to bait the hook this time. Next time you do it." Tâm threaded the hook onto the line, took one of the insects, and stabbed it with the fishhook. The grasshopper was dead, but its legs still squirmed.

"Now, drop the line into the water. When you feel a tug, pull it out and drop the fish into the net. Be patient and don't give up."

"Why?" Mai's gut twisted. "Where are you going?"

"To get more fruit." Tâm climbed off the rock and disappeared into the bush again.

Mai cautiously dropped her fishing line into the water. Yesterday her world had been normal. It was a world she could understand. She had her place in it. Today, she had no idea where they were or where they were going, and she was stuck with a fishing rod in her hands. Her parents and Sáng were dead, they had stolen a sampan, and all she had in the world was Tâm. While they were sisters, they were so different. She tried to imagine sharing a funny incident with Chị Tâm, as she did with Dung. Or her mother. She couldn't.

Mai wore her *nón lá*, but the sun, lazy and languid at dawn, was now fiery hot. The rock sizzled like a simmering cauldron, and Mai couldn't move without burning her skin. She had to stay where she was. She felt as if she was in a prison without walls. All because of a damn fish. She wanted shade, and she didn't want to keep going in the sampan. But Chị Tâm would say they had to eat, and they had to get to Saigon. She teared up in frustration and blinked quickly. Maybe this was all a bad dream. When she woke up, everything would be the way it had been before.

She wasn't sure how long she had been sitting, steeped in misery, when she felt a tiny tug on the line. She straightened. "Chị Tâm, Chị Tâm, I think I have a fish. What do I do?"

There was no answer. What had Tâm told her to do? Pull it up. Catch it in the net. She pulled up the line. Amazingly, a fish dangled, flopping on the hook. She had caught a fish! She knew she had to get the fish into the net, but the line was too long to do it deftly. Was she supposed to grab the fish with her hands? She looked for the spool on the rod that fishermen used to reel in their catch, but there was nothing. She was going to have to pull the line in another way. Fumbling with the rod, she managed to pull it in until the line was in front of her. The fish still struggled. She was afraid it would plop back into the river. Despite the heat on the rock, she got to her knees, leaned forward, and grabbed the line with one hand. With the other she grasped the line higher up. She repeated what she had done. It was working! The line and the fish were coming closer. She grabbed the line twice more.

The fish was now within reach. Mai picked up the net with one hand and grabbed the fish with the other. A sharp pain shot through her wrist, and she cried out. She had stabbed herself with the fish-hook. She tried to pull it out, but it was embedded in her skin and wouldn't budge. Panicking, she pulled harder. The pain was excruciating. She let out a piercing scream. Finally, she was able to pull out the hook. Blood gushed down her forearm. Her skin was torn. She burst into tears.

CHAPTER 7

TÂM

Tâm found Mai clutching a bloody fish. She was crying hysterically. Blood was everywhere, on her hands, her arms, even the rock. "What happened?"

Mai held up her wrist. "I stabbed myself with the hook. Then I pulled it out. Am I going to die?"

Tâm hurried to the sampan, where she'd stowed the sheet bundled with their clothes. She untied it and tore off several strips with her teeth. Then she ran back to Mai and helped her off the rock. Blood was still flowing freely—Mai must have nicked a vein. She took Mai to the river's edge and rinsed her wrist in the water. Then she tied the strips tight around the wound.

"That will help stop the blood. We'll put a new one on afterward. Can you squeeze your wrist with your other hand? That will help."

Mai nodded and wiped her tears on the strip of sheet. "Are you sure the blood will stop?"

Tâm tried to calm her sister. "It will." In her thoughts, though, doubt swirled. She should have never left Mai alone. Mai was too young, too inexperienced. Perhaps it was folly to head toward Saigon. Perhaps, despite her best efforts, she and Mai wouldn't make it.

Aloud she said, "You may have a scar, but you will be fine in a few days." *Unless an infection sets in.*

Tâm decided it would be safer to travel by night, so she spread the sheet down in a shady spot at the edge of the bush. Then she took the rod and caught two more catfish. Catfish liked to fight, and they flipped and flopped back and forth on the line until Tâm overpowered them. Their whiskers could sting as well, if she wasn't careful. She laid all three fish on the rock. The sun was now scorching hot. Chances were good they would be eating baked fish by sunset.

"Let's try to take a nap, and then we'll eat."

Mai sniffed. "What fruit did you find? Can we warm it like Mama used to?"

Tâm smiled sadly. Warmed fruit sliding down their throats had been a treat. "Let's try." She peeled the fruit and set it down beside the fish.

Two nights later Tâm paddled south on the Mekong, hugging the shore. Bright moonlight spilled down, making the sampan more conspicuous than she wanted. She was weary. It was difficult to sleep during the heat of the day; all she'd managed was a few hours. It wasn't much cooler at night anyway, and tending to Mai's wrist, providing food, and protecting them as best she could was draining her. There had been no time to mourn or plan what to do next. She watched the shoreline carefully, looking for any discrepancy in the muted shades of greenery that would suggest a potential stranger or enemy.

The whine of an engine startled Tâm. She paddled more strenuously. The noise woke Mai, who'd been dozing in the belly of the sampan. "Where are we?" she asked drowsily.

"I don't know. But without you paddling, we're not making much progress."

"What can I do?" Mai said bitterly. She held up her wounded wrist.

"I know. I'm just saying. . ." Tâm's voice trailed off. She wasn't angry, just fatigued and despondent.

Mai changed the subject. "What is that noise?" She sat up and twisted around. So did Tâm. A fishing trawler cruised behind them. Even in the dark Tâm could see it was about ten meters long, weather-beaten, and shabby, with scratches and dents on the side. A hiccup in the engine every few seconds told her that it wasn't in very good shape, either. Tâm wondered how many generations of fishermen the trawler had served.

Other ships and boats had passed them on the river, but Tâm ignored them and told Mai to do the same. This time, though, Mai looked straight at the boat. So did Tâm. No one was on deck. Of course. Most of the crew would be sleeping. Except whoever was at the wheel.

Mai kept gazing at the boat. Tâm was about to tell her to stop when its engine suddenly died. Fear climbed up Tâm's spine, but Mai cocked her head to the side. In an effort to put more distance between them, Tâm plunged her oar in the water, pulling with strong, powerful strokes.

"Wait, Chị Tâm." Mai pointed. "Someone's on the deck. He's waving at us!"

"We don't know who he is. We need to get away."

Mai let out a breath. "Chị Tâm, please. Let me try something."

"You are a child."

"And you are a grumpy old woman."

"My job is to keep us safe."

"How safe were we when I sliced my wrist on the fishhook?"

"I was wrong. I shouldn't have left you alone."

"And I should never have fished in the first place." Mai threw Tâm an indignant glance, swung her head toward the trawler, and waved back at the man on deck.

He called out. "Hello! Where are you headed?"

"Saigon," Mai answered.

Tâm was pulling away from the boat. "Stop, Chị Tâm," Mai said.

The man on the deck replied. "So are we! That's where we sell our catch."

In the bright moonlight Tâm watched him look them over. "It will take you days to get there by sampan."

"This is all we have," Mai said. "We had no choice."

The man nodded as if he knew or could imagine what had happened. Maybe he did, Mai thought. The entire country was in the middle of a war. He looked down. "If you don't mind the stink of fish, we could give you a ride. We'll be there tomorrow."

Mai grinned. "Really?" She twisted back to Tâm, who was already shaking her head.

"You can't board a stranger's boat. Anything could happen."

"Well, then you stay in the sampan. I want to get to Saigon."

"Mama and Papa would never permit this."

"Mama and Papa aren't here."

"Dirty Rabbit, please." Tâm's tone softened. "Please don't. We can make it to Saigon by ourselves. Why rush?"

"Because I'm tired. My wrist is throbbing. I'm dirty and hungry. I hate this." She paused. "And please don't call me 'Dirty Rabbit' again. It's absurd. So old-fashioned," she scoffed. "There are no evil spirits."

"What do you mean? What about the massacre?"

"You know what I'm talking about. No spirit will kidnap us. We're not children anymore."

Tâm sighed in defeat and lowered her head. She was exhausted too. She lifted her paddle out of the water and laid it across the stern.

Mai smiled and turned back to the man on the deck. "Thank you. We'd be grateful for the ride."

CHAPTER 8

MAI

S he'd done it. By herself. Yes, the fish odor was putrid and would linger in their hair and clothes for days. Yes, the accommodations were hardly better than the sampan—which was now tied to the back of the trawler. But they'd arrive in Saigon in hours, not days. Even through the grief and trauma, Mai sensed a hint of what life might be like going forward. A hint that said she could make decisions and control her destiny as well as her sister.

Tâm nodded at the man on the deck, whose name, he told them, was Phong. "Who else is on the trawler?" she asked.

"Just my father," Phong said. "He's asleep below."

Tâm checked her surroundings. They were alone on deck. She took the blanket he offered and lay down near the bow, instantly asleep. Mai sensed she was relieved her burden had been lifted for a few hours.

"Neither of us has slept in days," Mai said.

Phong nodded. He handed her a blanket. "We will talk in the morning. You can sleep on the deck."

Mai took the blanket with a smile. He smiled back.

~

The sun had climbed high in the sky when Mai woke. Happily, the breeze from the trawler's forward motion kept the worst of the heat away. Unhappily, the pervasive odor of fish had intensified overnight and permeated the air. Trying to ignore it, Mai stretched and got up. Tâm was still asleep.

Phong and an older man were seated in the stern drinking tea from a thermos. They faced the river behind them, rather than the girls' makeshift bedroom in the bow. Courteous, Mai thought.

"Good morning." She approached them.

The men turned around. "Good morning," Phong said. "This is my father, Bác Quang."

Slim and slight, he was losing his hair on top, and it was gray on the sides. When he smiled, she saw he was missing one of his front teeth. "Some tea?"

Mai nodded. He poured the tea into a cup and handed it to her. "We are grateful your son rescued us last night," she said, taking the cup.

"In these times, we follow in the steps of Buddha. He has shown us the path to travel."

If he was as devout as he sounded, he was probably a good man. She began to relax and peered over at the bank of the river. An occasional water buffalo stared back. The foliage wasn't as thick here, and fewer trees edged the shore. Here and there were groups of huts, some of them built on stilts. A few sampans with fishermen casting nets or lines dotted the water. It was hard to remember that just beyond the shores, a war nobody wanted was taking the lives of young Vietnamese men.

"The closer we get to Saigon," Quang said, as if reading her mind, "the fewer bombs and fire smoke we see."

Mai was glad. With every revolution of the engine, the horror of the massacre, the killings, guns, and blood, slipped further away. Saigon would be a better place. It had to be.

～

Tâm stirred. She lifted her head and saw Mai with the fishermen. She sat up and ran a hand through her hair, then rose and went over. After introductions, Quang poured tea for her. He bowed his head as he handed it over. "Cháu, you are the firstborn in your family." A statement, not a question.

Tâm nodded.

Mai chafed at his courteous attitude toward Tâm. Mai had managed to get them on the trawler, not Tâm. Of course, Bác Quang was just observing the custom. She bit back her irritation.

"What are your plans when you get to Saigon?" he asked.

Mai and Tâm exchanged glances. They had been so focused on surviving the massacre that they'd had no time to make plans. Saigon was their beacon, blinking in the distance like a golden light. It was the reason they'd stolen the sampan, fed themselves with whatever they could scrape together, and exhausted themselves. And yet, neither knew much about the city or what they would do once they arrived. Tâm had chosen it only because the U.S. soldiers were heading in the opposite direction.

Tâm answered honestly. "We have no plan. We've been living from moment to moment. The Americans . . . destroyed our village. Our parents and little brother are dead. We lost our family. Our home. Everything."

"Ah." Quang sipped his tea, studying the cup as if he could see their ordeal and trauma in the tea leaves. Then he looked to the shore of the river. "I have an idea. We'll dock near the fish market and sell our catch. Near it is the Binh Tay market. In the Chinese district. It's Saigon's biggest. You'll find everything you need. Clothing. Food. Perhaps even work."

"But we have no money," Tâm said.

"You have the sampan," Quang said.

Tam understood what he was saying. "It is yours. With grateful thanks. But it could not possibly be worth enough to buy what we need."

Phong whispered to his father. His father nodded. "We know

people in the market. They're good souls. They understand we are at war."

CHAPTER 9

TÂM

As they neared Saigon, fields gave way to homes built on the river itself. Those grew closer together until they formed a continuous ribbon of huts, most of them on stilts. In back of them trucks, cars, military vehicles, and motorcycles thundered by on the road. The huts gradually disappeared, and in their place, beyond the riverbank, were a series of tall, skinny houses, about five stories high but no wider than a few meters.

"What are those?" Tâm asked.

"Tube houses," Phong answered. "As Saigon grew there was no room to build out, so people built up instead."

Tâm studied them. "But they are so narrow. How can there be more than one room on a floor?"

"There aren't," Quang said. "Often there's a shop or restaurant on the ground floor, a kitchen and bath on the second, and bedrooms on the others."

"The top floors are often rented out," Phong said hopefully. "Perhaps you can find a place to live."

When we have money to pay the rent, Tâm thought.

They navigated off the Saigon River and docked in a busy shipping canal just after noon. Neither Tâm nor Mai had ever been to

Saigon, and while they weren't in the center of the city, the din of traffic, loud horns, and hordes of people on bicycles and cyclos unnerved Tâm. The war had brought nearly one in five Vietnamese citizens to Saigon as refugees, and the air was layered with the odors of gasoline exhaust and urine and the scent of cooking. Mixed in was the pervasive stench of fish. Tâm breathed through her mouth.

While Phong and Bác Quang talked business, Mai and Tâm went belowdecks to freshen up and change into their only remaining clean white tunics and black pants. When they returned, Phong and his father had sealed their deal. Three other men materialized to relieve them of their catch. The nets held mostly catfish, but there was carp, too. The men hoisted the nets out of the boat into huge bins filled with ice.

Afterward Phong and Quang washed up in a men's room behind the dock. Tâm and Mai still reeked of fish, but there was nothing they could do, since there was no corresponding room for women. Women worked just as long and hard as men. Some, like the woman in the neighboring village who wove *nón lá*, were astute in business matters. Generally, though, women were second-class citizens, at least in South Vietnam. Tâm had been told it was different in Communist North Vietnam. Women were equal to men. She wasn't sure she believed it. Men were men, no matter where they lived. Most were driven by power and sex and not much else.

The four of them twisted through narrow streets filled with people, many of them children in threadbare clothes who looked hungry. Mai, wide-eyed and cautious, clutched Tâm's arm. "Who are they? They look younger than Sáng."

Quang answered. "They are in Saigon because of the war. They build tent camps in the outer rings of the city, as well as Cholon, the Chinese district. Their families come to the market, and the children beg."

As if on cue, two boys approached, imploring them for a few *đồng*. Tâm threw up her hands and shook her head, but Quang fished a bill from his pocket. The boys practically snatched it from him, which made him laugh.

"They've won the prize," he joked. The boys bowed their thanks, ran back to a woman squatting on the sidewalk, and handed the bill to her. She caught Tâm's eyes and smiled. She must have thought Quang and Tâm were a couple. The woman wore the same white tunic and black pants as Tâm and Mai. Tâm swallowed. What would they do if they couldn't find work? Would she and Mai be forced to beg?

"The market is just ahead," Phong said.

The narrow sidewalk became more congested. Throngs of people pushed and shoved past one another. A few women, having staked out a patch of concrete at the edge of the street, cooked *phở* in pots with makeshift hot plates. In exchange for a few *đồng*, other people squatted down beside them, wolfing down the fragrant noodle soup with chunks of pork. Another woman wrung the neck of a chicken and calmly started to pluck out its feathers.

Mai nudged Tâm. "Mama taught us how to do that, remember?" She bit her lip.

Tâm kept her mouth shut.

When they reached the entrance to the Binh Tay market, Tâm realized it didn't matter that they smelled of fish. The scents of the market overpowered them: fish, *phở*, rancid body odor, and a sickly sweet smell she couldn't identify. She had seen markets before; her parents had taken her to Chau Doc, a two-hour oxcart ride away, where a larger, floating outdoor wet market bustled with fruits, flowers, cooked food, fresh fish, and cheap toys.

But she had never seen anything like this. The Cholon market occupied an immense two-story building that looked bigger than their entire village. Inside, more than a hundred stalls exploded with sights, sounds, colors, and scents. Food was packaged in cans or bags or just arranged on a counter. There was sticky candy. Household goods. Furniture. Carpets. Clothing. Paintings jostled for space with cheap plastic dolls, cars, and other toys. Jewelry with leather goods. American cigarettes, toothpaste, whiskey, and chewing gum. Covering everything, like a giant blanket, was a cacophony of noise from the brisk nasal tones of Vietnamese merchants selling, bartering, negotiating.

Phong and Quang led the way through the maze of stalls with confidence, twisting and turning at strategic points. Several merchants waved as they passed. The fishermen stopped when they reached an area where the aromas of cooked food like *phở*, *bún thịt nướng*, and other dishes overwhelmed everything else. Tâm was dizzy with hunger. Mai gazed ravenously at the food.

"Now you'll eat."

Tâm began. "But—"

Quang held up a hand and cut her off. He turned around and waved at one of the women serving *phở*. She waved back. He approached her and started talking. Tâm couldn't overhear. But when Quang pointed at them, she knew. A moment later, both men returned with steaming bowls of *bún cá*, rice noodles with large chunks of fish thickening the broth. Dumplings too. The fishermen gestured to a counter in front of the stall. Tâm and Mai squatted and attacked their meal. Tâm did not see money change hands. She must have missed it.

Tâm spoke around a mouthful of fish. "I don't know how we can repay you."

"I didn't pay. They buy our fish at a good price. We eat their *bún cá*. It's a fair trade."

"Thank you." Tâm templed her hands at chest level in gratitude.

Quang motioned her to go back to her meal. Within seconds, the noodles disappeared from their bowls.

"More?"

Tâm bowed her head.

"Don't be shy," Quang said. "You haven't had a solid meal in days."

Mai looked up. "Yes, please. And another dumpling."

Quang nudged Phong, who returned with another bowl, a dumpling, and chopsticks. Mai ate slowly, as if relishing every bite.

With a full belly, Tâm's mood improved. She might even have to revise her attitude toward men. Decent and generous, Quang was not seeking power or sex. He and his son seemed to be made of finer stuff. Karma had brought their paths together. Why? What made them so special? She didn't know, but she was grateful.

"The Buddha will honor you. As do we," she said.

Quang templed his hands at chest level, as if to pray. "You were in need. You will do the same for others, and the circle will be complete."

CHAPTER 10

TÂM

By the time Phong and Bác Quang said farewell, both sisters had a new change of clothes and a knapsack filled with toiletries from the market. They also were given sandals, since they had left their village barefoot. As Tâm looked for the correct sizes, Mai drifted over to browse the perfume stall. One of the women tended to Mai's wrist and put a real bandage on it. Tâm was relieved her wound wasn't infected. Most important, Tâm had the address of a restaurant on a scrap of paper.

"How long a walk is it?" Mai asked.

"The woman at the market said thirty minutes," Tâm said. "We should change clothes when we get close. We stink like dead catfish."

Mai giggled. That she could laugh, even feel hopeful after their ordeal, was good, Tâm thought. Normal. She ignored her own guilt that came with Mai's giggle. Young people adapted more easily to change. The three years between Mai and Tâm was not much, but to Tâm it felt like a chasm.

"Do you think we'll get jobs?" Mai asked.

Tâm shrugged. "We'll try. And then we'll go to the refugee camp the women told us about."

"But I don't want to live in a camp," Mai said. "I want—"

Tâm cut her off. "We have no choice."

"Promise me that as soon as we have money, we can search for a proper home."

"What is a 'proper' home, Mai? We lived in a hut with a dirt floor and a straw roof. I don't see any of those here." She swept her hand across the street.

They had left the dense thickness of the market and were now approaching the city center. Traffic was less crowded here, the roads wider. They walked down one street with islands separating the two directions of traffic. Buildings were larger too, with space between them. Some were painted yellow with graceful wrought iron or marble flourishes. Trees and flowering bushes lined islands and curbs, and urns filled with colorful blossoms dressed up entrances. The heat of the afternoon had crested, but a slight breeze made the walk tolerable.

Mai took it all in. "Dung was right," she said.

"What do you mean?"

"She said everyone in Saigon was rich." She pointed to a hotel. "I've never seen such a big hotel. And look at all those decorations."

Tâm studied a large building. "That is not a hotel. It is the post office."

"How do you know?"

"I've seen photos. At the library back home. It was built by the French during their occupation."

The memory of quiet afternoons at the one-room library in the Catholic school swept over Tâm. It was the most peaceful place she knew. When the heat became too much, the librarian would bring in a fan and place it on a tall counter, so the relief reached Tâm at a table a few meters away. She was one of the lucky students. Her father did not make her quit school to work when there wasn't enough money. He knew she reveled in the pure act of learning. While the family did need her at harvesttime, they allowed her to continue her education if she helped after school. She'd been grateful. But they were gone now. She needed to think about them in the past tense. The thought brought tears to her eyes, and she bit her lip.

They turned the corner and came to a huge structure with graceful arches, colored glass windows, and two steeples. "What is this?" Mai asked.

Tâm laughed. "It is a cathedral. For Christians."

"Really?"

"The French built that, too."

"For Catholics?"

"And now probably Americans as well."

As they kept walking, the neighborhood changed again. Rows of skinny tube houses Quang had pointed out lined the streets. Up close, most were only two or three meters wide. But what they lost in width they made up for in height, stretching up four or five stories. Crowded together like chopsticks in a drawer, they were painted different colors, tropical green, yellow, even pink. In most, shops occupied the ground floor.

"Look!" Mai pointed to a succession of tall, narrow structures. "More tube houses. Like Bác Quang told us about. Do you think the restaurant is in one of them? Perhaps they will let us live above it," Mai said hopefully.

"In return for what? We'd probably need to work a week just to afford one night."

Mai stiffened. "Well, you don't have to be crabby about it."

Tâm ignored her. Mai was always spinning dreams, most of them wildly unattainable. "There! We're here." Tâm stopped at a green tube building with five stories. A sign on the door of the ground floor indicated they'd reached the Saigon Café.

They peered inside. There were only ten tables squeezed together, with barely any space between them. A set of stairs lay at the back. Perhaps there were more tables upstairs? The tables were covered with white tablecloths, and Chinese lanterns in bright colors festooned the ceiling.

Mai smiled. "I like it."

"Let me do the talking," Tâm said.

Mai shot her sister a dubious look but didn't say anything.

Tâm sighed. "Let's find a place to change clothes."

In an alley nearby they changed into their new black pantaloons and white blouses. Mai dug inside her knapsack and pulled out a small bottle of perfume.

"Where did you get that?"

"At the market."

Tâm's eyes narrowed. "How did you pay for it?"

Wide-eyed, Mai's aggrieved expression said she was surprised that Tâm doubted her. "One of the women gave it to me. She said it would help with the fish smell."

Tâm wasn't sure she believed Mai, but now was not the time to challenge her sister. A few minutes later, in new clothes and doused with perfume, they presented themselves at the restaurant.

CHAPTER 11

MAI

"You're not from Saigon," the woman in the restaurant said after Tâm introduced herself and Mai. "Your accent is—You're from the country." Mai sensed the woman was trying to be polite and wondered what Saigon natives were supposed to sound like. The woman looked to be in her early forties, her mother's age, but not as pretty. Streaks of gray were threaded through her black hair, which was pulled back in a tight knot. She wore Western-style clothes except for her sandals, which had soft soles. Was she the owner?

"We are from a village in the Mekong Delta," Tâm explained.

The woman looked them up and down. "There is fierce fighting in the delta."

Tâm's lips tightened. "Mai and I are the only survivors of our village. Everyone was killed in a massacre."

"The NVA?" The woman looked concerned.

"Americans," Tâm replied.

The woman's hand rose to her forehead. "I'm sorry for your loss." Then she crossed herself. Catholic, Mai thought.

"My son enlisted in the South Vietnamese army. He left a few days ago. That is why we need help."

"We would be honored to take his place. Until he returns," Tâm said.

She eyed Tâm. "He washed dishes. Set up tables. Waited on customers on busy nights." She eyed them more intently. "Have you waited tables or worked in a restaurant before?"

Tâm hesitated. Mai wondered if she was going to lie. Mai would. But then Tâm said, "No, but we are fast learners."

"I need experienced workers. We're open for lunch and dinner. And many of our customers are Americans who only speak English." She gazed at Tâm as if she was asking a question.

Tâm winced. The idea of serving the people who had killed her family was abhorrent. It was clear, however, that she had no choice. At least for now. Aloud she said, "We need a job."

"Do you speak any English?"

"No. But we will learn."

The woman peered at them. "At least you're honest. Most of the girls who come pretend they can speak English. But apart from 'Yankee,' 'baseball,' and 'how much,' they lie." She laughed at her little joke.

Mai smiled politely. What was Tâm thinking? How were they supposed to learn English?

"Who told you about us?" The woman crossed her arms.

"A woman at the Binh Tay market who gave us lunch."

"Ah. I know who you mean. A nice woman." She dropped her arms and looked them over again. "Well, you don't need to speak English to work in the kitchen. By the way, our customers do not like Vietnamese food, so we serve mostly Chinese. My husband, who is Chinese, is the chef. He knows many dishes, but Americans love their egg roll and chow mein. Peasant food." She shrugged as if to say, *What can we do?*

She looked them over, then tipped her head to the side. "I'll give you two a chance.

You"—she pointed at Tâm—"will wash dishes." She turned to Mai. "You will help my husband. Chop vegetables. Cut up fruit. Stir soup." She paused. "You're pretty. If you learn enough English, you could be a waitress."

Mai smiled. She imagined herself in a beautiful silk kimono gliding around the restaurant taking orders, dispensing food, chatting with customers.

"The pay is 200 *đồng* per hour. Each."

Mai's face fell. "But that isn't enough. We need—"

The woman folded her arms. "How do I know you won't work just one or two days and then disappear? You stay, you learn, then we'll see about salary."

"But—" Mai pleaded.

Tâm cut in. "That will be acceptable."

"My husband's name is Wang. But you may call me Cô Cúc. You will meet my husband later."

"Pardon me, Cô Cúc," Mai said. "I did not see a stream or river nearby. Where will we wash the dishes? Is there a pump?" As soon as it was out of her mouth, she felt Tâm's elbow in her ribs.

Cô Cúc, taken aback, tapped her fingers on her arm. "You had no running water in your village?"

When Mai shook her head, Cô Cúc let out a doubtful breath. "We have indoor plumbing. Running water. Hot and cold." She hesitated. "Perhaps we shouldn't ... "

"When do we start?" Tâm said, an anxious smile on her face.

"Do you use an indoor toilet?"

The girls exchanged a glance and nodded. "They had them at our Catholic school," Mai said.

"Catholic?" She nodded. "Good." Cô Cúc fingered a gold cross on a necklace. Mai didn't mention that although they attended a Catholic school, they were Buddhists.

"So when do we start?" Mai repeated Tâm's question.

Cô Cúc looked at Mai, at Tâm, and then at her watch. "We reopen in twenty minutes. You have enough time to get an English dictionary at the bookstore across the street." She went to the cash register and pulled out a few *đồng*. "This will be deducted from your wages. She handed the money to Tâm. "When you return, I'll show you around the kitchen."

CHAPTER 12

TÂM

Two Weeks Later

T*he life span of some butterflies is only two weeks,* Tâm thought one night after work. If she'd been a butterfly, the past two weeks would have given her an enterprising, resourceful life. Both she and Mai were settling into their jobs at the Saigon Café. Tâm remembered Bác Quang mentioning a refugee camp in Cholon, not far from the Binh Tay market, so after their interview they walked back to check it out. During the Tết Offensive two months earlier, the North Vietnamese Army and their Communist allies in the South, the Viet Cong, had penetrated Cholon and held it for nearly a week before South Vietnamese and U.S. forces took it back. Since then, it had been generally peaceful. Tâm rationalized it was only a temporary solution, and it was free. The sisters spent their first week's wages on a tent and two mats and moved in.

The camp teemed with hundreds if not thousands of refugees from the south and central parts of the country. Like Tâm and Mai's, their arrival was the result of American retaliation for Tết. Space was cramped, conditions were unsanitary, and the level of noise during the day, whether it was children playing, adults shouting, or the din of Saigon around them, was oppressive. Tâm longed for the silence of the bush back home.

But there were benefits. Women set up makeshift markets in the camp, and the sisters could barter or buy fresh fruits and vegetables, *phở*, even cooked chicken and fish. Because of their evening hours, Tâm and Mai usually returned late, when the noise was muted, except for sporadic gunfire on the outskirts of the city.

By the end of the first week, Mai had befriended several girls around her own age. Some, like her, had jobs; others didn't. But all of them were of an age when they thought they knew everything about the world and could navigate the ocean of life with ease. When they gathered together, they chattered like magpies, offering one another advice about jealous boyfriends, overly protective mothers, or how to find a good paying job.

Tâm listened with half an ear when they met in their tent, instead studying the English phrase book they'd bought. She begged Mai to do the same, but Mai was unenthusiastic.

"Why must I study English?" she complained one night. "It's a waste of time. I'll never use it."

"Because a waitress who knows English makes more money than a kitchen helper." Tâm reminded her that Cô Cúc had said Mai was pretty and could waitress if she learned enough English.

"But I don't want to be a waitress."

"What are you going to do?"

Mai gave her a sly smile, as though she had a secret. "I may have other plans."

"What other plans?"

"You'll see."

"Mai, what are those chatterboxes filling your ears with?"

Mai shrugged. "If you're so eager for me to waitress, why don't you take the position?"

Tâm had no illusions about her own beauty. She was average— not ugly, not beautiful. She wasn't jealous of Mai's looks; she had never considered beauty a defining character trait. But beauty could be an asset in business, and that included a restaurant where a pretty waitress could make extra money. "What secrets are you hiding?"

"I'll tell you when I'm ready."

The stirrings of anger roiled Tâm's gut. She'd saved her sister from certain death after the massacre, made sure she had food and a path forward, even if it was by sampan. Yes, Mai had approached Anh Phong and his father's trawler, but that was just luck. Tâm had found them jobs and a place to live. And this was how Mai repaid her? Not with gratitude, but with secrets and smirks? Tâm understood how frustrated her parents had been with Mai at times. Sometimes Tâm herself wanted to slap her sister's face. But Mai was only fourteen. Not much older than a child, despite her pronouncements. Sixteen was the age of majority in Vietnam. So Tâm reined in her feelings and spoke quietly.

"Mai, you are the only family I have left. I love you, and I only want the best for you. But you are not old or wise enough to be responsible for your actions. When you are sixteen, you may do as you please. Until then, we'll have to talk before you make any important decisions. Do you understand?"

Mai nodded, then let out an exasperated breath and flounced out of the tent.

Despite Mai's cheekiness, their lives grew into the semblance of a routine. Tâm wasn't in love with her job either, but it was stable; Cô Cúc and her husband were fair and honest; and if she was careful, she could save a little every week. They'd both bought used bicycles with their second paycheck, and Tâm reminded herself how far they had come. They had survived a vicious massacre. Aside from Mai's wrist, they were uninjured. They had jobs. They would have food for the next day. And they could use their bicycles to get around Saigon.

They had survived for a reason. Perhaps it was their karma. They were supposed to be here, one step above poverty, even though she didn't know why. Tâm knew she would have to reckon with the why at some point. She grieved for the days when all she needed to do was study. Now she had to deal with what life threw at her each day.

CHAPTER 13

TÂM

South Vietnam's monsoon season begins in April, settles in during May, and continues through July. Dirty gray clouds edged in black formed in the South China Sea and brought in sheets of rain, usually in the afternoon. Back home on the Mekong, overflowing banks and floodplains meant everything slowed. Not in Saigon. When the streets flooded, sometimes higher than people's knees, traffic persisted. People simply took off their shoes and sloshed through the water.

By the end of April, the refugee camp had degenerated into a huge mud pit. Water seeped into tents, soaking beds, blankets, and clothing. Mold grew on canvas walls and flaps. Women no longer cooked outside, which meant more desperately poor and starving refugees. Theft was a constant problem. Those who could afford locks bought them.

Thinking no one would steal their pots and sodden blankets, which they'd bought at Binh Tay, Tâm didn't buy a lock. Two nights later when she got back from work, everything—blankets, pots, clothing, even their mats—was gone. When Tâm discovered the robbery, she squatted and hid her face in her hands. After all she'd done, all the sacrifices they'd made, she was crushed. The fact that everything had—again—been taken from them made her feel as dismal as if they'd been attacked by the Viet Cong. Although she normally wasn't one to show her emotions, tears spilled down her cheeks.

Mai entered the tent a few minutes later. Tâm didn't look up. For once in her life, she couldn't summon up the words to admit that she had failed. As Mai moved around the tent, Tâm heard her sharp intake of breath. "Where is my lipstick? And my mascara?" Mai snapped in an accusatory tone. "Did you take them?"

Tâm didn't answer. Mai crawled over to the back corner where they stowed their cooking and food utensils. "The pots are gone too?" She went to a loose drawer that held their clothes. Balanced on a cinder block, it was empty. "And our clothes?"

Tâm looked up. "We were robbed."

Mai squeezed her eyes shut. Then she opened them and shook her head. "That's it, Chị Tâm. I can't do this anymore. We would be better off if we'd died in the massacre."

Tâm rocked back, a sudden earnestness washing over her. "No. Never say that."

"Why not? You tried. But"—Mai pursed her lips—"after a month we are back to where we started. We have nothing." She squatted in front of Tâm. "I need to do things my way. Like I did with the trawler and Anh Phong." She paused. "That was the only smart decision we made. And it was my doing."

"Yes, it was," Tâm acknowledged. "But they were in our path for a reason. Buddha tells us so. What if you hadn't spotted them? What if you were asleep when they passed? What if—"

"Chị Tâm," Mai said, "you sound like our parents. Buddha did not help us. Religion is for children and people about to die. I want to survive. And that means earning more than a few *đồng* from a Chinese restaurant."

"You are still a child, Mai. How much money do you think you can make?"

Mai sniffed. "First of all, I will be fifteen soon, Chị Tâm. And second, I have been offered a job in Saigon that not only pays well but will give me a place to live."

Tâm inclined her head. "What kind of job? You have been scheming behind my back."

"It pays better than the stupid Saigon Café. And it's easier than waiting tables."

"What is this job?"

Mai raised her chin defiantly. "I'm going to be a hostess at the Stardust Lounge in District 1."

"What is that?"

"It's a bar and nightclub that many American GIs go to when they come to Saigon for R&R."

"What is R&R?"

"Rest and relaxation. Their break from the war."

Tâm folded her arms across her chest. "I see. You will become a whore."

Mai's cheeks flared. "No! You don't understand. I'm going to be a hostess. I'll talk to soldiers. Flirt with them. Bring them drinks. Encourage them to spend money. But I won't have sex with them."

It was Tâm's turn to shake her head. "You believe that? Who told you about it?"

"Hạnh." One of the girls she'd been hanging around with. "Her cousin, who is very pretty, got a job there. She says I am prettier than her cousin."

"Have you actually gone there? Talked to the people who run this —this nightclub? Or is this just another fiction on your part? And your new friends?"

Mai's chin quivered. "My friends are nicer than you, Chị Tâm. They care about me."

Tâm let out a breath. "How do you know it wasn't one of them who robbed us? Do they have jobs in a restaurant? Are they trying to earn a living? Or do they simply lie around all day and complain about their lives? Perhaps you should check their tents for our things."

Mai folded her arms across her chest but didn't answer.

"And now you'll go to a bar where you are expected to speak English to American soldiers. You'll flirt with them, get them drunk, but won't have sex with them? Mai, even though you're only fourteen, you can't be that naïve." Tâm shook her head. "And you're doing this because your new friends said you are pretty? How are you going to talk to these soldiers? You haven't picked up the English dictionary since we bought it."

"Chị Tâm, you don't know about these things. My friends do. And they are teaching me English." She pointed to the phrase book, lying in a muddy corner of the tent. "Not words from a book that no one uses, but words that will help me talk to American soldiers."

"Words like 'You want good time, sweetheart?' or 'I make you happy tonight'?"

Mai's face was scarlet now, her body rigid. "Chị Tâm, you never listen to me. All you do is tell me what to do. What to say. How to act. You don't believe I can think for myself." She waved a hand around the tent. "And where did it get us? This—this tent, this camp, this life? It isn't a life. Sometimes I wish I had died in the massacre."

For a brief moment Tâm looked stricken. The massacre's devastation had stolen from them any sense of peace and security. The trauma of seeing their parents and little brother murdered would be with them for a long time, perhaps the rest of their lives. But they had to go on. They couldn't allow the images of death and destruction to become a lodestone for their future. But to become a bar girl? Their parents would be ashamed. They would have blamed themselves for poor child-rearing.

"So you'll bring dishonor and shame on our family rather than work an honest day?"

"Family? What family? I have no family, Chị Tâm. Neither do you. We are alone in the world." Mai bent down to the drawer, saw nothing in it, and straightened. "Tell me, did the thieves leave us a toothbrush? A comb? A pair of chopsticks? Anything?"

"And what will you tell Cô Cúc? She gave us a chance. She's expecting you at the restaurant tomorrow."

"Tell her whatever you want. I'm done with you." Mai turned her back on Tâm and marched out of the tent.

CHAPTER 14

TÂM

Tâm told Cô Cúc about Mai's resignation the next afternoon. To her surprise, Cô Cúc didn't seem upset. "She is young and impatient. She would not have made a good waitress. Where did she go?"

Tâm shook her head, embarrassed to tell her the truth.

Cô Cúc didn't press her, which made Tâm wonder if she already knew. Tâm thought she saw a glimmer of sympathy in her expression. Then it disappeared and she said briskly, "You, on the other hand, might work out well as a waitress. I will start training you."

A few nights later, Tâm was filling in as a waitress. So much for beauty, she mused. When help was needed, the criteria for waitressing became more flexible.

It was late, and most of customers had gone. She was replacing a white tablecloth on one of the tables when the door opened, and the most elegant woman Tâm had ever seen glided in. She was petite and delicate boned, with almond-shaped dark eyes and makeup that looked perfect but not showy. Her hair was swept up in back with chopsticks holding it in place. She wore a pale blue silk blouse embroidered with colorful Chinese birds, and a pair of Western white linen pants that had no wrinkles. The sandals on her feet gave her an additional two inches of height. With her was a man, less memorable, Tâm thought, in a navy sport coat and slacks.

Cô Cúc greeted the woman with a big smile, which was effusive behavior for her, Tâm noted, and seated her at their number one table. The woman sat down gracefully, unfolded her napkin, slipped it into her lap. Napkins were rare back home.

Cô Cúc gestured at Tâm. "Bring us the wine menu."

Most people came for the food, not the alcohol, so the selection wasn't huge: three reds and three whites, as well as the requisite liquors. The woman took a quick glance and ordered the Bordeaux. Cô Cúc motioned with her chin for Tâm to get it and sat at their table. Tâm was surprised. Beyond a pleasant greeting or farewell, Cô Cúc rarely chatted up her customers. These must be important people.

As Tâm served their wine, she asked if they were ready for menus. "Not at the moment," the woman said. She looked Tâm up and down. "A new employee?" she whispered to Cô Cúc.

Cô Cúc waited for Tâm to retreat, then whispered back. She must be telling the woman Tâm's story, Tâm figured. The woman nodded at Cô Cúc, but her eyes lingered on Tâm, as if she was sizing her up for a dress. Tâm felt uneasy.

The conversation between the woman and Cô Cúc seemed intense, the woman gesturing with her hands. She was graceful even when she gestured, Tâm thought. She bit her lip, anxious to know what they were talking about but stayed out of earshot, lest Cô Cúc think she was eavesdropping. But ten minutes later, Cô Cúc waved Tâm over.

"No menus necessary, tonight, Tâm. I will order for them."

"Yes, ma'am." Tâm nodded. Cô Cúc ordered the house special, plus a noodle dish that Cô Cúc's husband made only on important occasions.

The woman smiled at Cô Cúc. "Thank you, dear Kim Cúc."

"I only wish the outcome had been better."

The woman shrugged. "We lost our best people during Tết. We overestimated our strength and underestimated the weapons used against us. We need to rebuild our forces."

Her voice was louder now, and Tâm, back at her station, could easily hear. When Cô Cúc sighed, the woman went on. "No disappointed sighs, my friend. We must remember what Hồ Chí Minh told the French twenty years ago."

"What was that?" Cô Cúc darted a glance at Tâm, who'd jerked her head up at the mention of Hồ Chí Minh.

"You can kill ten of my men for every one I kill of yours. But even at those odds, you will lose and I will win."

Tâm froze, startled by the frankness with which the woman spoke about the Viet Cong's losses during Tết. It was quite dangerous to openly support North Vietnam here in Saigon, the capital of South Vietnam. Who was this woman?

Then the woman did the oddest thing. She looked up at Tâm and raised her eyebrows, as if to say, *Isn't that right?*

Tâm opened and closed her mouth, bowed slightly, and backed into the kitchen. Her pulse was racing.

Before the massacre Tâm and her father had shared many conversations about the war. He disparaged the South Vietnamese government and the American presence. He tacitly supported the Communists, as did many in the Mekong Delta. They wanted a unified Vietnam. Not only did many still have family in the North, but the government of the South was notoriously corrupt. The Communist notion of equality for all, which Hồ Chí Minh advocated, was appealing.

Still, there wasn't much the villagers could do. Most were farmers or fishermen, and the struggle to feed their own families took all their time and energy. Some, including Tâm's parents, helped in small ways, by feeding the Viet Cong guerrillas.

Tết was supposed to be the battle to end the war. During the Lunar New Year on January 31, the People's Army of the Communist North and their Viet Cong allies launched dozens of coordinated surprise attacks on the South. Nearly 80,000 troops tried to overwhelm Saigon, Hue, Da Nang, Khe Sanh, and the American installations in and around those cities. Initially, the surprise worked, and the Communists penetrated the American embassy in Saigon, overran the American airbase, and stormed Hue, which they held for more than a month. Gradually, though, American firepower defeated them, and the Communists were forced to retreat.

But now, to hear a woman she didn't know voice thoughts similar to those her father had was a revelation. It meant she was not alone. That others felt the same way.

She needed to catch up on what she'd missed the past few weeks. She returned to the table with the house special, a Chinese dish flavored Vietnamese-style. Chicken and vegetables, it was one of Tâm's favorites. She set the plate down, bowed her head, and began to retreat.

The woman raised her chin. "What is your name, child?"

Tâm looked around, realized the woman was talking to her. "I am Trang Tâm, madam," she said.

The woman placed a graceful, well-manicured hand on her heart. "I am Dr. Đường Châu Hằng. I work for the government."

Confused, Tâm took a step back. "Excuse me?"

"The health department."

"You work for the South Vietnamese government?"

A smile slowly unfolded across Dr. Hằng's face. "Things are not always as they seem. Perhaps we could chat. I believe we have much in common. Lê Kim Cúc will give you my phone number."

CHAPTER 15

TÂM

During the first week of May, phase 2 of the Tết Offensive, what came to be called "Mini-Tết," began. Strategically, the North Vietnamese shifted the battlefield from the countryside to urban areas, in an effort to "bring the war to the enemy's own lair." Saigon became one of the primary targets. VC units wearing stolen U.S. Marine uniforms attacked Marine positions in the city center. They also attacked the Newport Bridge above the Saigon River, the Phu Tho Racetrack, and the Tan Son Nhut Air Base outside Saigon, a major installation for the Americans.

But again, the Viet Cong could not withstand the barrage of American airstrikes and heavy artillery, and a week later, the battles were over. The Americans, who measured progress by counting the number of enemy killed, claimed more than 3,000 North Vietnamese bodies, compared to a loss of less than 100 for ARVN and American forces.

There were still skirmishes. Late at night in the refugee camp Tâm could hear the spit of rifles and the whistle of mortar shells before they hit. On her way to work, she now bought a newspaper and discovered some of the skirmishes occurred in Cholon near the camp. No wonder she could hear the firefights.

She gazed around her damp, moldy tent. Mai had been right. This was no place to live. She had replaced a few necessary items: soap, toothbrush, hairbrush. She didn't need pots and pans, or even new bedding. Her bike was her only possession that hadn't been stolen—it was at the restaurant when the thieves pounced. Now she rode it to the public baths. She knew she was living a makeshift life. It wouldn't last. The fighting was moving closer.

At Cô Cúc's insistence, she'd written down Dr. Hằng's phone number and slipped it into her pocket, where it remained for a week. Tâm was intimidated by the doctor's elegance, grace, and self-confidence. She felt awkward and tongue-tied around the woman. However, after one particularly sleepless night, when the fighting sounded so close that she'd asked Buddha to protect her, Tâm knew what she had to do.

The French Quarter in District 1 was the most exclusive neighborhood in Saigon, quieter than the rest of the city. Chauffeured Citroën sedans and limousines glided down wide boulevards flanked by leafy trees. Also known also as the Colonial District, it was home to several historic landmarks built by the French, including a cathedral in the style of Notre-Dame; the architecturally elaborate post office with a yellow exterior that Mai mistook for a hotel; and a city hall in gingerbread beige with white trim, designed to resemble the city hall of Paris. In between were graceful mansions and apartment buildings in pastel shades of blue, lemon, pink, and green.

Except for her brief walk past the cathedral and post office on her way to the Saigon Café, Tâm had not visited this part of the city. Her only association with the French, Vietnam's former colonial rulers, was a few photos in a library book at her Catholic school in which mustached men in military uniforms decorated with medals wore stiff expressions that radiated power and confidence.

Dr. Hằng lived in an apartment on the third floor of an elegant pastel yellow stucco building with decorative white trim. Rainwater gushed through the wide boulevards, but traffic was light. Tâm rode her bicycle to the building. It was raining hard and water splashed her pants. By the time she arrived, she was soaked. She locked the bike to a tree.

A doorman in a navy blue uniform with gold buttons opened the door. He wore white gloves and a tall hat. Although dressed in Western garb, he was Vietnamese, and his expression was as haughty as the French officials'. Tâm had seen that before. At her Catholic school the Vietnamese janitor put on a sanctimonious air of piety worthy of a priest.

Now the doorman studied her through condescending eyes, as if she wasn't quite human. "May I help you?"

"Dr.—Dr. Đường Châu Hằng," she stammered.

"Do you have an appointment?" He stared at her wet pants.

She nodded, unsettled. Her tunic and black pants had been clean. Her long hair was swept back, and while she never wore makeup, she had washed up at the kitchen sink in the café when no one was around.

The doorman sniffed, then led her to what looked like a small metal cage in the lobby. He slid the front side open and gestured impatiently. Tâm hesitated. She had never been in an elevator before and wasn't sure she should enter. Did he plan to lock her inside? Her heart thumped in her chest. She took a breath and stepped in. He followed her, grabbed a handle, and closed the door. Then he yanked a large stick from left to right. She felt a horrifying lurch—she was sure they would drop to their deaths. But the cage slowly rose. There were no walls, and Tâm could see floors and ceilings as they crawled upward. Fascinated by the mechanics of the machine, Tâm felt her fear melt away. At the third floor they lurched to a stop, and the metal gate once again slid open.

"Left to the end of the hall," he barked.

Tâm exited and walked in the direction he indicated. When she glanced back, he was still watching her. She hurried to the end of the hall and knocked on a heavy steel door.

A moment later another Vietnamese woman who couldn't have

been older than Tâm opened it. She was dressed in a black dress with ruffles at the neck and sleeves. A small white apron was tied at her waist, and more ruffles lined its edges. Her hair was tied back in a complicated knot, and a white cap sat on top of her crown. She wore makeup and was quite attractive. She eyed Tâm curiously, then, as if she was either embarrassed or ashamed, refused to make further eye contact.

Tâm, for her part, was so surprised she couldn't speak. What was the woman wearing? Was this a costume of some sort? She wore silk stockings on her legs, and black shoes with heels. That was modern dress in Vietnam. The girl ushered her down the hall into a large room.

"The doctor will be with you in a moment," she said in Vietnamese. "You may sit there." She gestured to a plush sofa covered in a blue brocade material. Tâm nodded and lowered herself tentatively onto the sofa.

The girl disappeared but returned a moment later with a tea towel and handed it to Tâm. Tâm offered a grateful smile and tried to blot her clothes dry.

CHAPTER 16

TÂM

Tâm had never been in the midst of such opulence. The sofa was soft and velvety. The walls were covered with light gray wallpaper woven through with shiny silver branches and leaves. Silk, she thought. A low table with a glass surface and a highly polished wood base sat in front of the sofa. Two upright chairs, also polished wood, flanked it. Gold sconces with white tapered candles hung from the walls. Light gray curtains that matched the wallpaper filtered the light but didn't keep it out, and a thick oriental carpet in the middle of the room picked up those colors and more. The portion of floor not covered by the carpet looked to be marble. Fresh flowers with white, yellow, pink, and blue blossoms were arranged in vases. How did Dr. Hằng become so rich? Tâm tensed her shoulders and contracted her body in an effort to make herself smaller, as if by taking up too much space she would somehow soil or contaminate the room.

A few minutes later Dr. Hằng emerged. In contrast to the luxury of the room, she wore a no-nonsense navy business suit, nylon stockings, and navy heels. Her hair was pulled back in a knot, and her makeup, while perfect, was less dramatic than it had been on the evening they'd met. Tâm rose and bowed.

Dr. Hằng smiled. "Please sit. I am delighted you called and so pleased to see you again, Tâm. You are well?"

Tâm nodded, at a loss for words. The elegance, the taste, the sense of casual wealth, were overwhelming. She swallowed and tried to hide the tea towel with which she'd been drying herself.

"Don't worry. We're all clammy and wet during monsoon season." The doctor picked up a bell, which Tâm had not noticed before, and shook it. A silvery chime rang. "Let's have some tea."

The girl who'd opened the door for her came in. "Oui, madame?"

"Du thé, s'il vous plait, Marie."

"Oui, madame."

"Et des biscuits pour notre visiteur."

"Oui, madame." Marie turned and left the room.

"You speak French at home?" Tâm asked.

She nodded. "Est-ce que tu parle le français?"

"*Non*, madame. We only learned a few words at school."

"Ah. I see. Many Vietnamese do speak French, you know. It is considered an asset. Especially now."

"Why is that?"

Dr. Hằng smiled. "Americans generally do not speak French. Or Vietnamese, for that matter. It is a way for us to communicate when we don't want to be overheard."

"I see."

Marie returned, carrying a silver tray that held a teapot, two cups, sugar, lemon, milk, and a plate of cookies. She set down the tray on the low table between them and withdrew.

Dr. Hằng busied herself with pouring two cups. "How do you take your tea, my dear?"

Tâm looked at her and shook her head.

"Ah. I understand." The doctor picked up a lemon wedge and two cookies, placed them on the saucer, and passed it to Tâm. "This is French tea. A tiny squeeze of lemon sharpens its taste."

Tâm had never drunk tea with lemon. It was not common in her village. Dr. Hằng had peculiar habits. As if she preferred French customs to Vietnamese, even though the French, defeated by Hồ Chí

Minh at Dien Bien Phu, had finally abandoned Vietnam. Tâm took a small bite of the cookie. It tasted like a sweet, chewy coconut.

"A macaroon," Dr. Hằng said. "They are French." She sipped her tea. "Now, let's talk. First, please accept my condolences. I cannot imagine the horror and grief you have suffered."

Tâm looked down, as if doing so would keep her emotions under control. Her parents had taught her the display of feelings was not appropriate, especially with strangers.

"And I can see how hard you're working to control yourself."

Tâm didn't know what to say. She looked back up at the doctor, who smiled kindly.

"It isn't always a good thing to suppress them." She paused. "Sometimes." She paused again. "So. Cô Cúc told me about you. She is a fine woman. How did you find her?"

"A woman at the Binh Tay market gave us her name."

She nodded as if that concurred with her information. "You also have a sister, I understand. But she is no longer working at the restaurant?"

Tâm shook her head. "She found another job."

"And where will she work?"

"She will be a hostess at a nightclub."

"Ah. I understand," she repeated. A sympathetic expression came over her.

Tâm felt her eyes tear up. She blinked the tears back.

"Tell me, Tâm, were your parents Viet Cong?"

Surprised by the bluntness of the question, Tâm tried to put her thoughts in order. "I think they would have been, had they not been afraid it would put us in jeopardy." She paused. "We had a brother. Five years old. After two girls, he was the prince of the family. My parents protected him."

Dr. Hằng said, "Yet in the end, it made no difference."

Tâm couldn't help it. Her eyes filled again. She had not yet had time to mourn her family. She'd stuffed her feelings down while she tried to protect Mai and lead them out of danger.

"And now your sister has left."

Tâm nodded.

"Why?"

Tears silently rolled down Tâm's cheeks.

"She rejected your help?" Dr. Hằng took a napkin from the tray and passed it to Tâm. "I know." She soothed. "I know." She was quiet while Tâm let the tears flow. Tears of grief that had been bottled up for weeks. Grief that would take a lifetime to manage.

"And yet, despite her defiance, you feel guilty about it, don't you? You think it's your fault. That you failed your parents, your family."

Tâm looked at her. "How did you know?"

The doctor smiled and set her teacup back down on the tray.

Tâm took her time to pull herself together. "Why did you want me to visit you?"

"Why did you come?"

"I was hoping you could suggest a safe place I could move into. I'm in a refugee camp in Cholon, and there is fighting nearby. I'm living one step up from hell."

"Yes. The fighting has intensified. And that will continue," she said. "I can certainly help you find a new place, Tâm. But I think you want more than a room. I think you are looking for a purpose. A reason to go on. A way to turn the tragedy of your family and sister into something—constructive. Something good."

How did this woman know the inside of her soul?

"Tết was a failure for the patriots who want to see Vietnam reunited under one government. We lost many fine soldiers. We need to rebuild our forces with committed individuals whose goals align with ours. I think you may be one of those individuals."

"But I am just a girl. A student. What can I do?"

"What if I told you we have female fighting forces? Real Viet Cong patriots?"

Tâm's mouth fell open.

"It's true. The men call them the Long Hair Army. They are spread throughout our troops and are quite effective. Are you familiar with the Cu Chi tunnels?"

Tâm shook her head.

"Ah yes. Saigon is still new to you." She picked up a macaroon from the tray. "I can arrange a meeting with someone if you want. Not the Long Hairs but other fighters that need help. If it goes well, they would train you and then decide your assignment."

"Train me? To do what?"

"Whatever is necessary." She nibbled the cookie. "We all have our part to play."

"I-I don't know. I never thought I—"

Dr. Hằng cut Tâm off. "I realize that. Which is why I want you to think about it. And while you do, you can stay here. My husband is in Paris on business."

Her husband. Is that where their wealth came from? Was he a tycoon? Or did he inherit it from his family? Was he French? Or part French? Tâm had so many questions.

"I have an extra room. I will make contact with the right people on your behalf. If you decide, after meeting with them, that this is not what you want to do, we will find you a room in a safe place." Dr. Hằng picked up her teacup again. "But, if you believe in our mission . . ." She let the words trail off.

Tâm knew this was a test. What she said would determine her future with Dr. Hằng. She wasn't sure how to respond. "My father bought a transistor radio a few months before the—before he died. We would listen to the news broadcasts together. He said the Communists were our friends, not enemies."

"Why, if I may ask?"

"He said the Communists cared about poor people. That if they won, we would share the wealth that was previously held only by the rich. All people would be equal, and our suffering would cease."

"Did you believe him?"

Tâm straightened. "He was my father."

Dr. Hằng nodded. "He was a wise man."

Tâm shifted in her seat. *What does she want me to do?*

"And he has a wise daughter."

"May I ask you a question?" Tâm said.

Dr. Hằng nodded.

"The resurgence of the fighting around Saigon . . . Did you help plan it?"

Dr. Hằng laughed. "No. I don't get involved in military strategy or tactics. But I can tell you we will never give up. And we will win. We have already triumphed over the U.S. president. This war is the reason why he won't run for reelection." She paused. "He knows we will win. If only his generals felt the same way." She sighed. "They will. In time."

Tâm let out a breath. "Why me?"

"We need smart people. Brave people. And you have proven you're both."

Tâm felt her cheeks get hot. "I'm not sure about that."

"Think about the massacre, Tâm. Wouldn't you like to make sure it doesn't happen to a family in another village? Cô Cúc told me that you're always reading. That the sciences interest you. That you were a scholar. There is certainly a time for thought. For ideas. And then there is a time for action. This is a time for action."

PART II
SAIGON, 1968

Mai

CHAPTER 17

MAI

Mai rose from her cot and went to the mirror on the wall. Chipped and dirty, the mirror was marred by years of stains and smudges, but she didn't see its flaws. She planted herself in front of it, pursed her mouth, applied the plum lipstick, and smacked her lips.

"I love it!" she chirped to the girl in the room with her. "But does it make me look older?"

The girl hesitated for a moment, then said, "At least seventeen."

Mai grinned. "Perfect."

For the past few days Mai had been staying with five other girls in a cramped two-room apartment in a tube house in the heart of downtown Saigon. Although it was filled with shabby, threadbare furniture, the place was only a few blocks from the Stardust Lounge on Tu Do Street. Hạnh, one of the girls from the refugee camp, had been hired as a bar girl there, and Mai begged Hạnh to take her with her. Hạnh reluctantly agreed but couldn't promise she'd be hired.

"You're only fifteen. Girls must be seventeen to work."

"You're only sixteen," Mai shot back.

"Yes, but I'm tall for my age. I can pass. You . . ." She shrugged. "I don't know."

Mai, who in fact wouldn't be fifteen for another month, wasn't worried. With the right clothes and makeup, she was sure she could pass for seventeen. Hạnh told her all the girls wore Western-style clothing, so Mai spent the last of her wages from the restaurant at the market. She bought a shiny blue halter top with sequins, a pair of tight white jeans, three-inch white high heels, and cosmetics. This evening was her interview at the Stardust. She dressed, carefully arranged her hair in a French twist, and finished applying her makeup. She twirled around in the mirror, inspecting herself from every angle. "So, how do I look?"

Hạnh raised her eyebrows. "Beautiful. Now, let's go."

The Stardust Lounge, named for a famous hotel in Las Vegas, was one of a string of bars with names like Hollywood, Tahiti, Miami Beach, and Brooklyn, all designed to lure in American GIs. Hạnh opened the door, and Mai tottered in, still getting acclimated to the heels. Once inside, she planted one hand on her hip and looked around, inspecting the surroundings with what she hoped was a sophisticated expression.

Chú Thạc and Cô Thạc, the owners, according to Hạnh, were just opening for the night. The bar was at the front near the entrance. Behind it a large room contained booths covered in fake leather on the sides and tables with cheap chairs in the center. At the far end was a makeshift stage for performances, which Hạnh told her were rare. Each table and booth had a votive vase with candles that were lit when customers sat. Someone had painted a spray of stars and moons of various sizes across the ceiling in white neon paint, which glowed faintly in the semidarkness. The star design was repeated on the front of the menus.

The faint residue of cigarette smoke hung in the air, but six fans hung from the ceiling. Hạnh told her this made the Stardust a unique bar.

"Why?" Mai asked.

"Air-conditioning."

"Air what?"

"A machine that cools the air so it is not so hot indoors. They have a big unit in the back of the building. The fans circulate the air and keep it cool. It filters the cigarette smoke too. Well, a little."

"It isn't cold now."

"They haven't turned it on yet. You'll see."

Few of the bars were air-conditioned yet, which made the Stardust a popular draw for GIs used to chilled air in hot places. A girl could get used to it too.

Chú Thạc, a small, fleshy man, was behind the bar drying shot glasses with a towel. Two teenage boys, probably only a couple of years younger than Mai, mopped the floor. Hạnh had told Mai his wife did all the hiring, but Mai didn't see her.

"Good evening, Chú Thạc," Hạnh said. "This is the friend I told you about." She introduced Mai. "Where is Cô Thạc?"

When Chú Thạc looked her over, his eyes widened a bit, and he smiled. Mai smiled back. He approved. He waved his hand toward the back of the room. "She's in the kitchen making sure we have enough snacks."

The girls walked to the back, passing the younger boys. Both stopped mopping to ogle Mai, which boosted her confidence. A fleeting thought of the sampan maker's son from the next village flew into her mind. It felt like another life.

In the kitchen, which smelled of stale food and fresh disinfectant, Cô Thạc was counting out small packages of pretzels, nuts, potato chips, and rice snacks. When the girls came in, she finished her count before looking up. She was petite, like Mai, and moved with a lithe silkiness. Except for polished red nails that made her hands look like those of a Hollywood star, she wore no makeup. Frown lines were prominent on her forehead. Hạnh had said she could be cross if girls broke the rules. Now she nodded to Hạnh, then appraised Mai.

Mai felt like she was on display.

"How old are you?" The woman raised an eyebrow.

Her age? The first question? Crestfallen, Mai said, "Seventeen, Cô Thạc."

Cô Thạc shook her head. "You're not seventeen. Hạnh is only sixteen, and she towers over you."

Hạnh's jaw dropped. "How did you know that?"

Cô Thạc wrapped her arms across her chest, tapping her nails against her skin. "Do you think after five years of hiring bar girls I cannot tell how old you are?" She looked Mai over again and said scornfully, "You're barely fifteen."

There was no use lying about it, Mai thought. "That may be. But if I were still in my village, I would be promised in marriage already."

Cô Thạc grunted. "And you didn't want to marry the boy your parents arranged."

Mai nodded. That was a lie as well, but she and Hạnh had decided not to tell Cô Thạc about the massacre. Hạnh had made it clear that their wages depended on the presence of American GIs. Cô Thạc would not hire a bar girl who might harbor a grudge against them—or worse, might act on it.

Mai was devastated that the Americans had killed her family, but unlike Tâm, she didn't care about the war. The U.S. was all-powerful; the guerrillas would never win. For Mai to work at the Stardust, she was prepared to mentally cordon off what had happened back home. She would be consorting with the "enemy" every night. Persuading them to part with their money.

"You ever work in bar?" Cô Thạc asked in English.

Mai frowned. "Excuse me?"

She switched back to Vietnamese. "You do not speak English either. So. You are very pretty, but you are too young, and you do not speak English. Why should I hire you? Goodbye." She turned around and gave Mai her back.

Mai begged. "I am practice every day," she said haltingly in English. "And I work hard." Then she, too, switched to Vietnamese. "My parents—they were killed in an attack on my village. I am on my own. I was in a refugee camp. I don't want to stay there. Every night guns and bombs fire around me. I'll sell many drinks. You will see."

Cô Thạc opened a small package of peanuts, broke the wrapper, and popped a few into her mouth. She looked Mai over again as she crunched and swallowed the nuts. Mai knew the woman was making a decision. She couldn't go back to the refugee camp. She just couldn't.

Then, "You want to be a bar girl? You talk. You flirt. You tell customers you are seventeen. You bring them as many drinks as possible. You do not drink at all. We pay you half the price of the drinks. You want more money? That is your business. There is a small hotel behind us on the next block. It is clean."

Mai knew what she was referring to. She wouldn't be needing the hotel, but she kept her mouth shut.

"But you must, you must practice your English. You need to talk better."

Mai nodded. "I will. Every day."

She motioned to Hạnh. "You practice with her."

Mai nodded again. "When do I start?"

"Tonight," Cô Thạc said. "We shall see."

Mai grinned. She and Hạnh hugged each other.

CHAPTER 18

MAI

Mai let out an excited breath. She'd done it again! All by herself. Although Chị Tâm would disapprove, Mai wished her sister could see her now. This was the second time she'd succeeded, the first, of course, talking to Phong on the trawler. She was so proud of herself that she kept a silly grin on her face and found it difficult to concentrate as Chú Thạc explained the system to her.

Hạnh poked her in the side. Mai glanced over. Frowning, Hạnh stared at Chú Thạc. Mai would be a "personal" waitress. When a GI came in, particularly if he was alone, a bar girl would bring him a drink menu, then sit and help him decide on his order. The Stardust offered a wide range of tropical and American drinks. Once he decided, she would say she hoped he didn't mind if she joined him. She would go to the bar, where Chú Thạc would make his drink and give her a glass with colored water and ice. Her job was to take his money or, preferably, start a tab. She was to make sure the soldier's glass was always full. If a group of GIs came in, two or more bar girls could snag them. They should always smile, chat, dance, flirt. The more attention the bar girls showered on the GIs, the more drinks they'd order, and the more money they would all earn. Chú Thạc would record how many drinks each soldier and bar girl ordered. They would be paid every night at the end of their shift.

"How many bar girls are there?" Mai asked.

"There can be as many as twenty."

Mai did a quick calculation in her head. Drinks were on average 75 *đồng* each. If a GI had five drinks, and a bar girl the same, that was seventy-five hundred per couple. And half of that—Mai sucked in a breath—was a lot of money. Much more than she could earn at the Saigon Café.

It was eight PM when two GIs walked into the Stardust. The air-conditioning was running full blast. Already the blue haze of cigarette smoke floated toward the fans on the ceiling. Even so, Mai was delighted. No longer would she sweat in the hot, wet Saigon weather. The men headed to one of the booths. Hạnh and Mai made eye contact with each other, waited until the men sat down, then sauntered over. One man was taller than the other, so Hạnh approached him; Mai gravitated toward the other.

"Hi, boys," Hạnh said cheerfully.

The tall soldier replied. "Hello, sweetheart. What's your name?"

"Hannah."

"Well, Hannah, you just sit right down next to me, darlin.' I'm Chuck. Who's your friend?"

Hạnh sat down. "Maylinn. She just here to Saigon. She—how you say—afraid? Quiet?"

"She's shy?"

"Yes, shy."

"Well, Lenny here don't mind shy girls, do you, Lenny? You sit next to him, Maylinn."

Hạnh translated. Mai nodded and sat down.

"She doesn't speak English?" Chuck said.

"Yes," Mai said, "I speak."

"Well then," Lenny piped up. "That's good."

Mai looked over. He wasn't the worst-looking guy in the world. For a white man. But he wasn't really a man. He had pimples on his face, and his cheeks were as rosy as a baby's. She was surprised. Were American soldiers always this young? Or had he, like her, lied about his age? It didn't matter. His youth loosened her up, put them on an equal footing. She smiled. He returned it. "You are one gorgeous babe," he said.

Mai didn't know what gorgeous meant. "What is 'gorgeous'?"

"Beautiful," Hạnh translated.

"Thanks." May felt her cheeks get hot. "You want drink?"

"We'll start out with beers," Chuck said. "Miller, if you got it."

"We do," Hạnh said. "Come, Mai."

Mai rose and smiled at Lenny. When she and Hạnh were out of earshot, Mai asked, "What is 'shy'?" When Hạnh explained, Mai said, "But I'm not shy at all."

"They don't know that. Go along with it."

"That isn't me."

"You're working now. Think about playing a role. You are an actress. That's what makes it fun. Different GI, different role. Shy, not shy. Sexy. Loud. Whatever they want. As long as they keep buying drinks."

Mai ran her tongue around her lips. She could do this.

And she did.

When she returned with Lenny's beer and a glass, she set it down in front of him and poured his beer. She favored him with a shy—or what she thought was a shy—smile. A minute later, one of the boys who'd been mopping the floor came over to them with a drink, straw, and little parasol. "Thank you," Mai said softly.

"Oh man, I'm sorry," Lenny said. "I didn't know you wanted a drink, too." Mai nodded. Lenny tossed back his beer and gestured to the boy. "Two more, just like that, for us. And put them both on my tab."

The boy returned to the bar but hurried back less than a minute later with their drinks. Chú Thạc had already poured the drinks, Mai guessed.

"What do you call this?" he asked Mai.

She shrugged. She didn't know.

Chuck cut in. See that slice of orange on top?" Lenny nodded. "It's called an Agent Orange."

The two soldiers guffawed. Mai shot Hạnh a quizzical look. "Ask them what the joke is."

"What so funny?" Hạnh asked.

Chuck spoke in English. Hạnh listened, then turned to Mai. "He says the drink is called Agent Orange, for the chemical that strips the land and poisons it."

Mai remembered the fields around her village that had been defoliated. "That's not funny."

"They're Americans." Hạnh shrugged, as if that explained everything.

Lenny slipped his arm around Mai's shoulder. "You are so goddamned beautiful . . . I hope you don't mind."

Mai remembered to act shy. She went rigid for a moment, then looked at him. Then she gulped down a swig of her drink, looked over, and met his eyes. "Is okay."

Lenny's fingers brushed the back of her neck.

Two rounds later, the lights dimmed and slow music started. American music she recognized from listening to the transistor radio back home. Lenny started singing. "My girl, my girl . . ."

Chuck joined in. "Talkin' bout my girl . . . my girl."

"C'mon," Lenny said. "Let's dance."

"Okay," Mai said. He waited for her to slide out of the booth and walked her to the dance floor, where he put his arms around her and held her tight. She wrapped her arms around his neck. Together, they swayed to the music, not moving much. Over his shoulder she spotted Hạnh and Chuck in a similar embrace. Hạnh winked at her.

Mai had never danced like this with a boy before, and at first she felt self-conscious. Still, she enjoyed the warmth of his body pressed against hers. Then she felt his erection through his pants. Startled, she drew in a breath. What should she do? This was the first time she'd ever been this close to a boy. Was she supposed to be cross? To tell him it was not decent to dance this way? Or should she simply ignore it? She was about to withdraw from his embrace and go back to the booth when she decided he must know he was erect, but it didn't seem to bother him. So, if it didn't bother him, it wouldn't bother her. In fact, the only reason he was erect was because of her. She was desirable. Sexy.

She considered this new train of thought. If she was honest, she knew when she called over to Phong on the trawler that he would respond. Everyone said she was beautiful, and men worshipped beauty. Now, apparently, Lenny felt the same way. Vietnamese or American, men were the same the world over. She would remember that.

An hour later, Lenny and Chuck had polished off two more rounds and were slurring their words. Lenny leaned over and pulled Mai toward him. "I want to get to know you. All of you. Will you make love with me, Maylinn?"

No man had ever talked to her that way. She hoped she was blushing. But she was in no hurry to lose her virginity. Certainly not to the first man who asked. She pulled back and covered her mouth with her hand, pretending to be shocked.

It worked. He grimaced. "Oh, hell. I came on too strong, didn't I?"

She looked over at Hạnh, who translated for her.

"Tell him I—I'm not that kind of girl."

When Hạnh translated, Lenny said, "I'm sorry. Will you forgive me?"

She studied him, leaned forward, and kissed him on the cheek. Let him have some hope. "You come again."

"Okay, baby. I'll be back tomorrow night. Will you be here?"

When she nodded, he got up and lurched toward the bar. Mai wondered whether he and Chuck would make it back to the base.

The tab was five drinks and a beer for him, five drinks for Mai. A good start.

CHAPTER 19

MAI

It didn't take long for Mai to master the skills of a bar girl. The key was to know her customer. She would watch each GI as they arrived. Was he wearing a pair of nice pants, shirt, real shoes? Or was he dressed in jeans, a T-shirt, and scruffy Adidas? How did the soldier hold himself? Was his posture upright and proud, or did he slink in hoping no one would notice? What about his attitude? Was he interested in his surroundings? Curious about the other patrons and staff? Or was there a condescending, cynical look, a "just give me my booze" expression?

By choosing a man who met her criteria, she was two steps ahead. She would give the man time to get used to the lighting and the cool temperature. She was eternally grateful to Chú and Cô Thạc for installing air-conditioning because it always meant a full house. Once a "qualified" GI headed to a table or booth, she would glide over. In a quiet but cheerful voice, she'd say, "Hello, there."

She'd wait for the man's reaction. If his face lit up or if he smiled, she'd ask if she could sit. If he didn't respond, she'd adopt a little-girl-lost role. She'd tentatively ask if he could please help her. She'd just arrived in Saigon and was nervous about working at the bar, and she needed reassurance that she'd made the right decision. He could help by buying a drink from her. In the event the GI was a regular customer and already knew her, she'd greet him like a brother, make a fuss over him, and guide him to the table or booth at which they'd sat before, calling it their "spot."

One of those methods always worked, and within a few weeks, she was earning ten times what she'd made at the Saigon Café, and more than officials who worked for the South Vietnamese government, the girls told her.

The first thing she did was buy more clothes, all of them colorful and seductive without being slutty, mostly pants and silky tops. In order to maintain her popularity, she needed to retain some of the mystery and allure that American soldiers attached to Asian women, so she made sure her clothes flattered her slim build. Occasionally she wore an *áo dài*, a tight fitting tunic with slits on the sides, over loose pants, although Cô Thạc preferred they dress Western-style.

After a few weeks she and Hạnh pooled their resources and searched for a nicer place to live. They found a neighborhood boardinghouse run by an older couple who were hard of hearing. The couple ran a camera shop on the ground floor of their tube house; they lived on the second and third floors and rented out the fourth and fifth. Mai told the couple they were nursing students on the night shift and would be asleep most of the day. The couple said that wasn't a problem and showed them their largest room, on the fourth floor of the tube house. A small bath adjoined it. The room was large and clean and included two beds. The girls took it. They would move in two days later.

"I am so happy!" Hạnh clapped her hands together as they started back to the bar. "Here we are, from the country, and we're living on our own in Saigon. My family back home will not believe it."

"Where is home for you, Hạnh?"

"I am from the Central Highlands. A small village called Ba Na. Near Pleiku."

"Why did you come to Saigon?"

"I am the number one child, but the only daughter. The NVA

recruited my younger brothers. My mother didn't want me to be involved in the war. They recruit women, too, you know."

Mai nodded. "So your parents approved?"

Hạnh shook her head. "My father didn't. He is a committed Communist. My mother arranged for me to 'run away.'"

Mai bit her lip and went quiet. Then: "She must love you very much."

Hạnh didn't answer for a moment. "Yes." She said it almost reverently. "I miss her."

Their mood turned somber, and they walked in silence, both thinking about the families they had lost. They turned the corner and emerged from the French Quarter near the cathedral. A hot sun glinted off the stained-glass windows. Mai forced her mood to lighten. "We have each other now."

Hạnh slipped her arm around Mai. "We do. And we have good jobs, and now, a nice place to live." She smiled slyly. "And maybe something else."

Mai turned to her. "What?"

Hạnh's grin widened. "You know Chuck, the GI who comes in often?"

"Of course," Mai said. "He always asks for you."

Hạnh colored. "I know. I—I like him."

Mai's eyebrows arched. "And?"

Hạnh's face grew beet red. "He would like to have some 'private time' with me."

Mai was quiet for a moment. "And what would you like?"

"I would like that too," Hạnh said.

"Ah. I see." Mai turned her gaze from her friend to the street. "And you are hoping you can use our new apartment for this 'private time'?"

Hạnh nodded.

Mai was both jealous of and happy for her friend. A man wanted her. An American. If things worked out, perhaps he would take her to America. That was the dream of every bar girl. To get an American to fall in love with them and whisk them off to the States, where life was easy and there was plenty of money. Of course, they didn't talk about it to one another. No one wanted to confess to a dream that might not come true. They were under no illusions as to what the soldiers wanted. Some girls gave; others didn't. The rumor at the Stardust was that only one bar girl had ever left for the U.S. with her soldier prince. They were said to be in California, but no one had heard from her. But now Hạnh had a chance. It might happen.

"You are sure this is what you want, Hạnh?"

Hạnh nodded.

"Well then, of course you can," Mai answered. "Just let me know when, so I can make other arrangements."

Hạnh squealed in delight and hugged Mai. Mai wondered if that would ever happen to her.

CHAPTER 20

MAI

Even though the Viet Cong had been driven back from Saigon during the Mini-Tết of May, they tried again at the end of the month. In a new series of attacks, Cholon again faced the brunt of the fighting. A week later an American rocket misfired and killed Saigon's chief of police and five others. Mai worried about Chị Tâm, who, as far as she knew, was still at the Cholon refugee camp. Had she been caught in the crossfire? She considered going to the Saigon Café to make sure her sister was uninjured.

But she knew Chị Tâm would disapprove of her newfound affluence and how she'd come by it. Her sister clung to rigid values, values handed down by generations of villagers. But their village was gone, and they were in the middle of a war. Mai was just trying to cope. To survive. And that meant change. Doing things she'd never imagined before. She was meeting that challenge.

But Chị Tâm? Yes, she had made sure they survived the massacre and started them off on their journey to Saigon, but they had opposite approaches to life. Chị Tâm was a thinker; careful, methodical. Mai was all action; she would deal with the consequences later. She couldn't listen to Chị Tâm's lectures and rigid attitude. She never went to the Saigon Café.

～

During monsoon season, when powerful rainstorms pummeled the city, people in Saigon ignored the deluges. They went about their business, as if rain sheeting sideways was but a trifling matter and their schedules were too important to permit nature to interfere.

It was the same with the war, Mai discovered. Most Saigon natives paid little attention to the war unless they were directly involved with the military or artillery destroyed their homes. The attacks from the NVA and Viet Cong were considered nuisances, but nothing to change one's life over. But Mai had lost everything because of the war. She would never adopt such a cavalier attitude. She knew how quickly life could be destroyed, including her new life in Saigon. She was determined never to lose everything again. She just had to figure out how.

～

The Stardust packed in GIs every night, sometimes to an overflow crowd. Tables and booths turned over about three times an evening, which meant that Mai could make even more than she'd made last month. Hạnh thought it was due to the weather.

"Americans can't tolerate heat and humidity like we can," she said. "And we're one of the only bars with air-conditioning."

Mai shook her head. "It's because there are more Americans here. I overheard an officer say almost 500,000 soldiers are in Vietnam. Many more came because of Tết. Haven't you noticed? You can't go anywhere in Saigon without bumping into a uniform."

Hạnh thought about it. "I'm just glad they come here."

"I'm sure Chú Thạc and Cô Thạc feel the same way."

They were giggling when Cô Thạc herself approached. Both girls lost their smiles.

Cô Thạc didn't seem to notice. "I have made an important decision," she announced.

"What is it, Cô Thạc?" Mai swallowed. Had she done something wrong? Was her boss going to fire her?

"I want you to call me Madame Thạc from now on."

The girls stared at her. "Why?" Hạnh asked.

"We have big crowds now. Lots of Americans. 'Madame' is more elegant than 'Aunt.'" She smiled in a patronizing manner. "The Stardust should be the most sophisticated, most popular bar in Saigon." She paused. "So you tell the other girls. No more Cô Thạc. Madame Thạc is more suitable. The GIs will approve."

After Cô Thạc walked away, Mai and Hạnh exchanged glances and giggled again. There was never a dull minute at the Stardust. Still, Mai noticed that the mood inside the Stardust wasn't always cheerful and happy. Sometimes the bar thrummed with the subtle vibration of discontent. Drinking and jokes and flirting aside, she sensed an undertone of anger and despair. Most of the soldiers, barely older than Mai, were boys who found themselves thousands of miles away from home fighting in a country they'd never heard of.

Some of the GIs told Mai and the others their president, weakened by American opposition to the war, was throwing bodies into Vietnam as a last stand. Others thought the Communist threat was overblown. But most said they didn't know why they were here or what they were fighting for.

One night in June she was at a table with Châu, another bar girl, and three GIs. One was Lenny, whom she'd met the first night she worked at the Stardust. The other two were new to her: Dave from Texas and Freddy from Alabama. She'd been practicing her English with the GIs and Hạnh every day, and it was smoother, more colloquial. But the men's drawls and twangs were so thick she had trouble understanding them.

After a gloomy conversation between the men about "Charlie," the slang name the Americans called the Viet Cong, and what the gooks were doing devolved into silence, Mai changed the subject to something lighter. "I think to buy motorbike, but I know not much about. Do you?"

"Whatcha wanna know, babe?" Freddy said.

He wasn't bad-looking for an American, Mai thought. Tall, lanky, pleasant face. A striped shirt and khaki pants. The only drawback was his greasy black hair.

"I need know if price is—how you say—okay."

Freddy looked quizzical. Lenny cut in. "You mean if the price is worth it."

"Yeah, yeah." She favored him with a smile. "I don't want big bike. Little. Like me." She giggled.

Dave took a long pull on his beer. "Hey. The looie who shipped in a month ago says he has a Harley at home. What's his name?"

"First Lieutenant Bowden?" Freddy said. "The one who's in charge of weapons, armaments, and maintenance?"

Lenny nodded. "Right. Sandy or something. From Chicago."

Mai looked blankly from one GI to the other. "What is Harley?"

Dave launched into a long explanation of a Harley-Davidson, its size and power.

Mai shook her head. Between his drawl and the words he was throwing around, she was lost. She flipped up her hands. "Sorry."

Freddy grinned. "I'll show you." He curled his fingers, wrapped them around an imaginary handlebar, and pretended to shift gears. At the same time he growled, "Vroom-vroom!"

Mai made sure to chuckle. So did everyone else. "So Sandy know this"—she curled her fingers as Freddy had—"this 'vroom-vroom'?"

"Yeah, babe. Sandy knows vroom-vroom."

Mai got them another round of drinks.

CHAPTER 21

MAI

By the end of June a more festive vibe buzzed the Stardust. On the eighteenth of the month, 152 members of the Viet Cong had surrendered to ARVN forces after Operation Quyet Thang—Operation Sure Win—was fought in Pleiku, not far from Hạnh's village. It was the largest Communist surrender of the war to date, and the air of gloom at the Stardust lifted, at least temporarily. Unfortunately, Hạnh had to pretend she was happy. The fighting was so close to Ba Na, her home in the Central Highlands, that she worried about her family's safety.

Mai's birthday fell on the twenty-third of June. Vietnamese didn't celebrate on the day of their birth; everyone turned one year older on Tết. But Mai liked the idea that Americans did celebrate, and she decided to combine South Vietnam's victory with a small party for her birthday. She was officially fifteen, although she swore she was seventeen. Her favorite GIs bought her drinks, and she twirled the tiny parasols that came with them. She was sitting in a booth with two soldiers when Freddy walked in with another GI. When Freddy spotted her, he nudged his friend and waved to Mai. She grinned and waved back, motioning them over.

"Hey, babe. This is Sandy, the guy I was telling you about."

Mai looked him over. He was medium height, which meant he wouldn't tower over her as so many Americans did. He was almost as slim as a Vietnamese, and his wavy hair, like his name, reminded her of the beaches along the Mekong. He had a pronounced chin, unlike most Asians. But what caught her attention were his eyes, large pools of clear blue that seemed larger because of the glasses he wore. Something in those eyes, frank and appraising, made her nervous, and she looked away.

"This is the vroom-vroom guy." Freddy laughed.

Mai snuck a glance at Sandy. He was staring at her. Why?

"You're still interested in buying one, right?" Freddy asked.

"Oh yes," she said.

"Well then, he's your guy."

She replied with the few slang words she had learned, hoping they masked her jitters. "Far out. Cool. You want join us?" She looked around and saw Châu at the bar. She beckoned her to the table. Châu sat with them.

"This is Châu." Mai made introductions. "So, what you do in war, Sandy?"

"Ordnance."

"What?"

"Ammo. Munitions. Maintenance. Not infantry."

"In Saigon?" she asked.

"Near Saigon. Service Battery Seventh Battalion, Ninth Artillery. I deliver ammo to Freddy's platoon in the field."

"Because he knows so much about 'boom-booms.'" Freddy grinned, immensely pleased with his joke. "And he's an officer. You gotta be nice to him."

Mai didn't understand. "You have—what you call—Harley at home?"

"I do."

"Where home?"

"Rogers Park. Chicago."

She extended her index finger and lifted her thumb. "Al Capone. Bang. Bang."

"Naw . . . that's history. Chicago has the best blues music in the world. And deep-dish pizza."

"What deep dish?"

"You ask a lot of questions."

Mai wasn't sure whether to be flattered or insulted.

Then he smiled. "You know pizza, right?"

"We eat for dinner lots." A restaurant around the corner from the boardinghouse had started serving pizza, mostly to please Americans. It was different from the delicate flavors of Vietnamese cuisine. Much less subtle. GIs said it was lousy compared to what they got back home, but Mai liked the bold, cheesy taste. Best of all, it was cheap.

An hour and two rounds of drinks later, she and Sandy made a date to go motorbike shopping.

CHAPTER 22

MAI

A few days later, after the monsoon rains had poured their heart out, Sandy met Mai at the Stardust to go motorbike shopping. Mai had found a store in District 2 that was about three miles away; they rode a tuk-tuk to get there. Sitting in the back of the bicycle taxi, Mai had a visceral reaction to Sandy's presence, an itch she couldn't scratch. She was wearing jeans and a tank top, but her skin turned hot, then cold. She wanted to reach across and touch him. That she could feel an urge like that made her suddenly fearful. Did he feel the same way? She couldn't tell. He was silent, his gaze on the Saigon traffic ahead.

"It's still pretty wet," he said after a long silence.

May turned her head toward him. "Is problem? Will bike slide on road?"

"I don't think so." He looked over.

When their eyes met, her stomach lurched. She fumbled for something to say. "I—I—when you get to Saigon?"

"Two weeks ago."

"How long you stay?"

"My tour is for a year." His eyes, through his glasses, loomed large and curious. As if he'd asked her a question and was patiently waiting for the answer.

A rush of emotions tugged at Mai. Irrepressible joy; a year was forever. A pang of desire; she wanted to be with him every day of that year. And deep anxiety; what if he didn't want the same?

At the Saigon Scooter Center in District 2, Sandy changed from shy to a confident American with extensive knowledge about motorbikes. Happily, the salesman spoke better English than Mai did and answered his questions about horsepower, engine size, and cost. Unlike most of the stores in the city, crammed together in stalls or on the ground floors of homes, the shop was in a small but sturdy one-story building that had been built specifically for motorbikes and had a large lot behind it. Sandy went out to the lot, where most of the bikes were parked, and examined Vespas, Hondas, and Yamahas. He recommended a small bike for Mai, since she only planned to use it for basic transportation. She agreed. As they passed a huge motorcycle, however, Mai saw Sandy cast a wistful glance at it.

"That Harley?" she asked.

"Yup." A slow grin spread across his face. "You want to go for a ride?"

She bit her lip. The machine in front of her reminded her of a fierce dragon just waiting to swallow them whole. "Too big." Then she caught his disappointed expression. She changed her mind. "Sure. I go."

Sandy told the salesman they'd like to test-drive the Harley. The man nodded, gave them helmets, and wheeled it to the edge of the lot. "Only ten minutes, okay?"

Sandy nodded and showed Mai where to sit. He swung his leg over and keyed the engine. A ferocious growl erupted. Mai swallowed, strapped on her helmet, and nervously climbed on behind him. "Put your arms around my waist and hold on tight," he yelled.

His body was strong, slim, and yet smooth as a seashell. He smelled of American soap, cigarettes, and chewing gum. She forgot her fear. Sandy ran through the gears on the handlebars. Lenny had been right. The sound of the engine gearing up was *vroom-vroom.* They took off and flew through District 2, Sandy steering the bike around streets at what seemed like terrifying speeds. As they kept going, though, her hair flying, wind whipping her cheeks, Mai relaxed, and little by little her enjoyment grew. Never before had she felt a machine as powerful as this. The way it ate up the road as if the concrete was rice paper felt almost primitive. And liberating. They could go anywhere they wanted, she and Sandy, as long as she kept her arms around his waist and their bodies close together. Mai couldn't recall a more exhilarating time. The only sobering moment came when they crossed over the Saigon River on a concrete bridge and passed the pier where the trawler carrying her and Tâm to Saigon had docked. The memory of that day caused Mai to avert her eyes.

They left the motorbike shop with a sky-blue Vespa for Mai. Small and delicate—like her, Sandy said. It was the most expensive possession she'd ever owned, but to Mai it was money well spent. She would pay for it from her salary and tips. Sandy promised to teach her how to take care of it. She would be free to come and go as she pleased. Most of all, she would be looked at as a young woman of means. A woman to be admired and respected. What other girl owned her own motorbike? Certainly not Hạnh. Or Chị Tâm.

Sandy kick-started the engine, but he made her drive them back to the boardinghouse in time for her shift. When she pecked him on the cheek to thank him, he touched her cheek and kissed her lightly on the lips. It was her first kiss. His lips were soft and tasted salty. When he withdrew, he smiled down at her. "Thanks, Mai. This was the best time I've had since I've been in-country."

Mai smiled back. What a gentleman he was. "See you tomorrow?"

True to his word, Sandy spent time making her practice gear

changes, acceleration, when and how to brake, and basic bike maintenance. After she got her license, Mai and Hạnh rode back and forth to the Stardust when Hạnh's boyfriend, Chuck, wasn't around. Heads turned when the two attractive young girls scootered by. Mai and Hạnh loved the attention.

CHAPTER 23

MAI

Sandy supplied ammunition and weapons to his battalion four or five days a week but was generally back at the base for two days at a time. He would hitch a ride or borrow someone's motorbike and ride into Saigon to the bar.

Mai loved the way his face lit up when he spotted her at the Stardust. She would excuse herself and make her way to him. They'd hug, and she would invite him to join her at whatever table she was hosting. Within a few weeks it was clear to the other bar girls that Mai and Sandy were a couple, and they left the two alone.

When a steady stream of GIs poured in, which happened most nights, Mai would invite one or two other bar girls to join her until she was confident the new soldiers were in good hands. Then she and Sandy would slip away to a smaller table. When Cô Thạc, now Madame Thạc, occasionally tapped her on the shoulder, annoyed she was spending too much time with one customer, Mai would leave him for ten minutes, but she always found a way to return.

Mai made it her business to observe his expressions, mannerisms, and mood. She knew when he was tired, worried, or happy. Although her English wasn't perfect, she could tell when he was holding back and when he wanted to talk. Madame Thạc had said the best bar girls always knew their customer's mood and adjusted their behavior accordingly. But Sandy wasn't just a customer. Over the past month he had become her boyfriend, and—if she was lucky—perhaps one day he would be her fiancé. The girls had explained to her that he was an officer. More important than most of the soldiers who came into the Stardust. He could get her extras, like stockings, makeup, even jewelry from the PX on the base. But Mai didn't care about the swag of war. She wanted him. She wouldn't bother him with little things.

Gazing into his face one night at the bar, she sensed something wasn't right. "You okay, honey?"

He tossed back a scotch, asked for another.

She brought it to him. "What wrong?"

He threw back half of the second scotch. His eyes watered. Then he sighed. "I don't know, Mai. I don't know why we're here. I don't know who or what we're supposed to be fighting."

"Why?"

"I delivered ammo to Freddy's platoon, then drove to another in the same battery. It was about a three-hour drive. When I got to their camp, it was almost dark. A couple of squads had just come back from the field." He took another sip of his scotch. "Mai, they were really high."

She'd heard stories about GIs and drugs. Marijuana had always been an issue. She could smell it drifting out of dark alleys when she finished her shift.

"You are boss, right? You make them stop."

He smiled wistfully. "I'm a lieutenant. Not so high up. And I wouldn't know how. I think it's a lost cause."

Mai thought about it. The soldiers seemed to be drinking more at the Stardust as well. The brittle attitude that had briefly lifted in the spring was back and stronger now, tinged with a black edge of despair. It had touched most of the GIs. Including Sandy.

"Why this happen?"

"It's a lot of things," Sandy said. "Some of the guys were upset when Bobby Kennedy was shot." He looked at her. "You know, the brother of President Kennedy?"

Mai nodded.

"Well, he was running for president and was against the war. He could have stopped all this." He waved a hand. "Now there is no one. Except McCarthy. And he won't win."

He went on. "And they just replaced the general who commanded the war for the past four years. Westmoreland."

"Yes, I know name."

"Here's the thing. He told everyone we were winning. Seeing 'the light at the end of the tunnel.' We thought the war was nearly over." He tossed back more scotch. "Then there was Têt. After that he asked for 200,000 more troops. Two hundred thousand. He was a fucking liar. Made all those empty promises."

"I get drinks." Mai rose and went to the bar, thinking about Sandy's mood. He could sink into depression quickly. She felt responsible, that it was her job to cheer him up. But how? She brought the drinks to the table.

"In fact, this year more soldiers died in Vietnam than any other year of the war. And it's only fucking July. And you wonder why we all get drunk or high?"

Mai was quiet for a moment. "What about you?" she asked, half-afraid to hear his answer.

"Drugs aren't my scene. I'm just gonna keep my head down and get out of this shithole at the end of my tour. But . . ." His voice trailed off. "It's bad. Guys use when they're out in the field, not just at camp."

Mai tried not to think about his comment about the "shithole" that was Vietnam. "They are high when they fight?"

He nodded. "It's not just passing a joint back and forth, either. Some are scoring hashish, or horse—that's heroin—and ganja on the black market. Psychedelic shit, too, LSD, mescaline, and psilocybin."

Mai was quiet. She had no idea what these drugs were. Or did.

"It gets worse," he went on. "There are pills, too. Officers have started to dole out uppers to the infantry."

"What?"

"The higher-ups say it improves performance and boosts endurance on the battlefield. Then they give the guys downers for anxiety. The brass are sure they work. But they're turning guys into addicts." He shrugged. "I'm beginning to think those pills may be partly to blame for the atrocities—you know—the massacres. I wasn't here but I heard about that guy Calley. Supposedly his men were pretty strung out with all of that shit." Then, as if he'd just realized what he said, he sat up straight. "Oh shit. I'm so sorry, Mai."

Mai didn't know how to react. Sandy was the only person, besides Hạnh, who knew about the massacre of her family. She hadn't meant to tell him; it slipped out one night when they were talking about families. But she'd trusted him to keep the confidence. Indeed, she trusted him implicitly. But to think her family was killed by some drug-induced GI frenzy belittled her loss and the lives of her family. Her eyes filled. She choked back tears. He covered her free hand with his.

When they rode back to the boardinghouse on her Vespa that night, he climbed off and gave her a gentle kiss. This time, though, Mai felt an urgency for more. She wanted to get as close as possible to him. To climb inside him if she could. She wrapped her arms around him and kissed him long and deeply. The faint scent of motor oil along with mint gum and cigarettes wafted off his clothes. He responded and tightened his hold. When they broke apart, she had to catch her breath. She gazed into his eyes, saw the question in them.

He lifted her hand to his lips and kissed it. She eyed the fourth floor. It was dark. Hạnh was still at the Stardust. She looked back at him. Her dream was to go to America with Sandy. To marry him. The other girls had told her not to pressure him. And she had not. She hadn't even asked him to bring her little gifts. But tonight she couldn't help herself. "I would like to go to U.S."

"I would like to see you there."

Was that an invitation? Or just a casual comment? She didn't know. And not knowing was the answer to the question in his eyes. At least tonight.

"Good night, Sandy." She squeezed his hand.

CHAPTER 24

MAI

Mai fussed with her hair before her shift at the Stardust on a sultry day in late June. To stay cooler, she'd pinned it up. Hạnh was helping her twist it into a French braid when they heard slow but deliberate steps on the boardinghouse stairs. Then, a knock on the door. Hạnh opened it to Bà Phạm, the owner of the house.

"Cháu Mai, you have a visitor. Downstairs at the camera shop."

"A GI?" Mai asked, thinking Sandy was paying her a surprise visit.

"No. A woman."

Mai glanced at Hạnh in the mirror. "Are you expecting anyone?"

Hạnh shook her head.

"All right. Send her up."

Bà Phạm nodded and resumed her heavy tread down the steps.

A minute later a lighter gait trotted up to the fourth floor. Hạnh stayed by the door and opened it before the person had time to knock.

It was Tâm.

Startled, Mai dropped the comb she'd been using to tease her hair into place. "Chị Tâm."

"Hello, Mai."

"I'll go downstairs." Hạnh closed the door and made a speedy exit.

Mai took a good look at her sister. She was thinner and more sinewy. Her arms had definition they'd never had before, and her face was leaner. She'd cut her hair, too; it no longer hung down her back but was cut at her chin. She wore an *áo bà ba*, the black tunic over black pants that was common for women in the Mekong Delta but not in Saigon. Her sneakers were so soiled they had the same shade as dirt. As she noted her sister's appearance, she realized Tâm was examining her.

"How did you find me, Chị Tâm?"

"It wasn't hard," Tâm said. "I went to the Stardust. They told me."

Mai nodded, feeling awkward. Tâm was different, but she couldn't figure out how or why. And yet the air between them seemed charged with a peculiar energy. "Are you still working at the Saigon Café?"

"No. I have other work."

"What kind of work?"

"Oh, this and that."

Mai frowned. "What is this and that?"

"I—I have been studying."

"Your plants?"

"In a way. I'm here to tell you I'm going away, and I wanted to say goodbye. You're the only family I have." Tâm's face was blank, as if she was keeping rigid control of her feelings.

Mai's stomach pitched. Despite their problems, she never imagined Tâm would leave Saigon. Mai would be alone "Where—where are you going?"

Tâm ignored the question. "I don't know when I'll be back. Or if I'll be back at all. We may not see each other again."

"Wait. You are leaving, but you won't tell me what you're doing or where you're going? What if I need you? What if something happens? How will I find you?"

Tâm's features softened for an instant, but she quickly wrestled them back to the unrelenting stolid expression with which she'd come in. "You won't be able to."

Mai blinked rapidly. Before she could stop herself, she blurted out, "It wasn't enough for us to lose Mama, Papa, and Sáng. Now you're willing to lose me, too?"

Tâm stood motionless, her eyes scanning her sister's face. "It's always about you, Mai, isn't it? That's why we don't get along. I have dedicated myself to something that requires a selflessness you could never understand."

Mai's mouth opened. She crossed her arms. "You are serious? You have never thought about anyone beside yourself. You think you're smarter and more capable than me. You've always told me what I do wrong and how much better you are. How I'm a traitor to the family. You are not only selfish, but you are cruel."

"Of course you would say that." Tâm motioned with her hand. "Look around, Mai. What are you doing with your life? Prostituting yourself with our enemies? How many of them have you fucked? Two . . . five . . . ten? I don't have to tell you who or what you are. You know."

Mai raised her hand and slapped Tâm across the face.

Tâm raised a hand to her reddening cheek. "How do you know one of those American soldiers wasn't part of the squad that massacred our family? You have changed, Mai. Not only are you consorting with the enemy, but you continue to disrespect your older sister and have either forgotten or chosen not to honor your elders."

"You have no right to say that, Chị Tâm. You have no idea what I do or who I do it with. The important thing is that I am a survivor. I bring home more money in a week than Papa made in a month."

"It's tainted money. Only traitors would take it."

Mai took a step back. "You should hear what some of the girls at the bar say about Vietnamese men. How they watched their fathers or their neighbors beat their wives. Perhaps raped them. Then told them to go outside and feed the pigs. American men treat their women well. With respect. They are gentlemen in comparison. These girls say they will never marry a Vietnamese man."

"And you believe them . . . these girls? Did you ever see our father treat our mother that way?" Tâm snorted. "The Americans only treat you well until they get what they want."

Mai shook her head. "You're wrong. American soldiers are kind. And polite. They want to know what we think. How many Vietnamese men do you know who ask us our opinions? They're too busy drinking at night after work. Do they feed their animals? Buy food at the market and cook it? Wash their own clothes? We do it all. And why? Because they are men, and we are women. And women don't mean shit in Vietnam."

Tâm folded her arms.

Mai planted her hands on her hips. "Most of the women at the Stardust love their jobs. For the first time in their lives, they feel free. No one can take that away from them."

"Until the Viet Cong defeat South Vietnam. Then they will all become marked women. Anyone who consorts with the enemy will be dealt with. Including you. You could spend the rest of your life in prison. If you are not executed."

"The North will never win the war," Mai said defiantly.

Tâm stared at her in silence. Then: "You deserve everything you are going to get, little sister. I fear for your future. But you have brought it on yourself. Do not come to me for help."

Tâm turned on her heel, headed to the door, and slammed it on the way out. Mai heard her stomp down the steps.

CHAPTER 25

MAI

Mai's mood turned sour that night. She asked the bartender at the Stardust to mix her drinks with real liquor. The bartender cocked his head but did what she asked. Mai didn't have much tolerance for alcohol; after two drinks her rage at being abandoned by Chị Tâm had dulled, replaced with a sense of deep isolation. Chị Tâm was right about one thing, and Mai couldn't stop thinking about it. No one cared whether she lived or died, except, perhaps, Hạnh. To Chú Thạc and Cô Thạc, she was just a bar girl. To Bà Phạm, the monthly rent. She wasn't sure about Sandy.

Hạnh stuck close to Mai that evening, which Mai appreciated. Hạnh would never talk to her the way Chị Tâm had. Finally, though, Hạnh said, "I know you don't want to talk about your sister—"

"You're right." She cut Hạnh off.

"There's something you should know."

Mai threw Hạnh a wary glance. She hoped Hạnh wasn't going to lecture her too.

"I was outside the camera shop smoking a cigarette when your sister came out. And I saw something poking out of her pants pocket."

"What?"

Hạnh blinked. "It was a black-and-white-checkered scarf."

It took a moment for Mai to register. "Tâm had a *khăn rằn*?"

Hạnh nodded.

Mai's hand flew to her mouth. The *khăn rằn* was a common scarf worn in the Mekong Delta. Since the war started, however, it had become a symbol through which Viet Cong fighters, who had no uniforms and wore everyday clothes, recognized one another during combat. Wearing it now, of course, was illegal, and anyone found with the scarf could be arrested. Even executed. Astonished, Mai said, "My sister is going to fight with the Viet Cong!"

By the time Sandy showed up, Mai, on her fourth mai tai, was tipsy and loud. For her the evening had become a gray fog of cigarette smoke broken up occasionally by vivid colors like the paintings of those French painters the nuns from the Catholic school had showed them. When she spotted Sandy, she clumsily waved a hand in the air. He came over, sized her up, then glanced at Hạnh, who rolled her eyes.

Mai saw them. "You share secrets? What about?" Her words were slurred.

Sandy caught her arm in an effort to help her get up, but she pushed him away. "No." She shook her head. "I finish my drink."

"You've had enough," Sandy said. "Hạnh, get our princess some coffee." He had taken to calling her that. Usually Mai loved the nickname, but tonight she was so out of sorts she blurted out, "Not your princess." She leaned back against her chair and swiveled her head. The action made her dizzy and nauseous.

Hạnh came back with a steaming cup of coffee, but Mai pushed it away. "Too hot," she complained.

"Feeling cross, are we?" Sandy said.

Mai looked over. "Take me home."

Hạnh nodded. "Good idea."

Mai tried to get up but stumbled and bumped into the table. The coffee sloshed over the rim. Some spilled onto her dress. "Ayii!"

"I have an idea." Sandy picked her up and held her in his arms. "You're such a slip of a girl. You're lighter than my field gear."

Mai suddenly giggled at the thought of being carried into battle, but her mood darkened again. "My sister come today. She fight with Viet Cong."

Sandy look puzzled. Hạnh held up her hand to indicate it was a long story.

"Well," Sandy said, "we can talk about it. Right now, princess, I'm taking you home."

Sandy carried her from the Vespa all the way up to the fourth floor. The fresh breeze whipped up by the motorbike had sobered her somewhat, and she felt loose, as if nothing mattered. Sandy took the key from Mai and opened the door. Mai and Hạnh had divided the room with a flowered sheet so they both had privacy. Mai went to her half of the room and sat on the bed. Sandy sat beside her. Mai began to tell him about Tâm's visit, but he stopped her by gently touching his index finger to her lips. She stopped. The silence was broken only by the sound of their breathing. He leaned over and kissed her. She returned it. His fingers slipped behind her head and unpinned her hair. As it fell, their kisses became longer and deeper. He gently pressed against her until she lay back on the bed. He followed and positioned himself on top.

When she felt how hard he was, she knew what was about to happen, but this time she wanted it. Wanted him to fill the empty spaces in her body and her heart. He wanted it too, because his touch grew more insistent. Little by little, he helped her take off her blouse, her pants, and her underwear. She helped him with his clothes.

As he stroked her naked body, she shivered. She felt like an instrument whose strings he could pluck at will. He kept stroking. She began to move in a way she never had before, and with each movement, her desire mounted. When he explored her private places, which, up until now, no one had ever touched, soft cries escaped her lips. She arched her pelvis toward him. Finally, he entered her.

She gasped at the pain.

"You are a virgin?" he whispered, surprised.

She nodded.

"I didn't know."

"It's okay," she breathed. And it was. The pain was already subsiding.

He began to thrust. "Oh, Mai. Little Mai. Now you belong to me."

"Yes," she whispered back, equally surprised at how wonderful it felt. "Yes. I belong to you."

PART III
SOUTH VIETNAM, 1968

Tâm

CHAPTER 26

TÂM

Tâm knelt in the stern of the sampan on the Mekong River. Mai sat in the bow, her paddle across the gunwales. Streams of blood ran down Mai's wrist, the result of her wound from the fish-hook. "Why do we need to stay on the river?" Mai wailed. "Can't we take a bus to Saigon? Or get a ride on a truck?" Tâm didn't have an answer. Her own hands were raw and blistered from paddling. She gritted her teeth and dipped her paddle deep in the water. Suddenly a helicopter appeared above them, trailing orange smoke that drifted down to the sampan. "Smoke! The Americans are going to kill us!" Mai coughed and gagged. Tâm realized she was right. Death was imminent. The smoke, heavy and dense, descended into the Mekong, where it triggered powerful waves that crashed into the boat and flung them from port to starboard.

Tâm startled awake. Blinking away the dream, she slowly oriented herself. It was late morning, a sullen sun baking the air. She slouched in the back of a truck lumbering down a rock-strewn road. The jungle encroached on both sides, tree branches, leaves, and overgrown bushes threatening to engulf the narrow road. The uneven pitch of the terrain threw her from side to side. Six new recruits in the truck rolled with her. All of them were somber, perhaps thinking about the war to which they'd just committed. Wondering if they would survive. With the superior American firepower, the odds weren't good.

They were headed to a training camp for two weeks. Dr. Hằng had told her it was in a rural area but wouldn't say exactly where. Security, she said. But Tâm would be safe once they arrived; there was practically nothing near the camp.

"Two weeks?" Tâm had said. "Is that enough time? Will we be prepared to fight a war in two weeks?"

Dr. Hằng sighed. "Unfortunately, that's all we can manage. Continuing the war is consuming all our resources. Money, soldiers, and time. Our military commanders were overconfident. They expected Tết to succeed. Their plans were—how do you say it?—too ambitious. Unrealistic. Don't forget—we lost 40,000 men."

It had taken a month for Tâm to decide whether to join the Communists. But Dr. Hằng was persuasive, especially after Tâm accepted her invitation to stay at her apartment in the French Quarter. Thrilled to finally be leaving the refugee camp in Cholon, Tâm gave her few remaining possessions to a young woman with two small children.

The irony was that Dr. Hằng's apartment in the French Quarter was the most luxurious place Tâm had ever seen. She recalled how the French nuns at her Catholic school had declared the French were the most civilized people in the world. But when, as a student, she showed pictures of French civilization to her father, he'd hissed, "Power-hungry imperialists!" and disparaged the leaders who'd colonized Vietnam for more than a century.

Tâm was smart enough to realize her father's hostility stemmed from the occupation of Vietnam by China, France, and Japan. Like many patriotic Vietnamese, he longed for continuous independence. Where the French were concerned, however, Dr. Hằng didn't agree. It was complicated, she said. Yes, France exploited Vietnam for its resources, but they spurred development too. Their architecture, education system, even their cuisine helped raise the standard of living for many. And compared to the rest of Indochina, the French afforded the Vietnamese a higher social standing than Cambodians or Laotians. Tâm was confused. Precisely what was Dr. Hằng trying to say?

In fact, if she was honest, Tâm's decision to fight with the Communists might have had more to do with Dr. Hằng herself than with her history lessons. There was something puzzling, even mysterious, about this woman. Highly intelligent, a skilled professional who'd earned her medical degree in Paris, she operated at the pinnacle of South Vietnamese society. But she also was an eloquent advocate for the Communists. She could see all sides of an issue simultaneously, which made her a walking contradiction. It also made her dangerous. Tâm wanted to know more about her. What made her tick. And why she'd decided Tâm was worth fostering.

Tâm got an answer the night before she left for training. After a light supper of bread, cheese, and fruit, she and Dr. Hằng sat on the balcony watching twilight descend. One or two brave stars glimmered in the purple sky. The monsoon rains that afternoon had rinsed the air, and a fresh breeze promised a cooler night.

Dr. Hằng sipped a cup of tea. "Did you visit your sister?"

Tâm nodded but said nothing.

"It did not go well," Dr. Hằng said softly.

Tâm shook her head. "She is involved with U.S. soldiers. I think there is one in particular she is sleeping with."

Dr. Hằng tipped her head to the side. "That could be valuable." When Tâm flashed a quizzical expression, she replied, "Intelligence. If the two of you were on better terms, you might be able to discover and report back American troop movements and scheduled bombing raids."

Tâm shook her head again.

"Why not? Are you still too angry? Or do you not wish to manipulate her?"

Tâm's mouth opened, and she sucked in air. Dr. Hằng knew her too well. "Both, I suppose."

"What if that became your assignment after training?"

"Please, Dr. Hằng, I beg you. It would not work out."

"Sometimes we must do what we would rather not. For reunification. And our countrymen." She set the teacup down. "How did you leave it with her?"

"It was bad." She recounted how she'd told Mai she was no longer her sister.

A sad smile crossed Dr. Hằng's face. "At least you have family to be angry with."

"But your husband is alive and in Paris, yes?"

Dr. Hằng rose and went to the balcony rail, looked down at the garden in back of the apartment building. She didn't turn around. "We had a son," she said slowly. "He was about your age when he told us he wanted to fight the 'American War.' He was an enthusiastic recruit. One night he went on a mission to the airfield, not long after his training. He was killed by an enemy mortar attack."

Tâm sat without moving, afraid that if she did, even a little, Dr. Hằng might shatter into fragments of grief. A long silence ensued. Finally, the doctor turned to face Tâm. Her eyes were wet.

"You have been sleeping in his room. I redecorated it after he died. I vowed to fill it with new recruits as a memorial to him. I would only choose the best of the best. Young men whose courage and dedication reminded me of him." She cleared her throat. "You are the first woman."

Tâm was quiet for a moment. Then she said, "I am honored."

"To the Americans he was just one more number for their body-count statistics. But he was my world. I thought I would go insane after he died, but eventually, after many months, his death gave me purpose." She watched as someone on the ground below walked past the garden to their apartment. "Just as the massacre of your family did you."

Tâm was quiet. After a moment she rose, went to Dr. Hằng, and stood beside her. She and Dr. Hằng stared down at the garden until the darkening sky of twilight faded into night.

CHAPTER 27

TÂM

The camp wasn't much more than a clearing in the middle of the jungle. Tâm later found out she was in Phuoc Tuy Province, about three hours southeast of Saigon. South Vietnam occupied its capital, Ba Ria, but nearly 5,000 Communist troops had penetrated the countryside outside the city. Most depended on the support of friendly villages scattered around the province. Tâm recalled the meals people in her village had given the guerrillas, who, like ghosts in the night, materialized out of the bush. She would soon become one of those ghosts. If she survived.

As she dismounted the truck, she counted about fifteen recruits already there. Tâm saw only one other woman. They nodded to each other. She looked around. They were in the middle of a grove of rubber trees. A closer inspection revealed half a dozen small tents pitched among the trees. The tents, whose canvas sides were the same brown as the tree bark, provided a clever camouflage.

Their instructor met them at the truck. In his early twenties at most, he was slim and compact and wore a Western-style button-down shirt and jeans. His hair was on the longish side, probably to disguise his Northern allegiance and blend in with other South Vietnamese young men.

He hurried them off the truck. "I'm Nam. At least that is the name you may use for the next two weeks. Line up over there." He waved at something behind them. When the students, Tâm included, looked confused, he barked, "Now!"

This time he pointed to the clearing, which was edged by more rubber trees and others she couldn't identify. Hammocks were slung on three sides. A tarp covered one of the hammocks. They moved in a sloppy formation to the spot.

"Stop!" Nam ordered. "From this point on, you move in formation. One straight line, unless we order otherwise." The recruits assembled themselves in a line. Nam pulled out a stopwatch and timed them. "Too long. Seven seconds only. Understand?"

He didn't wait for an answer. He advanced to the hammock covered with the tarp and flung the tarp aside. In it lay at least twenty-four rifles. "How many of you have never used a rifle? Raise your hands."

Most of the recruits raised theirs, including Tâm. "First rule: Don't be afraid of them. They will become part of you, as familiar and intimate as your fingers and skin. That's why it is critical to get to know your weapon: its power, its range, weight, and most of all, its unique characteristics. Your weapon is your lifeline. Your shield between life and death. You must become a better shot than your enemy."

Each recruit was handed an assault rifle or light machine gun. Tâm didn't know the first thing about either, but she could tell the weapons in the hammock differed from one another. Tâm was handed an AK-47. Nam said that they stockpiled weapons from a variety of places. "We have a few old Soviet SKS carbines, RPD light machine guns, Chinese guns, and even M-16s, which we took from dead Americans." He grinned.

"Rule two: never leave anything in the field after an ambush," Nam said. "We use everything the Americans and ARVN discard and turn it back on them. Not only weapons, but ammo, field gear, other supplies, food. Even C-ration cans."

A young recruit laughed. "We eat the food?"

"We build explosives and stuff them in the cans to make grenades. You will prepare and demonstrate one for the group."

The boy stopped laughing.

Nam demonstrated how to carry the rifles, how to keep them close at all times, even when they relieved themselves. "Tomorrow you will be given ammo and you'll learn how to shoot."

Tâm's AK-47 was heavier than she'd expected. But she did what she was told and learned the different carry positions that would keep her and the rifle safe.

An hour later they were given a cold lunch and assigned to tents. She and the other woman, whose name was Phan Vân Chi, shared one on the edge of the grove of rubber trees. Chi was from the Highlands. Her two brothers were also Communist fighters and fought at Hue, one of the longest battles during Tết. Chi had not heard from them since the Americans retook the city.

Due to the heat, they spent the rest of the afternoon in political education. Nam and another man, who said he was part of the NLF, the political arm of the National Liberation Front, gathered at the edge of the clearing. The recruits sat on the hammocks or the ground. The NLF official, who wore glasses and looked about ten years older than Nam, lectured them about two important concepts: *đấu tranh*, "struggle," and *giải phóng*, "liberation." He summarized the history of the South Vietnamese Communists and how they'd expanded and grown over the years. Their success was due to their mastery of guerrilla techniques.

"You'll learn how to be guerrilla fighters," he said. "The NVA military, who come in from the north, fight traditional battles against the South and the Americans. But we concentrate on ambushes, sabotage, bombings, and assassinations."

Tâm leaned forward. She had known the Communists slipped in and out of the shadows, but she hadn't realized it was a calculated decision. She felt a little stupid at her ignorance.

"So. What do we mean by guerrilla warfare? The two most critical components are concealment and camouflage." The instructor pointed to the tents, then the hammocks. "You must let the jungle and the bush work for you. The tents are the same color as the tree bark. The hammocks the same green as the bush. That's camouflage. Concealment, on the other hand, is when we bury a land mine under the jungle floor and arrange leaves and foliage on top. Or we build a tiger trap. Does anyone know what that is?"

No one answered.

"It is a powerful weapon. We dig a large hole in the ground, fill it with wooden or bamboo spikes, then cover it with leaves and branches to conceal the hole. When an enemy falls into it during close combat, their limbs are impaled on the spikes. It takes considerable time to extract them—if they are still alive—without causing more damage to their body."

He looked around at the recruits. One or two looked green. Tâm swallowed.

"If you are fighting defensively, a spider-hole trap is also useful. You dig a hole in the ground, cover it with greenery, and hide inside it. When the enemy closes in, you stab them with your bayonet.

"The point is to disrupt your surroundings as little as possible, whether you are scouting, transporting goods, or, as we've discussed, preparing to fight. Many times, you'll camouflage yourself with leaves and grass to wear on your head."

Tâm worked a hand through her hair. There was so much to know about this type of warfare.

"At the same time, however, you must know your surroundings intimately. For example, many of you will be traveling up and down the Đường Trường Sơn—what the Americans call the Hồ Chí Minh Trail—to move positions, deliver supplies, or take wounded soldiers back north. Most of the trail is aboveground but there is a network of tunnels underground. We don't want you down in the tunnels without someone who knows them well. They are seeded with booby traps that can kill you if you don't know what or where they are."

"What is the purpose of the traps, if the tunnels are designed to help North Vietnam and the Communist troops?" someone asked.

"That is an excellent question." The instructor glanced at the recruits. "Does anyone have the answer?"

No one volunteered.

"The enemy discovered the tunnels, and for the past five years they've been trying to destroy them. They've used explosives. They've flushed the entrances with gas and water. They use dogs to sniff us out. They spray chemicals to defoliate the land and reveal them. They've even set fire to the grasses in an effort to expose the tunnels. They are likely the most bombed, shelled, gassed, and devastated site in the history of warfare. But the enemy has failed. Our tunnels have survived, even expanded. So now the enemy sends men down them on suicide missions."

"Suicide missions?" Tâm asked, surprised.

"They call them 'tunnel rats,' and they try to kill as many of us as they can before they are themselves killed. But we have many traps that prevent them—and their dogs—from succeeding. They are all usually killed, either by us or by the traps. That is why the people of Vietnam will defeat the enemy. We will be one people, one country, reunited."

Tâm wiped sweat from her neck. She hoped she would be ready for all this.

CHAPTER 28

TÂM

Two weeks flew by in a blur of activities, exercises, and lectures. Tâm worked with her AK-47. She carefully field-stripped it for the first time. Cleaned the parts with an oiled rag. Then, with Nam timing her, she reassembled, loaded, and assumed a shooting position. It took more than a minute.

"Not fast enough," he yelled. "You will be dead if the enemy knows you are there. Get it down to fifteen seconds."

Tâm nodded and did it again. Thirty seconds this time.

"Still too slow."

"This is the first time I've done this, sir."

"No excuses!" he shouted. "Unless you want to die."

She got it down to twenty seconds. Nam nodded grudgingly and showed her how to load a magazine with the correct ammunition. The AK fired a Soviet 7.62 round and used a standard thirty-round curved box magazine.

Once she learned how to shoot, Tâm was surprised at the thrill she felt when her shots rang true. To realize she held the power of life and death in her hands was intoxicating. Because she was a daughter and young girl, her family had emphasized an image of herself as weak and subservient. But with her AK she could end a life with a flick of her finger. What greater power was there? She almost laughed out loud. She didn't need to be told to get to know her weapon. She'd fallen in love with it.

They woke early, before sunrise. After tea and fruit, they practiced shooting, mostly tin-can targets if they had them; coconuts or jack-fruit if they didn't. After a few days, as she grew more proficient, they fitted her with a shoulder strap so it was more comfortable to carry.

The next activity was a commando crawl under cover for fifty meters with her rifle, after which she was to stop, aim, and shoot. The first time she tried, she sliced her ankle on barbed wire, but Nam gestured for her to keep going. As blood seeped from the gash onto the jungle floor, she pulled herself forward using her elbows and knees. She ignored the bugs and mosquitoes that buzzed around her head and tried to remember what he'd said about pain. It was to be expected, he said. "You must learn to accept it and keep fighting. The only time you stop is when you are dead."

They worked with bayonets as well, in endless drills where they camouflaged themselves with leaves and branches and scooted forward on their bellies holding the bayonet in an attack position. When a bell clanged, they ran to trenches, slid into them, then aimed and thrust their bayonets at burlap bags stuffed with garbage, rotten fruit, or straw.

They took turns arming and firing the two large grenade and mortar launchers in the camp, leftovers from World War II. They also practiced arming an older Chinese 75mm recoilless rifle, which required at least two soldiers, one to prepare the shot, the other to hold the shell. The camp did not have large artillery or infantry support weapons, but Nam passed around photos, which he described in detail. They needed to know about cannons, rocket launchers, and antitank weapons; they might be delivering arms or ammo to NVA troops in the field.

At the end of the first week, they moved on to explosives. Dividing into two-man teams, they carefully disassembled, then rebuilt grenades. They needed to work in teams, Nam said, because supplies were limited. He went over the parts of the grenade: the blasting cap or detonator. The fuse. The gunpowder. The safety lever or spring. The exterior shell. Ordinary matches. "By the way, dead GIs always have matches on them. Get them. We need them."

While they worked, Nam told them how one recruit blew himself up when he didn't place his thumb over the safety lever as the pin was pulled. Tâm shivered and hid her shaking hands. Nam saw her fear. "Push doubt out of your mind," he said. "There is no room for fear. We do this now so you will know how to control the explosion."

Tâm sucked in a breath. She could do this. She worked slowly and methodically to reassemble the grenade. Nam watched her, and when she finished, he grabbed it and trotted to other side of the stream behind the tents. Releasing the pin, he lobbed it into a barren area she hadn't noticed before. Five seconds later, the sudden burst of noise, smoke, and fire made the recruits cheer. Tâm let out her breath, unaware she'd been holding it in.

Nam encouraged them to invent new booby traps using sharp bamboo sticks or crossbows triggered by trip wires. Each recruit was given a utility knife. Next to her AK, it became Tâm's favorite weapon.

The recruits usually ate, then went to bed, exhausted, once darkness fell. Occasionally, though, Nam woke them up during the night to practice how to hide and melt back into the jungle. How to communicate. Communication between fighters during a mission would be a challenge; they didn't have two-way radios like the Americans. They couldn't afford them, and they didn't want them. It would be too easy to be overheard by the wrong people at the wrong time. Instead recruits practiced birdcalls or animal noises as a way of contacting or warning team members.

Better still, Nam said, "Make sure your attack plans are self-contained within your own team. We have limited access to NVA troops and their artillery. That's why we concentrate on booby traps."

Nam also talked about interrogation techniques. "Some of you will capture soldiers or citizens who support the South or other enemies of us freedom-loving comrades. There are important principles you need to learn when questioning your prisoners. If a prisoner refuses to answer, there are many tools you can use to 'encourage' cooperation, from starving prisoners to depriving them of sleep. If they still do not cooperate, you can move up to beatings, stripping off their clothing, and other activities that will sound unpleasant but are critical if we are to win this struggle." Nam was talking about torture, Tâm realized, after he described some of those activities. She squeezed her eyes shut.

They had no uniforms, but they were equipped with rubber sandals made from old tires. Tâm liked hers; they were much more practical and flexible for the jungle than the thick boots worn by the Americans and the South. Whether they were crossing rice paddies, bogs, or streams, rubber dried quickly, so foot rot wasn't an issue. The sandals were also easy to replace. Each recruit also was given a ruck-sack, a canteen, and a black-and-white-checked scarf, the *khăn rằn*. Tâm already had one.

Every afternoon when the heat of the day was overpowering, the recruits gathered in the clearing for political education. Some recruits had never been to school or had only a rudimentary educa-tion. An NLF officer took them through Vietnam's history: its dynas-ties and emperors, its close but uneasy relationship with China, its rejection of colonialism, its embrace of Communism. He told them about Karl Marx and Lenin, and how Hồ Chí Minh rose to power. He talked about French oppression, the Japanese occupation during World War II, the return of the French and their defeat at Dien Bien Phu in 1954, after which Vietnam was separated into North and South.

Tâm already knew most of what he was saying through her stud-ies. What she did not know, because she was too young, was the history of Ngô Đình Diệm, who became president of South Vietnam in 1955 after it separated from the North. She learned how Diệm and his brother were staunch anti-Communists. How they encouraged business development and education. Diệm's success impressed the U.S., which, hoping his regime would be the bulwark against Communism, poured money into South Vietnam. But Diệm was assassinated in 1963 by the CIA during a military coup, because, the instructor said, he wanted to open discussions with Hồ Chí Minh about reunification.

His eventual successor, Nguyễn Văn Thiệu, a former general, supported the coup. Although he, too, was anti-Communist, Thiệu turned a blind eye to corruption, lining his pockets with American aid. Furthermore, he was known to appoint loyalists rather than competent officers to lead the military, which was one of the reasons why the South was caught flat-footed during Tết.

The most critical point the political education officer made was the necessity of unswerving loyalty to Hồ Chí Minh and the Communist Party. Any disloyalty would be dealt with quickly; justice would be meted out with a knife or a bullet. That applied to civilians, not only soldiers. He described an incident in which villagers in Communist-controlled territory informed on a schoolteacher who did not precisely follow the North Vietnamese curriculum. The teacher was executed. If that could happen to a civilian, the NLF officer said, not without a simper or two, imagine what disloyal fighters would face. Tâm cringed. Dr. Hằng had never mentioned the brutality of the fighters. Indeed, the contrast between Dr. Hằng's polished sophistication and the soldiers' cruelty was startling. Was her omission by design? Disturbed, Tâm walked back to her tent, mulling it over.

CHAPTER 29

TÂM

Tâm's final training exercise was her first official mission as a Communist fighter. Nam assigned her and three other recruits to monitor the main road to Ba Ria, the capital of Phuoc Tuy Province. The enemy had enough sense not to travel on the road at night, but if supplies or other transport between Saigon and Ba Ria were necessary, there could be traffic during the day.

Their mission was to set a booby trap and lie in wait for a supply truck, preferably a U.S. vehicle, but an ARVN was also acceptable. Or Australian. Aussie troops were in Vietnam supporting the South and the Americans. The team would plant an explosive device, which, when a truck passed, would detonate and destroy the truck. If for some reason the explosive did not detonate, the backup plan was to ambush the truck, shoot everyone in it, and liberate whatever supplies could be useful. Nam said they had the afternoon and night to plan.

By the time he finished describing the assignment, a cold sweat had crawled up Tâm's back. Anxiety tightened her throat. The risks were enormous. What if they tried and failed? Would she be killed by the enemy? Or worse, if they failed and survived, would they be punished or even executed when they got back to camp? And what about the other three recruits? She knew the men; two were hardly more than boys. Nam was forcing strangers to trust one another with their lives with less than two weeks of training. No one was looking out for her. For the first time, Tâm questioned her decision to join the guerrillas.

She was swinging in one of the hammocks in the clearing, trying to push her doubts away. She was trying to remember everything they'd taught her about explosives and hand-to-hand combat when the other recruits found her. One, the only one who seemed close to her age, approached. She thought his name was Chinh.

"Good," he said. "You're here."

Tâm said. "Yes. I am—Biên." Nam had told them they must always use a pseudonym when they were in the field or conducting business with one another. It was their "Party name." They should never reveal their real names when they were Communist fighters.

"You?" She motioned with her chin to all three of them.

"I am Chinh." Tall and sturdy, he was clearly the leader. She assumed that was his Party name.

"Trai." Younger than Chinh, he was long-limbed but thin and his hair was cut short.

"Hiên." He looked to be younger than the others. Barely in his teens, she thought, with a mop of long hair that partially covered his eyes.

Chinh took in a breath. It puffed out his chest. "I have the plan," he said.

Tâm lifted her eyebrows. She hoped he did, because she certainly didn't. "Let's hear it."

"It's simple, actually," Chinh said. "We dig a spider hole in the middle of the road. Build or find the explosive and connect it to a trip wire. Lower it into the spider hole. When the truck rolls over the hole, the explosive will detonate, and we're done."

She noticed the younger boys nodding and smiling as Chinh described the plan. They wanted to believe Chinh knew what he was talking about. They weren't going to like what she was going to say.

"Hmm," Tâm said. "It is ambitious. But it will not work."

Chinh went rigid. "What do you mean it won't work?"

"It relies too much on chance. What if the truck tire does not roll over the spider hole? Its wheels could be riding on the edge of the road rather than the center. Which means it would avoid the spider hole altogether." She paused. "There is something else." She kept her voice neutral; she did not want to alienate him or the boys. They had to work together. "If the truck avoids the spider hole, it may not slow down, which would make an ambush impossible, and we will fail."

Chinh crossed his arms. "If you know so much, what do you suggest?"

She pasted on a smile, which she hoped looked conciliatory. "I'm not sure, but why don't we try to solve one problem at a time. For example, do you agree we need to set the trip wire or whatever we use to connect the explosive to the detonator across the entire width of the road?"

Chinh frowned. "And if I say yes?"

"It means we cannot use the main road. It is paved. We need a road that is not paved to dig a trench. And in order to find one, we need a map of the area." She motioned to Hîên. "Can you get one?"

"Where?" Hîên looked blank.

"Ask Nam. If he doesn't know, we can ask the NLF officer when he comes this afternoon."

"Then what?" Trai said.

The outline of a plan came to her. It wasn't firm, but hopefully they would clarify it together. She rose from the hammock, found a stick on the ground, and started to make lines in the dirt. "Here is what I'm thinking."

About a kilometer down the paved road was an intersection with a dirt road; on the west side, according to the map Hîên got from Nam, this dirt road took a winding path through several villages that were controlled by the Communists—which meant the chances of blowing up an American vehicle there were slim. The truck's occupants undoubtedly would know where the enemy infiltration was. They would never turn west and take the chance of being ambushed. On the east side, however, the road seemed to peter out in the jungle.

"If we can provide some sort of diversion that forces them to turn east . . ." Tâm made eye contact with Chinh, raised her eyebrows, and let her voice trail off.

"A diversion . . ." Chinh said. "Yes."

They brainstormed for hours. Even if they could stop traffic, there was no reason a truck driver would take the chance of turning off the only secure road in the province. "What if Trai and I wore South Vietnamese uniforms?" Hiên suggested. "Wouldn't that help?"

Tâm shrugged. "Not necessarily. They're not stupid. They could see it as a ruse."

"Well, what, then?"

She concentrated. "Something nonmilitary. Perhaps something that involves villagers. You know, a family."

"We don't know any villagers," Trai said.

Tâm thought about it. Then she grinned. "So we pretend. I will be the wife. You, Chinh, are my husband. You block the road. Wave your hands frantically. Call out for help. I am in an oxcart beside you. You tell them there has been an ambush ahead on the paved road, and I have been injured. You need to get me home so you can dress my wounds. You tell them they must not keep going down the paved road. That they will be ambushed too. And they should not turn west because they will run into Communist-controlled villages. That will help persuade them that we are loyal South Vietnamese."

Chinh cut in. "Yes. I see. But, they may not know what to do. What if they turn around and return the way they came?"

"Yes . . ." Tâm looked at each of the men in turn. "But even if they try, they will need to stop the truck to talk to us. At least slow down."

Chinh smiled. "So we place the explosive as close to the main road as we can. One of you"—he pointed to Trai—"will stay deep in the bush so you will not be hurt by the blast. I will stay on the main road and beg for help. Biên will cry out as if she is severely wounded."

"Exactly," Tâm said. "Meanwhile Hiên stays hidden at the edge of the road." She turned to him. "You wait until the truck slows down or they turn east off the main road. Once they do, you give Trai the signal. Maybe one of the birdcalls we've been practicing. He will detonate the explosive by touching the wire we have strung from the booby trap to the battery."

She turned back to Chinh. "What do you think?"

Grudgingly Chinh nodded. "It has a chance. But the timing is critical. Trai, you will be in the bush with the trip wire. And you, Hiên, are the most important. You will tell him when to touch the wire to the detonator."

They both nodded vigorously.

Tâm said, "Meanwhile we can hide our rifles under some blankets in the oxcart. You two have yours at your sides. If the shell does not go off, we shoot."

"But where will we find an oxcart?" Hiên asked.

"We'll get one from the villagers who bring us food at night." Friendly villagers appeared almost every night with huge bowls of *phở*, bread, and fruit for the recruits. Tâm thought of her parents, who had done the same thing. What would they think if they knew their eldest daughter was now one of them?

Chinh ran a worried hand through his hair. "Wait. What about our safety? Won't we be clipped by the blast if we're on the road?"

Tâm showed him with her stick. "We should be okay if we are to the west, this side, of the paved road. Here." She marked it with her stick. "That's why you are the critical link." She hesitated. "You must persuade them to slow down and turn east. Wave your arms. Yell at them." She demonstrated. Then she turned to Trai and Hiên. "You two should not be seen. Under any circumstance. Just stay where you are and wait for the truck to turn. Then Hiên, you signal Trai."

Chinh clapped his hands, his rancor gone. "Yes. That's it! It's good. Now let us divide up the tasks."

CHAPTER 30

TÂM

They waited until nightfall to put the plan in place. Tâm, all nerves, was restless, constantly reviewing, analyzing its strength. Were there any weak points? Anything they'd forgotten? Or miscalculated? What about the range of the blast? The shell that Nam provided them originally came from the U.S. military. After every battle, troops would scour the battlefield and round up any unexploded American ordnance to use against the enemy the next time. That payload—and there was a lot of it—made retribution sweet. It was ingenious, Tâm thought.

Now, to pass the time, she cleaned and oiled her assault rifle, her fingers sliding along the barrel, receiver, and butt. Then she loaded the magazine. She counted the rounds. More than thirty. Was that enough? Or did she need another magazine?

According to the map given to them by Nam, the main road to Ba Ria lay about two kilometers from the camp. When the last rays of daylight had fled and the sky was the color of ink, they hiked through the bush, carrying their supplies. The two younger recruits carried the shell gingerly.

Tâm was used to heat and humidity, but tonight uncertainty thickened the air, and she gulped down huge breaths to steady herself. Gray clouds shoved their way across the sky, first hiding, then revealing a full moon. Silvery moonlight bounced off the clouds, intensifying the light on the ground. No one said anything, each, like Tâm, likely wondering if they would be alive this time tomorrow.

When they emerged from the bush, the paved road stretched out in front of them. But that wasn't the road they were looking for. They kept going another kilometer until they came across the dirt road that intersected the paved one. They unpacked their gear at the corner of the intersection. Three of them hoisted shovels, and Chinh a pickax. They began to dig.

An hour later they'd dug a narrow trench about a meter from the intersection of the dirt and paved roads. The ditch, in the center of the dirt road, was just wide and deep enough to hold the artillery shell. Chinh placed the bomb in the ditch and attached a blasting cap with two wires protruding from it. He carefully stretched the wires across the road into the bush where Trai would hold a rectangular box that contained the battery. Two metal posts jutted out from the top of the battery. Chinh taped one of the wires to the negative post. Trai would hold the other wire in his hand. Both wires were stripped of insulation. As the truck slowed and approached the oxcart, Hiên would signal Trai, and he would touch the wire in his hand to the positive post. The shell should explode.

They filled the ditch with the loose dirt they'd dug up earlier and camouflaged it with leaves and small rocks. They buried the wires under the surface of the road. Then they took final measurements so they could make sure the oxcart would be far enough away from the blast's radius.

Once that was completed, Tâm realized too much time would elapse from the truck slowing and the blast. "If we give them time to get out of the truck and actually walk over to the oxcart, Chinh and I will die," she said. "Let's skip the birdcall signal. I'll scream as if I'm in agony from my wounds of the pretend ambush. That will be your signal to detonate the bomb."

Trai nodded.

"What about me?" Hiên grumbled. "What will I do?"

Chinh and Tâm exchanged glances. "You'll hide across the road in the bush," Tâm said. "If we've made an error and the bomb does not detonate, you shoot the tires on the truck to slow it down. We'll join in from our positions. Expect return fire. It"—she gulped down air —"will be dangerous." She searched for something optimistic to say to the men. "But remember, we have the element of surprise." She tried to smile.

They had decided earlier that they would stay overnight at the bomb site. The villagers would deliver the oxcart sometime that night, and Chinh thought that if a truck were to come, it might be at the relatively safer hour of dawn. Tâm agreed. Chinh suggested they nap in shifts, but Tâm was too edgy to sleep. The oxcart arrived right on schedule, along with some food.

She made camp at the edge of the paved road, half-hidden behind some bushes. A late-night breeze chased the clouds away and rustled the leaves. Jungle creatures chirred. Occasionally she heard the quiet caw of a monkey. A tiny burst of orange flared across the road, then disappeared. Chinh lighting a cigarette. He wasn't sleeping either.

CHAPTER 31

TÂM

A birdsong jolted Tâm awake. She was surprised she'd dozed off. The day hadn't yet dawned, but the moon was gone and the dark black of night had softened to gray. She picked up her AK-47 and chambered a round. No one sprang out of the bushes. No one came down the road. Still, she should make sure the others were up and ready.

She changed into her old black pants and a black shirt and headed over to the oxcart. The ox was placidly chewing grass and shrubs on the edge of the road. Tâm didn't want to disturb it, so she climbed carefully into the cart. The villagers had left blankets for them in the cart. Tâm arranged them so they covered the assault rifle. She'd just finished when she heard steps coming toward the cart from behind. She grabbed her weapon, but a voice whispered, "It's Chinh."

She put her rifle down.

"Did you sleep?" he asked.

She shrugged. "Not really."

"Neither did I."

"I saw you smoking."

He shifted. "I wanted to tell you something before—before it begins. When you pointed out the flaws in my plan, I didn't think you knew what you were doing. But I was wrong. The plan is a good one. If it doesn't work, it's not because of you. You anticipated everything."

She felt her cheeks get hot. "I don't know. There's always something you can't plan for." She wasn't used to compliments. She hung her head, almost as if she'd been criticized. Finally, in a low voice, she said, "You are a brave soul."

He didn't smile, but he nodded, a silent signal of sorts. "I'll get Trai and Hiên and we'll set up."

Daylight came, and with it the breeze gave way to the familiar heat and humidity of the jungle, and the night air that seemed so refreshing earlier grew close and stifling. Tâm drank from her canteen; her mouth was dry, but not from thirst. This could be the last day of her life. A sudden rush of rage washed over her. How could Nam have put them in this situation? After two weeks, they weren't equipped to make the kinds of decisions they'd made. To implement the plan with no guidance. They were still too raw, too inexperienced. Fear clenched her stomach, and the more she ruminated, the more tense she grew, until she wanted to cancel the mission altogether.

But she didn't.

The sun rose. In minutes sweat prickled her neck and forehead. She left most of her gear, except the canteen, in the bushes and climbed into the oxcart. Chinh reappeared shortly afterward. He was dressed in peasant clothes: a plaid short-sleeved shirt and black pants. He hid his rifle underneath the blankets next to Tâm's. They would grab them only if the explosion failed.

Then they waited.

Tâm reclined in the cart, her head on her elbow, watching the paved road ahead. Chinh walked back and forth across the paved road. There'd been no traffic on either the paved or the dirt road. An hour passed. Tâm's concentration wavered, along with the smattering of courage she'd been able to muster up. How could she have thought this would succeed? She wasn't a fighter. She was a woman. And women in Vietnam were shit, she recalled Mai saying.

Suddenly she heard a low thrum far down the paved road. Tâm sat up. Chinh, who had hidden a pair of binoculars under the blanket along with his rifle, grabbed them and focused.

"It's a truck!" he said loudly enough for everyone to hear. "Positions!"

The thrum expanded to a whine as a vehicle approached. Chinh focused the binoculars. "It's not military," he finally called out. "Let it pass." He dropped the binoculars, came over to the oxcart, where Tâm had squeezed under the blankets, and said, "Let me try to make you more comfortable."

Tâm realized he was playing the role of husband, and joined in. "Thank you, dear husband. The pain is getting sharper."

He grinned but wiped it off when they both realized the truck was slowing down. A cold weight settled in Tâm's stomach. This was the contingency she hadn't anticipated. Now what? She reached under the blanket to make sure her assault rifle was nearby. Just in case.

The truck, which bore the name of a Saigon grocery chain, rolled to a stop on the paved road, directly across from the oxcart. A man in the passenger seat called out in Vietnamese. "Hello, friends. Do you need help?"

"Tell them I'm in labor," Tâm whispered.

"My wife is in labor."

"Do you need a ride to hospital? You can get in the back and we'll take you into the capital."

"Tell them the midwife is on the way."

"Thank you but the midwife is coming to deliver the baby as soon as I get her home."

"You are sure?"

Tâm lifted her arm and waved to signal she was okay.

"Good luck. We will pray it's a boy."

"Thank you, friends." Chinh templed his hands.

The passenger waved. The driver put the truck in gear and drove off.

Tâm was about to say something when she heard another whine. Chinh heard it a moment later. He grabbed the glasses. "Positions!" he called out.

The truck was traveling faster than the grocery van. Chinh focused on the vehicle. "I can't see any markings. It might be military."

"Yes, but whose?" Tâm said.

Chinh jogged to the middle of the paved road and started to wave his hands. The driver didn't appear to see him, because the truck was still coming at him fast. Chinh kept waving his hands. Finally the truck changed gears and started to slow. Chinh put the binoculars down and waved more frantically. "I saw their faces. They're Americans. Or Australians!" he called out. "Get ready! Biên! Hiền! Trai!"

A wave of dread rolled through Tâm. For a single fleeting moment, she wanted to jump down from the oxcart and melt back into the jungle. But the truck was still coming at them. Dread turned into adrenaline, which surged through her.

The truck slowed to a crawl as it reached the intersection. Chinh was frantically waving and pointing to the dirt road that led east. The driver rolled down his window and stuck his head out.

"Out of the way, gook!" He motioned with his hand. "Or I'll run you over."

"No go!" Chinh yelled in fractured English. "No go! VC!" He yanked his thumb to indicate further down on the paved road, then waved his arms and shook his head. "No go! No go!"

The driver pulled his head back in and said something to a soldier in the passenger seat. Tâm guessed they were trying to assess whether this was an ambush or the truth. She could see their lips moving. She became aware she was holding her breath.

The driver stuck out his head again. "Who's in there?" He motioned to the oxcart. Tâm could see a muscle in his jaw pulse.

"Wife! *Người vợ!* Chinh shouted. "Wife!"

The driver pulled his head in again and conferred with the

passenger. Then, a moment later, he backed up, turned the wheel, and angled the vehicle toward the dirt road leading east. Exactly as they'd hoped. Tâm let out a blood-curdling scream.

Two seconds later, the world exploded.

A blast louder than thunder reverberated through the jungle. A fiery ball of flame engulfed the vehicle. A wave of pressure threatened to shatter Tâm's eardrums. The air left her lungs and it was hard to breathe. The flames rose and expanded, sweeping up black dust and projectiles and flinging them into the air. Seconds later they rained down to the ground. Tâm rolled into a fetal position to protect herself. She might have heard screams of agony from the truck's occupants, but she wasn't sure. Waves of black and gray smoke rose higher than the flames. She smelled rubber burning, the chemical odor of gasoline. Suddenly a second blast, not as powerful as the first, rent the air. The gas tank. The heat was intolerable. Tâm threw a blanket over her head. She hoped Chinh had managed to escape the blast.

Ten minutes later it was over. Tâm raised her head. Flames licked the carcass of what had been a military vehicle. Black smoke curled up from its desiccated hulk. The ground was littered with shattered glass, unidentifiable blackened objects, steel beams from the frame of the truck, and bits of white that could only be the bones, muscles, and sinews of men. The sky beyond the smoke was cerulean blue. A bird soared across it.

CHAPTER 32

TÂM

Back at camp that evening, Tâm and the three men waited in line at the side of a makeshift table in the clearing. The rest of the recruits occupied the hammocks. Nam was behind the table, on which lay certificates and medals. Tâm, somewhat embarrassed at the attention, looked down, but Chinh, who by some miracle was uninjured, stood proudly, his chest puffed out. Trai and Hîên, whose arm had been broken and was now encased in a cast and sling, stood behind Chinh, both with wide grins. They'd been jubilant since the return trip to camp, practically glowing from the praise and admiration of their fellow recruits.

Tâm and Chinh were more sober. While Tâm was grateful they were all still alive, the weight of what she'd done brought back the horror of the village massacre. Informants among the villagers near the camp told Nam the vehicle they'd destroyed was American. It was carrying four soldiers to the provincial capital for a meeting with their South Vietnamese counterparts. Tâm didn't regret the explosion. The Americans who annihilated her village had done far worse, taking the lives of not four, but ten times as many, including her family. And their bombing campaign was killing thousands of innocent Vietnamese who only wanted to be left alone to live their lives.

No, she didn't regret killing the four men in the truck. But with the success of the mission, she could no longer accept that she was more principled than the enemy. She had descended to the same level of violence, bloodshed, and killing. She, too, was now complicit in murder. Which made her no better than the enemy. And yet she was being honored.

Nam cut into her thoughts. "We honor these fighters. For their bravery, ingenuity, and loyalty beyond the call of duty." He recounted their mission and plan, how they'd come up with the diversion of the oxcart. He emphasized how they had all worked together—equally— as a team. How the spirit of belonging to a group that was bigger than each individual, the essence of Communism, had guided them. Tâm wished he'd stop. "For all those reasons we honor all four of you." He called each of them in turn.

"Biên, please step forward."

Tâm shuffled forward. Nam draped a medal on a ribbon around her neck and handed her a rolled-up certificate tied with string. "We rarely give out medals to our recruits. But I knew you were special. Your work proves it." Then he called Chinh and gave him the same medal and certificate. Boisterous cheers and applause rang out. Tâm and Chinh exchanged a glance. Tâm was surprised to see he looked as embarrassed as she. Nam repeated the ritual with the boys, whose unfettered pride and joy in being recognized made Tâm smile. When all four stood in front of the table, Nam said, "Please show your appreciation, comrades."

Most of the recruits were younger, like Trai and Hiên, and responded with cheers, whistles, and shouts. Nam had to signal them to quiet down.

"Tomorrow morning you will receive your assignments. I want you to know the NLF appreciates you and welcomes you into our family. We will survive the atrocities of imperialist America and its allies." He paused. "Now, go take the night off. We meet back here tomorrow at six AM."

The group dispersed. Tâm took off the medal around her neck and headed to her tent. Packing would take about thirty seconds.

Except for her AK-47, knife, and sandals, which she now wore all the time, she had very few possessions—just one change of clothes.

She was exhausted. They'd returned at midday and between reporting in, debriefing Nam, and the ceremony, she'd had no sleep. Now she arranged the mosquito netting above her mat, looking forward to a long rest. Her tent mate, Chi, snored lightly. Tâm lay down, still in her clothes, and for the first time in more than twenty-four hours, she felt her body finally relax. She was dozing, on the edge of sleep, when she heard a scratching outside.

By instinct she grabbed her rifle. Nam had told them wild animals attracted by leftover food sometimes prowled the area.

She sat up, unzipped the tent's flap, and chambered a round. She pushed the barrel of the AK-47 out first.

"Biên. Don't shoot! It's only me," a male voice whispered.

Chinh. She cautiously stuck her head out. "What are you doing here?"

He stepped forward unsteadily and squatted at the opening of the tent. "Nam gave me a pint of Jim Beam. We only drank a little and there is much left. I want to share it with you."

She frowned.

As if he knew her thoughts, he said, "Come with me. It is only fitting. We may hate the Americans, but they do make a fine whiskey."

Tâm wasn't sure this was a good idea, and she desperately needed sleep, but she didn't want to disappoint Chinh—or so she told herself. Without a sound she scrambled out of the tent. As they walked past the six tents she'd seen when she arrived at camp, she saw six more. Again they were the same colors as the surrounding leaves, bushes, and jungle foliage.

"I didn't know these were here. They are so well camouflaged," she whispered.

He pointed. "And there are six more behind those."

"Very clever." They approached the third tent. "What about your tent mate?

"I have no tent mate. I would raise hell if I did. The tents are hardly big enough for one person."

"I have a tent mate. Another woman," she said. *Because they know the women won't complain.* Vaguely irritated, she pointed to the bottle. "Give that to me. He looked surprised but handed it over. She took a swig and nearly spit it out. It was hot. Brazen. Almost spicy. She let it slide down her throat. She downed another slug. She felt suddenly warm.

"Hey, save some for me. Let's go inside."

"I thought you said it wasn't big enough."

"We will make it work."

She knew what he wanted. She looked him in the eye. "This will be my first time."

He stroked her hair. "Then I am glad it will be me."

Afterward, Tâm was too. It wasn't love; she knew that. It was the release from having lived through life-threatening danger. Not knowing from minute to minute if she'd be blown to bits. It was a celebration of survival. Of life. For the first time in weeks she let herself relax, his arm across her chest. She soon dropped into a deep sleep.

PART IV
SAIGON, 1969

Mai

CHAPTER 33

MAI

It wasn't until January 1969 that Mai discovered she was pregnant. She'd started her period only ten months earlier, and her cycle wasn't regular yet. She and Hạnh tended to get them around the same time; she'd been told that happened when women lived together. But she didn't get hers in May and August, so when it didn't show up after October, she forgot all about it. It was only when her breasts seemed heavier and sore, and when her pants and skirts grew tight, that she sought Hạnh's advice.

They were riding on the Vespa, enjoying the cooler weather on Sunday, their day off. They rode to the Binh Tay market to pick up a few things and stopped to enjoy some ice cream on the way home. As Mai described her current state, Hạnh's hand flew to her mouth, a worried expression coming over her. Hạnh had a penchant for drama, and Mai usually ignored her theatrics.

"Why are you acting this way, Hạnh? It's just a period."

Hạnh shook her head. "Mai, it's more than that." Hạnh lowered her voice to a whisper. "You're pregnant."

Mai scowled. "I can't be. I just started my period last April, and it hasn't settled down yet. I didn't get it in May. Or August. This is just more of the same."

"Are your breasts sore?"

"Yes, but—"

"Are you feeling nauseous in the morning?"

She nodded. "Sometimes."

"And you haven't been using birth control? The pill?"

"I didn't think I could get pregnant when my period is still so unpredictable. Where would I get pills anyway?"

Hạnh let out a breath. "Some of the girls use a doctor downtown. We'll get his name and make an appointment. He can do a test. You know, they say the pill is supposed to make your period more regular."

"How do you know that?"

"The doctor said so. I've been on it for six months."

"You never told me."

"I—I didn't know if you would want to know about things like that."

Mai frowned. What did Hạnh mean by "things like that"? She was reluctant to ask, unsure she wanted to hear the answer. She knew she'd gushed about Sandy to Hạnh. More now that they were lovers. Like the folktales her mother told her when she was little, he was the hero prince who would rescue her from the war—a devastating war that threatened to steal everything from her. She was able to cope with her losses because she had him. And he had the power to whisk her off to America, where they could build a new life. But a baby? It was too soon. Children were a dream far off in the future.

Now, though, as she absorbed the reality of Hạnh's words, a sense of dread washed over Mai. How would she tell Sandy? How would he react? She'd been careful not to make their relationship a drain on his energy. Sandy had enough to worry about with his job. She never said anything to him about the fantasies she shared with Hạnh. Except for the one comment back in the summer about wanting to go to America. He'd seemed receptive to the idea. What had he said? He'd like to "see her in America, too." They would have to talk about it if she was pregnant. She threw away the ice cream, its sweet taste now cloying and dense. Hạnh had to be wrong.

The next day Hạnh took Mai to a doctor in a part of District 1 Mai had stopped visiting. It wasn't dangerous, but it was crowded with people and market stalls, and the smells ranged from *phở* and cooked vegetables to urine on the sidewalk. His office, on the second floor of an older building, fortunately, looked clean. She submitted a urine sample, but after examining her, the doctor said he didn't need the test. It was clear she was about eight weeks pregnant. He was surprised she wasn't showing yet. Probably because she was so young. He advised her to come in once a month for checkups. He would deliver the baby in the hospital. She could pay him in installments.

On their way back to the Vespa, Hạnh said, "So you got pregnant sometime in November."

"It would seem so."

"I do not want to bring this up, but what if Sandy does not want the baby, Mai?"

Mai gazed at her. "What do you mean?"

"Will you still have it?"

"I don't understand. How can I not?"

"There are ways," Hạnh explained.

"If you are talking about abortion, it's very dangerous. I could never do it."

"You're wrong, Mai. It's a simple procedure. It's not legal, but several girls have had them. Madame Thạc arranged them. But you have to do it before your fourth month. So you'll need to decide soon."

Mai cocked her head. Hạnh was a fount of information. How had Mai not known about this procedure? "I'll talk to Sandy about it."

"Mai, it's your decision, not his."

"He's the father." Despite her sophisticated behavior at the Stardust, she was woefully uninformed. Did her mother know about this procedure? Had Tâm?

～

Sandy came to the Stardust late Friday evening with Freddy, the soldier who'd first introduced them. Mai had taken the time to look her best: oiling her hair, wearing a new dress, spritzing herself with the cologne she knew he liked. Sandy's expression came alive when he saw her; that was a good sign. She kissed him lightly on the lips, hugged Freddy, sat them both at a booth in the back.

"What are we drinking tonight?" Her English continued to improve, and she was proud of it. Freddy said before long she would be chattering away like a native.

"What's on draft tonight?" Sandy asked.

"The usual. Bud, Miller, and Coors," she said.

"Two Millers."

She returned with the beer and with Hoa, one of the newer girls, for Freddy. She was almost as pretty as Mai, and she noted Freddy's appreciative smile. "You always take care of me, babe." He nodded at Hoa, who seemed confused and kept her mouth shut.

No English yet, Mai thought. That would change. Mai laughed prettily, assuming her role as the cheerful, charming bar girl. Although her gut felt as cold and heavy as a block of ice, she exchanged lighthearted banter and explained to Hoa what was required of her. Was it only nine months since she had been the new girl?

It took almost two hours before she got Sandy alone. She served him a cocktail and sat next to him. Crowded in the booth, their shoulders touched. He rolled his glass around the table. Mai waited for him to talk. But he was quiet.

"Is everything okay?"

He looked through his glasses at her. The lenses made his blue eyes seem enormous. And sad. "I had my evaluation with my captain, Mai. I am going home in the middle of March."

Mai felt like she'd been punched in the stomach. "So soon?"

"It's been almost eleven months."

Mai bit her lip and glanced down.

"I earned high marks on everything. And then he offered me a promotion to captain, if I would stay another six months."

She looked up, eager. "What did you say?"

"I said no. I need to go home and start college."

Mai swallowed. "I see."

A long silence bounced from one to the other. Then they both spoke at the same time. "Mai, there's something I want to say to you."

"I have something to tell you, Sandy."

Their somewhat embarrassed smiles were short-lived. Mai signaled him to go first.

"I don't think I would have made it through this year if not for you. You are the light of my life. The only good thing I'll remember about this fucking war." He chugged his beer.

She wasn't sure how to say it. *Just tell him*, she heard Hạnh say. "Sandy, I'm pregnant. I am starting my fourth month. It is your baby. I want to come with you. To Chicago. Have our baby and raise it together."

Sandy blinked several times. He glanced at Mai, then looked at his beer. As if he had heard her words but didn't understand. The silence expanded and thickened into a heavy wall.

"Did you hear me, Sandy?" she asked quietly.

He nodded, still blinking. The noise of the crowd at the Stardust grew rowdier and shrill. "That why I not pressure you for little things, you know, like makeup or cigarettes," she blurted out. "Like other girls. I not want those things. I want you. I love you. I want to spend rest of my life together. I think you want same thing. I make you happy, yes?"

Finally he stopped blinking, took in a breath, and looked at her. "I thought you were on the pill."

Irritation snaked through her. "Who tell you that? Not me."

"No, but all the other girls said . . ."

"They tell you I am on pill? That is a lie."

"They say they are on pill. At least that's what the guys say."

There was no joy on his part. No excitement. His eyes were empty. Mai felt a sharp pain stab her. This was not going the way she'd hoped. Over the past year her universe had shrunk to a world of two people. Now one was sipping a beer, and the other was about to beg.

"You—you do not want me? Or baby?" She knew she sounded like a little girl whose balloon had suddenly been punctured. She couldn't help it. She felt alone. Desperately alone.

His sigh was audible. "That's not it, Mai. Not at all. Of course I want you. And the baby. He tried to smile, but it looked wooden, artificial. "But . . ." His smile faded. "I don't know. How would I . . . I mean, my family back home . . ."

"What are you saying?"

"My parents expect me to go to college on the GI Bill. Then graduate school. They want me to be a lawyer. Or a doctor. It will be hard to do that with a baby."

"Is not hard. I will work. Pay bills. Take care of baby. You study."

Another sad smile. "The money you bring in will not be enough. Things cost much more in the U.S. than here. Much more. And my parents don't have the money to support us."

The noise at the Stardust might as well have been thousands of miles away. She squeezed her hands into fists, equal parts rage and sorrow battling. "So I am right. You don't want baby. You don't want me."

Sandy shook his head. "I do want you. Who wouldn't? You are gorgeous. Sweet. Sexy. And of course I want the baby too."

Her eyes narrowed. "Prove it. We can get married here. At the courthouse."

"I—I do love you Mai." He covered her fist with his hand. "Let me think it over. I'll figure something out. I can—I can ask my parents for a ticket to fly you over after I'm home."

"Really?"

He nodded. "We'll figure something out. I promise."

She loosened her fists.

CHAPTER 34

MAI

S andy was often out in the field for a week or more, delivering and setting up armaments for various platoons. For a week Mai waited patiently for him to come back with an airplane ticket. But when he didn't show up by the middle of February, she started to ask around. One night she spotted Freddy at a table with two other GIs.

She casually dropped by. "Hello, Freddy. How are you?"

"Mai. Don't you look as pretty as a peach." She looked down at him, conscious that the other men were checking her out. Did she spot a trace of pity in his eyes? He introduced her to the others and pointed to one. "This is Hank. He just got here. We're giving him an orientation."

She dipped her head, not making eye contact with either man.

"Will you sit with us?"

"Freddy, have you seen Sandy? Is he okay?"

Freddy suddenly became absorbed in his beer, as if it was the most interesting object on earth. His lips tightened. "No, Mai. I haven't seen him." He looked up. "He hasn't been here?"

She shook her head. "Has—have you checked the KIA lists? Was he on one?" She knew GIs had access to the weekly lists the military produced of Americans who were killed in action.

"No. Nothing like that."

"You know something that you're not telling me."

"No, Mai. I don't. But if I see him, I'll let him know you're looking for him."

She nodded and floated off.

By the third week fear and despair took turns tearing apart her soul. Fear that he was injured. Despair that he had left her. Every time the door to the Stardust opened, Mai watched who came in. When it wasn't Sandy, which it never was, another pang of disappointment stabbed her. She lost her appetite. She didn't sleep. She couldn't think of anything else.

She began to ask every GI at the Stardust if they knew First Lieutenant Alexander Bowden. Most didn't. Neither did the familiar faces she'd seen over the past year. No one could or would tell her anything.

"I am here every night. Please let me know if you hear something," she said one night. She turned around to find Madame Thạc in front of her, hands planted on her hips. The woman pulled her aside. "You have been asking every soldier who comes in about this man, haven't you?"

"He is my boyfriend. We are engaged."

"Is that so. Where is your ring?"

"He—he said he will bring it the next time he comes in."

Madame Thạc took in a breath. "Mai, you are one of my best girls, but you must stop asking about this man. Your behavior is bad for business. The soldiers want you, not a young woman who mopes around, constantly talking about another GI. Do you understand?"

Mai nodded miserably.

"Keep your feelings for your day off. When you are here, you must be the charming, beautiful hostess I took a chance on, although she was only fourteen." The shadow of a smile passed across Madame Thạc's face.

"You knew?"

"Of course I did. I also know you are pregnant."

Mai stiffened. "How?"

"I'm a woman. I see the signs. The glowing skin. The clear eyes. The tiny bump. This is his baby?"

She nodded.

"It's not too late to get rid of it." Madame Thạc went on. "It's not yet a baby. It's—it's like a seed that is growing. But more important, you can't work here if you are pregnant. Men don't want to see that. And this place is no good for you or your baby." Madame Thạc pointed upward at the haze of smoke. "But I don't want to see you go. So I'll give you the name of a Chinese doctor. But you must keep it to yourself. It is illegal. I don't want to see you—or the doctor—get into trouble."

"Never!" Mai lashed out. "How can you even suggest such a thing? Sandy will be back. We're going to be married. We'll raise our child together."

Madame Thạc looked like she might respond but bit her lip instead. She gazed around the room, then back at Mai. "See that young GI over there? Drinking by himself?"

Mai followed her gaze.

"You go over there and make him happy. Right now. We will finish this discussion another time." She turned Mai around by her shoulders and gave her a little push in the soldier's direction.

For the rest of the night, Mai felt self-conscious, certain that everyone was talking about her and her missing soldier boyfriend. And that she was pregnant. She knew other bar girls who had become pregnant by U.S. soldiers. Most were still in Vietnam with their children, their boyfriends long gone. But she and Sandy were special. Weren't they?

How could he have left her? After all she'd done for him. How could he rip to shreds the fragile happiness she had glued together after the massacre? He couldn't—wouldn't—be that cruel. Waves of heat and then chills skimmed her body. He had told her many times how beautiful she was. How he wanted to be with her all the time. He'd even helped her shop for her Vespa. Her stomach knotted into a tight ball. Was it all a show? A way for him to casually pass the time? Where was he? It was the not knowing that was intolerable. If he wasn't wounded or hurt, there was only one other conclusion: the only man she had made room for in her heart had abandoned her.

CHAPTER 35

MAI

The next morning Mai set out on her Vespa for Bien Hoa Air Base, about twenty-five kilometers from Saigon. As she cleared the city and the shanties of the close-in suburbs, the Vespa kicked up a familiar fine red dust. It was the dust that coated the roads and fields back home. It even seeped into their hut at home, and it had been Mai's job to sweep the floor every afternoon. A swell of homesickness washed over her. Almost a year had passed since the death of her family and her escape to Saigon. She recalled Tâm saying they'd never had the time to grieve. On that particular subject, her sister had been right. Tears filled her eyes, and she pulled to the side of the road to collect herself.

A few moments later a sign said she'd arrived at the front gate of the Bien Hoa Air Base. The major base for the U.S. Army during the war, it was huge, sprawling across hundreds of acres. In addition to the army, the air force, navy, and marines stationed units there as well. This airfield was base camp for Sandy.

A couple of GIs walking by the gate slowed and stared at her but eventually went back to their conversation. She talked to the MP at the gate and explained why she was there. The MP stared at her. Sandy had told her that because of the base's size and its nearness to

Saigon, Viet Cong attacks were frequent. During Tết, Sandy said, Charlie would shoot soldiers from the shanties across the street. Did the MP Mai had just passed think she was the enemy?

"Please, sir. I really need to find out where my fiancé is. He was supposed to send me an airplane ticket to Chicago." She bit her tongue. "Please."

Finally, the MP gave her a brief nod and gave her directions to the check-in hut. Mai thanked him profusely and started to wheel the Vespa inside the front gate. "That stays here," the MP said. She nodded, leaned it against the fence, and walked inside.

Another soldier jogged by.

"Hello. Please, can you help me?"

He slowed.

"Where is check-in?"

He motioned to a wooden building about a hundred meters from the gate. "They're supposed to have a master list of everyone. Update it every day."

She nodded.

He squinted. "Good luck."

She walked to the wooden building. Several loud helicopters began to growl. They weren't close, but their noise was deafening. She shaded her eyes and watched as they rose into the air, dust clouds swirling. No sooner had their clatter receded when she heard the roar of several planes that, one after another, thundered down the runway and took to the sky. Moments later, the smell of jet exhaust, hot and tangy, drifted over.

Mai climbed two steps up to the door. It was unlocked. She pushed through. A GI in a khaki uniform lounged behind a battered gray metal desk. Although the noise outside was piercingly loud, it didn't seem to disturb him. He was deep into a book. She couldn't see the title, wouldn't have known it anyway. She could speak English. Reading it was another matter.

"Excuse me, sir."

He looked up and appraised her. She was holding her helmet in one hand. Her hair was pulled back in a ponytail. A knapsack hung from her shoulders. But she'd applied makeup and polished her nails.

"Chào em," he replied in Vietnamese.

She answered in English. "Good morning."

He cleared his throat and switched back to English. "What can I do you for?"

"I'm looking for a GI. Alexander Bowden. He a first lieutenant. Can you tell me where to find him?"

"Give me a minute." He got up and went behind the desk, where a door led to an office. The door was closed. A painted sign on a wood plank hung above the door, but she couldn't read it. A second soldier, beefy but short, in green fatigues, opened the door and headed toward Mai. The first soldier followed him.

"I'm Captain Shepherd. I hear you're looking for Lieutenant Bowden."

"Yes, please," she said.

He cocked his head, then shook his head. "He shipped out a couple days ago. He's on his way home."

Mai froze. "That's not possible."

"I walked him to the airfield myself. He applied for early release."

"What is early release?" She still had trouble with the "r" sound. She was embarrassed.

"It's approval to leave a month ahead of schedule. There was something about a college semester that he needed to register for."

"No. He is my fiancé. He was supposed to . . ." Her voice trailed off, and her hand flew to her forehead. Sandy had run out on her. He hadn't even said goodbye. She stared at the captain. Then at the clerk. She had no idea what to say. She dropped her hand, turned on her heel, and ran out of the building.

Mai never knew how she got back to Saigon. The tears started soon after she mounted the Vespa. She couldn't see more than a meter in front of her, and, in retrospect, it must have been the Buddha who guided her back. She thought she was back in control when she parked the bike and climbed her stairs, but she collapsed when she reached her room. Tears flowed. For Sandy, for Tâm, her parents, little Sáng. Her world had shattered. For the second time in less than a year.

Was this the life she was destined to live? To be robbed of happiness just when she was almost able to reach out and touch it?

What was she doing wrong that the gods above, whoever they were, wanted to punish her? Was it possible she had been marked for misfortune by one of the evil spirits? That despite her mother's name for her, Dirty Rabbit, it hadn't kept them away? Or was it just this war, this horrific war, that had destroyed her family, her future, and her happiness? She thought she'd been doing all right. Embracing her new life in Saigon. Working at the Stardust. Falling for Sandy. But now it was all falling apart. What was she doing wrong?

She didn't know how long she cried, but she spent the next two days wrestling with what to do. She felt her belly. Whatever was inside, she didn't want it. Sandy had no right to saddle her with this memory of him. If she was to be alone, she would make sure it was absolute. She would make an appointment with the doctor Madame Thạc had suggested.

But what if something went wrong? What if the doctor failed to take the "seed" out of her? What if he made a mistake? Would she survive? And what if she and the doctor were arrested? Abortions were illegal. Would they put her in jail?

There was always the chance that Sandy would send her a plane ticket. He was just getting home, registering for school. When he realized how much he missed Mai, he could decide he couldn't live without her. And the baby. If she followed through and went to the doctor, she would lose the slim hope she was still grasping.

No. Sandy was gone, and he wasn't coming back. She clutched a booklet he had given her one night. *A Pocket Guide to Vietnam*, it was a ninety-page booklet filled with advice and suggestions about dealing with Vietnamese customs, plus simple phrases in Vietnamese. They had laughed together about some of the advice, and she had taught him how to pronounce some of the phrases. It was the only reminder, the only tangible proof, that they had been a couple. She felt like tearing it to shreds, destroying it forever. She wanted nothing that would remind her of him. She would make an appointment with Madame Thạc's doctor. And she would never allow another human being to hurt her again.

CHAPTER 36

MAI

Mai took Hạnh with her to the doctor. She steered the Vespa around the shadowy back streets of Saigon, zigzagging through alleys too narrow, crowded, and dirty to be called streets. Storefront after storefront, most of them shabby and dilapidated, lined both sides of the alleys. Feral cats made themselves at home. Women squatted over pots stirring *phở* while hungry customers eagerly waited. Emaciated dogs whimpered for scraps but were swatted away, and the absence of sunshine intensified the fetid odors of animal waste, rotten food, and decay. Above it all was the nasal buzz of women gossiping and shopkeepers selling their wares.

Halfway down a cramped alley was a sign that said "For Dr. Jin" with an arrow pointing up.

"Is that the Chinese doctor?" Mai pointed to the sign.

"Yes," Hạnh said.

Mai frowned.

Hạnh replied quickly, "He is very good. Um—at least that's what I hear."

After parking the Vespa, Mai and Hạnh found a staircase behind the sign and climbed up. A closed door with another sign told them they were at the doctor's office. Mai shot Hạnh a worried glance.

Hạnh returned a wan smile, which Mai figured was supposed to reassure her.

"Go ahead. Knock," Hạnh said.

Mai nodded and tapped lightly on the door. A voice inside said, "Enter."

She twisted the door handle and they walked in. A man wearing a white doctor's coat sat behind a desk. His hair was graying at his temples, and he wore wire-rimmed eyeglasses. The desk and two chairs filled the room, but a half-opened door in the back led to another room, which looked bigger.

"You called?" he said in a businesslike tone. "Nguyễn Linh Mai, yes?" When Mai nodded, he squinted at her. "How old are you?"

"Fifteen."

"And you don't want the baby."

She nodded.

"You are sure?"

He glanced over at Hạnh.

"You look familiar. You have been here before?"

Hạnh tightened her lips and looked down.

Mai's mouth opened in surprise. "You never told me."

Hạnh shrugged. "It was before I knew you."

The doctor looked from one to the other. "So, did you tell her what to expect?"

Hạnh shook her head.

He frowned. "Okay, okay. Come with me. I'll show you."

"Right now?" Mai felt her stomach knot.

"Now," he said gruffly.

"But—but I'm not ready."

"Then why are you here?" Impatience laced his words.

"I—I wanted to know more about the procedure."

"You are wasting my time."

"Please."

Dr. Jin sighed. He pushed himself away from the desk and motioned for her to follow him into the back room.

Mai tentatively followed him. In the center of the room was a black leather examination table with straps on both sides. A white sheet was folded at one end of the table. The room was dim, but the sheet looked clean. Mai wrapped her arms around herself.

"What's that?" Her voice was tense.

"That is the table you will lie on when we do the procedure," Dr. Jin said.

"What are the silver straps?"

"The stirrups are where you will place your feet."

Mai swallowed. "How long will it take?"

"About twenty minutes," he said. "But you will need to rest for two days after."

Mai and Hạnh exchanged glances. Hạnh wasn't offering any more smiles. Suddenly, Mai felt her belly quiver. She dropped her hands to the spot. "What—what's happening?" she cried out.

The doctor approached her. "Let me feel your belly."

Mai staggered back.

"I will not hurt you."

Mai stood still. The doctor placed a hand on her belly and kept it there. Then he looked at her. "Your baby is kicking. Here." He reached for her hand.

Mai let him guide her hand to the spot. The quiver ceased. "I don't feel anything," she said.

"Wait."

She waited a moment. The quiver started again. She kept her hands on top of her belly, and a smile filled with wonder unfolded across her face. "This is my baby?"

The doctor nodded. "His foot."

"Hạnh," she said excitedly. "Come here. Feel."

Hạnh placed her hand on Mai's belly and squeaked in delight a few seconds later. "I can feel him."

"Or her," the doctor said. He looked at Mai with a quizzical expression, as if he was asking, *What now?*

Mai kept her hands on her belly. She had witnessed so much horror, death, and heartbreak over the past year. Was this part of the Buddha's teaching? To do what she could to reclaim life? She sounded like her sister. Despite the hostility between them, she smiled.

She ran her tongue around her lips. Maybe she could manage this. Lots of girls her age had babies. It wouldn't have to slow her down. And there was always the chance that Sandy would send her the plane ticket. Most of all, her own son or daughter would mark the start of her own family. Wasn't that what she'd dreamed about? She looked at the doctor. "I—I have changed my mind, Doctor. I do not want an abortion."

Dr. Jin's expression flashed with irritation, as if he'd known all along he wouldn't be making any money today. "Good. Now, go home and leave me alone. Next time think it through before you bother busy people."

CHAPTER 37

MAI

Mai made it through another month before Madame Thạc said she had to go. "You are showing now. You cannot work here anymore."

"But what will I do?" Mai asked.

"Find another job. After you have the baby we will see." Madame Thạc hesitated. "Before you started up with that soldier, you were one of our most popular girls. But now?" She waved her hand as if to shoo her away. "You go. Now."

Mai wanted to lash out at her. After all the business she had brought in, all the drinks she made sure customers ordered, the least Madame Thạc could do was be nice to her. But she did want to come back after the baby was born, so she kept her mouth shut.

But what was she going to do? Where could she find a job? The only place where she'd worked, other than the Stardust, was the Saigon Café, and she'd left under less than ideal circumstances. On the other hand, she now spoke English quite well, and Cô Cúc would see that as a benefit. Tâm had worked there, and she was Tâm's sister. If she was lucky, Cô Cúc might rehire her. So she swallowed her pride and went to the restaurant.

But Cô Cúc, behind the cash register, gave her a chilly reception.

Cô Cúc took a look at Mai, focusing on her protruding belly, and raised her eyebrows. "Your sister is no longer here."

"I know, Cô Cúc. I was hoping you might take me on as a waitress. My English is now very good."

"Is that so?" Cô Cúc asked in English.

Mai nodded and answered in English. "I learned at my last job."

"Where did you work?"

"At the Stardust Lounge. I was a hostess. Lots of U.S. soldiers are customers."

Cô Cúc switched back to Vietnamese and motioned toward her baby bump. "Being a hostess is not all you were doing."

"The baby's father is my fiancé. From Chicago," Mai lied. "He will be sending me a plane ticket soon."

"The Stardust didn't want you with that bump."

"It is not good for business." Mai nodded. She instantly regretted it. But it was too late."What makes you think it is better for me? Why should I hire you? Your belly will get in the way of serving customers. And if what you say is true, you will leave in three or four months anyway. I am sorry." She shook her head.

Mai wanted to say that her sister didn't work very long at the restaurant either, and it wasn't fair that Cô Cúc wouldn't give her a second chance. But something told her not to. She suppressed her anger. "I understand. Thank you anyway." She turned and headed to the door.

Cô Cúc's voice called out from behind her. "Your sister is doing well."

Mai spun around. "How do you know?"

"I heard a rumor she might be in Cu Chi. Driving a truck." The woman shrugged. "Of course, it could be a lie. The Communists are quite secretive about their plans." An area west of Saigon, Cu Chi was known for its tunnels, which were linked to the Đường Trường Sơn, the trail the North Vietnamese used to transport soldiers, weapons, and supplies for the Viet Cong.

Mai nodded and pushed through the door. She'd been debating whether to ask about Tâm and was glad for the information. Driving a truck was safer than serving on the battlefield. Curiously, Tâm was doing for the Viet Cong exactly what Sandy had done for their sworn enemy. She walked away from the restaurant, remembering their early days in Saigon. How Phong and his father had led them to the Binh Tay market. Mai stopped. The market.

Two hours later, Mai made her way home on the Vespa. She was hired by not just one but two merchants who ran stalls adjacent to each other. She would work part-time at each when they had other business to attend to or wanted a break. Together, her earnings would be higher than at the Saigon Café, but not nearly as much as at the Stardust. She hadn't expected to earn that much, of course, but with this wage, combined with her savings, she could make it through the pregnancy. Plus, one of the stalls sold baby goods, and she and the owner had already negotiated a deal. When her time was closer, she could barter for everything she needed in return for extra hours. All in all, it was a good solution. She could hardly wait to tell Hạnh.

She raced back to the boardinghouse, hurried up the stairs, and burst into their room. "Hạnh, you will not believe my good fortune!"

Hạnh's face flushed bright red. "Hello, Mai."

Mai stopped short. Another young girl was sitting on Hạnh's bed. She was very pretty, and it was clear that Mai had interrupted their conversation. "Oh, hello." She nodded to the young girl. "I am Mai. Who are you?"

Hahn answered for her. "This is Tuyết. She is from the Highlands. She just arrived."

Mai nodded.

"Well, Tuyết, I will see you at the Stardust tonight and will introduce you to Madame Thạc." She stood up.

"Thank you so much, Hạnh. Karma put you on the path of my life," the girl gushed.

Hạnh led Tuyết to their door. Was she in a hurry to get the girl out of their room? Mai sat heavily on her bed and waited for Hạnh.

When the door closed, Mai said, "What was that about? Why did you cut her visit short?"

Hạnh didn't answer for a moment. Then she cleared her throat, walked around the sheet that served as their room partition, and sat next to Mai. "I have been thinking a lot, Mai. Ever since you got pregnant—"

"Thinking about what?" Mai cut her off.

"Mai, you are like my sister, but we cannot live together after the baby comes."

A sour taste came into Mai's mouth. She tried to ignore it. "Why not? You're very good with babies. You told me."

Hạnh sighed. "Yes. That was one of the biggest reasons I left home. My mother worked in the fields. So I was in charge of my little brothers and sister from the time they were born. I did not want to do it. I wanted to go to school. But there was no one else—I am the number one daughter, as you know."

"You can go to school. During the day."

"Mai, I know what's involved with a baby. I do not want to hear it cry in the middle of the night or the morning when I am trying to sleep. I do not want to feed and clean it. Or change its diaper. In fact, I do not think I will ever want children."

"You won't have to do anything, Hạnh. I'm the baby's mother. I'll do all the work."

Hạnh chuckled nervously. "You say that now, but I know you, Mai. You'll want help. But I promised myself I was finished with baby care. So you'll need to move. That's why Tuyết was here. She and I know each other from back home. We're going to be roommates. I'm really sorry, Mai."

"That's why you wanted me to have an abortion, isn't it? Because it would be more convenient for you."

Hạnh kept her mouth shut.

"You say I'm like a sister." Mai's voice was sharp. "But even Tâm wouldn't treat me like this. I no longer meet your needs, and so you cast me off like a piece of garbage."

Hạnh looked miserable. "I'll help you find another place to live. And someone to babysit when you go back to the Stardust."

Mai shot off the bed and stomped to the door. "I don't want your help. Ever again." She slammed the door on the way out.

Mai tried to suppress her rage and despair at Hạnh's betrayal, but it seeped into her bones. Mai had thought she had a lifelong friend; someone to trust, someone in whom to confide. But Hạnh was just as selfish as everyone else. Eager to destroy their friendship just because Mai was pregnant. And bring in another roommate when Mai was not there. That made her deceitful as well. Once again, another person in her life had hurt her. Mai began to wonder if she was at fault. Sandy. Tâm. Hạnh. Was there something so evil about her that the people she loved went out of their way to abandon her?

She blinked away hot tears as she climbed on the Vespa. For the first time, she missed her parents and her village. Back then life was simple. Safe. Predictable.

Until it wasn't. She was cast adrift in a world at war, a world where people broke their promises and betrayed the people they professed to love. If that was the case, it was better not to love at all. She didn't need anyone.

CHAPTER 38

MAI

Spring melted into summer, once again bringing monsoons and tropical heat to southern Vietnam. With Mai's pregnancy, the heat this season was intolerable. Although she was used to a busy schedule, she was glad she no longer had to dress up, dance, and flirt with GIs who frequented the Stardust. She bought two fans at the market: one for home and one for the market stalls. The stall owners, two women whose husbands were cousins, they said, chattered all day long, much like the young girls Mai had befriended in the Cholon refugee camp. This time, though, Mai did all the work.

And these women discussed the war more than the young girls. In May, over ten days, American and South Vietnamese infantry troops fought significant battles at Ap Bia Mountain in the north, about a mile from the border with Laos. They had taken the hill, but the close-combat brutality and carnage had killed so many soldiers that U.S. journalists labeled it Hamburger Hill.

"Hamburger is American meat, yes?" Mai asked one of the women. The GIs at the Stardust often said hamburgers from home were what they missed most in Vietnam.

"It is meat from a cow, ground up. Americans eat it between two pieces of bread," the woman answered.

Mai wrinkled her nose. The women laughed.

The new American president, Richard Nixon, in office several months now, said that he wanted to gradually reduce the number of American troops. He was calling it the "Vietnamization" of the war.

"But who will fight?" Mai asked.

"The South Vietnamese army."

"But they don't have the same equipment as the Americans," Mai said. Sandy had told her many times that the South Vietnamese lagged behind the U.S. in firepower, equipment, and training.

"Apparently the Americans are going to train them before they leave," one of the women said.

The other woman shrugged. "Train the ARVN? They say our men run the other way when the fighting gets bad."

"And there are many rumors of corruption." The first woman shook her head. "This is not a good sign."

Now that Sandy was gone, Mai paid little attention to war news. She still thought about him constantly, but her fantasy, that he would return, plane ticket in hand, dimmed a little each day, like faded lipstick.

Even if he did come back, how would he find her? The cousins had helped her find and rent a new place to live in District 10, Ward 6. In an urban, working-class neighborhood, her new home consisted of two rooms in the back of a small house. One of the cousins lent her his truck, which she loaded up one night when Hạnh was at work so she wouldn't have to say goodbye.

While the new location was much less exclusive than the board-inghouse, there was an advantage. Families squeezed into small shacks crammed together on all sides, which meant people were always around. Especially older women, since many families living together spanned three generations. The women generally spent the day together making *nón lá*, cheap jewelry, belts, and other craft items. When Mai moved in, the aunties, as they were called, expressed their enthusiasm about the baby, and offers to babysit—for a price, of course—were extended.

Once again Mai seemed to have solved her problems on her own.

This time, though, she felt less smug about it. She was grateful for the offers of help from the aunties. She was even willing to concede that a power greater than herself might be looking out for her. Now she understood why her mother had assembled a small Buddhist altar in their home. She thought about creating one of her own.

When she mentioned it to one of the aunties, the auntie grinned. "Yes. Of course. It will be good for the baby. He or she will be protected." She paused. "And now we know what to give you when the child is born." She chuckled.

CHAPTER 39

MAI

By the middle of July, Mai could hardly walk without feeling as heavy and sluggish as one of the tanks at the Bien Hoa Air Base. She was grateful for the breeze from her Vespa, which, though hot, moved the air around. She was grateful, too, that it had been a normal pregnancy, with little morning sickness or bleeding problems. The cousins' wives at the Binh Tay advised her what to buy for the baby. A bassinet would do for at least the first year. They told her to buy a stroller as well and to stock up on baby towels, diapers, and a few one-piece outfits. "Oh, and a pacifier or two."

"Why?" Mai asked. She'd seen babies with the plastic nipple in their mouths. It looked like they could choke at any moment.

"You'll see." One of the women laughed. "Your own nipples will need time to recover."

One day during her ninth month, the cousins at the market surprised her with a manicure and pedicure. Long, a woman from a neighboring stall, came over with a small basket filled with tools. Mai had seen them in the market and was curious. She had always done her nails herself with an emery board and polish. But this woman made it into an art form. She made Mai sit down in one of the chairs at the counter of the stall, squatted in front of her, and placed a tray on the counter. The tinny noise of buyers and merchants in the market swirled around them, but Long seemed unperturbed.

She unwrapped each tool. In addition to the emery board was a cuticle knife, an orange stick, a nail clipper, three tools that looked like scissors, a pumice stone she explained was to get rid of calluses, creams and potions, and ten—Mai counted them—different colors of polish as well as clear varnish.

Long inspected Mai's hands. Since Mai was no longer at the Stardust, she hadn't paid much attention to them. At the market, she lifted, moved, opened and closed boxes, packages, and items like carpets, cushions, and clothing all day. As a result her nails were chipped and dirty, and there were patches of rough skin on her wrists and palms. Long scolded that she needed to take better care of her hands.

"They are the—the door to a woman's beauty. What did the French do when they first met a woman? They took her hand. Kissed it. Perhaps held it. You want men to have a favorable impression, yes? To linger on the beauty of your hands and wonder what other treasures you hold?"

"But we're not French."

Long smiled wistfully. "Sometimes I wish we were. The good ones were willing to touch us and make us feel beautiful. Not like our husbands, who won't hold our hands at all."

Mai's eyebrows went up. She'd never thought of her hands as beautiful. Her hands had always held something with which to work. A broom, a hoe, a shovel. Her little brother. A tray of drinks at the Stardust. The handlebars of her Vespa. Soon, an infant.

"And your feet." Long said. "Vietnamese women have beautiful feet. But we must make sure everyone sees their beauty. When I am done, you will no longer want to hide them from the world."

The delicate feet May once had at the Stardust were in her past. Now her feet were swollen and red from the pregnancy. She was under no illusions they could be made to look beautiful.

"Do not worry," Long said, as if reading her inner thoughts. "I know how to make your hands and feet so silky and tempting you will never feel the same way about them."

Mai recalled how perfect Madame Thạc's hands and feet looked; perhaps hers might be even better.

The manicurist took her time. First she soaked Mai's fingers in sudsy rose-petaled water until her skin was soft. She applied coconut lotion to make her skin even softer. She rubbed the pumice stone over her calluses, and they gradually disappeared. Then she carefully cleaned Mai's nails, lifting out all the dirt. She shaped, clipped, and filed them into perfect ovals. She pushed the cuticles back so that the tiny moons at the base of her nails were clear. The woman then buffed her nails until they were shiny.

"See?" Long looked up at Mai. "Look how pretty they are. You have good moons."

The woman applied what she called a clear base coat to her nails. "This will make them stronger, so they will keep the polish." Then she stood the ten tiny bottles of nail polish in front of Mai and asked her which one she wanted. The shades of pinks, roses, and reds made a glamorous display.

"Oh," Mai cried. "Which one should I choose? I love them all!" She picked up one bottle, then another, and brought them to her nails. "I can't decide."

Long laughed. "Come. If you don't like one, next time you choose another."

Mai finally chose bright pink.

"The color of passion." Long smiled.

After two coats of polish and another coat of clear polish, the woman spread a small towel in front of Mail. "You rest your nails here until they are dry while I start on your feet."

Long repeated the entire process on Mai's feet. When she was finished, Mai was astonished at how delicate and pretty they were. Her feet looked like those of a rich lady.

She felt pampered and beautiful. She had never realized there were such elaborate rituals attached to manicures and pedicures. She left the market flashing and flaunting her nails to anyone who noticed.

CHAPTER 40

MAI

Everyone in Vietnam was talking about the moon landing. In the second part of July America was sending astronauts on a journey into space, and if they didn't meet with some catastrophe, they would land and walk on the moon's surface in three days' time. Most of the people Mai knew were afraid. This was not the nature of things. America was tempting the gods, and the gods would punish them. They would meet with some disastrous misfortune if they disturbed the universe in this way. Others didn't believe it and said they'd heard it would be staged to fool people into believing the event was real, which it obviously couldn't be.

Mai was looking forward to watching the landing. One of the families in the neighborhood owned a television and invited everyone to their home. The day they were supposed to land, Mai was at work at the market. She was trying to find a comfortable sitting position when she stood up and water streamed down from her private parts.

"What is happening?" Mai asked.

One of the women cried out. "It is your time!"

"We need to get you home. Quickly," the other woman said. "Your contractions will begin soon. And then the baby."

"But I am to go to the doctor in the hospital."

"There isn't time. We will take you home in a tuk-tuk."

During the trip home, Mai's abdomen seemed to shift and heave, and sharp menstrual cramps stabbed her, so strong that she gasped and doubled over.

"No!" she shouted. "This is not right!" The woman with her peered at her with compassion.

Mai's eyes widened. "It will get worse?"

The woman put her arm around Mai. "It is better if you pant during the worst ones."

When the next contraction hit, Mai tried to pant but it did nothing to ease the pain. She wanted it all to stop. She'd made a terrible mistake. She should have had the abortion. She couldn't go through with this. She wanted her mother. Even Tâm would do. Or Hạnh. But there was no one except the aunties who gathered outside as the tuk-tuk deposited Mai at home.

Luckily, several of the aunties said they were or had been midwives. They took her inside. One spread two clean sheets over her mattress. Another rolled up a small towel for Mai to bite down on. A third boiled water for the birth and brewed *trà đắng*, a bitter green tea, which was supposed to dull the pain. She lay down on her bed, knees up.

Despite their ministrations, Mai screamed and cried and yelled. "Make it stop. I cannot bear it!" Her body felt like it was being torn apart, ripped in two. One of the aunties gave her the towel to chew on, but Mai swatted it and the woman away. "Don't touch me. I will choke. Please. Just make it stop!"

Another auntie stroked her forehead. Mai told her to get the hell away. The auntie nodded. Instead, she spooned tea into Mai's mouth during the lull between contractions, but the pain intensified. Mai sipped tea, tasting salty beads of sweat that had formed on her upper lip. Spots of blood stained the sheets, which were now bunched up under her. She thrashed and twisted, contorting her body, when the contractions were at their worst, trying to make them go away.

At one point, Mai lost her mind. She had no idea what time it was, how many hours had passed, what she was doing, or why. Nothing existed except the unspeakable pain, the murmur of the aunties, a fierce heat, and the brief respites in between. After several hours of nothing but excruciating pain and her stubborn attempts to survive it, one contraction at a time, Mai felt the urge to push. "I need to push!" she screamed. "I need to get this out of me! Help me!"

One of the aunties inspected her between her legs. A victorious grin spread across her face. "I see the head! Now you push with the contractions!"

Mai started to push. The contractions weren't weaker, but they had leveled off, and combined with the pushing, they seemed natural. It was then she noticed a few of the aunties darting in and out, filling in the others on what was going on with the moon landing.

"They have landed!" A young girl ran into Mai's apartment. "They are on the moon!"

A swell of gasps and amazement rose from the aunties. "Bring the radio," one said to the girl.

Mai didn't give a damn about the moon landing. All she wanted was this thing to come out of her. She pushed and panted, panted and pushed. Sweat drenched her neck and hair, matting it to her head. She had been wearing a T-shirt, but the aunties helped her take it off, replaced it with a fresh towel, and tried to wipe down her sweat. The auntie who inspected between her legs nodded and urged her on. "Good girl. It is almost over. Keep pushing."

The girl who'd run in earlier brought a radio and tuned it to the station that was broadcasting the landing.

Finally the auntie who was ministering to Mai held up her hand. "Stop. Now!" She reached her fingers inside Mai. Mai screamed, felt blood pour out of her, watched it seep into the sheets. When the woman's hands emerged, they were holding a wet, bloody creature with eyes squeezed shut and scarlet cheeks. The auntie swatted him on his rear end, wiped inside his mouth, and made sure he was breathing. Then she took a pair of scissors and cut the umbilical cord.

She swaddled him in one of the soft baby towels and handed him to Mai.

Mai's son was born at the same time that Neil Armstrong pronounced, "One small step for man, one giant leap for mankind." As if to punctuate the words, a lusty cry came from the baby. Mai laughed. He had Mai's black hair and a lot of it. But he had Sandy's wide-shaped eyes and light coloring. His eyes were blue. "He will need glasses." Mai said, still breathing hard, but now with a smile.

"Let him have your nipple," the auntie said. Mai cradled him and guided his mouth to her breast. He took to it right away. The pulling, sucking sensation was strange, but not uncomfortable.

"What are you going to name him?" one of the aunties asked.

Mai was quiet for a moment. "I will name him Đêm Nguyệt, the bright moon at night."

The auntie scowled, taken aback. "But Nguyệt is a girl's name. And I've never heard of any name that includes the word 'night.'"

Mai looked up at her. "He was born the minute men first walked on the moon. That will never be an ordinary event." She smiled. "And so my son will never have an ordinary name. Đêm Nguyệt is the only name he could have."

PART V

SOUTH VIETNAM, 1969

Tâm

CHAPTER 41

TÂM

The gears made a loud grinding noise as Tâm shifted from second to third. She grimaced as the truck lurched forward. She'd been at the wheel only two days, and this was the first time in her life she'd driven a vehicle at all, so her ability to manipulate the clutch and gearshift was crude. To make matters worse, the gearshift was actually behind her, so that she had to reach almost to the small of her back to shift gears.

She was driving on Highway 1 on the outskirts of Saigon in the middle of the night, which was a blessing since few vehicles were on the road. Still, she had to look out for enemy air attacks, especially as she approached the Hồ Chí Minh Trail northwest of Saigon. Which was where she was headed. With her was Đắc, another truck driver, who'd been assigned to teach her how to handle the truck and avoid the main roads during a bombing.

They were delivering a truck full of medical supplies to medics in the Cu Chi tunnels, two hundred kilometers of tunnels originally built by the French but upgraded and expanded by the North. The tunnels, not far from the southern tip of the Hồ Chí Minh Trail, were now the major transit route between North Vietnam and the Saigon area.

Tâm cruised down the highway. In the dark, it seemed to stretch out forever. She should step on the fuel pedal to gain some speed.

Đắc cut into her thoughts. "When did you get here?"

"Yesterday."

"Where are you from?"

She was intentionally vague. Better to be careful. "A training camp in the south. You?"

"I live in Saigon. Sixth district."

She looked over, surprised. Small and slim, he wore jeans and a T-shirt that bore the seal of an American baseball team. Very Western. "You didn't you go to a training camp?"

He shook his head. "But I know all the back roads. And I know these trucks." He pulled out a cigarette, tore the filter off, and lit it with a match.

Tâm scowled.

"You don't want to be a driver?"

Tâm had thought that as a result of her success at training camp, they'd give her a plum assignment. But either word didn't spread, or the commanders didn't want female fighters, because here she was delivering food, medical supplies, weapons, and ammunition. Away from the battlefield. At the very least, she'd hoped Dr. Hằng would put in a good word for her. She was disappointed, but she said, "I'm here to do my duty. Whatever that is."

Đắc grunted. "Spoken like a loyal comrade." He was quiet. Then: "The first rule of driving is that when Americans start bombing, you need to get off the main road as soon as possible. Particularly as you get closer to the tunnels and the trail. Most of the bombs come after midnight—they know we travel at night."

She glanced at both sides of the road. Nothing looked familiar. She could make out a few shacks, small businesses, and fields, but she had no idea where she was. "How frequent are the air strikes?"

"Maybe a few times a week. They used to be every day. I guess they think there is not much more to bomb." He laughed. "But as I said, on the trail, it is every day. Do you know what we call the bombs?"

She shook her head.

"The war against trucks."

Tâm peered at her companion. "Really?"

He nodded. "Thousands of these trucks carry supplies up and down the Hồ Chí Minh Trail every day. When the enemy strikes, you get off the road, camouflage the truck, and say a prayer that you'll find another road. You have a map? I will draw some of the roads I use."

"It is under your seat."

Đắc pulled it out and started drawing lines on it. "This is a Russian truck, you know."

"I didn't know."

"It's saved my life more than once."

She cocked her head. "How?"

"It has four-wheel drive. So you can drive it over logs, stumps, and boulders. You can even cross streams of water up to one meter deep. It also has a creeper gear that helps to grind its way up the steepest, most rutted trail." He went on. "All of which means if there's a bomb and you don't see a road close by, it is safe to turn off the road wherever you are and hope you outrun the blast."

Tâm swallowed. "Is it sturdy enough to withstand a bomb?"

Đắc shrugged. "It won't win a prize for beauty, but it's stronger than ten oxen."

Tâm shot him a wan smile. The truck was ugly, painted camouflage green with an open bed in back framed with skinny steel poles in case a tarp was needed to cover or hide the contents. The tires were thick, and the chassis underneath was old and dusty.

"If your truck does get stuck, it's fitted with a winch and a generous length of cable so you can hitch it to a nearby tree and pull yourself forward." He paused. "Of course, you will become its chief mechanic."

"What? Me?"

"You'll learn every screw, bolt, and wire of your machine, what it needs and when, and how to repair it. You'll be making those repairs. Ask questions when you bring the truck back to an outpost on the trail. Or when you come across other drivers." He twisted around and motioned. "There is a toolbox in the bed of the truck. That's where you'll find the cable and the winch." He cleared his throat. "Consider this your new home," he said. "You can even sleep in the bed of the truck. I do."

She nodded.

Suddenly a flash of light ahead of them flared, followed by a thunderous blast. Tâm jumped.

"*Ayii!* We have company tonight. Get off the road. Now!" He fumbled with a seat belt. "Watch for trees. Strap yourself in. Hurry!"

Tâm's pulse began to race. Fear snatched her breath. Was another bomb headed toward them? She shifted down to first, turned the wheel sharply, and stepped on the gas. The truck pitched forward into a field. Luckily there were no trees nearby.

Đắc shouted, "Look where you're going! Avoid boulders, holes, and bushes if you can."

Over the next few minutes the truck bounced and bucked like a young bull, but Tâm was able to put distance between them and the road. No bomb dropped on the field. "The bombers cannot track us, can they?"

"No, but they know we use this road. Keep going across the field. There will be another road in a kilometer or two. QL 1. Turn left onto it."

Another flash of light and explosion sounded behind them. Tâm arched her back. Part of her wanted to ditch the truck and run for cover. She didn't.

"You see?" Đắc yelled. "We would have been killed if you hadn't gone off road. Good job." He lit another cigarette and dragged deeply.

Tâm's senses were on high alert. The danger they'd narrowly escaped reminded her of her training mission. She barreled straight across the field, clutching the wheel so Đắc would not see her shaking hands. When she reached the alternate road, she turned left. The wheels squealed and the truck bounced again. This two-lane road was unpaved, and ruts were filled with water from the monsoons, but they were safer here than on the main road. She slowed, relief surging through her. Still, it took ten minutes before her breath returned to normal.

CHAPTER 42

TÂM

They reached the Cu Chi tunnel area an hour later. Tâm drove down on a dirt road that ended at a cluster of jungle-like woods. Spools of leftover chicken wire lay in random spots along the path. She slowed in case there were traps.

"Stop here." Đắc pointed to her left. "You see that low-hanging branch? The one that's almost broken off the guava tree?"

Tâm nodded.

"Head about twelve meters left of that, where there is a gap between trees. You should see tracks from previous trucks."

Tâm did what he said and turned her headlights on bright. Squinting through the windshield, she saw he was right. Rough tire treads in the dirt led deeper into the forest.

"Something like that"—Đắc gestured to the branch—"will always tell you where to go. It might be a broken branch, used chicken wire, flowers on a bush that don't belong, perhaps even a *khăn rằn*. Look for the signs."

Tâm wasn't worried about finding a signpost. She was knowledgeable about plants and bushes and trees. "But how will I know if the signposts are a decoy? I don't want to drive into a trap. Or an ambush."

"You'll learn." He took a drag on yet another cigarette. "One outpost might use flowers and suddenly change to fruit. Another may have used a scarf but changed to flowers. When you see other drivers on the trail, ask. They will tell you. We look out for each other that way."

Tâm steered the truck on the tire treads and drove deeper into the woods. About one hundred meters farther, a clearing suddenly appeared.

"We're here."

Tâm cut the engine and opened the truck door. Đắc jumped down from his side of the truck. "I'm looking forward to checking out the tunnels," Tâm said.

"You're not going into them tonight."

"Why not?"

"You don't have the right smell."

Tâm planted her hands on her waist. "What?"

"When the enemy comes looking for us in the tunnels, they bring large dogs. German shepherds. Because the dogs have such a sharp sense of smell, they can detect us underground. We have learned to wash with American soap so the dogs smell friendly Americans and won't bark. You need to get some American soap at the market and start bathing with it. Then you can go into the tunnels."

"I don't hear any dogs tonight."

"They can show up at any time."

"So we 'Viet Cong' are safe because of American soap," she said wryly.

Đắc smiled and shrugged. Then he sobered. "I'll tell them we are here. Come to the entrance so you'll know how to get in the next time."

He made his way in the dark to a large boulder on the edge of the clearing. He squatted next to it and rolled the boulder aside. "It's hollow." He kept his voice low. The resulting hole in the ground was a square shape about thirty centimeters on all sides. Đắc inserted one foot, then the other into the gap. Then he jumped down inside. Tâm saw only his torso from the waist up. He raised his arms over his head and slithered down even more. Now only his head was visible. He reached over, grabbed the rock, dipped his head, and slid the rock so it covered the hole. He had completely disappeared. Tâm's mouth opened in surprise.

Ten minutes later a group of twenty young troops emerged from the same hole and gathered at the back of the truck. Some wore green uniforms, but most were dressed like her in black *áo bà ba*. Nearly half were women. They formed a human chain between the truck and the tunnel entrance and passed supplies one box at a time to a young man whose torso, like Đắc's, was half-hidden beneath the ground.

Within fifteen minutes the operation was finished and the back of the truck was empty. The guerrillas bowed their heads and thanked Đắc and Tâm. Đắc asked if anyone needed a ride to the Hồ Chí Minh Trail.

He turned to Tâm. "You must ask every time you deliver something. The truck can carry more than twelve people. Usually someone needs a ride."

But this time no one did. The guerrillas returned to the secret entrance and slid back down into the tunnel. Five minutes later the jungle was quiet. It was impossible to tell that anyone had been there.

"Usually I stay and help them carry the supplies, but since we still have more driving tonight, I'll stay with you. But you should help."

Tâm was still astonished at the efficiency with which the entire operation was handled. "Does it always go this smoothly?"

Đắc laughed. "We hope."

Thirty minutes later, at Đắc's direction, Tâm headed northwest toward the border with Cambodia. She was managing the truck with more dexterity now. Her steering was more precise. Gearshifts became a challenge rather than a worry.

"Where are we going now?"

"An Loc."

"Why?"

"You will see."

It was still dark, but the moon made an appearance, shining a bluish silver backlight on the scrim of clouds. Tâm's watch said it was past three in the morning. Less than two hours until dawn. They were passing through farmland now, and the smells of hay and cattle rose from grassy fields and pastures. Their familiarity cut deep, reminding Tâm of home. Her village was farther south, and on the river. Still, the scents were a bittersweet reminder that she no longer had a home. Like a caterpillar that has been transformed and now dances in the sun, she was adrift, waiting for the transformation that would turn her into a butterfly.

Đắc said, "They bomb here every night. But the attacks are over for tonight. Even the enemy must sleep." He looked through the windshield. "And while they sleep, we work. Pull over and stop the truck."

"What are we doing now?"

"Now that the moon is out, we will search the fields where they have dropped bombs. If we can, we will take the unexploded bombs —there are usually some—and load them in the truck."

"Why?"

"We reuse them. Give them to the NVA if they are not damaged. Or make grenades and other explosive devices for ourselves." He paused. "One more thing. You should look for land mines as well. But be careful."

Tâm looked over. "How do I avoid them in the dark?"

"Use your flashlight. Walk slowly. If you find one, let me know. I can tell whether it is inert. If it is, we can reuse it to make a new bomb."

"Is there anything you do not want me to scavenge?"

Đắc shook his head. "We waste nothing. We can't afford to."

∽

As Tâm and Đắc searched the field for unexploded ordnance, she began to respect the Communists' ingenuity. Nothing—food, supplies, even enemy munitions—was squandered. The fighters saw themselves not as individuals but as part of a whole. If one soldier failed or was struck down, another would take his place. They shared an unwavering belief in their mission. Like everyone else in the struggle, Tâm was just a tiny cog in a huge machine.

CHAPTER 43

TÂM

Over the next few months Tâm developed a routine. She grew more comfortable with the truck, and it became her home. She kept a sleeping mat and change of clothes in the bed of the truck along with her newly purchased American soap. Her assignments took her from Saigon to the tunnels, then to points along the Hồ Chí Minh Trail. Sometimes she was part of a convoy; sometimes she drove alone.

The word "trail" was a misnomer. It consisted of nearly 20,000 kilometers of interconnected roads, footpaths, and riverways that had connected North and South Vietnam for centuries. Parts of it wound through Laos and Cambodia. Hanoi had expanded the trail several times. In 1965 engineers using Soviet and Chinese machinery widened the web of jungle footpaths into flat roads and strengthened bridges to support heavy trucks. The North Vietnamese taught everyone how to camouflage themselves and their vehicles while moving along the roads. In convoys that traveled at night, more than ninety tons of supplies were taken south to the Communist fighters every day. Tâm slept during the day.

North Vietnam had also built way stations to repair and maintain both the trail and trucks. Refueling facilities were located at every third to fifth station. As Đắc had promised, Tâm bumped into other drivers at these outposts, where they traded war news and gossip and discussed truck maintenance. Her truck had a diesel engine, and she noticed that sometimes, when it was hot, the motor kept running even after she turned it off. She learned it wasn't uncommon and was called dieseling. Every driver seemed to have a different solution. She tried them all, but mostly she learned to live with it. She learned how to change a tire, what to do if the gears started to slip, and how to judge when the brakes needed replacement.

Đắc was right about the enemy's "war on trucks." By 1969, America boasted it had destroyed more than 9,000 trucks on the Hồ Chí Minh Trail. The North Vietnamese acquired more trucks and deployed sophisticated antiaircraft artillery along the trail to protect them. The net result was that the U.S. couldn't stop the North from delivering supplies to the Southern Communists, and, despite a steady rain of bombs, supply levels steadily increased. So did the number of troops. At the peak of the fighting, North Vietnamese Army regulars traveling the trail poured into South Vietnam at the rate of 20,000 fighters per month.

All of which made driving the trail treacherous. Tâm was relieved when she was not assigned to a convoy. Her truck wasn't nimble, but compared to a line of trucks, she had more options when she was alone. She could swerve off road and race into the bush for cover.

At the beginning of September 1969, Hồ Chí Minh died from a heart attack. It wasn't a surprise; his health had declined over the years, and he had given up his leadership role. Even so, North Vietnam declared a week of mourning and told its troops to turn their grief at Bác Hồ's death into revolutionary activities to defeat the U.S. and liberate South Vietnam. The battles and the bombings raged on.

When the dry season began Tâm was assigned to drive a dozen North Vietnamese troops from the trail to the Cu Chi tunnels. When she picked them up, she was surprised to see they were women. They called themselves part of the Long Hair Army. Most were from the mountainous area in northwest Vietnam, and they seemed to know each other well. Armed with a patchwork of Soviet and old German antiaircraft guns and two portable missile launchers, they squeezed into the bed of the truck, their bulky weapons taking up most of the space. The woman who appeared to be their leader asked if she could ride up front with Tâm.

Tâm nodded. "But there could be enemy bombing runs. They usually happen at night. If they do, I will take immediate evasive action."

The woman smiled. "I expect nothing less."

Tâm grinned back. Apparently bomb blasts did not frighten this soldier.

"I am Lieutenant Diệp Hồng Bảo."

"Hồng Bảo. Great Protection. That is fitting. I am—" She was about to say "Biên," but something made her change her mind. She blurted out, "I am Trang Tâm."

"Solemn Heart." She appraised Tâm. "Why is that?"

Tâm shrugged.

Bảo was small and slim. Then again, Tâm had never seen a plump Vietnamese woman except for aunties and grandmothers. Bảo's dark eyes, wider than most, sparkled with a cheerful, sunny cast, unlike those of other soldiers. Most weren't much older than she, and their expressions were either frightened or veiled with a smug arrogance Tâm knew was feigned. When Bảo smiled, though, Tâm felt lighter. It was a feeling, she realized as she headed to the back of the truck, akin to joy.

"Help me with the tarp?" Tâm asked.

Bảo nodded, and they stretched the cover over the bed of the truck to conceal the women. Before she tied it down Tâm explained to the soldiers that the ride might be rocky if there were bombing runs.

"What should they do?" Bảo asked on behalf of her charges.

Tâm inclined her head. "Just hang on. And pray." But she smiled when she said it.

She went back to the front and climbed into the driver's seat. As Bảo jumped up on the passenger side, the damp scent of a freshwater river on Bảo's uniform overwhelmed Tâm. Her mouth dropped open. "You smell like the Mekong."

Bảo looked over. "We came down the trail through Cambodia. We slept on its banks for two nights."

Before the Mekong River flows into South Vietnam, it winds through Laos, then Cambodia, essentially splitting the country in half. The smell unleashed in Tâm a powerful yearning for her home and childhood. For the days when she trudged home from school to help her father plant vegetables. Or washed their clothing with Mai and her mother in the river. Or fed Sáng his bottle when he fussed. That a simple scent could evoke the past in such rich detail was unsettling. She thought she'd locked her past in a remote, unreachable place, but now it seemed to have escaped to haunt her.

"I grew up on the Mekong." She paused. "In the South."

"Oh? What village?"

Tâm paused for a long time, then shook her head. "It's not there anymore. The Americans destroyed it."

Bảo shut her eyes tight, but Tâm had the strange sensation that Bảo felt her sorrow through her closed lids. And when she opened them again, Bảo didn't appear to be the least surprised that Tâm knew it.

Tâm took a roundabout route to get to the tunnels. Fortunately, the journey was without incident. Tâm and Bảo chatted the entire way. Bảo herded goats and sheep on the mountains in North Vietnam. She had four siblings, but they were too young to join the NVA. She was the only one in her family who could read and write, and she took that responsibility seriously. The more she learned about Hồ Chí Minh and his promises, the more she wanted to help achieve them. That was why she'd joined the army and rose to the rank of lieutenant. She went wherever she was assigned. They had been protecting other troops along the trail with antiaircraft activity; now they were assigned to shoot down American B-52s that were carpet-bombing the tunnels and the adjacent area controlled by the Communists, called the Iron Triangle.

"Have you been through the tunnels before?" Tâm asked.

"Oh yes. Several times. Often, now that the Americans are carpet-bombing the area. This time we expect to camp in the tunnels for a few weeks, perhaps months. We will come out only at night for anti-aircraft action. At some point we will head down to the Iron Triangle to shoot down aircraft near the Bien Hoa Air Base."

"You have been there before as well?"

Bảo nodded. "During Tết. The Tết Offensive was planned in the tunnels, you know."

Tâm replied with a wry smile.

"Why do you smile?"

"I first came to Saigon soon after Tết. My sister and I stayed in the Cholon refugee camp. The NVA sent mortars and missiles and bombs in our direction. It might have been you who fired those mortars."

Bảo shot Tâm a look that was equally compassionate and sad. "If that is so, I am glad we missed our target."

A rush of heat flew up Tâm's spine. She knew her cheeks were red.

"Tell me about you, Tâm."

Tâm let out a breath and began. She told Bảo about her father, her sister, the prince that had been Sáng. What she saw and felt when the Americans destroyed their village. She talked about her sister's obstinacy and how they had quarreled. Bảo didn't interrupt but seemed to be listening intently. Tâm realized she'd never opened up like this to anyone. She didn't want the journey to end.

CHAPTER 44

TÂM

They arrived at the tunnels by dawn.

"Perfect timing," Bảo said as Tâm pulled into a thick forest and braked at a ramshackle abandoned hut, the floor of which led down into the first tier of tunnels. The entrance was closer to the north end of the sprawling network, rather than the southern portion she'd seen with Đắc, but Bảo knew the route.

"I want to go through them with you."

"Why?"

Tâm didn't tell Bảo it was because she didn't want their time together to end. She wasn't sure that was the only reason anyway. "I know there are many traps inside, as well as tunnel rats and dogs above. I have been bathing with American soap, and it is time I learned how to navigate the tunnels. I can be much more useful if I know my way through when I deliver supplies. Will you take me with you? So I can learn?"

"Do you not have another assignment to perform?"

"My schedule is—flexible." That wasn't the complete truth. Tâm could delay her return trip by claiming that a bombing attack or nearby fighting forced her off the road. But guerrilla fighters were desperately needed by the Communists. If she accompanied Bảo's squad, her superiors probably would not complain.

Bảo looked at Tâm with a knowing expression. She reached across and gently touched Tâm's arm. "You will have to do what I say. Follow my lead exactly. I know where the traps are."

Tâm nodded.

"When we arrive at the other end, I will find someone to guide you back to your truck."

Tâm nodded again.

Bảo flashed Tâm a radiant smile. "Then, yes. I will take you with me." Bảo's hand was still on Tâm's arm.

Inside the tunnels were passages where the women could stand and move quickly. Other passages were dark, dank, and claustrophobic and required them to crawl on their hands and knees. Had Bảo not been leading the way, Tâm would not have made it through. They always moved in single file, and no one spoke unless it was absolutely necessary, and then only in whispers.

There were three levels to the tunnels, with steps and trapdoors at strategic points leading up or down. Every so often, Bảo would slow or stop to point out the traps. They weren't hidden exactly, but they didn't call attention to themselves. Tâm recalled hearing about them at training camp. She saw the sticking trap, the armpit trap, the swinging-up trap, and the fish hook trap, all constructed with sharp pins or spear tips that could at minimum maim and—more likely— kill an enemy if he or she missed a step and bumped into them. She ran her hand up and down her arm, suddenly chilled.

The tunnels were hives of activity. In addition to providing a refuge during combat, as well as the ability to secretly advance or retreat, the tunnels contained air vents, hospitals, cooking areas, latrines, conference areas, radio and communication areas, caches of weapons, and sleeping quarters for hundreds of North Vietnamese fighters. Bảo told her that at the other end of the tunnels, in the North near Bien Hoc, villagers actually lived in the tunnels and had been doing so for years. Although air sometimes felt scarce, and the entire network was poorly lit by flashlights, spots, or in some cases, torches, Tâm had to acknowledge how remarkable was the self-sufficiency of the NVA fighters.

Tâm stayed with the group of Long Hairs as they made their way to their living quarters, two levels down in the tunnels. Here they could whisper and murmur without danger. Bảo made room for Tâm next to her mat. "Try to sleep," she said. "We will go up and out when it is dark."

The living quarters were pitch black, and Tâm slept surprisingly well. Bảo woke her before midnight. As she stretched and got up, she noticed two welts, one on each arm.

"What are these?" She asked Bảo.

Bảo aimed her flashlight at them. "Spider bites, probably." She bent down and rummaged in her backpack. "Here is some cream, but it will not do much."

Tâm thanked her and picked up her mat. Ants scurried from underneath. Tâm groaned and shook it out. "Are there biting ants as well?"

Bảo tilted her head. "Sometimes. The tunnels are not a paradise by any means. Besides ants and spiders, there are scorpions, and, of course, rats. When there is heavy bombing or fighting we must remain underground for days at a time. Many people get sick with malaria. And everyone has intestinal parasites."

Tâm took in a breath.

"But, on the other hand, the Americans have been trying to destroy them for years, and they have not succeeded. So that is good."

"Tell me about the human tunnel rats," Tâm said.

Bảo shivered. "They are the biggest danger. We never know when they will pop up. They have only one mission, and that is to kill us."

"So then why not sleep in the open? I could drive your troops to a safer part of the Iron Triangle."

"My assignment is to protect the tunnels. I cannot shirk my duty."

~

The bombers came that night. The Long Hairs fired well and often, but they did not shoot down any B-52s.

Bảo frowned in frustration. "Our commanders order us to shoot down B-52s, but our antiaircraft guns can't reach them. Our surface-to-air missiles can hit helicopters and transport planes. But the B-52s fly too high."

"Then why do they order it?"

She shrugged. "Perhaps they do not know."

"Do you believe that?"

"No."

~

It was close to dawn when the Long Hairs were satisfied that the carpet-bombing for that night was over. Bảo was happy none of her troops were killed or wounded. "We go back in now."

"No." It slipped out.

Bảo stiffened. "You are not coming?"

"Yes, but not yet. Come with me."

Her expression grew puzzled. "Where?"

"We'll go for a walk."

"I—I cannot. I must stay with my troops."

"Just a few minutes. We will come back."

Bảo relaxed, and a sly smile came over her. "Oh, Tâm. You are a devil to tempt me."

"Please."

Bảo glanced at her troops, who were waiting for her at the tunnel entrance, then looked back at Tâm. She walked over to one of the women and spoke quietly to her. The woman nodded and began to wave the others toward the tunnels. Bảo watched as they went back down and disappeared. She went to Tâm, whose pulse was beating so fast and loud she was sure it could be heard up and down the Hồ Chí Minh Trail. Bảo took her hand, and they headed into the woods.

As they walked, the air between them turned electric. Tâm was tightly coiled, aware of not only every movement she made, but Bảo's as well. Was her hesitation a rejection? Was the blink of her eye a good sign? What about the way she scratched her arm? Ahead of them was a thick rubber tree. Tâm slowed as they approached it.

Years later Tâm still didn't know if Bảo reached for her, or she for Bảo. But somehow they ended up in each other's arms, Bảo kissing Tâm's neck, her cheek, her forehead. Tâm pushed her against the tree, her fingers losing themselves in Bảo's hair. She pressed herself against Bảo, trying to mold her body to every curve, indentation, and fold of Bảo's. Then she cupped Bảo's head and cradled it between her hands. She kissed her lips. She had never tasted anything as full or sweet or exciting.

They never made back to the tunnels.

CHAPTER 45

TÂM

Tâm deserted her unit and left her truck for another Communist driver. She spent the next two months trapped between the elation of love and the despair of war. The American carpet-bombing campaign intensified, killing and wounding many fighters on the Hồ Chí Minh Trail. Fighters in the Cu Chi tunnels were forced to take cover underground for days. This time the continuous bomb attacks succeeded well beyond earlier efforts to destroy the tunnels, and couriers reported significant cave-ins and exposure throughout the tunnel network.

Still, the Long Hairs squad led by Bảo pushed south, covering a few miles a day underground. Tâm went with them. She carried her AK-47 and her utility knife with her gear, and Bảo promised to teach her how to fire an antiaircraft gun. They were headed to the Iron Triangle. The area would be a launching pad for further antiaircraft activity. Along the way they emerged from the tunnels at night to shoot down what they could.

Which left plenty of hours when they weren't sleeping, fighting, or heading south. Tâm and Bảo took advantage of that time, hiding in recessed alcoves and tunnel dead ends to make love. Tâm couldn't get enough of Bảo, and Bảo seemed to feel the same way. Tâm became accustomed to Bảo's warm body beside, beneath, or on top of her and felt bereft when they were separated. Her passion exploded when she touched Bảo. Running her hands down Bảo's body, inhaling her scent, tasting her skin, filled her with a desire she'd never felt, not even with Chinh. Her first efforts were shy and tentative, but Bảo, who clearly had more experience, taught her what to do, and their lovemaking quickly became fiery and wanton.

After their trysts, they talked. About their wonder at finding each other during a time when death and destruction reigned. About their progress over the South and the U.S. About their plans for their lives after the war.

Bảo turned on her flashlight and shot Tâm a smile that was both sad and joyous. "I want to spend my life with you, Tâm."

"I do, as well. But why do you seem sad?"

"There is much to do before we can lay down our arms."

Tâm snuggled closer to Bảo. "What about your family? What will they say if you bring home a woman as your partner?"

Bảo paused for a moment. "They will not be happy. But I hope they will accept that I've found someone to cherish." She stroked Tâm's cheek. "What about your sister?"

"I do not talk to my sister. I told you we are estranged."

"Because she is a Saigon bar girl."

"Because she is a whore. And a traitor."

"Do not think harshly of her. War makes people take unfamiliar actions." Bảo paused. "Look at us. Do you think we would have found each other if not for this war?"

"That is unfair. We did."

"But would we have become lovers?"

"Bảo, how can I answer that? I did meet you. For the first time in my life, I know how it feels to be loved. Wholeheartedly. Completely."

"Your parents loved you. And your sister."

Tâm shrugged. "There were always conditions."

"Have you ever been with a woman before?"

"No."

"What about a man?"

"Once."

"And?"

"It happened during training camp. We had just finished a dangerous mission. We were ecstatic to be alive. He was a good man."

"So, tell me. What is the difference between the man and me?" Bảo asked.

"You," Tâm kissed Bảo.

"No, really," Bảo persisted. "Do you think you are *đồng tính nữ*? A lesbian?"

"I think I am in love. And, yes, I'm afraid of being labeled. Perhaps even ostracized. But the person I am in love with happens to be a woman." Tâm propped herself up on an elbow. "What about you? You have been with other women."

"Yes."

"Am I different?"

"Oh, Tâm. Of course you are. I fell in love with you, too."

"But how can we trust this love? It happened so quickly. And I have nothing to compare it to."

Bảo traced a finger down Tâm's nose. "Yes. It was fast. But I am of the opinion that Buddha's love is everywhere, and we must honor it in all its forms around us."

Tâm rolled on top of Bảo. "Then promise me we will stay together. We can live in Saigon or Hanoi after the war. I do not care which. As long as you are with me."

"You do not want to live in the mountains?"

"Herding goats. Working all day. Planting. Harvesting. Reading." Tâm smiled. "Perhaps. Is there a library? Or a university nearby?"

Bảo giggled. "If not, I will build one for you."

"Then the mountains it is."

～

Other times their pillow talk was about the war. One night, or morning—Tâm wasn't sure what time it was since her schedule was now upside-down—Bảo brought up the Iron Triangle. "You know it."

"I've driven through. It is controlled by the Communists."

"Yes. And did you know that the U.S. built an airbase right there on top of the tunnels?"

"What?" Tâm said.

"When the U.S. came to Vietnam, one of their first tasks was to build a base in the Cu Chi District. What they didn't know was that they built part of it over the tunnels."

"No! That could not happen," Tâm said in disbelief.

"It did," Bảo went on. "It is said that it took months before the American Twenty-fifth Division realized it. They could not understand why their men were shot in their tents at night."

Tâm's mouth dropped open.

"Perhaps that is why they work so hard to destroy us now," Bảo said.

That night, a bomb attack struck the tunnels hard. The NVA antiaircraft soldiers were exposed outside the tunnels, their guns and even their surface-to-air missiles no match for the B-52s. A harsh slapping sound, a whistle, then explosion after explosion rained down. Tâm saw soldiers in a panic, rushing back to the tunnels, and she felt the ground shake beneath her. But the deafening blasts obliterated all sound. Tâm couldn't hear, which might have been a blessing, since she saw bodies falling and shrapnel flying. There must have been ear-splitting screams too, but the scene played out like a silent movie she once saw as a child.

In the ensuing chaos, Tâm couldn't find Bảo. She wanted to look for her outside, but she had to get back to the tunnels if she wanted to survive. Tâm's breath came in tiny bursts of air, and she raced for the entrance. Slithering down faster than she thought possible, she tripped and fell when she climbed to a lower level. She picked herself up and hurried to the group living quarters. There! Bảo and her troops had gathered. Tâm said a silent prayer. Bảo beamed her flashlight on each face in turn, assessing who was still missing.

"I am here," Tâm shouted, still breathless.

Bảo's face lit up with relief when she aimed her flashlight at Tâm. Her lips moved, but Tâm still couldn't hear what she was saying. She cupped her ear in response. Bảo nodded to indicate she understood. Suddenly the walls and ground under their feet shook and vibrated. Another blast. Possibly a direct hit.

Dirt and loose stones dribbled down from the ceiling. Some of the Long Hairs gazed at one another in panic. Others raced for the one exit in that passageway. Others squeezed their eyes shut and folded their hands in prayer. Bảo wrapped herself around Tâm, who hugged her close as if she was a warm blanket. Another blast split their ears, again far too close. The ground shook. More pebbles and dirt fell. The women cried out in terror. But it wasn't their time. The ceiling held.

CHAPTER 46

TÂM

T he attack ended as suddenly as it had begun. By then Tâm's
hearing had gradually returned. Bảo and her troops waited
until they were sure the bombs had stopped, then went back outside
to help scour the area for survivors. Finding bodies that were charred
beyond recognition was harrowing. Unless they were in the traditional green NVA uniform, or bore the scarf of the Communist fighters, it was difficult to identify them. Even then, the rapid turnover of
Vietnamese recruits and the scarcity of dog tags often prevented
commanders from ascertaining exactly who the soldiers were.

While troops carried the wounded in hammock litters from the
field to the underground hospital, Bảo methodically searched each
soldier's face. "I am missing one of my troop," she said. Ten minutes
later Bảo suddenly slowed as one of the litters approached. She held
up her hand, and the men carrying the litter stopped. A woman with
long hair lay without moving. Her face was burned, and her neck and
arms were already blistering. Bảo sucked in a breath. "She is mine."
She bent her ear to the woman's chest. "She is still breathing." She
looked up at the men. "Hurry. I will be there soon."

As the men trotted over to the entrance to the tunnel with their
makeshift stretcher, Bảo went back to the spot where they'd found

her soldier. She spotted the soldier's Soviet SA-7, a portable surface-to-air missile launcher, not far away on the ground.

"Tâm, come here." Tâm went to her. "Can you pick that up?"

Tâm bent over and did what Bảo asked.

"Slide it onto your shoulder." She did. "Can you handle it?"

It felt awkward and heavy in Tâm's hands compared to her AK-47. But she nodded.

"Stay here. I will be back. I will teach you how to use it. This is one of our two missile launchers. Tomorrow you deploy with us. One of the squad members will calibrate your targets."

Bảo taught Tâm the basics of firing the SA-7. They stayed outside until the sun rose and a field officer waved at them to come inside before they were discovered by the enemy.

Back in their sleeping quarters, Bảo and Tâm whispered as they lay on their mats.

"You are a good—no, a great leader, Lieutenant Diệp Hồng Bảo." Tâm rolled over so they were face-to-face, although in the dark of their quarters, they could not see each other. "Where did your dedication come from? Is that your nature? Who taught you how to operate the SA-7s? You were so calm tonight. Especially with the wounded soldier."

"So many questions." But Bảo's thoughts apparently were elsewhere. "Tâm, I have changed my mind. I do not want you to deploy with us. You must stay here."

Tâm frowned. "Why? I want to try out the SA-7."

Bảo was quiet. Then, "I have lost too many soldiers. Good girls, all of them. I still mourn their deaths. But if I lose you, I will not be able go on."

Tâm leaned across to stroke Bảo's hair. "If something happens to me, you will go on. You are the strongest commander I've ever met."

Bảo shook her head. "No, Tâm. I cannot lose you too. Not now."

"I will be fine. You are just upset because—"

Bảo cut her off. "Listen to me. Our chances are not good. Fewer than half of us will survive. If malaria doesn't kill us, the bombs will. I will never forgive myself if you are injured. Or worse."

Tâm pulled Bảo into her arms. Bảo was crying. Tâm kissed her neck, her cheeks, her tears, and whispered words of love and reassurance. It took some time, but Bảo finally fell asleep in her arms.

For Tâm, sleep was a long time coming. She knew she was walking an emotional tightrope. Her passion for Bảo was equal to her fear of death. Her yin and yang. But she also knew she was exhausted from not getting enough sleep, the lack of decent food, and the inherent dangers in the tunnels. Still, the reality of finally meeting her other half, the person who filled up the hole inside, was too precious for her to waste a single moment.

CHAPTER 47

TÂM

W hen they woke, Tâm went with Bảo to the underground hospital. Tâm waited outside. Bảo was inside for about five minutes. When she emerged, head down, trudging like a heavy boulder had landed on her shoulders, Tâm knew her soldier had died. Tâm put her arm around Bảo but Bảo pulled away, walking two steps in front.

The hospital was on the second level of the tunnels, and they made their way to the steps that would take them either to the first level or down to the living quarters. As they reached the steps, Bảo turned around. "I need to go outside for some air."

Tâm nodded. "I will go with you."

Bảo started to object, but at that moment, a blur jumped out of the dark and launched itself at Bảo. Tâm froze. For a split second she was unable to process what was happening. Then it registered. A man was attacking Bảo, overwhelming her from behind. Since she was facing Tâm, he was able to seize her under her arms and press a knife against her throat.

Tâm always carried her utility knife, most of the time in her boot. She bent down to retrieve it. At the same time, Bảo began to struggle against the man.

"Help!" Tâm shouted at the top of her lungs. "We need help now! The enemy is inside!"

But it happened too fast. Bảo was able to partially loosen his grip with her hands. She tried to slide out underneath his hold. Tâm rushed at him, knife in her hand, but before she could stab him, he tightened his hold on Bảo again and shoved his knife deep into her stomach.

The light inside was dim, but Tâm saw the blood oozing from Bảo's middle. Bảo's eyes rolled back in her head and she would have collapsed, except the tunnel rat was holding her up. He pried out the knife from her stomach and tore into her, stabbing her again and again, this time in her chest. Once more Tâm screamed for help, but no one came. The man let Bảo crumple to the ground, where she lay, not moving, between him and Tâm. The man pocketed his knife and gazed at Tâm with a satisfied grimace. She thought he was coming for her next, but he surprised her. He whirled around, scrambled up the steps, and disappeared out of the tunnel.

The first night without Bảo was torture. Yes, they had spent only a few months together, but Tâm had never imagined that Bảo would not be in her life. They had promised each other. If anyone perished, Tâm thought it would be her. Bảo was too good a soldier.

At first she lay on her mat, pretending Bảo was just checking the guns, cleaning weapons, or instructing her troops. She would return in a few minutes. When Bảo didn't show up, she thrashed from side to side, sleep impossible. Finally, she abandoned the pretense, got up, and headed to the hospital.

She headed through the tunnels in a daze. On some level she knew she wasn't reacting normally. Emotions were simmering under the surface, but she couldn't bring them to consciousness. What were they? Grief? Rage? Self-pity? Her inability to define them kept her removed from reality, and she felt as though she was floating through time and space without making a tangible impression. She might have been a ghost.

Help had finally come, but it was too late. Soldiers lifted and placed Bảo in a hammock litter. They raced to the hospital, where she was pronounced dead. Now Tâm entered the hospital. In a quiet voice she asked to see Bảo to say farewell. The staff searched a small cave they said was the mortuary, but they couldn't find Bảo's body.

Tâm was puzzled. "She was brought in only a few hours ago."

A female, probably a nurse, gave Tâm a compassionate look. "Sometimes we keep bodies to conceal the true body count from the enemy. Other times, we bury them in mass graves if it is possible. For sanitary reasons. The area aboveground is quiet today. They took her and many more. They will bury them after dark."

Tâm felt completely abandoned. She didn't have the chance to say goodbye. Or to find a small keepsake of Bảo—a lock of her hair, perhaps. A button from her uniform. A sandal. She turned away from the nurse and trudged wearily out of the hospital.

Two days later, while marching south with the Long Hairs, Tâm's mist of emotional detachment snapped. The woman who had taken Bảo's place as leader was rigid and controlling. She took Tâm aside one evening.

"You are not officially a member of our squad," she said. "You are from the South. You are . . ." She paused then spit out, "Viet Cong."

"What do you mean?" Tâm replied evenly. She knew she'd been insulted. Communist fighters usually didn't refer to themselves as "Viet Cong" unless they were insulting someone.

"We are NVA." The woman straightened. Arrogance tightened her face. "You do not have our training or discipline. You are a handicap to us. All you were was Bảo's lover."

Tâm gazed at the woman. She could not believe what she was hearing. "We are all on the same side."

"In a way. But you do not know how to operate our weapons, and you—"

"Bảo taught me how to use the SA-7."

The woman cleared her throat. "Let me say it this way. I do not have confidence in your ability to fight with us. You are a weak link. Bảo was selfish to bring you in." She smirked. "But Bảo thought she was invincible. Like Triệu Thị Trinh."

The woman was referring to a famous, almost mythical female Vietnamese warrior who, during the Chinese Han dynasty's occupation of Vietnam nearly 2,000 years earlier, rebelled against Han oppression. Legend had it that Lady Triệu, as she was known, waged thirty successful battles against the Chinese before being defeated. But Bảo's successor was not complimenting Bảo's leadership skills.

"Bảo was never the heroine she thought she was. And we do not promote concubines to be soldiers. You are no longer welcome. Go back to your truck."

Time splintered into before and after. Tâm's reaction to the woman's venom was overwhelming. The leader didn't understand their relationship. Or she did and resented it. Or she was jealous of Bảo. Rage suffused Tâm's core. Anger pierced her veil of blankness, replacing it with purple fury. How dare this woman debase Bảo's memory? How dare she relegate Tâm to the role of concubine? Tâm wanted to tear the woman apart, limb from limb. Mortally wound her and watch her die a painful death. She towered over this woman. She could take her down. Finish her off with her knife. Her fingers itched. She forced herself to breathe. Once. Twice. Three times.

Then she had a better idea.

CHAPTER 48

TÂM

The next morning Tâm cleaned her knife and attached it to her belt. Then she stole two grenades from the cache of weapons and armaments. She went to the kitchen and told the cooks she was going on a mission and needed food for twenty-four hours. Equipped with her canteen, food, and weapons, she slung her AK-47 over her shoulder, then climbed up to the highest level of the tunnel, just beneath the ground.

She stalked the tunnel entrances looking for a spot to stake out. She needed enough room to survive an exploding grenade. Thanks to Bảo, she now was familiar enough with the traps to identify them on ceilings, behind doors, or sometimes at the bottom of steps. Along the way she collected a couple of handfuls of small rocks and pebbles and dropped them in her rucksack.

After tramping a kilometer, she found a location that would work. The tunnel entrance was on the ceiling at one end of a passageway that dead-ended about forty meters in the opposite direction. The only way out of it, apart from the ceiling entrance, was a hidden trapdoor at the other end of the passageway that led down to a fishhook, which could seriously injure whoever fell or was pushed into it. She reached up to the ceiling of the tunnel and lifted the cover of the concealed entrance. The lid was a square of grass that fit snugly against the rest of the grass in the field. Grass was one of the most common covers for tunnels. Instead of moving it back in place, she left it slightly askew. Any tunnel rat looking to climb in would notice it. That man would be her target. Hopefully, it would be the rat who killed Bảo. She settled down to wait.

There was a tight ache between her shoulder blades. An hour went by. Then another. Her head drooped. She hadn't slept since Bảo was killed. She forced herself to sit up, to pay attention. Did she hear something outside? Or was it just a Huey overhead? She waited. No NVA soldier would dare to approach the tunnels in broad daylight. The sound died away, and there was silence again. A shaft of sunlight poured in from the slightly askew tunnel lid, but it was enough to take stock of her bearings.

She wasn't sure how much time had passed when she heard it. A quiet bark. From a distance. A dog was scenting on top of the tunnels. Her pulse quickened, throbbing in her ears. She took her knife out of the makeshift sheath she'd cobbled together and placed one grenade at her side. Then she took out the stones and pebbles and put them on the floor within easy reach. A few minutes passed. The dog's bark was louder, more insistent. She hadn't been bathing with American soap recently; she hadn't been bathing at all. She knew the dog was scenting her.

Soon, the barking dog was close. She thought she heard him snuffle, followed by the sound of a man praising the dog. "Good boy. Good boy."

Tâm straightened up. She waited. Tried to hear what was going on outside. Was there a conversation? She wasn't sure, but the dog was going crazy. She sat still, not moving a muscle, taking short silent breaths, watching the shaft of light from the tunnel lid. As soon as it changed, she would launch her plan.

Suddenly the shaft of light widened. Someone was moving the cover of the tunnel entrance. Tâm squeezed against the phony dead end of the tunnel. The sunlight was so bright it temporarily blinded her. All she could see was the outline of a man. Grasping something in his hand. Probably a revolver. Slowly, quietly, he lowered his legs into the tunnel. He was so quiet that her own breathing sounded like the engine of a truck. Every few inches he stopped as if he was scenting the air. The dog still snarled and whined, but she couldn't see it. Someone must have it on a leash. Still, the dog knew there was something foreign in the tunnel.

Tâm watched every movement the man made as he lowered himself into the tunnel. When she was sure he couldn't easily get out again, she threw a handful of pebbles against the trapdoor. The man flicked his revolver up and fired three shots in quick succession. The deafening shots, exploding like firecrackers in a small space, must have alerted the soldiers below, but Tâm couldn't wait. She hit the ground, picked up the grenade, and pulled out the pin. The tunnel rat dropped down into the tunnel and quickly realized he was facing the wrong direction and his shots had gone nowhere. He whipped around, crouched, and aimed his revolver in Tâm's direction. Tâm tossed the grenade at him. Folding herself up to make herself as small as possible, she pulled her head down and waited for the explosion.

Nothing happened. She looked up. The tunnel rat had caught the grenade in his free hand. How had he done that? Tâm recoiled. This was not the plan. The tunnel rat, his eyes now adjusted to the light, advanced toward Tâm, the grenade in one hand, revolver in the other. He aimed and fired. The shot went wide. Tâm pulled out her knife and dove for his feet. She came up short. But he was clutching something in both hands. If she could reach him before he flung the grenade back or fired again, she had a chance. Adrenaline flooded her system. Her heart hammered in her chest. She lunged at him and sliced her knife through the air, aiming for his leg. The knife connected. She pulled it across his shin, trying to deepen the wound.

He roared in pain and dropped the gun. His other arm, the arm holding the grenade, instinctively flew up to protect his face. She jumped up, grabbed the grenade out of his hand and leopard-crawled to the trap door. She opened it, spun around, and lobbed the grenade back in his direction.

The explosion lifted his body into the air, and the tunnel rat disappeared in a haze of smoke, dirt, bone, gristle, and blood. The blowback pushed Tâm through the trapdoor, and she fell onto the fishhook below. The spikes, sharp as tigers' teeth, gouged and penetrated her legs. Blood spurted through her pants and sprayed the walls of the tunnel. So much blood. She was bleeding out. The pain was excruciating.

The blood turned gray and the tunnel walls darkened. Tâm felt herself slipping away. The last thing she heard was the faint bark of a dog. Then everything went black.

PART VI

SAIGON, 1970–1975

Mai

CHAPTER 49

MAI

Mai didn't expect to love her baby. She hadn't wanted him. He was the reminder of a love affair gone bad, which made her by turns angry, sad, and lonely. Before he was born, she fretted that an infant would chain her to an endless routine of cooking, cleaning, and serving his needs. Like it had with her mother. True, she'd abandoned the idea of abortion when she felt him kick, but loving him? That was not going to happen.

But after Đêm Nguyệt was born, washed, and swaddled in a soft blanket, Mai couldn't believe the wonder of him. She counted his fingers and toes dozens of times. Ran the tips of her fingers over his perfect lips, his eyebrows, his silky hair. The fact that she had produced this perfect, tiny being was a miracle. She remembered Sáng, her brother, and the joy with which her parents had greeted him. At the time she thought it was simply because he was a boy. Now she understood.

And this little miracle of life was hers. He might be the only person—she was loath to say possession, but if she was honest that's what he was, at least for a while—that belonged to her. And no one else. More important, though, he needed her. He might have been the first person in her life who did. She vowed never to let him down.

Never to let him think he was alone in the world, like she was. She would shower him with the love and affection she'd never felt. He would know he was wanted.

One of the aunties supervised her first breastfeeding, although Mai didn't need much help. "You are in luck." The elderly woman laughed. "Look how greedy he is for your nipple."

Mai giggled when he sucked. After the surprise of the first time, it no longer pinched, and while he took in her milk he gazed up at her before he drifted off. That this tiny being was dependent on her for everything was not the burden she'd feared. In a strange way, it was an honor that had been bestowed on her. Meeting that honor would be the most important goal in her life going forward.

In a way, too, Mai felt like Sandy had come back. Every time she gazed at Đêm Nguyệt, she saw Sandy's eyes and the shape of his chin. She still hated Sandy for abandoning them, but simply by dint of his birth, Đêm Nguyệt filled the hole in her heart that Sandy had carved out. In time, she might even forgive him. She dreamed of one day introducing him to his son. The chances of that were tiny; still, she imagined how it would go. Sandy would be overcome with fatherly love. He would beg Mai to let him come back so they could be a real family. She wasn't sure what she would say, but she had fantasies of the three of them on a Harley, Đêm Nguyệt on her back, roaring through the streets of Saigon.

For the next three months, the baby was never more than a breast's length away from Mai. One of the aunties cobbled together a baby carrier, a canvas bag with holes for his legs and straps that that tied around her waist. Mai was able to take him with her on the Vespa when she shopped, did errands, or went for a manicure at the market.

Manicures were now a weekly activity for Mai. They'd been a small, inexpensive way to spend thirty minutes lavishing attention on herself, but now that Đêm Nguyệt was here, she loved to watch the market women fuss and coo over him. He was a healthy, sturdy baby, they'd say. He would soon be strong and smart—look how much he'd grown in just a week's time.

One day Mai put on her best jeans and a tank top and made sure her hair and makeup were perfect. Then she and Đêm Nguyệt rode over to the Stardust nightclub for a visit. Though barely six months had passed, Chú Thạc was behind the bar as usual, a little heavier, perhaps, and grayer at his temples. He looked tired but greeted her profusely.

"Everyone always asks about you, Mai. The GIs want to know when you're coming back."

Mai smiled. "Please thank them, Chú Thạc. I will return soon, I hope." Then she introduced him to Đêm Nguyệt. Chú Thạc rolled his index finger under the baby's tiny fingers, which Đêm Nguyệt promptly grasped. Chú Thạc stifled a smile and said solemnly, "It is an honor to meet the son of Linh Mai."

Mai smiled. "No. It is my honor to introduce you to him." She paused. "Is Madame Thạc in the kitchen?"

Chú Thạc shrugged and motioned to the back. As Mai entered the kitchen, Madame Thạc glanced up from the snacks she was counting out for the tables.

Madame Thạc arched her brows and tightened her lips. "So you ready to come back?" she said as if Mai had been gone only a few days, not six months. The woman gave only a passing glance to Đêm Nguyệt. A spit of irritation came over Mai. Then again, a baby was not a revered object at the Stardust. It represented a failure. A mistake. At the very least, human carelessness. Mai was that human.

"I am ready. How are you, Madame?" As soon as she asked, she wasn't sure she should have. Like Chú Thạc, Madame looked tired, Mai thought. Frazzled.

Madame sighed. "I do not know anymore."

"Why? Tell."

"Our customers have changed. The GIs are different. They do not care anymore. Not the way they used to. They are reckless. I know they do drugs in the alley. Then they drink on top of the drugs. It is to forget. Not to be happy. They tell us what the Viet Cong do to enemy prisoners." She shook her head. "The stories paint such horror, they say they will kill themselves rather than become NVA prisoners. We are in a dark place."

Mai kept her mouth shut. Đêm Nguyệt started to fuss in his baby carrier. Mai ran her fingers through his hair, which had thickened since his birth.

Madame Thạc, perhaps realizing she had said too much, forced a smile. "But maybe you can help when you come back. They love you, Mai." When her lips parted, Mai spotted an empty space where a tooth used to be. Mai didn't comment on it. Instead, she asked, "How is Hạnh?"

Madame Thạc let out a breath and shook her head again. "She does drugs with the soldiers."

Mai stepped back, surprised. "How? Why?"

"A new boyfriend. She is high every night. When she works. Ever since you left, she has been—unreliable. I want to fire her. But I decided to wait until you were back. Maybe you can . . ." Madame Thạc's voice trailed off.

"We did not part on good terms. But I will talk to her." She changed the subject. "Business is good?"

Madame sighed again. "It is all right. For how long, I do not know. The U.S. will begin to pull out their soldiers soon. I do not like it, but I understand. Like I said, the Americans do not care. They are afraid of being captured by Viet Cong. Or getting malaria in the jungle. I am happy you are coming back. Perhaps you will lighten their spirits."

CHAPTER 50

MAI

Mai went back to the Stardust at the end of November. She made arrangements for two of the aunties to babysit Đêm Nguyệt. They were experienced mothers themselves; Mai knew he would be in good hands. Because he was a boy, they would treat him like a prince. Still, her heart ached to leave him. She tried to put him to sleep before she left so he wouldn't realize she was gone, but the aunties waved her off and told her not to worry. What she didn't say was how jealous she was that they would have more time with him than she. What if he came to like them more?

Within a week of going back, she was exhausted. She worked at night when Đêm Nguyệt was, for the most part, asleep. But he slept much of the day too, so she learned to nap when he did. However, a series of naps did not compensate for a good night's sleep. She wasn't a cat. When she complained to the aunties, they had little compassion.

"You are young, dear Mai. And strong. You can do this. We did, and we survived."

They had a point, she had to acknowledge. She'd turned sixteen only a few months earlier. Sixteen. Hardly more than a child herself. With a baby, a job, and a Vespa. Not the life she had imagined for herself. But the life she had. For Đêm Nguyệt's sake, she would make it the best she could.

The Stardust seemed a little shabbier and more tattered than she remembered. She could ignore it when the lights were dim and the spray of iridescent stars and moon on the ceiling drew her attention. Or the candle votives on the tables flickered, lending the nightclub a classy, sophisticated air. But when the lights shone bright, she saw the tears in the upholstery of the booths and the chipped corners of the tables.

For the most part, a new crop of fresh-faced soldiers occupied the bar. But on her third night Freddy, the lean, lanky GI with greasy hair from Alabama who had introduced her to Sandy, showed up. He caught her up in a tight hug. "Mai, you're still as pretty as a peach! Better. The whole damn orchard!"

She threw her arms around him. "Now I know I'm back." She laughed.

"I heard you had a little boy."

She nodded excitedly and drew him to a table. "First round is on the house," she said. "You still drink bourbon?"

"Does a pig like mud?"

She came back with two bourbons, one for him and one for the GI he was with, a solid, muscled man named Joe.

"Thank you, ma'am," Joe said. He was a nice-looking American, with steel blue eyes, a dark complexion, and lots of dark hair on his arms. He wasn't tall, but he looked tough and strong.

Mai flashed him a smile, then turned back to Freddy, who told her he'd been promoted to sergeant. "I signed up for another tour of duty."

"Why? You not want to go home to Alabama?" It was good to practice her English again. She'd neglected it during the pregnancy.

"To tell ya the truth, babe, I don't have much to go back to. My pappy passed, and my ma and I never got along. When I do get state-side, I'll probably take off for Florida."

Florida sounded exotic and mysterious to Mai. They said the

climate was as close to South Vietnam as you could get in the U.S. "Because of the climate?"

He laughed and swilled down his bourbon in one gulp. "No. I hear they got beautiful women down there."

She laughed, then grew serious. "You used to be infantry. Are you still?"

"No, ma'am," he said. "They moved me to quartermaster. Cigarettes and booze. My favorite things." He laughed. "And safe as a june bug at Christmas."

"Do you remember when you introduced me to Sandy?"

"Yeah." He averted his gaze.

"Do you hear from him?"

He paused, then said, "Nope. You?"

She shook her head.

"I'm sorry, babe. That wasn't good, him running out on you like that."

"You're right," she said, her voice tight. "I still do not understand why. But." She sniffed and shrugged and tried to smile. "I now have a beautiful son. And he has his father's eyes."

Joe listened to their conversation.

A crop of new girls worked the Stardust. Mai answered their questions, doled out advice, and quickly became their unofficial leader. She nudged them when a GI came in alone, paired off two or three girls with a small group, and monitored them to make sure there were no problems.

While she still longed to be home with Đêm Nguyệt, it was clear he had become used to the aunties. He babbled all the time now, and everyone pretended they knew what he was saying, which made him babble even more. When she came home or woke from a nap, they filled her in on all the feats he had mastered. "You must see him sit up, roll over, and bounce on his feet when you hold his arms," they exclaimed. "Surely this child is destined to be an important man."

Mai knew she would probably miss him say his first word, take his first step, ea his first sweet. Although the aunties would capture these milestones on their Brownie cameras, she would never see them as they happened. Those precious moments ought to be worth something, she thought.

The next day Mai went into work early and into the kitchen, where Madame Thạc was preparing snacks for the evening.

"Madame Thạc, how are you this evening?"

The woman looked up from the counter and smiled. "Good evening, Mai. We are happy you have come back to our little family. The crowds are almost what they used to be."

"I am pleased. And honored." Mai dipped her head. "I have a small matter to discuss with you."

"Yes?"

"I think you know how hard it is for me to be away from Đêm Nguyệt. You have two sons. You know how a child changes one's life. My son has captured my heart in a way I never thought possible. But, much as I want to spend every minute with him, I must work to feed and support him."

Madame Thạc looked like she wanted to interrupt.

Mai went on. "Of course, I do not mind. The Stardust has been my home away from home, and you know how much I care about you and Chú Thạc. Did you know I have been informally training the girls and looking after them? I am making sure the girls are cleaner and more attractive. They are learning English. I do not mind the extra work, even though it is in addition to my own duties as a bar girl. I am glad to do it. However, because of this, my own orders at the bar have dropped. Under my guidance, the girls are making the money I would have brought in. As I said, I do not mind, and I want to continue to do both, but—"

"How much?" Madame cut in.

Without missing a beat Mai proposed a number. "Two hundred đồng per drink plus an hourly salary of 400 đồng."

Madame laughed. "Impossible. I cannot afford that."

Mai glanced at her side-eyed. "I see how Chú Thạc waters down the drinks. And there have been no empty tables in a week."

Madame hesitated, pursed her lips, and countered. "One hundred and a 100 *đồng* fee."

Mai considered it and split the difference. "One hundred fifty *đồng* and 200 hourly."

Madame stared at Mai. Then she nodded. "You will continue to make sure the girls obey the rules."

"Of course." Mai bowed, suppressing a smile. "Thank you, Madame. I am honored."

CHAPTER 51

MAI

Hạnh was still a problem. Their relationship was awkward, almost hostile. Mai wanted to forgive Hạnh for kicking her out of the apartment. The two rooms in which she and Đêm Nguyệt lived now were small, modest, and farther away from the Stardust, but Mai was now surrounded by women with decades of experience raising children and who loved her son. That was so much more important. And satisfying. She was grateful to Buddha for leading her to this place.

Mai invited Hạnh out for lunch or dinner, but Hạnh refused. Mai tried to understand Hạnh's resistance. Was it coming from her boyfriend? He was an American corporal from New Jersey, wherever that was. But he never smiled, and he hustled Hạnh outside every few minutes. It was as if Hạnh was in a trance and only paid attention to him. Her duties as a hostess were an afterthought.

Madame was right. Hạnh had become careless about her appearance. She looked unclean, and her hair was listless and flat. She wore too much makeup. She was starting to look emaciated, and when Mai took hold of her arm one night, she saw track marks. She and Hạnh exchanged a worrying glance; then Hạnh shook her off and hurried out of the Stardust.

Mai understood. Hạnh must be humiliated to be seen by her closest friend when she was in such a state. Three months earlier Mai would have tried to help her friend get clean, but now she wasn't inclined to. Hạnh had made her decision when she asked Mai to leave the apartment they had so gaily decorated the year before. Their lives had taken different paths. Đêm Nguyệt was Mai's priority now. She had no idea what Hạnh's was, but Hạnh wasn't the girl she had been. Mai admitted defeat and let her go.

Madame was right about something else. The talk among the GIs had changed. One night she joined a small group at a table. There were three soldiers and three girls, but the girls spoke only rudimentary English, and their puzzled expressions told Mai they didn't understand what the soldiers were discussing. They shared an intense conversation, ignoring the girls except to ask for more drinks.

"You hear about Operation Greene Bullet up in Pleiku?"

The second soldier shook his head.

"Third Battalion, Twelfth Infantry Regiment and First Battalion, Thirty-fifth Infantry?"

"Yeah?"

"One night they were able to rescue a few POWs from Charlie when the zips were out shooting their asses off." He took a long pull on his beer. "But, apparently, the shit's getting pretty deep. Our guys were tortured."

Mai heard a sharp intake of breath from one of the GIs.

Another asked, "How bad?"

"They said the gooks screeched at them day and night. Wouldn't let them sleep either, always waking them up when they drifted off. Starved 'em too, kept them in chains, and pissed on them whenever they felt like it. Then they covered their heads with a bag and poured water down their throats."

One of the girls tried to insinuate herself into the conversation. "Water dun troats?" She smiled sweetly. "What is that?"

The GI glanced over. "Something you never want to experience, sweetheart." He glanced back at his pals. "You think you're going to drown. You don't know when it's gonna stop, so you choke."

"Fuck me." The soldier grimaced.

The girl who'd spoken must have thought the soldier was telling a joke, because she giggled. Pasting on a stern expression, Mai pointed a finger at the girl and shook her head.

"Said the motherfuckers beat them with billy clubs. Poured gasoline on them and attached hand-cranked generators with leads to their dicks, then cranked 'em up. One guy's dick is all fucked up. He's going home for an operation."

The second solider gagged on his beer.

The GI who'd been speaking chugged down the rest of his, tipped the empty glass in the girls' direction. "Another round here."

The girls scurried toward the bar.

"And for what? Just to find out where the next fucking skirmish is? It's shit. Total bullshit."

"Assholes, all of them," the third man said grimly.

The one who had gagged got up. "I'm going outside for some air."

"Sure you are, pal."

Mai swallowed, unsure what to say. The first solider went on as if she wasn't there. "Those fuckers'll use anything they can find to kill us. Grenades, bombs built from land mines, ripped off from our supplies, even TNT that's been smuggled into Saigon. And their women hide shit in pineapples, bread, and other food. Even in their bras."

Mai thought back to the soldiers who had ambushed her village. Their violence and their cruelty were unforgiveable. She could never accept what had happened, but they were fighting a war. Doing what they were instructed. For them it wasn't personal.

She compared them to the Viet Cong, with whom Tâm was now fighting. Is this what her sister was doing? Mutilating human beings, just because she could? Drowning them with water? If so, Tâm had become a monster.

CHAPTER 52

MAI

More troubles erupted during the rainy season of 1970. At the end of April the American president announced that the U.S. would invade and bomb Cambodia. He claimed it was to disrupt supply chains along the Hồ Chí Minh Trail, which swept through Cambodia at certain points, and to destroy North Vietnamese base camps, many of which sat just on the other side of the border in Cambodia. In reality, the bombings had begun before they were announced by the president, and for the Vietnamese who lived near the border areas, his pronouncement was too little, too late.

Nonetheless, a wave of protests erupted in the U.S., some of which became violent. Four students were shot and killed at Kent State University in Ohio by their own military. But the effect of the escalation on GIs already in Vietnam was like a touching a lit match to gasoline.

"This is a civil war, goddammit," a pal of Freddy's said at the Stardust. "What the fuck are we doing in the middle of it, anyway? Nothing's changed in six years in this armpit of a country, for Christ's sake!"

Joe, the soldier who seemed to be with Freddy all the time now, had a different take. "The South needs us. Their army doesn't know how to fight guerrilla warfare."

"You think we do?" The first guy fumed. "Why do you think our body count is still so high? We march through the jungle and rice paddies with fifty pounds of gear on our backs, covered from head to toe, wearing thick boots and socks that give us fungus. We can't run if there's an attack. We're fucking sitting ducks. I just don't know anymore."

Joe nodded. "I get it. I want out, too. But things are winding down. Thousands of GIs are going home. It'll be our turn soon. Just hang on a few more months."

The first man snorted and went outside. Five minutes later, a fistfight broke out between him and another soldier who was still pro-war. Freddy and Joe raced out the door to break it up.

It was on nights like this that Mai couldn't wait to go home to Đêm Nguyệt. Standing over his bassinet after the fistfight, she watched him sleep, his face so fresh and peaceful that a tiny thrill buzzed her nerves. He was a quiet sleeper; he didn't fuss or squirm. He was so quiet, in fact, that she leaned over the bassinet to make sure he was breathing. This child was not just her salvation; he was her object of unconditional love.

He was almost a year old and had been sleeping through the night for months. It was time to trade the bassinet for a crib. Soon he would be taking his first steps. Then he would be getting into everything. After that he would start talking. He was growing. But what kind of boy was he growing into? She thought about the war. He knew nothing of it, and she prayed he never would. He deserved to grow up in a place of sunshine and peace, to play with friends without fearing a bomb attack or mortar shell or Communist torture.

He deserved a father as well. A man to love and look up to. Sandy was on the other side of the world, but that didn't mean she couldn't find a man here. Maybe when he was a toddler she would consider it. She would make a wiser choice this time. She would be driven not by passion but by practicality. The man she chose, Vietnamese or not, had to love Đêm Nguyệt as if he was his biological son. He must not expect her to be his maid, either. She would have a profession, although she didn't know what, and he must respect it. Anything else was unacceptable.

When Đêm Nguyệt woke in the morning, Mai brought him to her breast and clasped him tight. She loved his baby smell and how it mingled with the smell of her milk. No matter who became his father, no one would ever come between her and her son.

As the number of bombing attacks raining down on Cambodia climbed, so did the withdrawal of American troops. Fewer GIs came to the Stardust, and the ones who did were depressed to be fighting a war no one thought they could win. Empty tables began to be the norm, and the lines to get in disappeared. The atmosphere at the bar grew dark and grim. Bar girls were no longer seen as charming or flirtatious. The soldiers seemed to view them as either whores or vinks to be ignored. At the same time, an anti-American mindset, even on the part of the South Vietnamese, was rising. The war had stretched for seven years. The country was exhausted, disillusioned, and out of patience. Where the Vietnamese had welcomed Americans before, now soldiers had to contend with insults and hostility. It was less unpleasant—and safer—to stay on the base and get high.

Madame Thạc had to let some of the girls go. Mai wasn't one of them, but she couldn't ignore reality. Even with the extra money Madame was paying her, fewer customers meant fewer drink orders. She needed another source of income. She went to the manicurist at the Binh Tay market and negotiated a payment plan for a basic basket of equipment and tools. Back at her place, she gave each auntie a manicure over the next few days. They were delighted with the results.

Then Mai asked hopefully, "Do you think that instead of money, I could give you a manicure instead? Just once in a while. Perhaps once a month."

For the first time since she had moved in, the aunties told her no.

"We need to eat, too," one said. "Manicures are a luxury. But they don't put food on our tables."

So Mai went back to the market and asked the manicurist if she needed any help. The woman shrugged and said no. "I don't have enough clients myself." But she did recommend a salon not far away in the heart of Chinatown, and Mai was able to get a part-time job there.

It meant more time away from Đêm Nguyệt, but she needed the money. She made an extra effort to spend every moment she wasn't working with him. She took him to the park, the zoo, and the market. He was becoming a real person now, imitating the inflection of language and words, and pulling himself up on a chair or table. He was her joy, her delight, and when he clung to her, crying when she had to leave for work, she was secretly glad.

CHAPTER 53

MAI

By 1971 the crowd at the Stardust had dwindled to a core group of GIs. More bar girls were let go, and Madame cut everyone's hours, including Mai's. Mai saved as much as she could, but between the cost of babysitting, gas for the Vespa, her rent, food, and clothes for Đêm Nguyệt, she was stretched thin. Around the middle of the year, Madame motioned her into the kitchen.

"I can't pay your extra salary anymore. We are just hanging on. I must let more bar girls go."

Mai had been expecting it. She nodded unhappily.

"There is something else."

Mai looked up, suddenly frightened. Was Madame going to fire her?

"We have been thinking we must allow Vietnamese men to come into the Stardust. Otherwise, we will be forced to close."

It was an unwritten rule that Vietnamese and other Asian men were not welcome at the Stardust. Americans had been given priority for years. Madame Thạc said Vietnamese men didn't tip like Americans. Or drink as much. It wasn't intentional; a Vietnamese paycheck was much lower than a soldier's.

The girls would have to adjust, Madame Thạc said. Mai was

relieved that she hadn't been fired. "Is there no other solution, Madame? Perhaps if we advertised more, we—"

Madame Thạc cut her off. "We have tried to come up with ideas, but they either cost too much or will take too long to show results." She bit her lip. "I know it is not the best solution, but you're our top bar girl, Mai. Will you stay under these new conditions? The girls who are still here look up to you. If you stay, I think they will."

Mai thought about it. Allowing Vietnamese men in the Stardust would fundamentally change the Stardust. She would end up making even less money. Freddy, his friend Joe, and some GIs still came in, but empty tables yawned at her every night. On the other hand, Đêm Nguyệt needed clothes. Food. A babysitter. Mai had no choice.

So Mai stayed. She tried to make the best of it. She still tried to look her best. Over the year she had developed a flair for fashion, and on her everything, whether jeans or an *áo dài*, looked good. She had admirers, both white and Asian.

Many of the other bar girls depended on her to help them socialize with the men, and she didn't let them down. Perhaps it was misplaced loyalty, but she remembered how Hạnh had helped her when she first came to the Stardust. Although Mai was only eighteen, she felt almost motherly toward the other girls. Perhaps her love for Đêm Nguyệt had softened her heart. Despite her need for extra money, she often let the other bar girls take money for the drinks she helped them order. She told herself she would make up the difference by offering manicures.

One night Joe, Freddy's GI pal, sat down at the table they usually took, a table that would seat up to six. Mai assumed Freddy would be joining him shortly so she didn't say anything about the size of the table. Twenty minutes later, though, after a bar girl had brought him a Jack Daniel's and he'd waved her off, Mai went over.

Joe tossed back the Jack Daniel's.

"You want another?" She smiled.

He nodded but didn't return the smile.

She brought him another. He downed it in two gulps.

"Slow down, cowboy," Mai teased. "You don't want to lose your cool."

He patted the empty chair next to him.

She sat. "Where's Freddy? And the others?"

He stared at her. "I have bad news, Mai."

Her stomach twisted. "What?"

He let out a breath. "Freddy is dead."

Mai sat stock-still, as if any movement on her part would verify what Joe told her. If she didn't move a muscle, it wasn't true. They could rewind the conversation and start over fresh.

"Did you hear what I said, Mai?"

She swallowed and squeezed her eyes shut. After a long moment, she said in a low, throaty voice she hardly recognized, "What happened?"

Joe tapped his empty shot glass on the table. "It was a freak accident. He was with another soldier and they took a jeep out from base to a meeting with a South Vietnamese lieutenant about some equipment. He drove over a land mine. It was over like that." He snapped his fingers.

Mai's eyes teared up. Freddy had been like a brother to her. An American, but a good and trusted friend. She remembered the night he'd brought her a fruit from his mess hall. An apple, he'd said. She'd heard of apples. They grew everywhere in America. But not Vietnam. He'd sliced it in half and made her eat it. She loved its crisp, part-sweet, part-tart taste, but more than that, she loved Freddy for caring enough to bring it to her. Why did he have to die? Why did all the people she loved leave her in the end? This war had robbed her of everyone she was close to. Her mother. Father. Brother. Tâm might as well be dead. Sandy. Now Freddy. The only person left was her son.

Joe's voice cracked. "And I'm shipping out soon."

Tears filled Mai's eyes and slipped down her cheeks. "Where—where are you going?"

"Home. Indiana. Munster."

"Where is that?"

He told her. "It's not far from Chicago. Mai, I'd like to stay in touch with you. May I give you my address?" He jotted it down on a napkin.

"Of course," she said, trying to wipe her tears away. "But I will never go to America. Do you plan on coming back?"

"Who knows?" He passed it to her. "Now give me yours."

"But I do not know how long I will be there. Everything is so—so uncertain."

"Give it to me anyway. Just make sure to tell the landlord when you move where you are going."

She smiled sadly. "Okay." She wrote her address on another napkin and gave it to him, then picked up the one on which he'd scribbled. "Okay," she repeated. "Mr. Joe Hunter. From Munster, Indiana. And what if you move?"

"That is my mother's home. If I'm not there, she will know how to get in touch with me."

Mai laughed. "How true that is."

"Freddy used to say your beauty, kindness, and good cheer helped make his time here bearable." He dug into his pocket and brought something out. "Freddy was half in love with you, so I think he would have wanted you to have this." He handed it to her.

It was a heart-shaped medal bordered in gold. The center of the heart was purple, with the profile of a man on it, also in gold.

"It's a Purple Heart. It just came in. It's given to soldiers who are wounded or killed in battle. His captain decided Freddy should have it."

Mai fingered it gently. She teared up again. "But what about his mother? Shouldn't she have the medal?"

Joe nodded. "I think Freddy would rather you have it. At least for a while. Show it to your son when he's old enough. Let him know there were Americans who lost their lives trying to do the right thing for your country." He almost smiled. "And when you come to the States, bring it with you, and we will give it to his mother." Joe rose and extended his hand. "I'm glad I got to know you, Mai. Good luck to you."

Through her tears, she felt suddenly shy. It wasn't common for men and women to touch in public. She extended hers. "Thank you, Joe."

He held her hand for a moment, then went to the bar to pay his bill. He left through the front door.

In September, a bomb exploded inside one of the most popular GI bars on Tu Do Street, only a block away from the Stardust. The Tu Do Night Club provided entertainment every night, and the bomb went off during the middle of a show, killing fifteen people and injuring fifty-seven. The ceiling and front walls of the two-story Tu Do Night Club were destroyed. Debris tumbled down on tables, and shards of glass were found as far as a block away. The bomb also demolished half a dozen motorbikes parked outside.

Despite an official investigation, the perpetrators were never found, but most were sure it was the Viet Cong. It was one more reminder of growing anti-American sentiment in Saigon, and now physical danger, for those who supported them.

The Stardust closed at the end of the year.

CHAPTER 54

MAI

One of the aunties died at the beginning of 1972. Mai feared it was an omen of things to come, and the year's events proved her right. Her most pressing worry was still money. She had a part-time job as a manicurist, but that alone wouldn't make ends meet. Her salary at the Stardust had provided most of her income, but that was gone. Madame and Chú Thạc had left too. Rumor had it they moved back to a hamlet in the northeast where Madame Thạc grew up.

Mai combed the shopping district of Chinatown and Saigon's central downtown, looking for hostess jobs. But the ones available paid less than the Stardust. Frustrated, she considered revisiting the Saigon Café, where she and Tâm had worked when they first arrived, but figured Cô Cúc would laugh her out the front door.

She went back to the Binh Tay market and walked the stalls, looking for work, but times were hard, and no one wanted to pay her what she and Đêm Nguyệt needed to survive. Her options were narrowing. Her situation was so dire that she had to sell the Vespa. She bought a used bicycle with the proceeds. She recalled how she and Tâm had bought bicycles when they first came to Saigon.

Only one profession would pay her the money she needed, but

she refused to consider it. Depressed and hopeless, she crawled into bed and stayed there. Đêm Nguyệt, who was now walking, toddled in several times and climbed into bed next to her. "Play now, Mama?" he asked in toddler talk.

Her eyes filled and she held him close, whispering, "In a few minutes, son. Yes, we will play." But then she wouldn't get up and Nguyệt would toddle out to one of the aunties. After a few days, one of the aunties came in and sat on the bed next to Mai.

"You need to get up," she said.

"Why?" Mai said in a dull tone.

"Đêm Nguyệt needs you."

Mai didn't move. "I have nothing to give him. I do not know how we will survive. I cannot get a job that pays enough."

The auntie didn't say anything for a while. "You know, Mai, I am not from Saigon. I lived in a village near Hue. I came here fifty years ago, when the French ruled Indochina."

Mai rolled over.

"I was a beautiful young girl. Like many Vietnamese women. Like you," she added.

Mai looked up.

"I was with a French officer for a year. His mistress. We had a child. But she died in infancy." The auntie went on. "After that the officer did not want me anymore. I was alone. No money. No place to live. No job. I was desperate."

Mai propped herself up on her elbow. "What did you do?"

"There is no shame in any work when survival is at stake. All of us have been desperate at some point in our lives. You have a son. You do what you must do. For him."

They looked at each other for a moment. Then Mai sat up and embraced the auntie.

"Thank you, Auntie."

The auntie nodded. "I will tend to Đêm Nguyệt when you work."

∾

And so Mai began work as a prostitute. She started in downtown Saigon and went to the hotel that Madame had suggested years ago for bar girls who set up trysts with soldiers. The Stardust was not the only GI bar that had closed, and the hotel's business had fallen off. They agreed to Mai's request for a lower room rate. Once that was negotiated, she focused on a radius of streets around Tu Do Street, guessing that American GIs who still came downtown would flock to the restaurants, fancy hotels, and expensive shops. Eventually the soldiers would take a stroll. When they did, they would find brothels filled with available Vietnamese women.

But Mai didn't want to be tied down to one bar. Many of the girls did drugs along with the soldiers, like Hạnh. There were men, too, she learned, who found customers for the girls and took a cut of their money in return. She didn't want to split her earnings with anyone. After inspecting the area around the hotel carefully, she chose the corner of Tu Do and Lam Son, which was a few yards from the better restaurants and clubs, as her turf.

If she was going to make it on her own, she had to be better than, or at least different from, the other girls. The Vietnamese called whores "Butterflies of the Night," and Mai was determined to be the most beautiful butterfly. She took pains to look attractive and stylish. No trashy or sloppy clothing. Her hair was scented, her makeup and nails flawless. Her outfits were seductive but carried with them a flair of elegance.

Like the other women, she would demand payment in advance. But some girls ran a racket where they took their customers' money and disappeared before having sex. She would explain she was not that kind of woman. Her customers would be with her from the moment they paid until they left her afterward. As for her price, the going rate, including the hotel, was about 9,500 đồng, or 18 dollars American. Mai charged 12,500, or 24 dollars. If her customers were American, she could make her goal of 50,000 đồng a night with fewer tricks.

A light rain fell on her first night on the streets, but it didn't affect the crowd. Plenty of Vietnamese men approached her, but she either looked the other way or shook her head. She watched their reactions. Some, hostile at her rejection, hurled insults at her. Others just shrugged. She inhaled the wet but surprisingly pleasant scent of rain on the concrete sidewalk and prayed for an American to pass by.

But few GIs were out tonight, and those who were already had girls hanging on their arms. She remembered when Madame Thạc opened the club to Vietnamese men in addition to Americans. It was clear she would have to do the same.

A few minutes later, when an older, slightly drunk Vietnamese man approached her, she forced a smile. When she told him her price, he stumbled backward and waved her away.

"*Con điếm!*"

It was Mai's turn to shrug.

Eventually an Asian man in Western clothes came up to her with a broad smile. She returned it, and he asked in Vietnamese, "How much?"

When she told him, he looked her up and down. "You better be worth it."

Mai suppressed the impulse to retaliate in kind, took his arm, and giggled. She was supposed to pretend she found him irresistible. Together they rounded the corner and headed to the hotel.

Mai hadn't had sex since Sandy left, but she did manage to get birth control pills through the aunties. The room looked clean but was tiny, with a single bed and a window that looked onto a brick wall. She sat on the bed, unsure what to do next.

"Would you like to watch?" She gestured taking off her clothes.

"Do it now. Quickly."

She did. She didn't realize how embarrassed she would be to stand in front of a stranger totally naked. She felt so self-conscious that she almost ran from the room. Then she thought of Đêm Nguyệt. She turned to face the man and gritted her teeth. "How do you like your women?"

He didn't reply but unzipped his pants and started to masturbate. Mai forced another smile. "Let me do that."

He kept going. "Shut up and lie down."

When she was on the bed he threw himself on top of her. He shoved himself inside. He smelled like day-old sweat, with rancid breath. Fortunately, ten seconds later he was done.

CHAPTER 55

MAI

It didn't become a routine as much as a business. Every night Mai prettied up herself, found her spot at the intersection of Lam Som and Tu Do, and waited. Like she had at the Stardust, she favored men who looked clean and not too old and seemed polite, although that was hard to tell. She was the object of catcalls and whistles and had her choice of johns. When other prostitutes noticed how she attracted men, they tried to home in on her turf. But Mai stood her ground and chased them away.

A wink, a stare that lasted a beat too long, a smile from a passerby, were signals to saunter up to them with her pitch. She started with "Do you want to be happy tonight?" That evolved to "Let me show you how you should be loved" and to "You will never forget this night."

Her customers ranged in age, from soldier to businessman, Asian to white. Some were polite; some quibbled about price. Some tipped her. Some did not. Some played rough, and occasionally it turned violent. Once a john demanded his money back after he couldn't get hard. She'd tried hard to please him with her mouth, but for whatever reason, he couldn't get an erection. He punched her in the face and gave her a black eye. Another with the same problem broke her wrist. She missed a week of work because of him, a week where she and Da Nguyệt ate nothing but noodles and fruit.

There were less dangerous but equally unpleasant parts to the job. While the men she chose looked clean, it was never a guarantee, and the body odor of a man who did not bathe was offensive. If they sweated too much, it dripped on her, and she'd have to shower afterward. Their hair was sometimes greasy, and the rank odor of their dirt disgusted her. Some of their faces were so unattractive she could barely look them in the eye. Then again, she would rationalize, that's probably why they were coming to her in the first place. Her job was to make them feel desirable. The after-sex smell, a yeasty stench, permeated the sheets on the bed, and while she paid for an extra set of clean sheets, their dingy look made her doubt how clean they were.

She found herself remembering sex with Sandy while she was with customers. She allowed that she might have exaggerated Sandy's sexual prowess during those times, but it made what she was doing more tolerable. But even that didn't work all the time. There were many times she came home and scrubbed her skin to wash away the stink and shame.

There was another problem as well. A month after she started, it became painful to urinate. A putrid-smelling yellowish green discharge began, and her privates grew swollen and red. Her insides cramped. The aunties said they could cure it with herbs and creams. They couldn't, and her condition worsened. She paid a visit to the doctor who'd confirmed her pregnancy, surprised he was still practicing in the back streets of District 1.

After examining her, he said. "You are lucky you came in when you did."

"Why?" Mai asked.

"If you had waited any longer, you might have died. As it is, I doubt you will ever conceive again."

Mai sat up. Her eyes widened. "Why? What is it?"

"You have one of the worst cases of gonorrhea I've ever seen. You are using condoms, yes?"

She looked up at him. "I try to, but sometimes . . ."

He let out a breath. "You must use one every time you have intercourse."

"But . . ." Mai faltered, searching for something to say. The truth was that some men refused to wear condoms. Rather than return their money, she would comply. She'd been careless. And these were the consequences. But she didn't want to admit she was a prostitute. Not to the doctor. "My—my boyfriend says they are not reliable."

"For getting pregnant, maybe so. But for preventing a venereal disease, they are crucial." He folded his arms. "You need to talk to your 'boyfriend.'"

"Why?"

"It seems he may not have been faithful to you."

He gazed at her with a knowing stare. She suspected he already knew what she did for a living but was giving her an out. She was grateful for his discretion.

"Of course." She lied. "I will." She feigned an angry scowl.

He went to a cabinet in a corner and returned with two bottles of antibiotics. "You must both take these. Take all of them. Come back if you are not better."

As she rode the bicycle back to her rooms, she chastised herself. This would never have happened if she and Sandy were still together. It was at moments like these that she missed him. But she had been innocent then. And careless now. She finished the bottle the doctor gave her and saved the other pills in case there was a second time.

The North Vietnamese Easter Offensive, one of the fiercest attacks by the NVA and Viet Cong in years, began at the end of March 1972 and lasted until October. South Vietnamese forces were ultimately able to withstand the North's invasion, mostly because of American airpower. But in some ways it was a Pyrrhic victory. The North hung on to much of the territory they captured, placing themselves in a stronger position at the Paris Peace Talks.

For Mai, business was both better and worse. More American soldiers flocked to Saigon for R&R during the offensive, but many, bitter and depressed, wanted Mai to do drugs with them before sex. She refused. Some GIs eschewed sex altogether. Lonely, afraid, and depressed, they cried on her shoulder. That she understood. She took them in her arms and held them, caressing their backs, running her fingers through their hair, and comforting them the way she might comfort her own son. When their time was up, she offered them their money back. None took her up on the offer.

The only time she was rattled was on a hot July night. The choking heat and humidity made sweat prickle her neck and forehead, and she was fanning herself, longing for the air-conditioning at the Stardust, when she spotted Joe Hunter, Freddy's friend, walking down Tu Do Street with another GI. She ducked into the shadows of a shop door, not knowing whether he'd seen her, then edged around the corner to avoid him.

Shame and embarrassment cracked her careful façade, and Mai was suddenly exhausted. Tired of the pretense of enjoying what she was doing, tired of her growing fear that South Vietnam would not win the war, tired of the guilt of being separated from her son. The difference between what she did at night and how she felt when, returning at dawn, she brushed her fingers across Đêm Nguyệt's peaceful face was beginning to tear her heart in two. He could never find out what she did. The next day she caught her reflection in the glass of a shop door. She was just nineteen, but she felt as if she had lived ninety lives.

After seeing Joe, Mai moved to a different spot in Chinatown, in District 5, not far from where she and Tâm had stayed at the refugee camp. What she hadn't known then was that Chinatown was a popular red-light district. She found another hotel above a Chinese restaurant that reminded her of the Saigon Café. Because Chinatown was a tourist area, she hoped to find visitors out for a good time, preferably white men who spoke English. She took a spot a few yards from a Chinese restaurant and bar.

At the same time she felt a gnawing resentment that she was forced to be there in the first place. The American War was beginning its eighth year. She wasn't locked up, but she might as well have been; the war had claimed her as its prisoner. Saigon itself, which as a young girl she considered sparkling and sophisticated, now looked dirty and tawdry. The noise was no longer exciting; now it grated. The food, which had once seemed glamorous, had grown tasteless. She knew that incense was a Buddhist tradition, but too often, she realized, it masked the fetid detritus of the river and streets.

The people she once thought were so cosmopolitan gossiped only about the war, their moods swinging from hope to despair depending on the day and the most recent battle. Her resentment deepened when she thought about the leaders on both sides who were either incompetent or corrupt or both. Why did they keep fighting when it was clear no one was winning? Could they not see the chaos and futility and grief they'd created?

Mai was just returning to her turf one evening on the busy Cholon street she'd commandeered when just ahead of her, a man slapped another girl in the face. Then he punched her in the gut. The girl cried out and doubled over. He kicked her in her groin and she crumpled to the ground. Rage and horror flooded through Mai. After the black eye and fractured wrist, she'd vowed to never allow a man to be violent with her. She ran over to the man.

"What are you doing? Stop it! You can't do that to a woman!"

He whirled around, his fists tight and elbows rigid, as if he was going to hit Mai in the face. "Who the fuck are you?" He took a step toward her.

Mai realized she might be in danger, but stubbornness made her stand her ground. "Who are you?" She bent down to the woman he'd assaulted, who was still on the ground moaning in pain. "Are you all right? Shall I take you to hospital? Or a doctor?"

"If you know what's good for you, you'll get away from her," the man barked.

Mai rose and gazed at the man. He was Vietnamese, she could tell, and was dressed in jeans and a T-shirt. He had a tattoo on his arm. She knew it was a Chinese word or expression, but she couldn't translate it.

He cocked his head and gazed at her. "This is a transaction between us. You have no business here. Get lost."

The woman on the ground rolled over, clutching her hands to her stomach. In a voice interspersed with groans, she sputtered, "He works for the Mad Horse."

A shiver ran through Mai. The Mad Horse was a powerful mobster in Cholon, second only to the Yellow Dragon, the head of a Chinese mob that controlled prostitution, gambling, drugs, and nightclubs in Cholon. The Mad Horse was almost as powerful as the Four Great Kings who controlled the entire Saigon underworld. Mai had been careful to avoid organized crime—until now.

Mai planted her hands on her hips. The woman on the ground was hurting. "She needs help," Mai said. "Let me take her to someone."

The *ma cô* stared at Mai. "I told you to get lost." When Mai didn't move, he added, "You don't go right now, and I will mess up your pretty face."

The woman on the ground made a feeble attempt to wave Mai away. Mai took the woman's advice.

The next day Mai was still mulling over what had happened. She wasn't surprised by the pimp's violence toward his whore; she knew it was part of the game. But to experience it firsthand was a reminder that this was no game. How long would it be until some pimp— maybe the man from last night—forced her to fuck his customers and pay him a cut? The aunties had said, more than once, how surprised they were that it hadn't happened already. They cautioned Mai to stake out "neutral" territory that wasn't under the control of whatever mob was dominant at the moment. She thought she had. Now, though, her time was running out.

That evening before setting out, Mai walked over to the Binh Tay market. She went to the cousins who owned the adjacent stalls for whom she'd worked when she was pregnant. She knew one of them had contacts with the Mad Horse. She told their wives what had happened and asked whether one of their husbands could help her. The two women considered it, then nodded.

Mai folded her hands in front of her heart. "I am thankful for your kindness."

That night, a sultry heat and humidity overpowering everything, one of the cousins met her at her spot near the Chinese restaurant. He lurked in the background, waiting for Mai to give him the signal. She expected the Mad Horse *ma cô* would come back.

She was right. About midnight, the man sauntered down the sidewalk approaching Mai with a smirk on his face. Mai nodded to the cousin, who approached the man and delivered a blow to the man's cheek, followed by an upper cut to his chin. The man staggered back, lost his balance, and fell backward on the concrete. The cousin sat on him, pulled out a revolver, and squeezed it against his cheek.

"Don't you ever bother my woman again. Do you hear? I will report you to Đại Cathay himself." Đại Cathay was the most powerful of the Four Great Kings in Saigon. "Do you understand?"

The man nodded and swallowed. "Now, get out of here," the cousin growled, "and don't let me see you again."

The man scrambled up and ran away. Mai never saw him again.

In January of 1973, after five years of negotiations, North Vietnam signed a peace agreement with the U.S. A few weeks later what was left of the depleted U.S. military fled Vietnam faster than the flutter of a hummingbird's wings. Half of Mai's customers disappeared. There was no way she and Đêm Nguyệt could survive on half her income. It hadn't been a fortune to begin with, and what she made at the nail salon was a pittance. She lost her appetite. Sleep was out of the question. She spent most of her sleep time tossing and turning, trying to come up with a plan.

Although she'd vowed never to return to the Saigon Café, she decided after another sleepless night that she had to swallow her pride. Cô Cúc didn't pay well, but now that Mai could speak English almost fluently, perhaps she could negotiate a higher salary. One evening before work she rode her bike to the restaurant, locked it against a tree, and was about to go in when a figure inside the restaurant passed by the window. Mai froze. Was that Tâm?

Mai clapped her hand over her mouth and ducked under the window. Most Vietnamese considered ghosts powerful spirits. They could pull out a human soul and heart, even come alive for a moment to wreak havoc or revenge. Mai, the sophisticated bar girl, had scorned such primitive beliefs a year ago. Now, though, given what she'd gone through, she wasn't so sure.

She blinked, carefully rose, and snuck another glance through the window. It wasn't Tâm. It was a woman about the same age and build carrying a tray to a table. Tâm was probably dead anyway, Mai thought. Her head had always been buried deep in books or wrapped around nature; Mai couldn't imagine Tâm as a fighter. She had probably been killed by an American bomb. Mai's shoulders slumped and tears welled in her eyes. She couldn't work in the restaurant. Too many ghosts. She unlocked her bicycle and rode back to Cholon.

CHAPTER 56

MAI

Two months later, on a night with air as dense as bricks, Mai walked the streets in Cholon. She was barely making ends meet and had no plan for the future. She was trying to take it one day at a time, but that wouldn't last. She was depressed, thinking about the desolate night ahead, when an Asian man approached her. He was wearing a black double-breasted jacket with three gold stripes around the cuffs, the uniform of a South Vietnamese navy officer. Although the Americans were gone, North and South Vietnam were still locked in their bitter war; a new offensive by the North had just begun.

He came closer, but then paused. She noticed his posture was erect, his hair combed. She wouldn't call him handsome, but he was slim and lithe, and his face, with a flat nose and chin but kind eyes, was pleasant. It flashed through her mind that he was somehow different. She smiled at him.

He smiled back. "You are available?" he asked politely. Most men barked, "How much?" When she nodded, he said, "Good."

She approached him, took his arm, and led him around the corner to the hotel. She told him her name.

"I am Phan Trúc Vinh." He'd given her his full name. Not just a first name. Or an obvious phony name, she thought. That was different.

Inside the small hotel above the restaurant Mai stopped at the front desk, picked up a key, and motioned him to the stairs. They climbed to the fourth floor. She opened the door and went to the bed and sat.

"First we take care of the money, then—" She cut herself off. She was going to say, "I will make sure you never forget this night," but it sounded hollow—she must have recited it a hundred times. This time, she simply told him her price. He slipped the bills out of his pocket and handed them over.

"Thank you. What would you like, Anh Vinh?"

"You." He hesitated.

"Here I am." She bit her lip. "Would you like to watch me take off my clothes?"

He reddened. "Anything will be appreciated."

She smiled. He inclined his head, as if puzzled. "It's not you," she said. "It's just that no one has ever said that to me before."

"They should have."

Afterward Mai started to put her clothes back on, but Vinh lay still naked under the sheet, hands behind his head. "Could we talk? I'll pay you for another tryst."

She stopped dressing. She should take the money. She needed it. "What is so important?"

He shrugged. "I—I do not have anyone else to talk to."

Mai's mood darkened. She wasn't here to soothe an unhappy husband whose wife didn't "understand" him. She had heard it before. Men liked to feel sorry for themselves, she'd discovered, and rarely thought they had any responsibility to make their *wives* happy. She was about to ask for another 12,000 *đồng* when she stopped and gazed at Vinh. Something about him seemed sincere. Honest.

Perhaps a bit naïve about love. Perhaps she should give him an extra few minutes.

No. She changed her mind again. She knew nothing about him. What if he was an undercover cop? The police had started to crack down on prostitution in Saigon. Or perhaps he was loosening her up for something truly evil. She debated with herself. Then she ventured a smile. She would hear him out. "All right. But just for a few minutes."

"How much do I owe you?"

She shook her head.

He smiled then, a smile so radiant that Mai was glad she'd taken the risk. "Come lie down with me," he said.

She did. He slipped an arm around her and started to talk. He was a senior captain in the Vietnamese navy, one of the highest ranks there was. He was married with two children.

"How old?"

"Eight and six."

She was surprised. She had expected them to be older. "My son is three."

He laughed. "A wonderful age. They soak up life in huge chunks." His happy expression faded. "My wife is—concerned with her position in society. For her it is the only thing that matters. She doesn't spend much time with the children. Or me. We have a *bảo mẫu*, a nanny. And a cook. She married me because of my career. I understand that. She came from nothing. A very hard life. So I make sure she wants for nothing."

"Where did she grow up?"

"A village in the Mekong Delta."

"That's where I am from."

"Then you know," he said, "how desperately poor the people are."

She nodded.

"She never loved me," he said. "And, you know, I can live with that."

"Did you love her?"

His eyes took on a reflective cast, as if he had never had the thought before. "I thought I did. But now . . ." Then he smiled. "I adore my children. They shower me with their love and trust. With them it is simple. It just comes naturally. Sometimes when I'm with them, I feel like I am stealing a tiny piece of their love to keep in my heart when I'm away."

"I feel the same way about my son. I spend every free minute I have with him. Perhaps you should spend more time with your children. They'll never be this age again, you know."

He leaned over and brushed his fingers down her hair. "You're not only beautiful on the outside."

Mai's felt her cheeks get hot. They had just met; how could he act as if they'd known each other for years? For some reason, though, she said nothing.

He cleared his throat. "But, as I said, there is more."

Mai tensed.

"It is the war. I have been fighting since 1968. I am tired. So are my men. We want it to be over. To be honest, who wins no longer matters to me. But I cannot share that with anyone. Least of all my wife. She's pinned everything on my career and the South's victory. How can I tell her I want to quit? And now that the U.S. is gone, it's just a matter of time. I fear the end will be ugly."

"You believe the Viet Cong and the North will win?"

"They are more committed. They've already formed shadow governments in the areas they've conquered, ready to pounce once the war is over. Nor do they care how many of their own soldiers die. They only care how much territory they've gained."

A buzz skimmed Mai's nerves. She had always assumed the South would somehow win. Most of the important battles, at least the ones she heard about, had ended with a Southern victory. To hear a South Vietnamese navy captain say he doubted it was shocking. She propped herself on an elbow.

"When will it happen? And what will happen to the South?"

"That I do not know." He looked steadily at her. "Now I want to talk of more cheerful matters. I have a confession to make to you."

Mai's alarm rose. What was he going to say to her? Did he know Tâm? Or one of her other relatives? Were they all dead?

He smiled. "Don't be worried. It's not bad. It's that I have seen you before. I have studied you several times from across the street, and I have seen how you look when you do not think anyone is watching. You are a beautiful woman, but I see how sad you are."

Mai swallowed but didn't reply.

"You don't want to be here. Doing this."

What woman, if she is honest, does? Mai thought. Still, she said nothing.

"I don't want you to be here, either," he said. "Which makes me think we have something in common. I have dreamed of this moment for weeks. But I had to work up the courage. Now that I have, I want to make you happy. So that the beauty of your heart"—he touched her chest gently—"matches that of your body." He cleared his throat again. "Mai, I would like to have the pleasure of your company again. Tomorrow evening. For the entire evening. I will arrange for a hotel. And I will pay in advance as much as you require."

CHAPTER 57

MAI

Mai saw Vinh the next night. And the one after that. By the third night, she felt so safe and cared for that she didn't want morning to come. After two weeks of seeing each other every evening, he asked if they could arrange a more permanent situation.

Mai was taken aback. What did he mean? What more did he want from her?

"I think you know I have fallen completely in love with you, Mai," he began.

She touched his face. "I love you too, Anh Vinh."

"Will you let me take care of you? And your son?"

She glanced at him side-eyed. "And in return?"

"We will spend as much time with each other as possible."

"You want me to be your mistress."

"Will you do me that honor?"

She thought about it. For about a second. "Of course."

Mai retired from the "profession" and hoped she would never be forced into it again. She returned to a daytime schedule. That in itself was a joy: to move and live and eat like the rest of the world. Best of all it meant she could devote more time to Nguyệt. He was almost four years old and went to nursery school in the mornings. Now she could to pick him up every day, usually with lunch for them both. Together they would share a picnic, then explore Saigon. She showed him the cathedral, the many small temples hidden behind storefronts, the zoo, the pier, even the markets. She ignored the boarded-up stores and bars, the detritus of bombed-out buildings that had yet to be cleaned up, and other destruction that reminded her they were still at war. The time they spent together reminded her of when he was an infant and she couldn't tear herself away from him.

She and Vinh discussed how and when he should meet Nguyệt—Vinh wanted to get to know him. At first Mai was reluctant; she wondered if, in some vague way, she was being unfaithful to Sandy. She worried that Vinh would reject Nguyệt because of his Caucasian blue eyes and sharp chin, both of which had become more pronounced as he grew. Then she realized she was being selfish. Nguyệt needed a man in his life, and Vinh was eager to take on that role. Eventually, she decided they would meet at a pier on the Saigon River.

A few days later, on a bright, breezy afternoon, Mai and Nguyệt went to the pier for a picnic. They were finishing their lunch when Mai said, "I have a surprise for you."

His face brightened and he replied eagerly. "What? What?"

Mai shaded her eyes and pointed. "You see those big ships and tankers out there?"

Nguyệt shaded his eyes. "Those big boats?"

"Yes. How would you like to meet the man in charge of one of them?"

Nguyệt's mouth dropped open. "Yes!"

"He is a friend of mine," Mai said.

"Oh boy!"

A few minutes later Vinh strolled up in his uniform. He'd pinned a spray of colorful badges and medals on his lapels. Nguyệt stared at them with his mouth open. Mai stood up, but Nguyệt was so excited it made him shy, and he hid behind Mai's skirt.

Vinh was carrying a small paper bag. He kissed Mai on her cheek and gazed around from side to side, pretending to search for someone.

"Mai, I thought a little man was going to be here."

Nguyệt giggled from behind Mai.

"Did you hear something, Mai?" Vinh said.

"No. Did you?" she said.

More giggles.

"I suppose not. That is too bad, because I have a gift for him."

Nguyệt poked his head around. "Here I am!"

"Ah. So you are. Come out and let me see you, little man."

Nguyệt sidestepped around until he was facing Vinh. Mai introduced them.

"Well, what a surprise. That is the name of the little man whose gift this is."

Nguyệt looked up at Mai. "May I have it, Mama?"

When she nodded, Vinh gave Nguyệt the bag. He opened it and took out a box. Inside was a tiny model of a tanker. Nguyệt's face showed his delight and he promptly started playing with it on the grass beside the pier.

"What do you say, Nguyệt?"

"Thank you." He looked over at Vinh. "Where did you get all your medals?"

"I will tell you later if you wish."

"Oh yes," Nguyệt said. "I would like that."

By the end of the summer, Mai and Nguyệt had moved out of their rooms in District 6 back to District 1, where Vinh rented a modest apartment for them. Mai said tearful goodbyes to the aunties who had taken such good care of Nguyệt, promising to bring him back for visits. Overwhelmed with its space and light, Mai loved the new apartment from the moment she saw it. There were two bedrooms, a kitchen, and a parlor. The building even had a garden plot in back, which, because of the war, had been neglected. She began to tend it, trying to remember how her mother had grown vegetables out of what seemed like dry sandy soil.

Whenever Vinh came to visit, he always brought a small toy or book for Nguyệt. Sometimes, in what Mai thought was an ingenious idea, Vinh brought a miniature flag of a nearby country, to introduce Nguyệt to geography.

Mai asked him to stop. "You will spoil him." But Vinh didn't. His thoughtfulness made Mai realize what a unique man he was. And how grateful she was to have him in their lives. In fact, his kindness was contagious, and Mai noticed she was softening, too. It was easier for her to consider forgiving the people in her past who had hurt her, because of the peace and joy now in her life.

One night, after Vinh left, Nguyệt asked, "Mama, is Chú Vinh my father?"

An icy fear raced up her spine. She had prepared for this moment. Then again, perhaps he was too young to learn about Sandy. He had asked a simple question. She would reply with a simple answer. The next question after that would be the key.

"No, Nguyệt. But he is your uncle."

"My uncle?"

"Yes. Uncle Vinh."

"Oh. That is good. I love him."

Mai threw her arms around him, relieved she did not need to tell him about Sandy yet. "He loves you too, *con yêu*."

The next time Vinh came to visit, Nguyệt ran to Vinh, who scooped him up in his arms. "Mama says you are my uncle."

Vinh's neck reddened. He grinned. "Yes. And I am so proud to be."

CHAPTER 58

MAI

Two years passed. Đêm Nguyệt started school in the neighborhood. Mai was the happiest she'd been since she was a little girl. She loved Ahn Vinh, not with the passion she'd felt for Sandy, but with a deeper, more gentle love. He was her best friend, her companion, and a willing, eager lover. For the first time she experienced the exquisite pleasures of sex, a pleasure she'd previously thought was just a lie to coax a woman's compliance. Now she knew.

She worked part-time giving manicures and pedicures, tended the garden in back, and was a full-time mother to Đêm Nguyệt. But the war dragged on, and she could tell from the deepening lines on Vinh's face that it was not going well. After the American soldiers left, the North made steady inroads into the South, capturing more territory in their sweep toward Saigon.

By the second half of April 1975, Mai could no longer ignore reality. A palpable anxiety had gripped Saigon. The wealthy tried to flee, taking their wealth with them. As days passed and the North closed in, though, wealth no longer mattered. What mattered were trains, ships, and airplane tickets. The city grew increasingly chaotic, as both rich and poor grabbed whatever they could and hastened to escape.

Mai couldn't sleep. She lost her appetite. She remembered what Chị Tâm had told her the last time they'd seen each other. When Vietnam fell, Mai would be marked for having "entertained" the enemy at the Stardust. For all she knew, it might be Chị Tâm who reported her to the authorities before she died. And now, as the mistress of a South Vietnamese navy captain, she might as well have a target painted on her back. At best, she would be sent to a reeducation camp; at worst, imprisoned, even executed. And because Đêm Nguyệt was of mixed race, he would not only be taken away from her, but probably subjected to discrimination. The Vietnamese, no matter whether they were from the North or South, frowned on mixed-race children. It was proof that some women, in this case Mai, were amoral, that they had consorted with American GIs.

Vinh was preoccupied with helping his troops and trying to arrange his own family's safe passage. Because he wasn't with her, Mai grew frantic. She had a little savings, but not enough for two plane tickets out of Saigon. She had no car or motorbike. She might be able to buy train tickets to Cambodia, but passing through newly captured North Vietnamese territory would be impossible, and the situation in Cambodia wasn't much better.

She avoided raising the subject with Anh Vinh during the few stolen hours he spent with her. But as the days passed, and the North closed in on Saigon, she grew desperate. He was her only hope. They were on her couch after Nguyệt fell asleep the night of April 29 when she spoke up.

"Anh Vinh, I have tried not to bring this up . . . I hate to burden you . . . but I have no choice. I know you are planning to flee when the North takes Saigon. Can you help Nguyệt and me? They will kill me if I stay here. They will take Đêm Nguyệt away from me."

He turned toward her and cupped her face in his hands. "Em, my beautiful Mai," he said. "Did you think I would abandon you?"

"I—I didn't know."

"Never. Ever. You are part of me. Deep in my heart. I could never leave my heart in Saigon. Of course I am planning to get you out." He tightened his hold. "I'm so sorry you have been frightened."

Tears rimmed her eyes. "I know you have been preoccupied," she said tentatively.

"Em Mai. Have faith. I am working on it. But it is difficult to plan. We do not know exactly when we will go. It depends on the North."

Her voice was edged in panic. "So, what should we do?"

He released her. "First, try not to worry. You must stay strong. For you and your son. Tonight you should pack only what you need. What you cannot live without. For Nguyệt as well." He stopped. "I'll try to call you an hour before I come for you. If the telephones are down, I'll either come for you myself or send a car. But you must turn on your radio and keep it on so you can track the progress of the Communists. It won't be more than a day or two, now. They are just outside the city."

She shivered. "Are—are you sure you will come for us?"

Again he wrapped his arms around her. "Once I know my family is safe, it will be your turn. I will not leave Vietnam without you."

"But how do I know that? The city is near panic." She could not stop trembling. Her life, and that of her son, again depended on a man. She'd vowed never to let herself be in that situation again. To let a man have power over her. To be fair, though, this time it wasn't simply one man. It was an entire army.

Anh Vinh released his hold on her, got up, and started to pace. "I am going to tell you something that is top secret. If you tell a soul, we will both be in great peril. Do you understand?"

She nodded.

"Captain Đỗ Kiểm is the deputy chief of staff for the South Vietnamese navy. He has a secret plan to evacuate the navy and our families. He has assembled a flotilla of thirty-five navy vessels that will sail from an island fifty miles off the coast in the South China Sea. The flotilla will join the U.S. Seventh Fleet and head for Subic Bay in the Philippines. My only task is to get my family to that island. You and Nguyệt will be two of the passengers." He gave her a wan smile. "So, you see? It is arranged."

Knowing the end was near, Mai packed a small suitcase for herself and Nguyệt. A change of clothes for them both, the two toys he played with most, and a beautiful necklace with emeralds Anh Vinh had given her, which she might have to sell at some point. She also tucked Freddy's Purple Heart and Joe Hunter's address into the bag. She tried to sleep but it was useless. She rose and took a shower.

Anh Vinh did love her and she loved him, but family always came first. He had an obligation. Ironically, that had been Chị Tâm's attitude after the massacre seven years earlier. She understood her sister better now. Chị Tâm was fulfilling her duty as she saw it, but Mai had been too young and self-absorbed to appreciate it. She was older now, with a family of her own. She wished she hadn't been so ungrateful to her sister. But the awful words she and Chị Tâm had spoken to each other the last time they met could never be unsaid.

She brewed a pot of tea and paced back and forth.

CHAPTER 59

MAI

On April 30, Mai turned on her radio at eight AM. At half past ten, the president of South Vietnam, General Dương Văn Minh, who had gone on radio and television earlier to announce his administration's surrender, appealed to all Saigon troops to lay down their arms. While he was speaking, scores of North Vietnamese tanks, armored vehicles, and camouflaged Chinese trucks rolled toward the presidential palace.

Where was Anh Vinh? She needed to know he was coming for them. She knew he was not in his office. Logic told her he was taking his family to safety, but Mai's anxiety made her pace restlessly. Even Đêm Nguyệt, absorbing the stress without knowing why, grew cranky. Mai suggested he play with his toys and opened his toy chest. It struck her that this would be the last time he played with them. After a few minutes, though, Đêm Nguyệt lost interest. He went to the window, where he looked out at the front of their building. She hadn't told him they were leaving today and was surprised he seemed to sense it. But no car was there. Nothing to see. A preternatural quiet descended on the city, punctuated only by an occasional shout, and glass shattering when looters broke windows to steal what they could.

The radio announcer reported sporadic fighting at various spots in Saigon, and she could hear the stutter of gunfire between the whine of helicopters and planes overhead. She learned later that most were Air America airplanes, and they were rescuing important government officials who hadn't left Vietnam yet and ferrying them to waiting ships.

Lunchtime approached. Still no Anh Vinh. Or his car. At noon, Communist tanks rolled into the presidential palace and hoisted the red and yellow flag of North Vietnam. Mai was desperate. Anh Vinh should have been here by now. Which meant he wasn't coming. What were she and Nguyệt going to do? Once again, a person she'd dared to love had abandoned her.

She started to cry. If Nguyệt had not been there she might have thrown herself out the window. Men always abandoned her. What had she done in this or a past life that was so evil that her karma was to face her fate alone? To be imprisoned, perhaps executed, when the Communists found her? Her stomach knotted. She grabbed Nguyệt. They would run away. Then she realized she had no idea where they would go.

The island. What was its name? Anh Vinh hadn't told her. He didn't want her to know.

That afternoon, the former president went on the radio for the final time to announce, "I declare the Saigon government is completely dissolved at all levels."

The war was over.

Mai made dinner for herself and Đêm Nguyệt, but she couldn't eat. There was nothing to do but wait to be captured. In a way, she hoped it would be soon. She couldn't keep up the pretense that everything was fine in front of Đêm Nguyệt. Exhausted by the lack of sleep the previous two nights, she and Đêm Nguyệt lay down on her bed and were soon slumbering.

∾

It was dark when an insistent ringing woke her. Her doorbell. She rushed to the door and the intercom but hesitated at the last minute. Was it the police? Perhaps yes, perhaps no. Still, she was cautious. Đêm Nguyệt solved the problem. He pressed the button and in his five-year-old voice asked, "Yes, who's there?"

"Đêm Nguyệt, it's me."

"Uncle Vinh?"

"Tell your mother to come down. You too. Hurry."

Mai slumped against the door. Tears filled her eyes, this time tears of relief.

Once they were settled in Anh Vinh's official chauffeured car, Mai said, "What happened? Where were you? I feared you changed your mind."

"I told you once my family was safe I would come for you, darling Mai." He drew her close.

She sniffed. "I know, I know, I just—"

"You had no faith."

"I thought you would be here earlier."

"There was a problem." He went on. "The Americans didn't show up. Remember how I told you how the U.S. is helping to evacuate us? Many boarded U.S. Navy aircraft carriers and steamed out of Vietnam. Others boarded helicopters from the U.S. embassy. Still others were taken on Air America flights. The CIA's airline."

"Yes, yes."

"Do you also recall the other night when I told you about Captain Kiểm's secret plan?" She nodded. "Well, he thought it was all in place. But somehow the U.S. forgot they were to escort us to Subic Bay. A destroyer had to circle back to the island, which, fortunately, has not yet been occupied by the North Vietnamese. It delayed our departure many hours. I didn't have a chance to call you. I apologize."

"But we're going there now?"

"We are." He tipped her chin up and looked into her eyes. "You look tired, my dear. Lean on me and try to sleep."

~

They reached the southern coast of Vietnam just as the sun came up on May 1. A small motorboat was waiting for them. Vinh woke Mai and Nguyệt, who was also sleeping. Half an hour later they arrived at Con Son Island in the South China Sea. More than thirty South Vietnamese navy ships plus dozens of fishing boats and cargo ships gently rocked in the water, packed with people desperate to evacuate. Mai had never seen so many ships. Or people.

The motorboat stopped at the side of one of the cargo ships. A ladder was tossed over the side. Men helped Mai and Nguyệt climb aboard. Vinh followed them and made sure they had a spot on the deck. Then he went back to the ladder.

"Wait," Mai called to him. "Aren't you coming?"

"I must go with my family. They are aboard another ship."

She ran toward him. "But what will become of us? You and I?"

"We are all going to Subic Bay in the Philippines. We will see each other there."

To say goodbye. Mai tightened her lips. Once more tears rimmed her eyes. "Oh, Anh Vinh."

"Never doubt that you are a kind, loving woman, Mai. You have been the love of my life."

"Will we be together?"

An anguished look swept over him.

"Oh, Anh Vinh."

His lips tightened.

She threw her arms around him. He held her tight. Then he embraced Đêm Nguyệt. "Take care of your mother, little man. She is the most precious cargo on this ship."

"I will, Uncle Vinh."

"And so are you, my son. I know you will grow up to do great things."

Mai watched him climb down the ladder and step into the motorboat. Without either of them acknowledging it, Mai knew this would be the last time she and Đêm Nguyệt would see Anh Vinh.

PART VII

SOUTH VIETNAM, 1970–1973

Tâm

CHAPTER 60

TÂM

Flashes of light burst through Tâm's head, disturbing her soft, peaceful darkness. Fortunately, not many of those moments, because they brought with them excruciating pain. She tried not to open her eyes when the light pulsed, sensing that if she kept them closed, the pain wouldn't materialize. She was wrong. The pain attacked even when her eyes were closed. Bright colors pushed against her eyelids, the way colors did when she squeezed her eyes shut in brilliant sunshine. She wanted to cry out, but her body wouldn't obey. She was helpless against the onslaught. When she didn't think she could bear it any longer, the black returned.

Her conscious moments of light with its accompanying agony grew more frequent. She heard noises through the pain. A door opening, the soft soprano of a woman, the tenor of a man. She was being rolled somewhere. A cold room. Questions were asked and answered. Her wrist was pricked with a sharp needle, which brought back the blessed darkness.

It lifted in tiny increments. The pain was still there, not as raw but still steady and harsh. Gradually she was able to determine it came from her abdomen and her leg. The next time she surfaced, she forced her eyes to open. It was an effort to make it happen. She blinked several times. She was in a bed in a room. White walls, white blankets, white window shades. A hospital. Something had gone wrong. What? She couldn't remember. Only that it had been unspeakably horrific.

The next time a sting in her shoulder woke her. A nurse, giving her a shot. She cracked her eyes.

"You're awake," the nurse said in an artificially cheerful voice. "Welcome back."

"Where am I?" It took tremendous energy to formulate the words. Her voice was hoarse and splintered.

"You're in the hospital in Saigon. They brought you from the Cu Chi Hospital."

"Cu Chi?"

"You were in bad shape. We didn't know if you would make it. You've been here about a week."

"The tunnels." Her mouth was dry.

"Tunnels? Where?"

"Water."

The nurse looked confused.

"Need water."

The nurse grabbed a glass of water and helped Tâm sip through a straw. As she swallowed, she began to remember what had happened. The tunnel rat. Tâm had gone after him with a grenade. What happened to him?

"What happened to who?" The nurse asked.

Tâm hadn't realized she'd spoken aloud. She shook her head. "To me? What happened?"

"The doctor will talk to you. I will tell him you are awake. He will be happy."

A few minutes later a man in a white coat with a stethoscope around his neck knocked and came in. "I am Dr. Giang." He smiled. He was wearing glasses, but he took them off and slid them into a pocket. "And they told me you are Tâm." When she didn't reply, he went on. "You have been through more than most of our wounded, Tâm. You are lucky to be alive. We didn't think you would make it.

"We understand you were in the Cu Chi tunnels when a grenade exploded. The blast propelled you backward, and you fell into a Viet Cong booby trap. You suffered third-degree burns on your legs and arms. We have already performed two skin grafts and will probably do two more. At the same time, the spikes and hooks of the trap caused quite a bit of internal and external damage. The gash in your left leg cut into an artery and you lost a lot of blood."

Tâm grunted. "But—"

"Let me finish," Giang said. "The people who brought you in were able to apply a tourniquet, which likely saved your life. But the most serious complication is what we call compartment syndrome in your right leg. It occurs when internal bleeding is trapped inside part of your body. Pressure builds up and prevents blood flow. The muscles and tendons can die, and if we can't get to it in time, the area is usually amputated."

Tâm's stomach lurched. "So—"

"We were able to operate right away, and we saved your legs. Both of them. But it was touch and go."

Tâm's eyes closed in relief. "Thank you."

"I'm not finished. Your spleen was ruptured as well. But that will heal." Dr. Giang was looking down at her with suspicious eyes. It occurred to Tâm that he must know she was fighting for the Communists if they found her in the tunnels. But she was in a Saigon hospital. He could turn her in for betraying the South and have her locked up. She would be imprisoned, perhaps executed. Why go to the bother of saving her?

As if he knew what she was thinking, he ran his tongue around his lips. "Tâm," he said quietly, "they said you were trying to save a tunnel rat. An American who courageously climbed into the tunnels to kill the enemy. Unfortunately, he died. As you very nearly did, too. You were very brave. And foolhardy. As I said, you are lucky to alive. But your fighting days are over."

CHAPTER 61

TÂM

It was a long convalescence. Tâm was in hospital until the first week of May, 1970. Two more skin grafts were performed. The ruptured spleen healed slowly. So did the gash in her left leg, but she would have a limp for the rest of her life. During the final month, they got her out of bed so she could learn to walk again.

She didn't know why Dr. Giang lied by claiming to the authorities that she was a South Vietnamese fighter when he had to have known she was fighting with the North. Perhaps he harbored his own Communist sympathies? She had no visitors the entire time she was hospitalized, but she didn't expect any. It was a time for mourning and reflection. She mourned Bảo's death and grieved the loss of their passion.

When Tâm was finally released, she felt bewildered. She couldn't think of anyone in Saigon she could call a friend who would take her in for a night or two. After some thought, however, she realized she did. She made her way to Dr. Hằng's apartment in the French Quarter, the last place she'd lived before she joined up. At least she would not need to pretend who she was and what she'd done.

Was it her imagination or did the building look a bit shabbier, a bit grimier than she recalled? The doorman was still there in his ridiculous uniform, but he, too, looked a bit rumpled, his posture bowed and tired. His eyes widened when he saw Tâm limp toward him.

"Mademoiselle, you are back!"

Tâm nodded.

"You have been injured."

"I am here to see Dr. Hằng, please."

"Of course."

A few minutes later, Tâm knocked at Dr. Hằng's door. She opened it as if she'd been expecting Tâm.

"Tâm!" She opened her arms. "I am so happy to see you. I was hoping you would come here after you were released."

"You knew?"

"Dr. Giang is a friend from the health department. He has given me regular reports on your progress."

Ah, Tâm thought. That made sense. "He took good care of me."

"He saved your life." She ushered Tâm into the plush living room.

"Yes. He did." Tâm's response was muted.

"You were a brave, courageous fighter."

"I tried." She pointed to her leg. "But it is over now."

Dr. Hằng faced Tâm. "Who told you that?"

"Dr. Giang for one. And everyone else. Look at me. I can barely walk."

"Wars are won by loyal soldiers performing whatever they are ordered to do. Not all of those orders include combat."

"I am finished with the war. Or should I say it is finished with me."

Dr. Hằng bade Tâm sit down on the elegant silk sofa. "I know you fell in love with a woman while you were near the tunnels. And her death triggered your—run-in with the tunnel rat. I am truly sorry for your loss." She placed a sympathetic hand on Tâm's arm. "But I have something new in mind for you. Something at which I know you will excel."

"I was thinking I would—"

Dr. Hằng cut her off. "A man will be visiting tonight. He is an important officer. He will tell you about an upcoming mission. I think you would be the perfect candidate for it. But you can decide after he talks. Fair?"

Tâm agreed, but questions nagged at her. How did Dr. Hằng know Tâm would come here after she was released from the hospital? Tâm hadn't told anyone where she was going. And how did she know to arrange a meeting for them on Tâm's first night here? Either Dr. Hằng was clairvoyant, or her flow of intelligence was so precise that she could manipulate people without them realizing it. Was that what Dr. Hằng had done when she recruited Tâm to fight with the Communists? Ingratiated herself. Invited her to stay in her dead son's room. Complimented her bravery and talent, although Dr. Hằng had no proof Tâm had done anything of note. Tâm wasn't eager to be manipulated again. She had almost died the first time.

～

Dr. Hằng cooked dinner that night, the young girl in the French maid's uniform having left a month earlier, she claimed. Had she tired of Dr. Hằng's manipulation, too? After dinner, she and Tâm relaxed on the balcony.

"What do you think of the American withdrawals?" Tâm asked.

"It is not important what I think," Dr. Hằng said elliptically. "But I can tell you that in America they do not think it is fast enough. The anti-war activists are incensed that the U.S. is helping South Vietnam invade Cambodia. It had to be done, of course, but it has triggered protests, some of them dangerous, like those college students shot in Ohio."

"The bombings are supposed to wipe out the NVA forces that massed near the border, yes?"

"Yes. But they did not succeed. More troops are gathering there as we speak."

"It seems a bit desperate at this point," Tâm ventured.

"On whose side?" Dr. Hằng peered at Tâm. "The South and the

U.S. invading yet another country to 'protect' the world from Communism?"

"Or the NVA invading another country to seize more territory and push south?"

Dr. Hằng threw Tâm a shrewd smile. "I see your experiences have turned you into a skeptic."

"The war has been going on for six years now, Dr. Hằng. Even World War II had ended by that time."

"Vietnam is but a pebble compared to the boulders of England, France, Germany, and America. We fight slowly, but methodically. The North may not have adequate resources, but we will win. It will take more time, more soldiers, but Vietnam will be reunified."

Tâm didn't reply.

"You must believe that."

"I believe you believe that."

A knock on the door interrupted them. A man in his forties, dressed in black farm pants and a black tunic, entered. A holster around his waist held what looked like an automatic pistol. He wore glasses, which softened his military bearing and expression. He was followed by a younger man, identically dressed. Dr. Hằng greeted them warmly.

"This is General Ngô Văn Minh," she introduced him to Tâm. She faced General Minh. "This is the woman I have been telling you about." She turned to Tâm. "The general is with the Viet Cong, but he used to live in the North. He was a student of General Võ Nguyên Giáp, whose reputation I believe you are familiar with."

Tâm rose and extended her hand. She couldn't help but be impressed. General Giáp was one of the greatest military strategists of the twentieth century. If this man studied with Giáp, he must share Giáp's deep knowledge of guerrilla as well as conventional strategy and tactics, tactics that became the guiding principles of the North's war philosophy. In the company of such an important man, Tâm felt self-conscious. Was he here to talk to her? What could she possibly do for him? Did Dr. Hằng know every North Vietnamese official?

General Minh nodded at her. "I have heard reports of your ingenuity. And your bravery. And your struggles. Particularly with the Long Hairs."

Tâm felt her cheeks burn. "Thank you, General. I have tried. But now . . ." She motioned to her leg. "I am not fit for fighting."

"Those who serve do so in many ways. I want to tell you about a mission that Dr. Hằng and I think you can handle."

General Minh was one of the most important generals in the war. And he had singled her out from every other soldier. Who was she to say no? "I am honored," Tâm said quietly.

CHAPTER 62

TÂM

Three days later, Tâm was on a bus to the city of Tay Ninh, in the province of the same name. It wasn't far from Binh Duong Province, where the Cu Chi tunnels were located. The irony was not lost on Tâm. Still, as the bus passed by the road leading to the tunnels, the loss of Bảo and the love they'd shared felt less like a sharp knife slicing her heart. More like a dull ache that would always be with her.

Her mission, according to General Minh, was to gather intelligence. She was to go undercover and assume the role of a South Vietnamese villager, accidentally wounded when she fell into a guerrilla booby trap, which, of course, was the truth. "Tay Ninh is the seat, the Holy See, of Cao Đài. Do you know it?"

"The religion? Of course. Some people from my village practiced it."

Cao Đài, an indigenous monotheistic Vietnamese faith founded in the 1920s, was a fusion of Buddhism, Christianity, Taoism, Confucianism, and even Islam. Its supreme deity, Cao Đài, was believed to have created the universe. Caodaism hoped to unite all religions, and also to provide a means of spiritual evolution. A basic principle was "All Religions Are One" and, as if to prove it, practitioners heralded as saints such eclectic luminaries as Victor Hugo, Joan of Arc, and Sun Yat-sen. Tâm had studied it herself at one point but thought it too diffuse and reverted to Buddhism.

"Then you know that Cao Đài's Great Temple is only a few kilometers from Tay Ninh's city center."

She nodded. "It is a beautiful temple. At least from the photographs I've seen."

General Minh went on. "Much of the Cao Đài hierarchy comes to Tay Ninh for meetings, synods, and other ecclesiastical events. Unfortunately, Cao Đài is staunchly anti-Communist. Which is surprising, since Diệm first supported them. Then he changed his mind. After that Hồ Chí Minh expected them to support us. But they have not."

"Excuse me, General," Dr. Hằng cut in. "The Cao Đài know they have no place in a secular Communist Vietnam. They are well aware that once the Communists win, they will be forbidden from practicing their religion. Or persecuted if they do."

"Perhaps," he said, nodding, "that is why some of their church members have infiltrated our ranks and are spying on us for the South."

"But why?" Tâm asked. "Caodaists are pious. They strive for inner harmony to avoid bad karma."

General Minh laughed. "Bad karma, is it? We have information that our activities in the area and across the border in Cambodia have reached the wrong ears. We have narrowed it down to three Caodaists, but we need to know who, where he or she is getting their intel, and whom they're giving it to. Once we do know, they will indeed experience bad karma."

"Three? How do you know?" Tâm said.

"Lieutenant Khuyên will tell you when he briefs you." The general motioned to the younger officer.

"We believe they want to stave off victory by the Communists for as long as they can, Tâm," Dr. Hằng said.

"But how do you know there are three?" Tâm repeated.

General Minh sprawled on Dr. Hằng's silk sofa. "A U.S. military base occupies the western outskirts of Tay Ninh. The city itself is only twelve kilometers from the Cambodian border. Recently the base has been used as a staging area for U.S. units invading Cambodia. However, in four months time the entire base will be formally given to the South Vietnamese army by the departing U.S. military. It appears that these three have visited the designated commander of the base, Colonel Thian, at different times. Soon after those visits, it became clear that the colonel knew our plans in advance and thwarted our push south. One of our people traced those 'visitors' back to the Cao Đài church."

Tâm tried to understand. "Why would they betray us? Because they are anti-Communist?"

"The Cao Đài will need South Vietnamese protection at some point, and they are buying it in advance." He shrugged. "It is a pity they will not achieve their goal."

Tâm folded her arms. "But, General, how can I do what you ask? I do not practice Cao Đài, nor do I know any Caodaists. How will I be able to find out who the spies are?" She rubbed the back of her neck. "And, if what you say is true, almost any Cao Đài would want to protect their religion from the North, yes?"

"That is all true," General Minh replied. "But we are quite interested in who revealed our plans to the Caodaists. Which is why we need to identify the messengers."

"But if I am to pose as a regular South Vietnamese citizen, how will I penetrate the Communists' ranks? I fear you are overrating my abilities, General."

"You are underestimating your skills." He paused. "We recognize your mission will take time. It should. You must spend months, perhaps a year, becoming a trusted and loyal member of the church. Once you have identified the Southern messenger, he or she will lead you to the traitors."

"General, I am honored by your trust, but I do not—"

The general cut her off. "I know you will do whatever is necessary." His tone made it clear any further discussion on the subject was closed.

"We will get information to you when necessary. And you will send us intelligence when you have something to report."

Dr. Hằng added, "You will be provided with a stipend for necessities, but you must work a job too, so you will not raise suspicion."

General Minh motioned to the younger officer. "Go into the dining room with Lieutenant Khuyên. He will brief you on the three suspects and how to pass information to us."

Tâm followed the younger soldier into the dining room, where he instructed her how to send and retrieve messages and how to use dead drops. He described one in the back of the market along a stone wall that she could use right away. He also showed her how to write coded letters, and, in an emergency, make a coded telephone call.

Then he described the three suspects. There were two men and a woman. One man was a priest and a womanizer. The second—they weren't sure of his position in the church—was a gambler. They had no information about the woman.

When he handed her the bus ticket, Tâm's jaw tightened. There was no way to refuse this mission. If she did, there would be a price to pay. They might even kill her. Perhaps not tomorrow or next week, but in time. It was clear Dr. Hằng had orchestrated everything. She'd assumed Tâm would comply. But since Bảo's death, Tâm's heart was no longer in it.

As the bus drove on, she stared at fields that had been destroyed by Agent Orange. She leaned the back of her head against the seat. What had she gotten herself into?

CHAPTER 63

TÂM

Tâm stayed at a hotel near the temple that night. The next day, armed with a map of the city, she had tea and rice cakes at a nearby food stall and asked where the market was. It was within walking distance, so she made her way there despite her bad leg. She bought a used bicycle and started to ride back, but pressing down on the pedals was painful. She hadn't realized how weak her wounded leg had become. She pedaled slowly, hunched over the bicycle like an old woman. She hoped her strength would return. She was only twenty years old.

Once she was close to the temple, she rode around the area on her bicycle, trying to suss out the grounds. The temple sat in the center of a large complex that included dormitories and kitchens for resident priests, a high school, and small hospital, plus a large clearing, probably for religious processions. She guessed the entire area was about two kilometers square.

The main temple—there were two—was a huge rectangular structure, not unlike the cathedral in Saigon. Here, though, were two graceful square towers, each with tiny balconies. The sides were flanked by arched walkways. The exterior was painted in warm beige tones, with blue and rose railings, flourishes, and windowpanes. It looked gracious and inviting, not at all pompous or overbearing.

She locked the bike around a small tree and wandered inside. Compared to the exterior, the interior was surprisingly elaborate. At least two dozen thick pink pillars supported the roof on both sides of the nave. Wrapped around the pillars were spirals of painted dragons with red tongues out, ready to swoop down on some unsuspecting creature. Patterned tiled floors, bright, airy stained-glass windows, and a vaulted ceiling of blue sky with puffy white clouds made her feel like she had ascended to a pastel heaven where angels, fairies, and even dragons frolicked together.

At the far end above the altar was a massive globe with one eye in the center. Several men knelt below it, two in everyday clothes, one in a white robe with a red hood and belt. What were they were praying for? Redemption? Forgiveness? Or something more practical, like a good harvest, a healthy baby, perhaps an end to the war?

Tâm watched for a while, then forced her mind back to her assignment. How was she supposed to discover who was leaking military information to the South? She would have to make subtle, indirect inquiries. Follow suspects without them knowing. Spy on their comings and goings. Tâm prided herself on being direct and honest, although some didn't want to hear what she said. Now she would be cloaked in deceit. She would befriend people, gain their trust, only to possibly betray them later. What if the Caodaists discovered she was a spy? Caught her in the act? Despite the heat, an icicle of fear crept up her back.

She headed back to the entrance of the temple. Near the door, set back in an alcove, was a reception area. A woman about her age sat behind a high counter. Splayed across the counter were brochures in pastel colors. She approached the counter and saw the brochures were in different languages: English, Vietnamese, French, and Chinese. She picked up the Vietnamese version, which included a schedule of services.

She glanced at the woman seated behind the counter. Dressed in a traditional pale blue *áo dài*, the woman kept her face downcast, as if she preferred to glide through life without people, places, or situations clinging to her. Was she the messenger to the South?

Tâm thumbed through the brochure. Services were held every six hours, night and day. "Excuse me, but are services open to the public?"

The woman glanced up, nodded, and looked down again.

~

As Tâm rode her bike back to the hotel, the glimmer of a plan emerged. She would try to get a job in the kitchens where food was prepared for the residents, visiting priests, and church officials. Her restaurant experience should count for something, even if she only washed pots. And everyone knew kitchen workers loved to gossip. Working in the kitchen could yield valuable intel. Tomorrow she would attend the morning service.

~

But Tâm slept late the next morning, so she went to the noon service instead. Everyone sat cross-legged on the floor in a sea of white, men on one side, women on the other. Sporadically a slash of a red, blue, or yellow robed priest sliced through the throng of white. Birds swooped and dived from one end of the temple to the other. The light of the noon sun pouring through the windows seemed to make the tile floors glow.

After the service Tâm asked the young woman at the front to whom she could speak about working in the kitchen. The woman stole a glance at her.

Tâm needed a new Party name. She was, after all, conducting business, and she'd been taught to use a different one for every encounter. "I am—Linh. I come from a village south of here on the Mekong River. I was critically wounded by a Viet Cong land mine months ago and just got out of hospital. I am so grateful to be alive that I thought of coming here to express my gratitude to the god who protects the Cao Đài."

The woman frowned. "You are Cao Đài?"

Tâm shook her head. "But I am so thankful that Buddha or Jesus or another deity saved me that I want to learn."

The young woman nodded and looked down. Did she believe her? Tâm cleared her throat. "What is your name?"

"I am Yến," she murmured.

Tâm nodded. "So who must I talk to?"

She pointed to a priest in white with a yellow robe who was just exiting the temple. "He is the one who supervises administration, but he will not be back until the start of the next service." Which wouldn't be until afternoon.

By late afternoon Tâm had a job in the kitchen. When she asked the priest about a room to rent, he said there was nothing on the temple grounds but suggested she talk to Yến, the girl at the front. She lived a few blocks away with an ailing mother. She might be able to help.

Tâm returned to the front desk. "You seem to be the one here with all the answers." She smiled. "Do you know of a room or boarding-house nearby? The priest suggested I ask you."

Yến still refused to look her in the eye. Tâm decided that was progress. The girl seemed painfully shy. Or was it something else? Then she nodded. "Come back in an hour."

CHAPTER 64

TÂM

"Where are we going?" Tâm asked when she returned to meet Yến. "Should I bring my bicycle?"

Yến nodded, walking quickly. "It's not far away."

Tâm followed with the bike, walking as fast as she could, but within moments her limp put her behind. Yến slowed. "I'm sorry. I shouldn't walk so fast."

Tâm, surprised Yến had voluntarily chosen to initiate a comment, shook her head. "It doesn't matter." Still, she was relieved to slow her pace.

A few blocks from the temple grounds, the city of Tay Ninh began to thin out. Homes and shops on the ground floor of tube houses popped up between buildings. Similar to Saigon, narrow cobblestone alleys cut across streets.

Yến led Tâm down one of the alleys. They turned left about thirty meters down, then right. Deep in the bowels of the city, many of the passages were no longer paved with cobblestones, just sandy dirt. Women stirred pots filled with *phở*; men squatted nearby, slurping the soup or chewing fruit. Children dashed back and forth, and cats slinked by prowling for scraps. Doors on both sides of the alley marked the entrances to small dwellings crammed together, peeling paint and uneven thresholds attesting to their age and disrepair. Odors that Tâm couldn't identify wafted through the air.

The narrow passageway they walked down abruptly opened up to a sandy lot surrounded by some bushes, a scrawny tree or two, and some random heavy boulders. About five or six young men huddled, their conversation heated. Near them on the ground were two wire crates with a rooster in each.

A cockfight. Tâm hadn't seen one since before the massacre. A popular form of entertainment, cockfights were a staple of rural life. Men usually gathered in teams, each team betting on a rooster who, when the gate was opened, would fight the other to the death. And provide dinner for its owner. The excitement, pitched shouts, and competition during the fight itself used to fascinate Tâm. Now, though, she felt indifferent.

Tâm and Yến watched as the crate doors opened and the birds emerged from their cages. Both had bright red combs; one was nearly white with brown splotches, and the other was all brown. After an initial period in which the birds circled each other with clawed feet, the brown one hopped forward, invading the white bird's turf. The white bird pecked him defensively. The brown one retaliated with a peck. Soon they were pecking each other over and over, fluttering their wings, hopping forward, backward, and to the side, all the while issuing high-pitched guttural chirrs.

The men cheered and shouted and exchanged money throughout the fight, until, about twenty minutes later, the white rooster succumbed. Exuberant shouts erupted from the winning team; bills and coins were exchanged again, and five minutes later, the men dispersed.

Yến approached one of them and started an earnest conversation, occasionally pointing at Tâm.

At last they both sauntered over. "This is my cousin Lý Viên Đức," Yến said. "His mother lives alone but likes to rent out her extra bedroom. No one is there at the moment."

Tâm's eyebrows rose. "That sounds perfect."

"She is my mother's sister and looks after my mother sometimes," Yến said.

"We'll go there now," Đức said.

The priest had told her Yến's mother was ailing. Tâm was curious but decided it would be impolite to ask for details.

As they walked, Đức was still exhilarated by the fight. "Did you see that, cousin? I bet on the brown, and I won!"

Yến nodded. "I hope you will save your earnings and not waste them on beer or"—a flush crept up her neck—"more of these games."

Đức laughed. "Of course not." But he turned to Tâm and gave her a wink. Tâm rolled her eyes.

"Who were the men?" Yến asked. "I only recognized you and Lành, but the others were new faces."

"I didn't know them." Đức shrugged. "Does it matter?"

Yến kept her mouth shut.

～

Tâm took the room. On the second floor of the house, it was tiny, no bigger than a closet, but it was clean and dry and had a small window that looked out on a field littered with beer cans, broken glass, and garbage. She reminded herself to be grateful that it wasn't a tent in Cholon with mud seeping up through the ground. Or a pup tent covered with mosquito netting she'd shared during her training.

Bà Thảo, the woman who rented the room to her, looked to be in her sixties and was hunched over from arthritis, but she was friendly enough. Bà Thảo had moved from Trang Bang village when the North Vietnamese first moved into the area. She wasn't around much during the day; she either babysat or took care of an elderly sister who was blind. Yến's mother, Tâm realized. That was her "ailment."

Bà Thảo would provide breakfast if Tâm wanted; for the other two meals, she was on her own.

Tâm brought her things over the next day.

CHAPTER 65

TÂM

Working in the temple kitchen could be described in one word: hellish. As the weather warmed up and the monsoons came in, the heat inside was intolerable. In the furnace-like atmosphere created by the giant ovens and stoves plust the lack of air-conditioning, rivers of sweat poured from the workers every day, and frequent water breaks were a necessity. Fortunately, the temple knew kitchen workers were critical and allowed them unlimited breaks, as long as the chefs permitted it.

Tâm and three other workers lounged under a rubber tree outside the kitchen one morning a few weeks later, sipping weak iced tea. She was one of only two female workers; the others were strong-looking young men. That didn't include the head chef and two sous-chefs. Sometimes they took breaks with the workers, sometimes not.

Tâm was surprised how friendly everyone was. In fact, she couldn't remember the last time she'd worked in such pleasant company, Bảo excepted. The workers considered themselves lucky to work at the temple, and if the grief and suffering of the war had marked them, they didn't talk about it. By the end of the first week Tâm felt she'd known them for years. Maybe there was something to the Cao Đài religion.

As she'd hoped, they loved to gossip. Ly, who alternated between kitchen duty and waiting on church officials at meals, put down his tea. "Did you see how Father Nghĩa treated visitors this morning? You would have thought he was Jesus himself."

The others giggled, including Tâm. Then she said, "I'm confused about something. I know a yellow robe is for Buddhist priests, red for Confucius, blue for Taoists, but what is the color for Christianity?"

"I don't know," Thủy, the other female worker, said. "The Catholics I know are always in white."

"Almost everyone wears white," Ly went on. "The colors are just for special ceremonies, like when an important leader comes to visit, and the bishop wants them to know how inclusive we are."

"I see." But Tâm wasn't altogether sure she did.

"You see, Cao Đài is based on three religions, but there are five doctrines, which include tenets of the other great religions of the world," Biên, the other male worker, said.

"Anyway," Ly resumed his story. "Father Nghĩa said he was anticipating the Catholic pilgrims and tourists who will be visiting this summer, and he wanted the church to build him an altar so he could offer them communion."

"Really? What did Bishop Huỳnh say?" Bishop Huỳnh was the head of the temple, although there was an archbishop to whom he reported.

"He said, 'Father Nghĩa'"—Ly tried to imitate the bishop's metallic voice—"'you are Cao Đài, not Catholic. Perhaps you should move to a Catholic school down along the Mekong. They will be happy to offer communion.'"

Thủy's eyes grew wide. So did Biên's. "What did he do?"

Ly's eyes filled with amusement. "He got up from the table in a huff and walked out."

"What did the bishop do?" Thủy asked.

"He folded his arms and winked at me."

They all burst out laughing.

"Well, Father Nghĩa is pompous," Ly said, standing and dusting off his black pajamas. "All right. Enough fun. We go back into hell now."

Tâm had the early shift and was able to go home when most of the preparations for dinner were done. Riding her bicycle was easier now, and she was pleased that her wounded leg was strengthening. Winding through the alleys back to Bà Thảo's home, though, she still had to dodge children, cats, and women cooking on their hot plates. After a close encounter with a kettle of *phở*, she admitted defeat and walked her bike the rest of the way.

When she arrived, Bà Thảo was pouring tea, which she placed on a tray and brought to the small front room. A woman sat on a chair. Tâm could tell from her milky but vacant eyes that the woman was blind. Not as old as Bà Thảo but much older than Tâm, she had long hair threaded with gray which was pulled back in a bun. She wore black pajamas and a white tunic.

Bà Thảo introduced them. "This is my sister, Anh. I take care of her a few days a month when Yến goes on her missionary work." She set the tea down, went back to the kitchen, and returned with a plate of rice cakes. She took Bác Anh's hands and folded them around the teacup so she could hold it herself.

Yến's mother. For a reason she didn't understand, Tâm was taken aback. She remained where she stood, letting the image of the two women imprint itself in her mind.

Bác Anh broke the silence, almost as if she had read Tâm's mind. "It was from Agent Orange. I was in the fields when they sprayed. An infection set in and I lost my eyesight. When the war is over, I will learn Braille and go to blind school."

"I am so sorry for your loss," Tâm said quietly.

"Why? You are not American."

"No, but . . ." Confused thoughts swirled through Tâm. She had been fighting Americans. They had retaliated with the poison. Had her involvement indirectly contributed to Bác Anh going blind? It wasn't logical; she had nothing to do with Agent Orange. Still, it was becoming increasingly difficult for her to determine who was right and who was wrong in this war, and what her part was. Perhaps it didn't matter. It all led to the same results: too many Vietnamese dead, wounded, or tortured. Too many families torn apart.

"Come here, my dear." Bác Anh smiled. "Let me feel your face. My daughter Yến said you are very pretty."

Tâm felt her cheeks get warm. She moved over, sat in a chair next to her, and let Bác Anh touch her face with light fingers.

"Yes. I can feel it." She dropped her hands. "Please, could you hand me a rice cake? Chị Thảo makes the best ones in South Vietnam."

Tâm handed her one and watched Bác Anh take a bite. Bác Anh smiled, clearly taking pleasure in the sweet. Then: "Tell me, Linh, how did you come to Tay Ninh?"

Tâm repeated her cover story. This time she added to it. "My uncle was Cao Đài. My father didn't approve. We were Buddhists. But I was always curious. I wanted to find out more. When I recovered from my injury, I came."

"And what of your family, my dear?"

"They were killed in an American massacre of my village."

"Ah . . . this war." Bác Anh shook her head. "Yến lost her brother. Chị Thảo, where are you? When are we going to end this carnage?"

Thảo sat down and rubbed the back of her neck. "Soon, Em. It cannot last forever."

Tâm spoke up. "You said Yến does missionary work. What does she do? Where does she go?"

Her mother answered. "All Cao Đài are encouraged to reach out to like-minded Vietnamese and try to bring them into the religion. Yến goes once or twice a month to smaller towns in the province."

"That's when she brings my sister here, so I can look after her," Bà Thảo said.

"I'd like to speak to Yến about that work," Tâm said casually. "Perhaps I can learn something."

"I don't know," Bác Anh said. "She doesn't like to talk about it. Not even with me. I don't understand why." She shrugged.

The serious mood ended when Bác Anh told an off-color joke. Something about two oxen and a man who didn't know how to drive them. Tâm didn't hear all of it; Bác Anh spoke in a low voice, almost a whisper. At the punch line, though, Bà Thảo roared with laughter. She had an infectious laugh. Tâm couldn't help it. She laughed too.

CHAPTER 66

TÂM

Two months later, the kitchen of the temple thrummed with activity. A two-day synod with most of the church's bishops and archbishops would begin at a luncheon in a few hours. The casual kitchen demeanor was absent today; both chefs and sous-chefs were short-tempered and impatient. Some of the resident priests had volunteered to help, so the kitchen staff had doubled.

Tables were set for nearly seventy-five people in a dining room in one of the dormitories. Everyone helped serve. Even Tâm with her limp was tasked with refilling water glasses and replacing bowls, chopsticks, and spoons. They all worked without a break for several hours; thankfully, the heat had moderated and the monsoons were over.

In between meals—they would begin preparations for supper in an hour—the workers gathered outside to gossip.

"The archbishop seems to be in very good spirits," Biên said, gulping down a quick cup of tea.

"He always is during these events," Ly said. "Gives him a chance to show off the temple and the new additions."

"What's new?" Tâm asked

"I know there are some new relics of the saints," Ly said. "I'm not sure what else, though."

"Did you see the bishop from Da Nang?" Thủy said. "He looks as angry as a tiger whose prey has escaped."

"Father Mạc?" Ly said.

"If that's his name," Thủy said.

"It could be because his girlfriend broke off their affair," Ly said in a low voice.

"Girlfriend?" Tâm asked. "I thought priests were celibate."

"The monks are. And a few priests who devote themselves to Cao Đài. But most priests are not, nor are they expected to be. It's the higher clergy, anyone above the title of priest, who are required to be celibate," Biên said.

"And you can see how that goes." Ly grinned.

Everyone laughed.

"Did you see how Father Mạc eyed us when we were waiting on him at lunch?" Thủy asked Tâm. "I saw him checking you out. You're probably on his list now. Don't be surprised if he makes a move. You are very attractive."

Tâm felt heat rise up from her neck. "I hope not," she said. "I don't want any trouble. I thought men and women had to sit separately, anyway."

"Only during prayers," Thủy answered.

"And even that doesn't stop the Eye." Ly raised his finger and pointed in the direction of the temple, where the giant eye rose above the altar.

Everyone laughed again.

"Stop. Now you are teasing me," Tâm said good-naturedly, realizing the double entendre.

"Not really," Ly said. "He's quite the ladies' man."

"More than the priest who left a few months ago?" Biên asked.

"What priest?" Tâm said, hoping she sounded casual. General Minh's lieutenant had said one of the possible spies was a womanizer.

"Like I said, Cao Đài doesn't care what you did before you joined the church." Ly arched his eyebrows. "There was a resident priest with us for about a year. But he left suddenly. No one knows why. But some church members swear they used to see him in town with prostitutes."

Tâm sipped tea. "So the higher clergy forced him to leave?"

"Who knows?" Thủy said.

"Tell me, where were those *other* church members going when they claimed to have seen him with whores?" Ly said. "When it comes to the inner workings of the church, we can only speculate."

Tâm put down her mug of tea. Suddenly she had two prospects for the "womanizer" spy. She needed to report back to Saigon. "What was the priest's name? The one who left?"

"Why?" Ly joked. "You having troubles with your boyfriend?"

Tâm laughed. "I don't have a boyfriend. But you never know." She tried to joke back.

"What was his name?" Ly asked the others. "You remember. The man who was too vain to wear his glasses. He was always bumping into things."

"Usually women." Thủy grinned.

Biên bit his tongue. "Let me think. Father Huỳnh Van Hoa. Yes. That was it. From Hue."

That night after supper at the church was cleared and the dishes were washed, Tâm rode her bike to one of the dead drops Lieutenant Khuyên had described. It was a fence on the eastern side of the market. At one point, it broke for a stone wall. She was to insert a note in one of the hollows of the stone and leave a mound of pebbles in front. She wrote the names of the two men and made sure to say she did not have proof of their espionage, but their names had come up among the staff as womanizers. One of the men had left the church soon after he was accused of fraternizing with whores. She thought it was information the general should have. Did they want her to go to Hue and discover more about Father Hoa? Or find out more about Father Mạc? She would wait for their response.

CHAPTER 67

TÂM

Since Tâm had worked late at the dinner, she was allowed to skip the breakfast shift. She planned to go to a morning service to observe Father Mạc, but she was so tired she slept through it. She awoke to the cheerful chatter of women in the front room. She dragged herself out of bed, threw on some clothes, and sneaked out to the front room. Bác Anh and Bà Thảo were nattering like magpies. As Tâm yawned, Bác Anh broke off their conversation.

"Good morning, Linh."

Tâm's eyes widened. "How did you know I was here?"

"I heard you yawn." She paused. "Also, there's your scent. It's not bad, not at all, but it is distinctive. It's Linh." Bác Anh smiled.

Tâm smiled back before she realized Bác Anh couldn't see her. A scent of her own? Was it sweet? Foul? Bitter? She thought of Mai, whose name she'd stolen for her new Party name. Did they share the same scent? She made her way to the kitchen and poured tea. The women resumed their conversation. Tâm joined them. Three people were the most that could comfortably fit in the tiny front room.

"Yến is so shy," Bác Anh was saying. "She never used to be. But after her brother was killed in a Viet Cong ambush, it changed her."

She looked in Tâm's direction. "That's when she began her missionary work."

For a moment, Tâm felt like Bác Anh could see straight through her: fears, thoughts, secrets. Her pulse started to speed up. She cleared her throat. "I know what that feels like. American soldiers massacred everyone in my village, including my baby brother. And my parents."

Bác Anh nodded as if she already knew. But how? Had she, in some unguarded moment, told Yến about the attack? She couldn't recall, and that unnerved her. Bác Anh went on. "We have all lost people dear to us in this abominable war."

Tâm's muscles loosened, and she breathed more easily. She was just suffering a flash of paranoia. Still, she had to be more careful about what she said and to whom.

"Yến likes you, Linh," Bác Anh said. "I wish you could get to know her better. Maybe it will help her become more like her old self. I have tried, but I am just her old blind mother."

"You are a fine mother," Bà Thảo declared.

Bác Anh shook her head.

"I can try," Tâm said." Perhaps she and I could go out for a meal." She usually ate her meals in the kitchen. It was one of the benefits of working in the kitchen. But she could spend a few *đồng* at a restaurant in Tay Ninh. "I used to work at a restaurant in Saigon," Tâm continued. "Chinese food. Very elegant. Is there one here you would recommend?"

Suddenly she bit her lip. She had been careless telling them she worked in a Saigon Chinese restaurant. They could ask around and find out which one it was. And discover who she really was. Then, just as suddenly, she relaxed. She now knew why she'd been instructed to use a Party name. They didn't know her real name, and they never would. Still, a stab of guilt nicked her. She liked Bác Anh and Bà Thảo. She was ashamed at her own deceit.

～

Over the next few months Tâm and Yến took walks around the temple complex during breaks, shared meals, and once in a while went out for ice cream. Tâm found she liked the young woman. Unlike Mai, Yến did not chatter all the time. Their silence was easy and natural. But Yến did not have a cheerful disposition, and Tâm tried hard to elicit a smile from her.

Their relationship was the inverse of her and Mai's, Tâm thought. *She* had been the grumpy one. In retrospect, Tâm wondered if Mai's constant chatter was not just about Mai and what she wanted or thought she deserved. Perhaps part of it had been Mai's attempt to draw Tâm out, like Tâm was doing with Yến, so they could feel closer.

She wanted to find out more about Yến's missionary work and why she was doing it, but she needed to tread carefully. They were not close enough yet; she didn't want Yến to use Tâm's curiosity as an excuse to shut down.

Tâm had returned to the dead drop three days after she left the note. A message, presumably from General Minh via Lieutenant Khuyên, told her to keep doing what she was doing in Tay Ninh. There was no need for her to further surveil the two men whose names she had reported.

Relief washed over her; she hadn't wanted to go to Da Nang or Hue to spy. After a decade of war, a deep fatigue had overspread Vietnam. It was rarely expressed; nonetheless, it was dispiriting. The truth was that Tâm felt like a stranger in her own land. What had seemed so clear to her, so compelling before, was now muddied. Both the North and the South seesawed between victory and defeat, each proclaiming victory when in reality there was nothing to celebrate. All Tâm saw was suffering and sorrow. Thousands of young men and women killed; each side responsible for unspeakable acts of cruelty and brutality.What had happened to her country?

CHAPTER 68

TÂM

It was just before Tết in 1971 when news arrived that two Cao Đài clergymen had been abducted, tortured, and executed by the Viet Cong. The victims were identified as Father Mạc, the bishop of Da Nang, and Father Hoa from Hue.

Biên was the first kitchen worker to announce it during their morning break. "Did you hear about Father Mạc and Father Hoa?" he said breathlessly.

"Who?" Tâm asked.

"Two Cao Đài priests. They were tortured and killed by the Viet Cong!" Biên said. "Everyone's talking about it."

Tâm inclined her head. "Those names sound familiar."

Ly stared at her. "We talked about both of them a few months ago. The ones who were . . ." His voice trailed off but he made a motion with his hands that indicated exactly what he meant.

"No!" Tâm cried. Her shoulders hunched and her body tensed. "What happened?"

Ly, who clearly already knew about the men, shook his head. "No one knows."

Tâm shrank into herself. "Was it because of their adultery?"

A flash of anger lit Ly's face. "I just said no one knows."

Thủy cut in. "We're all upset, Ly. Don't take it out on Linh."

Ly didn't say anything for a moment, then lowered his eyes. "Sorry."

Tâm nodded.

"But from what I picked up, it was horrific. The Viet Cong are brutal. The last thing a soldier wants is to be caught by them. You die a thousand deaths."

All eyes slid toward Ly. "What do they do?" Thủy asked softly.

"What don't they do?" Ly gazed at each one of them in turn. "You have no doubt heard how the North Vietnamese and Viet Cong scavenge weapons, undetonated bombs, and land mines once a battle is over?"

The others nodded. Tâm's heart was thumping so hard and fast she was sure they could hear it.

"Well, they're even more innovative when it comes to torture. They are trained to imagine their enemies as hateful and evil. Without a shred of humanity. To them, we are monsters who have no right to breathe the same air as they do."

Tâm wanted to ask how Ly knew this. It wasn't a lie, but he made the Viet Cong sound repulsive. Morally corrupt. Without a morsel of empathy. Her breathing grew shallow. She kept her mouth shut.

"Once the priests were captured," Ly continued, "the VC would have taken them somewhere where their screams would not be heard. Maybe into their tunnels and caves. Or deep into the jungle. If they had not already been beaten with clubs or whipped with ropes they would be. If the prisoners cried out, they would be beaten even harder. Perhaps a leg or arm twisted the wrong way and broken."

Her throat tightened. Why was Ly going into so much detail? Was he enjoying this?

"Then the fun would begin. Since psychologically their prisoners are less than human to them, anything would be possible. Perhaps because Father Mặc and Hoa were adulterers, the Viet Cong castrated them. Tied their genitals to an electrical generator and turned it on. If there was no generator, pliers would work. While they were doing this, of course, they would demand responses to questions they knew the priests could not possibly answer, say, about traitors, spies, or South Vietnam's military plans."

"What do you mean they couldn't possibly answer?"

"Do you really believe those priests are—or should I say *were*—spies? They may have been loose with the ladies, but how can you think they were engaging in espionage? They were just priests." Ly spat on the ground.

No one said anything. Tâm was afraid to breathe.

"So," Ly went on, "at that point their Viet Cong captors would be deep into their disgusting fantasies of purifying the earth of these hideous creatures. They would have continued their torture with water, or perhaps slicing off their fingers or prying out their fingernails until the priests would have told them anything to make it stop. And they probably did. Even then, however, the Viet Cong would not have stopped. If the priests were still alive, the VC would have slashed and carved them up piece by piece. After that, they would have mutilated—"

Tâm couldn't take any more and started to gag. Clapping her hand across her mouth, she bolted to her feet, sprinted around the corner as fast as her bad leg permitted, and vomited in the grass.

It was clear to Tâm that she had sent two priests to their deaths. She had no proof that they were spies. No proof they were even womanizers. All she did was report their names to her superiors. She had condemned them on the basis of idle gossip. It did not matter that she never thought General Minh and his lieutenant would act on her information. It did not matter that she assumed they would dig up the truth before they acted. She had been naïve.

They had rounded up, captured, tortured, and killed two men whose only sin was that they were talked about by the Cao Đài staff. What had she done? A hulking guilt settled on her shoulders. How would she live with herself?

CHAPTER 69

TÂM

Six months after Tết, in June of 1971, Yến dropped off her mother at Bà Thảo's so she could spend the bright, sunny afternoon with Tâm.

"Take your *nón lá*," Bác Anh said. "It is quite hot and dry today. You will need water as well."

Tâm grabbed her hat. She should know by now that Bác Anh could describe the weather without seeing it. She and Yến started out. First they bought rice cakes from one of the women in the alley. Then they strolled around the neighborhood.

"Yến," Tâm said, "I hope you don't mind me asking about your missionary work. Where do you do it? Do you find it gratifying?"

Yến tensed, and her voice was sharp. "Who told you about that?"

Tâm paused. "Your mother and your aunt. They both said the days they spend together are usually the days you are doing missionary outreach."

Yến let out a breath. "Oh. Yes. I go to different temples in the province. They bring me in to talk to young people about joining Cao Đài."

"Do they?" Tâm asked. They were passing a large field. "Join, that is."

"Some do. Some do not." Yến pointed. "Look. There is a cockfight on the field. Let's go watch." She paused. "Maybe my cousin is there."

Tâm nodded, and they walked over. Yến's response to Tâm was clipped. Reluctant. The flicker of suspicion Tâm been nursing since Bà Thảo first told her about Yến's missionary work flared.

As they approached the group, Yến said, "There is Đức." She shook her head. "I wish he would stop wasting his money this way. He rarely wins. Then when he is out of money, he tries to borrow *đồng* from me. He always promises to pay me back, but . . ." Suddenly her voice trailed off.

Tâm glanced at Yến. Her demeanor had changed from that of a sister mildly scolding her brother, or, in Yến's case, her cousin, to one of surprise. Tâm studied the group of men. She picked out Đức chattering to another young man at his side. Probably working out their bets on the cocks. She squinted and looked more closely. Something about that man was familiar. She knew him.

She slowed and let Yến walk in front of her. Tâm angled her *nón lá* so her face was hidden while she tried to figure out who he was. Young, intense, wearing loose black pants and a Western-style T-shirt. Long hair flopped on his forehead.

Hiền! From the Communist training camp. Along with Tâm, Hiền, Chinh, and Trai were a team when they sabotaged the truck and tricked its occupants with the oxcart. She remembered how young and enthusiastic he'd seemed at the camp. He was taller now, leaner, and older. He had broken his arm during their "exercise," she recalled. What was he doing in Tay Ninh? What would he think she was doing at the Cao Đài temple? She was undercover; no one, as far as she knew, suspected her real purpose. But Hiền could blow her cover merely with a friendly wave.

Panic skimmed her nerves. What if he recognized her? They hadn't known each other for long, but they had shared fear, anxiety, and stress. Together the four of them had approached the edge of death. Contemplating whether they would survive the next day. That kind of intensity was hard to forget. Or disguise.

Goose bumps rose on Tâm's skin as she frantically tried to figure out what to do. It was too risky to abruptly flee. She and Yến were the only women there; they were already conspicuous. Slowly she took a few steps backward until she was lurking at the back of the group. Hopefully, Hiên wouldn't notice her.

Yến, on the other hand, threaded her way through the crowd and walked up to Đức. Tâm couldn't hear her, but from her expression Tâm could see Yến admonishing him for gambling away his money. Hiên, flanking Đức's other side, watched, not saying anything, but a small smile appeared on his face, as though he found Yến attractive. Why not? Yến was attractive, when she wanted to be. Yến turned to Hiên.

But Tâm was startled at what happened next. When their eyes met, a clear sign of recognition passed between them. Then, as if Yến realized she might have been too overt, she looked down, probably pretending a bout of shyness had overcome her. When she did look back up at Hiên, his smile widened, and he spoke to her. Yến replied. Đức headed over to examine the two birds, a scrap of paper in his hands. While he was gone, Yến engaged Hiên in a long conversation. He nodded a few times. A few moments later, though, Hiên's eyebrows arched and his smile faded. His gaze swept over the group, clearly looking for someone. It stopped at Tâm.

Tâm felt naked. Her *nón lá* didn't offer enough protection. Liquid fear poured over her. Yến had outed her. Hiên's eyes narrowed as *he* tried to figure out who *she* was. It wouldn't take long.

She was right. When he recognized her, his eyes widened. His mouth opened and closed. He took a step toward her, but at that moment, the cages opened and a swell of shouts went up from the crowd. They closed in to watch the cockfight. Hiên was temporarily trapped.

Tâm wheeled around and ran as fast as she could.

∼

Bà Thảo and Bác Anh were not home when Tâm, breathless and terrified, returned to her room. She quickly packed her few possessions and left some money on the table for Bà Thảo. Then she quickly scribbled a note expressing her gratitude. She rode her bike to the bus depot and waited for the next bus back to Saigon.

While she waited, she tried to put the pieces together. She now knew the identities of the "gambler" and the "woman" leaking information to the South Vietnamese army. Yến's missionary work was a cover for her to take the bus to the South Vietnamese army airbase not far from Tay Ninh and deliver her intel.

No wonder she was reluctant to talk about her outreach work. Shared secrets were a risk. Indeed, they could be lethal. Tâm's only question was whether Đức was part of it. She suspected not. He was too immature.

Now she knew why Yến liked to watch cockfights. Ostensibly there to scold her cousin, in reality she was there to meet her contacts. And those contacts included Hiền. Did that mean he had turned against the North and the Viet Cong? If he had, why? Was it for money? Was it true that he was an inveterate gambler, or was that just his cover?

Perhaps he was a double agent, using gambling as a cover to get information about the South Vietnamese army's plans and pass them back to his Viet Cong handlers. It was possible. But she had no way of knowing the truth. It was all becoming too complicated.

But she did know two things. There was no way she would report the two to General Minh. One had been her comrade-in-arms, the other her friend. She could not condemn them to death. The other thing she knew was that her own cover was blown. She would be considered a traitor to General Minh because she fled without completing her mission. And Hiền, whatever his motives, would make sure "Linh," her Party name, surfaced when he reported back to his superiors. That would eventually get back to General Minh. He and Dr. Hằng would know right away that "Linh" was Tâm. If they ever caught her, she would suffer the same fate as the priests.

Perhaps she shouldn't have fled. Perhaps she should have gutted it out. Pretended she didn't know Hiền. Was meeting him for the first time. As far as she knew, no one in Tay Ninh suspected that she was gathering intel for the Viet Cong. She suspected Ly, the head kitchen worker, didn't trust her, but he didn't trust anyone, and he had no proof of anything.

Nevertheless, Tâm had allowed panic to replace reason. She wasn't cut out to be a spy. And that wasn't the worst part. If the South Vietnamese discovered what she'd been doing the past few years, she would be hunted down and arrested as a defector, thrown into prison, and possibly executed. She was a traitor not just to the North but also to the South. She was trapped.

PART VIII

VIETNAM TO U.S., 1975–1978

Tâm and Mai

CHAPTER 70

MAI

Mai was violently seasick during the voyage to Subic Bay. She'd played for years along the placid Mekong, but compared to the river, the ocean, with its rolling waves, hot sun, and sudden squalls, was a ferocious dragon. She stayed belowdecks and vomited during most of the three-day journey, trusting Đêm Nguyệt to a woman with a son about the same age. Luckily, Đêm Nguyệt fared better than Mai and became fast friends with the little boy.

After they docked and disembarked at Subic Bay, they boarded yellow buses that took them to an evacuation center. American officials, with the help of translators, asked their names, how many were in the family, and where they'd come from.

Mai answered the questions in English.

"Excellent!" The American grinned. "Where did you learn to speak so well?"

Mai shrugged. She wasn't sure how much to reveal. What if it got her in trouble? Then again, wouldn't Americans approve of someone who already spoke the language? "Here and there."

The official nodded, as if he understood her reluctance to be candid. "Well, you're certainly ahead of the game, miss."

The refugee camp was a riot of sights, sounds, and smells. An improvised tent city rose up after the volume of refugees exceeded the number of of arracks normally occupied by U.S. soldiers. Mai and Đêm Nguyệt were assigned to an eight-person tent. Laundry hung outside on clotheslines; women cooked rice and grilled meats over charcoal, just as they always had. Once Mai felt better, she chose two dresses for herself and pants and shirts for Đêm Nguyệt at a free "store" where donated clothes were available. A makeshift Buddhist temple occupied a space nearby, where children played and laughed in tubs filled with water from hoses.

The camp offered classes in English, which Mai attended. Though she already understood and spoke English, she had never learned to read and write. Đêm Nguyệt came with her. He needed to learn right away. She was disappointed when she discovered the teacher's knowledge of English was limited to a song that cited all the letters of the English alphabet. Mai and Đêm Nguyệt memorized them anyway.

Another American official interviewed her a few days later. When he asked how she had come to be on the boat, she told him the truth. Did she have a passport or any official papers, he asked? She shook her head. He made a note in a file. Now she understood why Anh Vinh had her board the ship he did. He and his family must be on a ship where they already had papers. She wondered where Anh Vinh was. He had told her he would meet her in Subic Bay, but she never spotted him. Was he already in the United States? Did South Vietnamese officers have a VIP ticket to their new homeland? Should she ask the official about him?

Three weeks later Mai and Đêm Nguyệt boarded a plane and flew to the island of Guam. Her first time on an airplane; Mai was terrified. She was sure the airplane would fall out of the sky with every bump. Her grip on the armrests was so fierce she was sure she would pull them out from their base. Đêm Nguyệt, on the other hand, loved the ride and kept pointing out how far above the clouds they had soared.

∽

Guam was similar to Subic Bay but much larger. Where Subic Bay housed about 1,000 refugees at a time, Guam, a U.S. territory with a huge American military presence, took in 50,000 refugees at its peak. More than ninety percent of the 130,000 Vietnamese refugees from the war passed through the island.

Mai and Đêm Nguyệt were assigned cots in a large tent on the beach with about a dozen strangers. Guam had hospitals, churches, galleys, showers, another free store with clothes and toys. There were classes in English, American food, and what to expect when they reached the States. Mai found some nail polish at the store and offered partial manicures to the women. It was always a good idea to learn what was really going on. When women were in a relaxed setting, they typically shared information, news, and gossip she wouldn't otherwise hear.

She was right. They were full of chatter about where they would be sent and what would be done for them once they settled. Some were thrilled at the prospect of becoming Americans. They talked about buying houses and cars, how their husbands would find high-paying jobs and their children would learn English and go to university one day. Others were bitter and complained about the American military invasion. "After what they did to us, they should be doing much more," they argued. Still others, from rural villages mostly, didn't appear to understand where they were going or what to expect.

Although the refugees were treated well, a layer of fear wrapped around the camp like a morning mist in the Vietnamese mountains. Thousands of Vietnamese had been abruptly uprooted and fled with only the clothes on their backs. The entire refugee population was suffering trauma and shock.

Though Mai was frightened, the seven years since the Americans massacred her family had changed her. Had the massacre not occurred, she would have stayed in the Mekong Delta in a dusty village. She might never have understood the world as she did now. The vicious mendacity of some. The unexpected generosity of others.

CHAPTER 71

MAI

Mai's interview at Guam was more thorough than the one at Subic Bay. An army official and a translator were both present, but Mai spoke in English, which the army man noted on a file with Mai's and Đêm Nguyệt's names at the top. The man asked her what she did in Vietnam, and what she'd like to do in America.

"I have many jobs," she said, telling them about her work at the Stardust Lounge, the Saigon Café, and the Binh Tay market. "I like giving manicures and pedicures the best." She thought back to Madame Thạc. Were there places like the Stardust in America? Would the American official expect her to be more ambitious? "I will also like to manage restaurant or nightclub."

"You have big plans." The army man smiled. "It's good to dream."

Mai arched her eyebrows, unsure what he was saying. He explained. "In order to go to the U.S. you will need a sponsor."

Mai frowned. "What is this sponsor?"

"A friend, a relative, or maybe an organization that will look out for you. Help you get settled. Find a job. Make sure you have enough food and clothing to start out. Do you know anyone in the U.S. you could ask to be your sponsor?"

Mai immediately thought of Sandy. "I do."

The official raised his eyebrows. "Really? Who?"

"A lieutenant in U.S. Army. Alexander Bowden. He was in Vietnam in 1968 and 1969."

The official took a look at Đêm Nguyệt, with his light coloring and blue eyes. He didn't say anything.

Mai knew what he was thinking. "He lives in Chicago. Rogers Park." She still had problems with her "r's sounding more like "l's."

"And he will vouch for you?"

She nodded.

"Do you have any kind of letter from him or other documentation that says that?"

"We had to leave Saigon quickly."

The official nodded and wrote something in the file. "We'll try to contact him."

"Really?"

"We'll try. But don't get your hopes up." He glanced at the file and cleared his throat. "I do have one piece of advice." He paused. "Miss Nguyễn."

"Yes?"

"If you're willing to take any job available, we can get you there quicker."

Again she was unsure what he was saying. Any job? Was he telling her to be a prostitute? She would not go to America if that was a condition. This time was going to be different. She eyed the man. What did he want to hear? He was waiting for her response. He looked sincere, not deceitful. Perhaps she did not understand. "I will work at anything. As long as it is permitted by the government. What is the word?"

"Legal."

"Yes. Legal."

The man made another note in the file. "Good."

"What're you writing down?" Mai asked.

"Don't be afraid. We are making a file for you. So there is a record and everyone will know you are in the United States legally." He emphasized the word.

She smiled.

~

In Mai and Đêm Nguyệt's English class, the teacher gave them an ABCs coloring book and crayons. They studied the letters by singing the alphabet song they learned in Subic Bay. Mai realized she knew more words than she thought.

Over the next three months, despite the classes, manicures, and taking care of Đêm Nguyệt, there was time to reflect. Her thoughts invariably circled back to Sandy. She had survived the war. They were on their way to America. It had to be a sign. Surely this was the path Buddha wanted her to take.

Sandy was Đêm Nguyệt's father. He would want to see his son. Any father would. Maybe when he did he would— No. She forced herself to stop. No more fantasies. And what about Anh Vinh? She loved him too. What would she do if he came back into her life? Whom would she choose? She honestly didn't know.

One afternoon she was filling her laundry tub with water when a soldier offered to help her. She thanked him, then asked where he was from.

"Chicago."

Mai's lips parted. Was this another good omen? "I know someone in Chicago."

"Really."

"His name is Alexander Bowden. He was a lieutenant in Vietnam in 1968."

The soldier shook his head. "There are millions of people in Chicago. And thousands of soldiers from Chi-town."

"Of course." Mai chastised herself for her naivety.

"But Chicago is a great city. You would love it. People are straight shooters. You know, direct. And friendly. They'd give you the shirt off their back if you needed it." He laughed. "There's only one thing."

"What is that?"

"The weather."

"It cannot be any worse than Vietnam."

"Well, there are no monsoons. And it never gets as hot as it is here."

"That is good."

"But we do get to twenty below zero." He explained how cold it got in the winter. All the snow that fell. How it lined the streets from December through March. Then he told her about the Hawk.

"A bird?"

"The wind. It's so bad sometimes it gets under your coat and hat and you get so cold you think the wind is clawing at your skin."

Mai shivered. "Oh no."

"Don't worry. You'll end up in Southern California like everybody else. You'll love the weather there."

But life had other plans for Mai and Đêm Nguyệt. After three months in Guam, they boarded a plane bound for Fort Indiantown Gap in Pennsylvania.

After changing planes in California, they landed in Pennsylvania at the end of August on a hot, hazy summer day. The Americans complained about the heat, but to Mai it was cool compared to Vietnam. They climbed onto a bus, and Mai kept her eyes glued to the window. Was she finally in America? She wanted to drink it in right away.

The shapes of trees were different, the color of the sky as well. The air was fresh and sweet compared to Vietnam, and the sunlight wasn't as harsh. Most of all, she was astonished at the highways. Vietnam had one or two highways with two or three lanes. Here they were flying down a highway with four lanes dotted with yellow lines, all of them crowded with cars and trucks. How did they keep from hitting one another?

Fort Indiantown Gap, in the south-central part of the state, was smaller than Subic Bay, but the U.S. military made sure that, like the other refugee camps, they had ample food, temporary housing,

English classes, and cultural training. This time, Mai and Đêm Nguyệt were assigned to barracks with other mothers and their children. The room was divided into two sections of bunk beds and a section of single beds in the middle. Đêm Nguyệt promptly climbed to the top of one bunk. "I want this bed, Mama," he said.

"Of course." Mai smiled.

It had been four months since they'd fled Vietnam; four months of feeling unanchored and stateless; Mai was more than ready to start her new life. But she had to be patient. Several charitable organizations were working to find sponsors and cities where refugees could be resettled. "Catholic Charities, for example, is working hard to find you a new home," one of the counselors told her. "You could be resettled anywhere."

She was interviewed twice by yet another team of officials who asked about her work experience. Didn't these people have her files from the previous interviews? Apparently not. Once again she repeated her work history and her knowledge of English. This time she added that she would love to be moved to Chicago.

One of the officials raised his eyebrows. "Do you have friends? Or relatives there?"

Mai was a little savvier this time. "Not really, but soldiers keep telling me how much I'd like the city."

"Your English is very good," the official said.

In the end, she was glad she'd volunteered that information. At the end of October, she learned that a Catholic church in Chicago would sponsor her. Her head started to spin. Had they found Sandy? Did he know they were coming? Was he going to be their sponsor? She would find out soon. They would be on a plane in two days.

CHAPTER 72

TÂM

July 1971–1975

T âm took the bus back to Saigon from Tay Ninh; she didn't know where else to go. Most of the trip was an eight-hour ride on bumpy, shelled-out dirt roads. She considered going back to the Saigon Café, but it was far too dangerous. If she ran into Dr. Hằng, or people who worked with her, she would be vulnerable. In fact, if she came across anyone she'd met while she fought for the Communists, it could mean her death. Unfortunately, the same was true if she came across any South Vietnamese fighters who knew her story.

During a sleepless night at a hotel in Cholon, she realized she'd made a foolish decision returning to Saigon. She would leave the next morning. She thought about trying to find Mai; she was family. Then she remembered how they'd parted. Tâm, full of self-righteous indignation, thought Mai was an opportunist taking the easy way out, and she'd let Mai know it. But the truth was that no one, whether North or South Vietnamese, had an easy way out. This country, torn apart by endless war, had made captives of them all, whether they were behind bars or not. Whether they lived in the North or the South, the Vietnamese people were controlled by the whims of greedy politicians and military commanders with grandiose plans but not much else.

Tâm felt abandoned and alone. The only person who'd loved her was dead. She recalled how Bảo had talked about the beauty of the Central Highlands where she grew up. How a morning mist curled around the mountains and a gentle sun warmed the plateaus. How she and her siblings would play hide-and-seek in the pine forests and collect cones. The temperate climate of the Highlands, compared to the rest of Vietnam, made it possible to grow a wide variety of flowers, vegetables, and fruit. Bảo's family raised broccoli, asparagus, and artichokes, as well as elegant hydrangeas, marigolds, and petunias bursting with color.

Tâm wondered if Bảo's family had been notified of her death. Chances were they didn't know. She decided to take a train to the city of Da Lat, which was quite close to Bảo's village. She would find them and deliver the sad news.

Da Lat rose 1,500 meters above sea level and because of its cooler temperatures was called "The City of Eternal Spring." Originally developed by the French as an Alpine-style retreat for high-ranking government officials , it was replete with hotels, spas, and boarding schools for the offspring of the ruling class. Because of its French heritage, they sometimes called Da Lat "Little Paris."

With the French now gone, stories about ghosts haunting abandoned Da Lat villas and homes circulated around Vietnam. Tâm wasn't a believer. She had outgrown her mother's fear that she would be kidnapped by evil spirits and barely remembered the nickname her mother had given her for protection. "Stinky Monkey." That was it.

So far Da Lat had been spared the worst of the war's carnage. Curiously, by tacit agreement, the city was a popular destination for R&R for soldiers on both sides of the war. Perhaps the spirits haunting the hills around the city were more benevolent than people imagined.

∽

"Are you the mother of Diệp Hồng Bảo?" Tâm said two days later when a short, matronly woman came to the door of a small house in Lam Dong Province. She wasn't old, but deep lines on her brow and cheeks told a story of hard work and sorrow.

The woman dipped her head and looked up at Tâm in fear. Tâm smiled. "I am Nguyễn Trang Tâm. I fought with your daughter in the war."

"Is she still alive? We have heard nothing for over a year. Has she been wounded?"

"May I come in?"

"Of course." She opened the door wider and gestured for her to come in. Larger than Tâm's family hut, the wooden structure had several rooms. Bảo's mother led the way to a kitchen, where a young woman was cutting and shaping hydrangeas. The young woman had to be Bảo's sister. She had the same wide, cheerful eyes, but her nose was larger and her chin not as chiseled.

Tâm swallowed before she spoke. "I am sorry to tell you that Bảo was stabbed and killed by the enemy in the Cu Chi tunnels in 1969."

Her mother sucked in a long breath. Then she nodded and her lips tightened. "We were afraid of this. But it is kind of you to tell us officially. Are you an officer as well?"

Tâm shook her head. "She was a wonderful leader. Brave, smart, but cautious. The Long Hairs adored her." Tâm swallowed. "So did I."

Bảo's mother inclined her head but said nothing.

"How long were you under Bảo's command?" the sister asked, carefully packing the flowers in a box.

"Only about two months. I was there when she—she died." Tâm bent her head and looked down. "I believe I killed the tunnel rat who killed her."

Bảo's sister straightened. "You believe? What do you mean?"

"It's impossible to know with certainty that the man I killed was the one who stabbed Bao, but I suspect it was. There are few enemy soldiers brave enough to climb into the tunnels and attack us."

"You risked your life, didn't you?"

"Why? Why did you do this?"

Tâm hesitated. Then, "Because I was in love with her."

Bảo's mother crossed her arms and went rigid.

The sister glanced at her mother, then back at Tâm. "She does—did not approve of Bảo's—how do you say it—attraction to other women. She thinks it is a sin," she said apologetically.

Bảo's mother started making brushing aside motions with her hands and pointed to the door. She was clearly telling Tâm to leave.

Tâm took the hint and headed for the door. She turned to face Bảo's sister. "I am sorry to bring such sorrowful news. I thought you would want to know. I miss her every day."

Bảo's mother's voice oozed a distinct undertone of contempt. "*Dồng tính nữ*. Lesbian. Get out of my home."

Her sister shook her head and gave Tâm a sad smile.

CHAPTER 73

TÂM

Back in Da Lat, Tâm walked to Da Lat University. Situated on a hilly area near Xuan Huong Lake, it had been founded by Vietnamese Catholic bishops, and Tâm had attended the Catholic school in her Mekong River village. She had no idea how she would pay for classes, but she was sure the familiarity of a Catholic school was an omen that she should continue her education. She found the central administrative office and waited for the woman at the reception desk to finish a telephone call. While she waited, she browsed through a book with all the educational programs and curricula.

Finally the woman hung up. "How can I help you?"

"I am interested in your degree in agriculture and forest management."

The woman raised her eyebrows. "Silviculture?"

Tâm nodded. It was as close as she could get to the study of botany at the university.

The woman looked her over, then shook her head. "Women do not study forest management."

Tâm ignored the comment. "What are the requirements to apply?"

The woman held up a finger and looked down at a telephone list taped to her desk. She punched in a number. "I have a young woman here who is interested in our agriculture program. May I send her to you?" She listened and nodded. "Right away."

The woman gave her directions to the agriculture building. When Tâm arrived, a man in khaki overalls and a plaid shirt was typing at a desk. He looked up. "Do you have your transcripts from your last school?"

Tâm shook her head. "I attended a small Catholic school in the Mekong Delta. I—I graduated in 1968," she fibbed. "I was planning to go to university to study botany, but my village was attacked and my family killed." That was the truth. She had never returned for the graduation.

The man spread his hands. "I am sorry, but there is nothing I can do without your records. Can the school mail them to us?"

Tâm equivocated. She didn't want anyone to know where she was, and giving them a forwarding address for her transcripts was too risky. "No." She hesitated. "Isn't there some test I could take to qualify? An entrance exam?"

"I am sorry." He looked back down at the typewriter and started to peck the keys.

Her shoulders slumped, and she turned to leave. She was halfway to the door when the man said, "Wait."

"Yes?" She slowed and peered over her shoulder.

"I may be able to find you a job as a farmworker. If your supervisor thinks you have promise, you could audit a class on a provisional basis."

Tâm turned around and grinned.

Tâm knew as soon as she began working the land that this was what she wanted. She'd helped her father when she was young. Back then it felt like a chore. Now, though, working on a farm about ten kilometers from Da Lat, Tâm loved to coax young flower buds to blossom and sprouts to become vegetables. She loved the smell of warm, wet soil and hot, dry sun. The fields resembled carpets woven from rich hues of green. And, of course, the perfume of fully grown flowers. To choose what species of herbs or vegetables to plant adjacent to each other to control pests. She even liked to weed.

She was creating life rather than destroying it, and she imagined the Buddha was smiling, pleased with the occupation she had chosen. She sometimes wondered if raising a child was in some tiny way similar. She would never have children of her own—she intuitively knew that—but she suspected that mucking around in soil to help seeds sprout and flowers bloom required a similar love and dedication.

After the first year, her supervisor told the Agriculture Department of the university that he was pleased with her progress, so the university allowed her to audit a course at night. It was a good solution. They would permit her to take the exam at the end of the course. If she passed, she would get half a credit. It would take longer to get the degree, but as long as she had work and money for food, she would stay in Da Lat as long as it took. Years, probably. Despite the hostility of Bảo's mother when she first arrived, Da Lat had begun to cleanse Tâm's soul.

⌇

Still the war dragged on. The U.S. formally exited the fighting in 1973, leaving Vietnam in civil war. The Communists were driving the momentum, and by 1974 the North was steadily gaining territory in the South, installing Communist officials to run the local governments of Southern cities and provinces they now controlled. With their control, though, came demands for higher taxes, loyalty tests, and increased conscription. Anyone who dared to side with the Saigon regime was captured, imprisoned, and sometimes executed.

In November of 1974 four officials from Lam Dong Province visited the farm where Tâm, who was one of five farmhands, worked. The bureaucrats lined up all five and demanded their names, place of birth, names of family members, and how long they had been in Lam

Dong. The four other farmhands were local, and their responses did not cause concern. Then they questioned Tâm.

One official asked how she had come to Da Lat. Why had she not returned to the Mekong Delta? She told them about the American massacre of her village. Another asked what she had done after the massacre. She told them she'd worked at the Saigon Café and then spent time at the Cao Đài temple. She didn't tell them she fought for the Communists. How did she get her limp? another asked. She told them she was injured during a bomb blast in Cholon.

Forced to repeat her answers three times, she was as suspicious of them as they were of her. How much did they know about her? Had General Minh tracked her to Da Lat? Was this a trap? Was she on the verge of arrest? She tried to hide her fear, but her throat closed up, and her voice caught in her throat. The officials scowled, and she thought they might take her in. But the owner of the farm, Chú Dũng, told them it was the middle of the growing season and he needed her. The officials, whose expressions indicated they were irritated, said they would come back after the harvest.

Five minutes after they left, Chú Dũng crooked his finger at Tâm. They went into the greenhouse, where the seeds were raised. He shooed out his wife, who was watering. When they were alone, he said sadly, "You know what I am going to tell you."

Tâm nodded. "I hope I have not caused you trouble."

"We will be fine. My brother-in-law works for the province. But you cannot stay."

"I understand."

"Is there something in your past you do not want to tell me?"

She looked down.

Chú Dũng let out a breath. "I do not know when they will be back. It could be tomorrow. It could be never. If they do return, I will tell them that you left the day after they questioned you. That I hardly knew you. And that I am grateful they came. That you were clearly a disloyal citizen and you needed to be 'weeded out.'"

"Yes, of course."

"Pack your things. I will tell the university." He paused. "But see me before you go. Every farmhand who works as hard as you deserves a bonus, and you have been one of my best."

Tâm's heart filled with gratitude. Despite the horrors of this war, despite the fear that now wrapped around her, a few generous souls still clung to their humanity.

CHAPTER 74

TÂM

Tâm took a train back to Saigon with no plan. She no longer had a destination or a goal to chase. Everything she believed in had turned to dust or death. With a clouded and uncertain future, she reverted to the past. She went to the Binh Tay market and used some of Chú Dũng's bonus money to buy a tent and bedding. She pitched it at the Cholon refugee camp, the place that marked where she and Mai had begun their journey; perhaps she could figure out what she should do next. The Cholon camp would be relatively safe. She would be one of many lost souls. Hopefully, no one would pay attention to her.

A few days later she took a bus to the Saigon Café. It was risky, but she wanted to find out what had happened to Dr. Hằng. And how much General Minh knew about her. But the restaurant was closed and boarded up. She wasn't surprised. Now that the Americans were gone, their business must have languished; most Vietnamese locals couldn't afford the prices. The restaurant occupied the ground floor of a five-story tube house, so Tâm went to the other entrance of the building and climbed up the steps, hoping Cô Cúc and her husband still lived above the restaurant. But they were gone, and a new family had moved in. The occupants said Cô Cúc had left no forwarding address.

She told herself it was even riskier to visit Dr. Hằng's apartment. It wasn't that she expected Dr. Hằng to be waiting for her. But she might run into someone: a doorman, a maid, or a neighbor who recognized her and would tell Dr. Hằng they saw her. Dr. Hằng might tell General Minh, and his men would start looking for her in Saigon.

On the other hand, despite her fears, she might not be considered a person of importance to either Dr. Hằng or General Minh. Her mission had begun three years earlier. That was a long time. Perhaps no one cared one way or the other about a double agent whom they had sent to spy on the Cao Đài. Perhaps they assumed she had been uncovered, arrested, and executed.

But Tâm didn't want to live in constant fear of being exposed. So she walked to the apartment house in District 1 where Dr. Hằng lived. The exterior of the yellow building looked dingier than before. Cracks ran down the stucco walls, and some of the decorative white trim had broken off. The front door was open, but she didn't see a doorman. Was he on break? Or could the building's occupants no longer afford the luxury? With the South now bearing the brunt of the war, times were hard. Money was scarce.

She walked up to the door and peered inside the lobby. A man in a janitor's uniform was sweeping the floor. "Excuse me, but does Dr. Hằng still live here?"

"Who?"

"Dr. Đường Châu Hằng."

"I have only been here one year. I do not know anyone by that name."

"She lived on the third floor at the end of the hall."

He stopped sweeping and leaned on his broom. "Oh . . . *her*." He ran his fingers down the broomstick. "She and her husband were arrested by the South Vietnamese military and executed for treason."

Tâm sucked in a breath. Her hand flew to her chest. "What?"

"She worked for the health department, yes?"

Tâm nodded.

"But she was secretly collaborating with the Viet Cong and North Vietnamese."

"When did this happen? Her arrest?"

"Just before I was hired."

"Are you sure the man arrested with her was her husband?"

He shrugged. "That's what I was told. But the person who told me, the doorman, is gone."

"I see. Thank you." She started back to the bus stop, trying to put it together. Someone had betrayed Dr. Hằng. Was it Cô Cúc? General Minh? Perhaps Cô Cúc or her husband had been forced to expose her. Officials might have surveilled Dr. Hằng and discovered she was close to Cô Cúc. They could have threatened to close down the restaurant if Cô Cúc didn't tell them what she knew about Dr. Hằng. But Tâm thought General Minh was behind it. When she first met him, he seemed to be an ally of convenience for Dr. Hằng. But if Dr. Hằng failed or if General Minh was under pressure from higher-ranking officials, Tâm suspected he would turn on Dr. Hằng without a backward glance.

Tâm shivered. Had he betrayed her to the Communists as well? She didn't know. But she did know she'd need to stay as inconspicuous as possible, even if it meant remaining in her dank, muddy tent until the war was over.

Five months later, on April 30, South Vietnam fell. The Americans helped evacuate thousands of South Vietnamese with close ties to the United States. Some were shipped out before Saigon collapsed, but most of the 130,000 evacuations occurred within a month after North Vietnam declared victory. Then the American rescue operation waned.

Tâm's situation hadn't changed. In fact, it was worse. If the Communists believed her to be from the South, she would suffer persecution, perhaps be sent to a reeducation camp. But if the North Vietnamese found out she had fought for the North and had gone AWOL, they would kill her. She had to get out.

CHAPTER 75

TÂM

Months later Tâm heard about the boat people: Vietnamese escaping the country on fishing boats, trawlers, rafts, even sampans. Their goal was to cross the South China Sea to the Philippines or Malaysia. But the vessels were often rickety and overcrowded, and people with no experience piloted them. The journey itself could be treacherous during monsoon season, when sudden squalls might capsize boats and drown passengers. Some estimated that only half the refugees who fled survived the voyage. But these were desperate times for many, who, like Tâm, saw no future in Communist Vietnam. Time was running out.

Tâm was leaving the Binh Tay market two days later when she remembered Anh Phong and his father, Bác Quang, the fishermen who had picked up Tâm and Mai up the Mekong River and given them a ride to Saigon. They'd docked at a busy shipping canal off the Saigon River to sell their catch. It wasn't far away from the market, she recalled. She hurried over. But it was midafternoon, and fish were bought and sold in the morning when they were fresh and the temperature cooler. No one was there.

She went back early the next morning, but again, she saw no trace of them. The next day either. She decided to try one more time before she lost all hope. It was on the fourth morning that she saw Bác Quang on the pier negotiating to sell his catch. He was piloting the same trawler. He had aged along with his boat. A sad dignity haunted his face, now craggy with deep lines, and reached to his eyes. She looked around for Anh Phong. He wasn't there.

She waited while Bác Quang finished his business. Before he boarded the boat again, she approached. "Do you remember me, Bác Quang?"

He squinted. "You look familiar, but—"

"Seven years ago you brought my sister and me to Saigon after the Americans massacred our village."

Bác Quang's eyes widened. "Oh yes! I remember now. Both of you. Where is your sister?"

"I do not know." Tâm felt her cheeks get hot. "We—we separated." She hesitated. "How is your son?"

He swallowed. "The army drafted him. But he was a fisherman, not a fighter. He stepped on a land mine near the Cambodian border. Three years ago." Bác Quang looked out at the water, the pain of his son's death clearly still visible.

Guilt lashed Tâm's soul. Anh Phong could have stepped on one of the inert land mines she had scavenged and given back to the Communists.

He cut in. "But you are limping. You were injured as well?"

She hung her head and nodded.

"So, what brings you here?"

Tâm looked up. "I must leave Vietnam. I am hoping to find someone with a boat. I thought—well—I thought you might know someone." Her voice trailed off.

"Ah. I see." He canted his head and examined her as if what she had just told him revealed a new dimension to her personality. "It is quite dangerous, you know."

She nodded.

He sighed. "I can't make any promise, but come back in two days."

CHAPTER 76

TÂM

Two days felt like two weeks. Now that Tâm had made the decision to leave, she wanted it to happen right away. Every hour she stayed in Saigon brought her closer to disaster. After two sleepless nights, she hurried to the canal just after dawn. Bác Quang was already there. A young man stood next to him. Tâm's pulse quickened. She hoped he knew of a boat.

When Quang saw Tâm, he waited for her to approach. Then he said, "I'll leave now. May the Buddha's spirit accompany you on your journey." He gave her a half smile, turned, and walked away.

The young man was terse. "We have a trawler. I will pilot. The price for a spot is now 250,000 *đồng*. You bring the money with you." She agreed. Since the fall of the government, rampant inflation had weakened the currency. This would wipe out her savings, but getting out was worth it. "We leave from this dock in five days. Saturday. At midnight. You may not bring more than one kilogram of added weight. Most of that should be food. It should be a three-day journey to Subic Bay if we're lucky."

~

The trawler could fit a dozen people comfortably. But more than forty passengers were crammed aboard. She paid her fee and looked around. The trawler sat quite low on the water. Tâm staked out a small space near the bow, squeezed between other passengers, their elbows and shoulders jabbing her. Still, it was her space, and she would stay in it. Standing up to stretch was no guarantee her spot would not be taken.

They pushed off from the dock in the dark. By morning, the weather was clear and sunny. The travelers, initially nervous, slowly relaxed and started chatting. Tâm had brought six baguettes, cheese, and fruit from the market. She ate her breakfast, trying to space out the baguettes so she would have enough for nine meals. She had also bought a compass and length of rope. She checked the compass to see if they were traveling in a northeasterly direction. They were. And they were making good time.

By afternoon, though, rolls of inky-black clouds unfurled on the horizon. A monsoon. Conversation died, and the passengers grew quiet. The trawler's motor drove the vessel, but there was a mast as well. Rain pelted them. Tâm dug the rope out of her bag and tied herself to the mast. The wind picked up, and waves crashed over the boat. The trawler dipped and listed heavily on both sides. Visibility dropped to nothing. The pilot tried to hit the waves at a ninety-degree angle—at least he knew something about sailing, she thought—but with high waves lashing them first one way, then the other, the ninety-degree angle kept changing, and he could not control the boat. The trawler rolled so far to port and starboard that it took on water. One fierce wave shoved the boat almost horizontal to the sea.

Water crashed over the deck and stung Tâm's eyes. The woman next to her fell and slid to the edge of the trawler before her husband grabbed her by her legs and pulled her back. Three other passengers weren't as lucky and were swept overboard. Had Tâm not tied herself to the mast, she would have been the fourth. Screams, shouts, and cries of horror competed with the sound of the storm. The captain yelled for someone to throw them a rope. No one did. The wailing from the refugees' loved ones rose above the wind. So did the screams of the three drowning passengers. Those screams would haunt Tâm's nightmares forever.

As suddenly as it started, the monsoon stopped. Ten minutes later, the sun was out and the monsoon had moved west. The drownings had cast a pall over the passengers, but except for the families whose loved ones had died, the others slowly came out of it. Chatter began again. People brought out soggy biscuits, fruit, and fish. Tâm untied herself and shared her food with a little boy whose mother had drowned.

When she checked her compass, they were off course, heading southeast instead of northeast. She went to relieve herself wondering whether she should point out the misdirection to the pilot. She decided he had enough to worry about. If he didn't correct the course in a few minutes, she would say something. Unfortunately the storm had swept some of the petrol cans overboard. Fuel made up the bulk of the extra weight in the trawler. Tâm wondered if they still had enough to reach the Philippines.

Eventually conversation turned to what they should say to American officials when they were interviewed at Subic Bay. Everyone wanted to go to the United States. Some refugees thought they should present themselves as academics, doctors, or lawyers who could blend into American society due to their knowledge and intellect.

Others thought that was the wrong approach. America already had plenty of smart people. What they needed were manual laborers: farmers, factory workers, cooks. Tâm was not sure what she would say. She was educated and still harbored the dream of studying botany, but her work at the Saigon Café and the Da Lat farm might mean the difference between resettlement in America and resettlement in another part of the world.

Another monsoon hit the next day, but it wasn't as strong as the first, and the trawler weathered it without mishap. They had been warned that bands of Thai pirates preyed on refugees, but no pirates confronted them. Out of food and water, tired, dirty, and fearful, the refugees reached the Philippines five days later.

The trawler came ashore off course, seventy kilometers south of Subic Bay, at a coastal town called Bagac in the Bataan Province. Tâm remembered studying the Bataan Death March of World War II, in which hundreds of Filipinos and Americans died because of Japanese brutality. Now, though, she was so relieved to be alive and ashore she could have kissed the ground. The passengers disembarked and hitchhiked north to Subic Bay.

CHAPTER 77

TÂM

A rriving at Subic Bay, Tâm discovered she and the other passengers were at the tail end of the U.S. military's rescue operation. Most of the refugees who'd passed through the refugee camp had already been resettled. As a result, her first interview with the American official and a Vietnamese translator seemed perfunctory and not particularly welcoming, as if both men were weary. Either that, or was there something problematic about the passengers from the trawler? Tâm worried she would say the wrong thing and they would send her back to Vietnam. She sat across a table from them, coiled and rigid.

"Where are you from?" the official opened the conversation, detached. Bored.

"The Mekong Delta," she answered cautiously.

"How did you get here?"

"I was aboard a trawler that left Saigon six days ago."

"How old are you?"

"Twenty-five."

"What did you do in Vietnam?"

"I studied botany. Then I worked in a restaurant for several years, and two years on a farm. I was trying to make enough money to go to university."

He looked up from his notes, as if he was more interested. "I see."

She didn't. What was he thinking? She straightened up.

The American scribbled something on his paper, after which the translator and interviewer made eye contact. Tâm felt like she had come uninvited to a party, but they were too polite to say so.

"Where would you like us to send you?"

"America."

"What would be your second choice?"

She shrugged. She hadn't thought about that. "Canada, I suppose."

"And your third?"

She frowned. Were there too many refugees in the U.S.? Were they going to send her someplace else? After a moment, she said, "France."

The American nodded. A second Vietnamese translator joined them. The first translator shook his head and tapped a pencil on the table at which they sat. "Half the Vietnamese we wanted to get out didn't, and half who did get out shouldn't have."

Now she understood. The refugees on the trawler were not wanted. They were not important people. They had not been invited, like the South Vietnamese officials who preceded them. But she was here now. A buzz skimmed her nerves. What if they sent her back? What would she do?

"So you worked on a farm?"

She took that as a good sign, took a breath, and nodded. "In the field and the greenhouse. I raised seedlings. Helped grow fruits and vegetables. Harvested them when they were ready."

"And you have restaurant experience?"

"In the kitchen and waiting tables."

The American made more notes, but there was a satisfied look on his face.

It took another three months but by December she was sent via

Guam to Southern California, where she was hired to work on a farm in Orange County.

CHAPTER 78

MAI

Mai and Đêm Nguyệt were met at the airport by a tall, lean, gray-haired man who introduced himself as Dave Chapman. He and his wife, longtime members of the Catholic church of Chicago, had agreed to sponsor them.

Once they had their suitcase, which she'd been given at the Pennsylvania camp, Dave opened the door to walk from the baggage claim to the garage where his car was parked. Mai let out an immediate yelp.

"Ayii!" she shouted. "What is this? It is cold!"

Đêm Nguyệt shivered too and threw his arms around his mother.

Dave laughed. "Didn't they tell you about Chicago weather?"

Mai hugged Đêm Nguyệt and ran her hands up and down his arms to warm him. She vaguely recalled someone saying something about buying coats as soon as they arrived. But she hadn't been paying close attention. "Is it like this all the time in Chicago?"

Dave laughed and opened the trunk of his car. "Not at all. We have a lovely summer, but it is November now, and it will be very cold until April." He stowed their suitcase and pulled out a blanket. "My wife told me to bring this. Wrap it around yourselves for the ride."

They piled into the biggest car Mai had ever been in, a giant gray Chevy, Dave told her. It had enough space for six people and reminded her of the limousines she had occasionally seen in Saigon, floating down the streets bearing important American officials. Dave circled the garage, pulled out, and started to drive. Mai tried to wrap Đêm Nguyệt in the blanket, but he was so excited he pressed his face against the window of the back seat for the entire journey, pointing out all the new and astonishing sights.

At first Mai was so overwhelmed she tried to pretend that she was merely in a Vietnamese city, rather than halfway across the world. It didn't work. The signs on the streets, for one thing, were a jumble of words and letters she hadn't yet mastered, and the giant skyscrapers rushing by the car's windows were intimidating. But it was the traffic, teeming with huge cars and powerful engines but never moving more than a few meters at a time, that terrified her. No motorbikes or tuk-tuks or bicycles on these roads. How was she supposed to navigate through them? She had hoped to buy another Vespa, but these machines would run her down in an instant. It was clear she had been transplanted into a different, strange world.

Their apartment was on the North Side of Chicago on Argyle Street. A second-floor two-bedroom apartment, it was huge compared to their tiny apartment in Saigon. There was a room for each of them, a kitchen large enough to accommodate a tiny table, and a living room with a couch and chairs. Mai clapped her hands in delight.

A woman was boiling water on the stove. Dave's wife, she said. She was almost as tall as her husband, and almost as lean. She had seen a lot of tall, massive, and muscular GIs, but was everyone in America a giant?

The woman didn't speak a word of Vietnamese but gave Mai a warm hug of welcome. She tried to pantomime a few things and grew flummoxed when Mai giggled.

"I speak English," Mai explained.

"Wonderful!" The woman switched to English. "My name is Irene

Chapman and we will be spending time together until you are settled and on your way. The first thing we will do is register your son for school."

Mai translated for Đêm Nguyệt, who clapped his hands, like his mother had. "Will I start today, Mama?"

Mai asked Irene.

"Probably not until next week. He will find it difficult at first—it is all in English—but he is young. He will learn quickly. Plus, there are other Vietnamese children at the school. It is quite close by." Irene smiled. "For now, though, why don't you unpack? Later we will go to the grocery store, and then my husband and I will take you and your son to dinner at a real American restaurant."

Mai was overwhelmed. "But I cannot pay you for these groceries. Or the dinner."

"You do not owe us a penny. We are your hosts. Your sponsors. And, hopefully, your friends."

The next few days flew by. They registered Đêm Nguyệt for school. At six, he would be in first grade and would start the following week. The supermarket was another head-spinning experience. Mai couldn't believe all the foods, cans, fresh fruit, and produce, all stacked neatly in endless aisles or behind counters. Most of it was unfamiliar, and even familiar foods looked foreign. The only way to tell what kind of food she was looking at was the picture on the label, if there was one. She recognized apples, the fruit that Freddy had brought her from his mess hall. A picture of one had appeared in one of Đêm Nguyệt's English readers for the letter "A." She bought three of them, anxious for her son to taste them.

A chicken already cut into parts and packaged with cellophane was rare in Vietnam. The same with fish. But it was the beef that made her feel lightheaded. She had never seen so much red meat carved and sliced in so many different ways. Did Americans eat beef every day? How did they know if it was fresh?

The smells were odd, too. Actually, there were few scents in the store, with the exception of a light fishy aroma at the fish counter.

Clearly, American shoppers did not judge the quality of food with their noses.

After they carried six bags of food up to her apartment, Mai made tea. Irene had suggested she buy a box of Oreo cookies for Đêm Nguyệt, and after asking Mai's permission, she opened the box and gave him one. He bit into it and his eyes grew as round as saucers. He wolfed it down in two bites and held out his hand for another.

"You'd better ask your mother, son." Irene pointed to Mai.

"Just for today," Mai answered. "A special treat."

Đêm Nguyệt waited for Irene to put it in his hand. He was about to grab it when Irene said, "When someone gives you something you want, we say, 'Thank you.'"

Mai grinned. "He knows. *Cảm ơn cô*, sweetie."

"Cảm ơn cô," Đêm Nguyệt said. "Tank you."

Irene laughed. "Excellent!"

Over tea Irene told Mai she was a lucky woman. "A very famous actress in America—her name is Tippi Hedren—visited a Vietnam refugee camp in Northern California. She wanted to help Vietnamese women find jobs in the States. So she brought in seamstresses and typists to help train them. But when the women met her for the first time, they wanted something altogether different. What do you think it was?"

Mai sloshed her tea. "What?"

"They were dazzled by her long, beautifully polished nails, and they wanted to paint their nails the same way."

"Manicures!" Mai clapped her hands. "I did them in Vietnam."

Irene grinned. "I know. We received that information."

Mai was grateful, and a little surprised, that information from at least one of her interviews at the refugee camps had reached America.

"So Tippi changed her plans. She found a local beauty school that taught and trained the women how to give manicures. One of the women who was trained is on her way to Chicago and wants to open her own nail salon. She will need help. Are you interested?"

Mai's jaw dropped. "Of course I am! It is perfect! I can't believe it. Buddha's compassion truly is infinite."

Irene chuckled. "Maybe because he is working with Jesus Christ our Lord."

CHAPTER 79

MAI

Two weeks later Mai, now wrapped up in a red wool coat with a white hat and gloves, met Huỳnh Hồng Liên for tea. Chị Liên's husband, a former major in the South Vietnamese army, wanted to open a restaurant, but once Chị Liên met Tippi Hedren while they were still in California, they decided they wanted to open a nail salon in Chicago.

"My husband will run the business, and I will manage the employees," Chị Liên said. "Of course, it is just a temporary situation for us. We expect the North will release our money, which we could not bring out before we left. And once that happens . . ." She intentionally let her voice trail off.

She still called them the North, Mai noted. But the North were Communists and they now ran the country. She almost wished her luck getting her money out but decided it was wiser to defer to her potential new boss. "Of course," Mai said. "I understand."

Chị Liên sniffed, as if Mai's submissive attitude was her due. She stirred her tea. "I understand you have experience in manicures?"

"I gave manicures in Vietnam. Women love them."

"What is there to love?"

Mai sipped her tea. She remembered when the cousin's friend at the Binh Tay market gave Mai her first manicure while she was pregnant. "We have such busy lives. Working jobs, caring for children and husband, keeping the house clean. A manicure is a special time for a woman. When I had my first one, I felt pampered. As if I had gone on a tiny vacation. And when it was done, I felt beautiful. Every woman deserves to feel that way."

Chị Liên cocked her head, as if Mai was an odd species of animal she was examining. "I need someone to help me start the business. Run the shop. And bring in customers. If you are interested, we will pay you twenty-five percent of what we bring in."

Mai shifted. "Twenty-five percent?"

The woman nodded.

"You want me to help you set up, run the shop, attract the customers. What will you be doing?"

"We are supplying the financing. And my husband will keep the books."

"You want to hire me as your employee. Yet you want me to do the work of a partner. If that is the case, fifty percent is fair."

Chị Liên put her teacup down and folded her hands in her lap. "Thirty-five percent. And that is my last offer."

"Forty," Mai countered. "In writing. For one year. We renegotiate after that."

"You seem very sure of yourself."

Mai smiled. "I have experience. My English is very good. And I am a hard worker."

They found space in an Uptown strip mall just two blocks from Mai's apartment. Major Hồng, or the Major, as he liked to be called, assembled a crew of workers who sanded the floor, painted the walls, fixed up the bathroom, and built shelves and two manicure stations. Mai printed flyers in Vietnamese, Chinese, and English. She persuaded Chị Liên to charge less than the other salons in the area, sure that more female clients—she suggested they call them "clients" rather than customers; it was more respectful—would try the salon if the price for a manicure was ten dollars or less. Of course, that was ten times more than it had been in Vietnam.

Mai recognized how much more expensive everything was in the U.S., but she didn't know why. The Chapmans tried to explain that each penny of that ten dollars ended up paying for rent and utilities, supplies, wages for employees, and taxes, both federal and state. Whatever was left—and they should always try to have some left— was profit. Wasn't that also the case in Vietnam, they asked?

Mai remembered negotiating top-dollar rates when she was a prostitute, but her price didn't include these costs. She had never paid taxes and doubted most small businesses in Saigon did. Money changed hands differently in Vietnam, she said. "Overhead," as the Chapmans called it, was a new concept. The Chapmans didn't pursue the matter.

She and Chị Liên planned a festive grand-opening party during Tết 1976. Mai and Đêm Nguyệt distributed flyers all over the neighborhood as far east as Lake Michigan and as far west as Ashland Avenue. Mai cooked spring rolls and *bánh xèo*, a Vietnamese crepe. Chị Liên brought cookies and cake. They agreed to hold a raffle for five free manicures.

The crowd overflowed the shop. It seemed as if everyone in the Chicago Vietnamese community, which was expanding daily, came to the opening of the Lotus Nail Salon. Mai scribbled down appointments all afternoon; Chị Liên and the Major acted like Asian royalty, sauntering around the room and nodding graciously. Mai didn't mind; she had created it. She knew it would succeed.

After a few weeks, word spread and the salon grew busy from the time it opened at ten AM til it closed at six PM. Mai was the only staff on hand. The Major came in two or three afternoons a week to go over the books, he claimed, although when Mai saw him, he was usually behind a desk looking off into space, hands clasped behind his head. Chị Liên hardly came in at all.

Mai would walk Đêm Nguyệt to school, then get herself ready for work. She needed to be well groomed, her nails looking perfect, so that her clients were confident in her ability. She'd work all day, then temporarily close the salon while she picked him up and brought him back with her. Many times her clients brought their children, too, and they would play in the back of the shop. That gave Mai an idea to propose to Chị Liên at some point. At the end of the day, the Major would total up their receivables and take out some for overhead. Mai would get forty percent of what was left. She loved getting money every day.

Within a month, they had to hire a second manicurist. There were more than twenty applicants, most of them Vietnamese, because the girls only needed to learn a few phrases in English to get by. Most of their customers were Asian anyway. She chose a sweet young girl named Kim Hoa, after Hoa gave Mai a manicure and Mai was sure she knew what to do.

Đêm Nguyệt settled into school, just as Irene Chapman had promised, and learned English at an astonishing rate. He made friends easily, both Asian and American. Mai learned about Cub Scouts, sleepovers, birthday parties, and carpools. All of it took money. She was making it, but just barely, and was grateful that her rent was subsidized by Catholic Charities for the first year.

Mai thought back to the years of war, with its death, chaos, and uncertainty. She recalled the miserable years when she had nothing to sell but her body. She no longer recognized the young girl from a Mekong village who thought the world owed her its best. She wasn't the same person. She thought, too, about Anh Vinh, who had saved her from whoring. And she thought about Sandy. He was the primary reason she'd lobbied to come to Chicago. The first man to whom she'd given herself completely. And now the Buddha was blessing her. It was time for Sandy to meet his son.

CHAPTER 80

MAI

According to the Chicago telephone directory, Sandy still lived in Rogers Park. At least Mai was pretty sure: his middle name was Frederick, and there was only one A. F. Bowden listed. She wrote down the address and asked Hoa to substitute for her the following Monday. It was a mild February day, but she bundled up and made sure Đêm Nguyệt was wearing a hat, scarf, and gloves. Đêm Nguyệt had started to call himself "Witt," an approximate pronunciation of his Vietnamese name. When Mai balked, he said it made him feel American.

"All the kids have nicknames," he said.

"But you were named for the American moon landing. You were born when the first man walked on the moon. It is an important, a historical name."

Đêm Nguyệt scowled. "I don't care. I want to be Witt."

He was right, one of her clients at the nail salon said. "Back in Vietnam, we showed our affection by giving them carefully chosen names, but here they shorten those names to something that's easy."

In some ways he reminded Mai of herself. Only six years old, but he already knew what he wanted. She shrugged and said okay. In a way she was behaving like her mother, who raised Mai to think she could have it all. Her mother was wrong, but her intentions were loving. Mai wasn't sure she wanted Đêm Nguyệt to think the same way, but what else could a parent do? He would learn, like she did, that the world was not that generous; with luck his spirit would not break, as hers almost had.

~

Now they took the el then walked a few blocks to West Morse Street. Mai found 1156 across the street. It was one of several narrow redbrick rowhouses with one shared wall between them. Evergreen bushes flanked the edge of a tiny yard. A concrete path led to a stoop with three steps up to the front door. This was the house Mai might have lived in with Sandy, she thought. Regret tugged at her.

She took a breath, squeezed Đêm Nguyệt's hand, and was about to cross the street when the door opened and a little girl and boy scampered out. They both looked younger than Đêm Nguyệt, the girl four, the boy maybe five. Like Witt, the boy wore glasses. He had the same color hair as Sandy. The same pointed chin. A woman, blond and petite, followed them. The little girl had her coloring. The woman was walking a dog of some kind.

They turned right and walked down the street. Mai shaded her eyes and spotted a playground on the next block with swings, a slide, and small children playing on the equipment.

Witt pulled on her arm. "Can I play with them?" He pointed. "On the playground?"

Mai deliberated. She could take Witt to the playground. She could tell the other mothers she had just moved into the neighborhood. She could even chat with the children's caretaker. Was this woman his wife? A babysitter? Or perhaps his sister, bringing her children to the park? She should find out. She hadn't come this far just to be thwarted by the appearance of another woman. There were a multitude of possibilities. Perhaps Sandy had moved away and this wasn't his family. Whatever the situation, Mai had the right to know. Witt was Sandy's son.

Still, Mai felt rooted to the sidewalk. The woman had to be Sandy's wife, just as the little boy was clearly Sandy's son. When had Sandy met this woman? Did he know her before he met Mai? Could he have been married or promised in marriage to her *before* he came to Vietnam? Was he lying when he claimed he wanted Mai and no one else? Was he deceiving her—and this woman too—the entire time he and Mai were a couple? Did he leave Vietnam early because of Mai's pregnancy? That would make him a liar and a coward.

Mai looked down at Đêm Nguyệt, still tugging on her arm. Đêm Nguyệt was the love of her life, the reason she had worked herself beyond exhaustion. The reason she had become a prostitute. She had to provide for him. So he would have the chance to build his own future. And she had done it. All by herself. Well, mostly.

And yet, here she was, tethering herself to the past, when this man, her first love, had deceived her. Broken her heart and moved on. She had come all this way, kept him in her heart for years, only to see that he was, in all likelihood, taken by someone else. She squeezed her eyes shut. How was that moving forward? Embracing the future? She was Đêm Nguyệt's family. Not Sandy. Anh Vinh had been more of a father to Đêm Nguyệt than Sandy. His birth father was just that. Nothing more.

Mai wrenched herself back to the present. "No," Mai said. "Not this time." She glanced down at Đêm Nguyệt. She would never have known love like this if she hadn't become pregnant. In another world, in another time, perhaps she would be grateful to Sandy. It was because of her pregnancy that she had been forced to grow up. To realize she wasn't the center of the universe. It had been a rocky journey, but it was worth it. Her son, her cherished son, had taught her how to love someone more than herself. And Sandy had made it possible.

For now, though, she took her son's hand, tucked it in hers, and brushed away a tear with her glove. "I made a mistake, Witt. These are not the right people." They took the el home.

CHAPTER 81

MAI

By spring of 1977 Mai was physically exhausted. She had worked at the Lotus Nail Salon nearly eighteen months, usually eight hours a day, with one short break to fetch Witt from school. The Major came in only once a week. When he did, it was to account for the revenue and pay Mai her wages.

But there was a problem. Mai was being shortchanged. She was not receiving forty percent of their proceeds. There was always a different excuse: the new girl's salary had to be split between Liên and Mai; Mai had ordered too many new colors of polish and they would only pay for some of them; the heat cost more last month and she should have been more careful with the temperature.

As a result Mai was feeling resentful and short-tempered. The way she'd felt about Chị Chi Tâm all those years ago when Tâm told her what to do. She hadn't put up with Chị Tâm then. Why should she put up with the Major?

There was another problem as well. When the Major wasn't complaining about the money, or she was able to talk him out of reducing her paycheck, he reminded her that she owed him gratitude. When she said she was grateful, he demanded that she show him.

The first time he said that, she was shocked but tried to laugh it off. "Major, I know you are joking with me. I will not take it personally." She hurried out of the back room. Luckily, a client had just come in. A week later, however, after handing over her paycheck, he did it again, and this time he unzipped his pants. Mai bolted from the back room, grabbed her coat, and fled.

After that Mai knew her days at the salon were numbered. Joy would be snatched from her hands yet again. But this time it was different. She had help. That evening, she called the Chapmans and invited them to tea at her home. She talked about being short-changed financially by the Major but left out his sexual advances.

"I've been thinking. I want to open my own nail salon. I would like to ask the bank for a loan. What do I need to do so they will give me the money?"

Dave was silent. Irene looked at him as if waiting for him to answer. He cleared his throat. "I think it is wonderful that you are ambitious, Mai. Not many immigrants have your moxie. But you need—"

She cut in. "What is this 'moxie'?"

Irene laughed. "Moxie is an American expression for a person, often a woman, who has a lot of energy and determination. Like you, my dear."

"This is good?"

"Very good." Dave smiled. "But you are still very young. You have no credit. It's not your fault, of course. You just came to the U.S. But the bank will think they are taking on a lot of risk with someone like you."

"I took a risk coming here to America. I will tell the bank I am not afraid to work hard. I have been doing that all my life."

"You're not even twenty-five, are you?"

"I will be soon," she lied. Some things never changed. "And because of Liên and her husband, I know how to run the business. I can manage it myself. And I know what I want to do with it. I have ideas to make it grow."

"That is all good. But you will probably need someone to cosign the loan with you. In case it doesn't work out. How much money do you want to borrow?"

"I think 2,000 dollars."

"Do you have any financials on that?"

Mai held up her hand. She went to Đêm Nguyệt's room and returned with a piece of accounting paper headed with "Income and Expenses." Items were neatly filled out under each appropriate section. "Witt helped me," she said proudly.

Dave and Irene looked it over. "We'll think it over," he said. "There may be a solution."

~

Three months later, in August, Mai's Nail Boutique opened on Lawrence Avenue, one of the main thoroughfares running through Chicago's Uptown. The Chapmans agreed to guarantee the loan, and Mai vowed they would never need to pay a penny out of their own pockets.

She set up three manicure stations with comfortable chairs for clients, and stools with trays for her employees. She hired Hoa, the manicurist who worked at Chị Liên's salon, as her second employee and advertised for one more, part-time manicurist. It was a perfect job for a woman; she could choose a morning or afternoon shift. She selected one from more than twenty applicants.

Mai also decided to apply the idea she'd first thought about for Lien's salon. The idea came to her when Đêm Nguyệt played in the shop. Instead of setting up a fourth station, she hired a babysitter part-time. For a small fee, her clients could completely relax for forty-five minutes and let the sitter take care of the children.

Women, primarily Asian, flooded the salon. And on Saturdays, a line often formed outside the door. Mai wasn't sure if it was the manicure or the babysitter that attracted them, but she didn't care. In 1978 she opened a second salon closer to their apartment on Argyle, near Kenmore, paid off the bank loan, and was out of debt. Witt was flourishing. They weren't rich, but she could afford to buy him whatever he needed. And she was now twenty-five years old.

CHAPTER 82

TÂM

The sun in Orange County was not nearly as brutal as Vietnam's, but that didn't keep Americans from complaining. Tâm was working on a farm not far from Westminster, California, a city in which thousands of Vietnamese refugees were settling. The farm was owned by a Japanese family whose grandparents had crossed the Pacific at the turn of the century. She appreciated the irony of working for one of Vietnam's fiercest enemies. Her father, who had suffered at their hands during World War II, would have been horrified. But in the United States former enemies shed their animosity. They were all Americans now, each with the goal to become rich and prosperous.

The hottest months of the American summer were about the same temperature as the coolest months in Vietnam. The farm grew strawberries, beans, broccoli, flowers, and other crops with which Tâm was familiar. The biggest problem was irrigation. With a desert climate, rain was intermittent and undependable, but farmers had huge motorized water-dispensing machines that advanced across an entire field. Tâm had heard of such machines but never seen one, and it made her realize how advanced American farming was. With the

exception of Da Lat, and some spots in the North, Vietnam still struggled with its farmland, either waterlogged or contaminated from
Agent Orange. Was this was the benefit of capitalism? The ability to
control the elements? All for a steep price, of course.

The Japanese owners were actually third-generation Americans
and paid her more than the so-called minimum wage, the lowest
amount, according to the government, that employers were required
to pay workers. It was ten times her wages in Vietnam. Then again,
everything here cost ten times more. It took time for Tâm to adjust to
the scale. Everything was bigger and bolder.

Tâm rented a room in Westminster, which was already being
called "Little Saigon" due to the crowds of South Vietnamese living
nearby and re-creating what they missed most from home. She wasn't
sure it was a good idea for her to spend time in Little Saigon, so she
kept to herself, with one exception. She signed up for a class in
English.

It was in that class, held at the Westminster Catholic Church, that
the teacher, a young, earnest university student, told them about
educational opportunities.

"There are state universities all around us, depending on what
you choose to study. There is also a two-year college, if your English
needs improvement." He reeled off half a dozen schools by name.
"And you should know that California residents are treated preferen-
tially, that is, before students from other states."

Tâm found it hard to believe. There was so much more of everything in America. So many choices. Even in education. She decided
her goals for the next year would be to buy a motorbike so she would
not be dependent on others for rides, and to apply to night school at
the closest two-year college. She registered for a library card and
quizzed herself on her English skills by checking out children's books
with pictures and simple words.

∼

In the fall of 1976, almost a year after she'd arrived in Southern California, she was invited to spend a day at Disneyland by the owners of the farm. It was an annual event for farmhands and their families, a thank-you for their hard work. Tâm had watched Disney movies at her Catholic school when she was very young, and she recalled Mickey Mouse in vivid detail. But she had no idea what to expect.

They "carpooled"—an American term she'd learned—to the nearby park and were given tickets to see whatever they wanted. Even before they entered, Tâm was stunned by the image of Mickey Mouse's face in flowers on a gentle rise near the front gate. Apparently, the flowers that formed his face changed depending on the season. Today violas for the black and alyssums for the white made a dramatic rendering. She smiled in amusement. Only in America would thousands of flowers be used to create a cartoon figure. She felt as if she'd been transported into an alternate universe.

That feeling continued as three-dimensional Snow Whites, Donald Ducks, and human-sized stuffed animals shook her hand; rocket carousels promised rides into the future; pirate ships took her back to the past; a monorail glided around the park; puppets danced. The tune of a song, "It's a Small World After All," wouldn't leave her head. Two years earlier she would have denounced the attraction as an example of capitalist excess. Indeed, it was exactly that, but watching children and adults enjoying themselves made her rethink her rigidity. The Americans had an expression one of the farmhands had taught her: "Live and let live." She could live with that.

That evening the farmhands, two of whom were Vietnamese in addition to Tâm, decided to go to a newly opened Vietnamese restaurant in Little Saigon. Tâm didn't have the chance to bow out; she was in someone else's car. Although she'd worked in a restaurant for years, she had rarely been a customer. The scents of ginger and coriander mingling with lemongrass and mint hit her as they pushed through the door. She was content to lose herself in the aromas of the past, the aromas of home. She ordered curry and vegetable rolls. She was waiting for her meal to arrive when a woman came over from another table and motioned to Tâm.

"You are Nguyễn Trang Tâm from the Mekong Delta, yes?"

Tâm stared. The girl looked familiar, but Tâm couldn't place her. A wave of fear washed over her. Friend or foe?

"My name is Hue Lanh. We were in Catholic school together. You were a year ahead of me."

Friend. Tâm let out a relieved breath. "I remember." She was safe. She tried to be affable. "When did you get here?"

"I was in what the Americans call the first wave. My brother was an officer in the army. I work in a shop down the street. You?"

"I came about a year ago. I work on a farm a few kilo—miles out of town."

"You have a sister, Mai, right?"

"Yes, but we have lost touch."

"Really? I may be able to help. In Guam, I ran into a friend we both knew. Mai was sent to a refugee camp in Pennsylvania. She wanted to settle in Chicago."

"Chicago?" Tâm was surprised.

Hue Lanh nodded. "She has a son. He is half-American."

Tâm jerked her neck back. "What? How do you know?"

"I don't recall." Hue Lanh smiled. "What about you? Will you go there and reunite with her?"

"I don't know. I am studying to be an agricultural engineer. It is a rigorous course." She shaded the truth just a bit.

"How interesting," Hue Lanh said in a voice that clearly meant the opposite. "You always were the smart one. I am so glad you made it out. The reports coming out of Vietnam are dreadful."

"That's what I hear," Tâm said. "It is very sad."

"We are the lucky ones. Well, Tâm, it was wonderful to see you. I wish you well."

"And to you."

Tâm sat down, disturbed and distracted. Her appetite vanished. Mai was here in America. How had she managed to get to the States? And why Chicago? She'd heard the weather was unbearable, with snow as deep and high as the roofs of cars. She supposed it didn't matter anyway; for her Chicago was as far away as Vietnam. She could not afford to visit. Nor she did know what sort of reception Mai would give her. Tâm had torn the fabric of the family into shreds; she doubted it could be repaired. She expected to be alone for the rest of her life.

CHAPTER 83

TÂM

Over the next year the plight of people trying to escape Vietnam, mostly by boat, worsened. The Communist regime governed with an iron fist, appropriating land, homes, and, of course, money through taxation. The situation was so dire that many Vietnamese people, particularly those in the cities, were starving. Either there was not enough food available, or people could not afford it. The Communists were vengeful as well, using minor pretexts to arrest, punish, and even execute anyone they labeled a traitor to the state. The government began eyeing hostilities, perhaps even another war, with Cambodia, where dictator Pol Pot and his Khmer Rouge allies were doing unspeakable things to its citizens.

Who were these Communists? Tâm didn't recognize the former North Vietnamese and Viet Cong. They weren't the idealistic recruits with whom she had trained. *Their* motives had been pure. Noble. They had been fighting for the common man, whose rights and welfare had been crushed by a corrupt system. But the new government sounded just as corrupt as the Thiệu government and the Diệm regime before it. The oppressed had become the oppressors.

South Vietnamese ex-officials and military officers who settled in America harbored a bitter hatred of the Viet Cong and North Vietnamese. When they encountered someone they didn't know, most would launch a series of questions until they were satisfied that person was the friend of a friend or a relative, or offered tangible proof they were indeed on the right side—the South's side—of the war.

If it could be proven that someone had lied about their wartime activities, their life would be miserable. They would be ostracized from the rest of the community. They would be unemployed or fired if they were working. Their homes would be vandalized. News of fatal accidents, sometimes assassinations, would surface. She'd believed that once Vietnamese refugees settled in the U.S., the old animosities between them would be forgotten. She'd been wrong. Even in America, it was a dangerous time for the North Vietnamese and Viet Cong.

So far Tâm had managed to conceal her wartime activities. She hailed from the Mekong Delta, and her village had been destroyed by the Americans, two facts that boosted her credibility. When she was asked what she did during the war, she stretched the truth by extending the time she worked at the Saigon Café as well as her "studies" at the Cao Đài temple in Tay Ninh. But she was always cautious, prepared to flee or hide if someone from her fighting days showed up.

It happened one night in October after her English class. Tâm was climbing down the stairs on her way out of the building when a woman, on her way up, suddenly stopped when she saw Tâm.

"Hey!" the woman said. "Don't I know you?"

Tâm stopped and stared at the woman. Her pulse started to race, and goose bumps broke out on her arms. She knew this woman. She was the one who, after Bảo was killed by the tunnel rat, told Tâm she couldn't stay with the Long Hair squad. That Tâm was an interloper, a mere concubine for Bảo, and was not to be trusted or welcomed. She was part of the reason Tâm had gone after the tunnel rat who may have killed Bảo. Her grief at Bảo's death and fury at this woman's insolence had driven her to action.

How had this woman escaped Vietnam? And what was she doing here, at the same night school Tâm attended? A flash of recognition lit the woman's face, and they exchanged hostile glances. Then the woman's expression morphed into a malicious smile, as if she had just realized she had the upper hand.

"We must talk, you and I. I know who you are."

Panic washed over Tâm. Was this woman now hunting former North Vietnamese fighters? Had she convinced the South Vietnamese in the U.S. she was worth more to them as a spy than an enemy? Was it her job to turn in people like Tâm? Perhaps the woman was even more treacherous. Perhaps she had been staking her out, waiting for the opportunity to confront Tâm.

Tâm didn't stick around for answers. She clattered down the rest of the stairs and hit the door at a run.

CHAPTER 84

MAI

At the beginning of 1979 Mai opened a third nail salon, this one in Skokie. Although it was primarily a working-class area, she hoped her lower prices would attract new clients. She expected the women to be more diverse; Skokie was slowly becoming home for immigrants from all over the world, not just Southeast Asia.

Her bet paid off. The salon was a hit from the day it opened. College girls from nearby Northwestern and the teaching college, Asians, and even black women came in for a manicure or pedicure and the free babysitting. Witt, almost ten now, worked at the salon on weekends. Mai wanted him to understand the importance of hard work. He kept the place clean and helped her with the receipts.

Mai had to laugh. She was now in Sandy's territory. She wondered if his wife might drop in at some point. The babysitting service was clearly a draw. Then Mai realized she didn't really care. She imagined herself being polite, even friendly to the woman. It wasn't her fault she had married a coward.

~

The Vietnamese neighborhood center for refugees, which had opened in Uptown a few years earlier, organized a Tết celebration for the Lunar New Year. As a successful member of the Vietnamese immigrant community, Mai was invited to give a short speech about her achievements. The night before the party, a snowstorm dumped six inches on the ground, but more than fifty people managed to slog through Chicago's frigid streets to attend.

The "Community Room"—there wasn't much more to the center yet—was decorated with paper dragons, crepe paper streamers, and paper flowers. Since 1979 was the Year of the Goat, two crepe paper goats welcomed in the New Year. A buffet spread included both Chinese and Vietnamese food, like rice noodle rolls, *bun thit nuong*, *bánh xèo*, Vietnamese crepes, spring rolls, dim sum dumplings, and more.

Mai made sure to look her best that morning and wore a brand new red brocade *áo dài* one of her clients had sewn for her. She rehearsed her talk with Witt the night before but asked him to stay close by. She was too nervous to eat anything and was afraid to have tea. What if she had to relieve herself in the middle of the talk?

They'd been there for forty long minutes before the head of the center motioned her to the front of the room. His introduction gushed with flattery; how ambitious she was, how industrious, how she had assimilated so quickly, and, of course, spoke English like a native. Mai didn't recognize herself. When he finally finished, it was her turn. She took in a long breath and spoke in Vietnamese.

"*Kính thưa quý vị.* Good afternoon." She smiled, but butterflies fluttered in her stomach, and she was sure her voice sounded as shaky as she felt. "I almost did not recognize myself from that introduction. Thank you so much. I am happy to tell you my story as we celebrate the New Year. But I must warn you: there is no magic to it. It is not a fairy tale. There are parts which I am still ashamed about.

"My journey started when the Americans massacred our tiny village in the Mekong Delta in 1968. My sister and I were the only survivors. Our father, mother, and baby brother were slaughtered, along with about thirty-five other people. My sister and I stole a sampan and paddled toward Saigon. When we stopped, my sister taught me to fish with just a hook and a line. I wasn't very good." She held up her wrist, where her scar was still visible. The audience laughed.

Mai told them about the trawler that picked them up, the tent in Cholon, the job at the Saigon Café, and her rebellious nature, which made her look for something that paid more. "I am not proud of it, but I became a bar girl at the Stardust in Saigon." There were nods from the crowd; they clearly remembered it. She went on to talk about one GI in particular, whom she fell in love with.

"I expected us to marry. To come to America and settle down. Of course, I was just one of many Vietnamese girls with the same dream." More nods from the audience. "It didn't last, of course. He left and I haven't seen him since. But the love of my life, my son, Đêm Nguyệt, was the wonderful result. He was born the night the American spacemen walked on the moon."

She then talked about her father and how the idea of hard work had been instilled in her. When it was harvesttime, she was expected to stay home from school to help. She resented it, she said, but she did it. As a young woman, there were many situations she resented as the war dragged on, but she had to accept them. She had no choice. She had to provide for her son. "How I got here was pure luck. I was fortunate to know a South Vietnamese navy captain who arranged for us to board a ship that was part of the American rescue operation. Eventually, I landed in Chicago. In short, I grew up during the American War. I learned I was not so special, but if I worked hard, tried to be kind, and picked myself up after something bad happened, I might—just might—make it. That is my story."

When Mai concluded, the burst of applause, loud and sustained, lasted at least thirty seconds. A short ceremony followed during which she was given a plaque that had her name engraved above the words "Entrepreneur of the Year." Mai was surprised and thrilled. For one of the only times in her life since working at the Stardust, she felt safe and accepted. Part of a larger whole. Was this was what "home" felt like?

She was nibbling on a plate of food from the buffet when she spotted a woman in a corner of the room. The woman was lean, taller than Mai, and her hair was cut short like a boy's. She squinted at the woman, whose plate was piled high with food, which she wolfed down like she had not eaten in days. Slowly, recognition dawned. "Chị Tâm?" she asked in a tremulous voice. "Is it really you? You are alive!"

Tâm looked up and stopped eating. Then she nodded. As she walked up to Mai, Mai noticed a limp.

"What are you doing here? How did you find me?"

"Someone from the Catholic school we attended heard you were here."

"But—but, why are you not in Vietnam with the Communists? And why are you limping?"

Tâm raised a finger to her lips. "Please, Mai. If these people know, they will arrest me, put me in prison for treason. I am limping because of a skirmish with a crazy American they called a tunnel rat."

"Is that why you never came back after you left the Saigon Café?"

A guilty look came over Tâm. She changed the subject. "I understand you have a son. I would like to meet him."

Mai smiled. "He is the light of my life."

Tâm returned it. "I loved your speech. I am so proud of you for everything you have accomplished."

Mai remembered the harsh words they had spoken when they last saw each other. "Proud of me?" She spoke in a low voice. "That does not sound like the sister who told me I would be jailed, perhaps executed, for having been a bar girl."

Tâm winced.

"Tâm, what do you want after all these years? Why are you here?"

"It is hard to know where to begin. I was—"

Mai cut her off. "Do you need money? A job?"

Tâm nodded.

"A place to live?"

She nodded again.

Mai studied Chị Tâm. Compared to some of the other Vietnamese refugees in the room, Chị Tâm had not prospered. She looked old beyond her years, her face wrinkled, her hands a mess, thin to the edge of gauntness. She wore old clothes, dirty sneakers, and a jacket totally unsuitable for a Chicago winter. She glanced around everywhere, but her gaze did not rest on anything. Whatever had happened to Chị Tâm had made her fearful, as if she was prepared to flee at any moment. A wave of compassion swept over Mai. They had switched places. Mai was now in a position to help her sister.

"You are going to need a warm winter coat," Mai said. "I have an extra. I will give it to you."

At that moment Witt came up to them with a plate of his own. Mai said, "Đêm Nguyệt, this is your auntie. My sister. The only member of my family still alive."

The boy stood stock-still. Then: "Really?" When Mai nodded, he turned to Tâm. "You are my aunt?"

"I am."

"You look like my mother." Witt grinned.

"Your mother is beautiful. I am not."

"Witt," Mai said, "give us a minute, please." When Witt left them alone, Mai said, "Tell me where you are staying."

"I just arrived on the bus. It took five days. I do not have a place to stay."

"I see," Mai said.

"You are all business, aren't you?" Tâm sounded abrasive, as if she was angry at Mai for her success. The old Tâm.

Mai eyed her sister. "Chị Tâm, I want to help, but I don't know if I can bring you back into in my life. Đêm Nguyệt has been my only family for some time. You hurt me time after time. You said terrible things. How can I trust you?"

Tâm opened her mouth, but nothing came out.

"Even if I did," Mai went on, "the risk that you might be targeted by South Vietnamese refugees if they discover your history is real." A new thought occurred to her, and she raised her index finger. "Is that why you want me to take you in? Are you depending on my protection to keep you safe? Do you believe no one will touch you if they know you are my sister?"

Tâm recoiled as if Mai had slapped her. "Those thoughts never occurred to me. I—I want to make amends. I was harsh and rigid. I thought I knew what was best for both of us. I was wrong. I was hoping we could become a family again." Tâm gazed at her sister with both longing and fear. Longing for a reconciliation. Fear that Mai wouldn't accept it.

Mai bit her lip. Chị Tâm must have suffered greatly during the war. She seemed like a different person. Still. "I don't know, Chị Tâm. It is safer here, much more than Vietnam, but the war is not over. Not here. Not yet. If anyone finds out who you really are and what you did during the war, it could be dangerous for all of us. What if something happens to Đêm Nguyệt? What if they use him to get to me so I'll give you up? I have so much at stake now. My son. I can't run the risk." She hesitated, then said softly, "I am sorry, Chị Tâm, but choices have consequences. I cannot bring you into my life right now. But I will help you get situated."

Tâm hung her head and nodded once, as if she felt shame for accepting her sister's charity.

CHAPTER 85

MAI

With three salons to manage, Mai's life was a nonstop whirlwind of work. She promoted Hoa, the girl she'd hired at the Lotus, to manager at the original salon and was training one of the other girls on Lawrence to be manager of that shop. Mai was now considered one of the most successful entrepreneurs in Chicago's Uptown, but her work ethic didn't change. She was saving to buy a house in a better school district for Witt. If not that, tuition for a Catholic high school. She was working as hard as ever.

But she was exhausted. Granted, she wasn't doing backbreaking work, but it was hard for her to get up in the mornings, hard to have enough energy to carry her through her day, hard to be present for Đêm Nguyệt in the evenings. Her menstrual cycle was also a mess; her periods had become irregular and brought intense cramps that reminded her of labor.

She made an effort to cook and eat healthy meals three times a day, figuring that would help her regain her strength. But when the time came to prepare meals, she had no appetite. Still, she put on a brave face; she'd learned all those years ago at the Stardust to be cheerful and charming no matter how she felt.

When, after two months, her strength didn't improve, she went to a Vietnamese herbalist who prescribed several treatments. Among them were black cohosh, cramp bark tea, evening primrose oil, and fennel for nausea and weakness during menstruation.

By the summer she felt better. Her appetite returned and she had more energy. She maintained contact with Tâm. She'd found her a job with a florist in Uptown and a room in a boardinghouse a few blocks away in West Rogers Park. Tâm registered for night school, and her English was improving. Mai noticed that her confidence was returning bit by bit, and Chị Tâm looked less anxious, which made some of the lines on her face less visible.

Mai met her for dinner, sometimes with Witt, sometimes just the two of them. They skipped the Vietnamese and Chinese restaurants in the area, and Chị Tâm developed a fondness for Greek food, pizza, and ice cream. Mai made sure to bring a few gently used clothes with her. One night after dinner she drove Chị Tâm back to her room.

"I have a surprise for you," she said.

Tâm inclined her head. "Yes?"

"But I'll need to come up to your room."

"Of course," Tâm replied. Mai grabbed a bag from the back seat of the car and followed Chị Tâm up two floors. She couldn't help recalling the only time Chị Tâm had come to her room, the one she shared with Hạnh when she first worked at the Stardust. "Do you remember when you came to see me in Saigon?"

Tâm blinked and shook her head. "I would like to forget that. I was—well, I was full of myself then. I thought I knew it all."

Mai giggled. "We both did."

Tâm didn't respond for a moment. Then she grinned. "Our parents' daughters. Remember how Papa always lectured us about history and politics?"

"And Mama never listened to a word of it." Mai laughed. Then her smile vanished. "I can't remember what they looked like anymore. All I remember is how they smelled. Papa like the pigs, Mama like incense."

Tâm nodded. "For some reason, though, I remember Sáng perfectly."

They were both silent for a moment. Then Mai picked up her bag and made Tâm sit on the bed. "Now, you cannot look in the mirror until I am done."

Tâm swallowed, looking worried. "What are you going to do?"

"You'll see."

Mai withdrew the cosmetics she'd bought at the drugstore. Foundation, blush, eyebrow pencil, mascara, and eye shadow. With a few quick, deft strokes, she applied the makeup to Chị Tâm's face. When she was done, she inspected her work. "Now. Stand up and go to the mirror."

When Tâm saw herself in the mirror, her eyes widened. "Who is this woman?"

"You look gorgeous," Mai said.

Tâm turned and gave her a shy smile. "Really?"

Mai smiled back. "Now I will show you how I did it."

The reports from Vietnam continued to be worrisome. More boat people were trying to escape, but they weren't making it to America. U.S. Immigration was more restrictive, and even if they did make it here, asylum was harder to prove. Illegal immigration through Canada was growing, and Vietnamese communities were forming in Europe, Australia, and Hong Kong.

A program to bring the half-American children of U.S. servicemen and Vietnamese women to the U.S. had begun in Vietnam, but Mai learned that wealthy Vietnamese were actually buying children from their mothers on the black market so they would qualify for visas. Mai thanked Buddha for helping her immigrate with Đêm Nguyệt at her side.

By the fall of 1979, Mai was feeling weak again. She doubled the quantities of the herbs she was taking, but their potency had flagged.

She kept to her schedule, but she was always exhausted, and her menstrual cramps returned. She went to the Buddhist temple and prayed, but when her health didn't improve, she grew frightened.

She was at the Rogers Park salon one Saturday when the scent of nail polish remover overpowered her. She began to get lightheaded. She stood, thinking she would go to the back office to rest. The room started to spin. Then it went black.

CHAPTER 86

MAI

When Mai woke up she was in a private room at Evanston Hospital. Witt and Hoa, the manager of the Rogers Park salon, were at her bedside.

"What happened?" she asked in a quiet voice.

"You fainted at the salon," Hoa said. "The doctor wants to do some tests."

"No tests," Mai said. "I will be fine." She tried to sit up.

Hoa shook her head. "You need to find out what is going on. Did you really think I did not notice how tired you look? All the time?"

"Yes, Mama. I want you to be well."

She turned to Đêm Nguyệt. "All right, son. Since it is you who ask, I will let them do their tests."

It didn't take long for the diagnosis. A few days later, Dr. Standish, a white-haired man with a solemn expression, came into her room. She was alone.

"You have advanced ovarian cancer, which has spread to your uterus and kidneys. "We could have done more if you'd come in sooner. Surely you had symptoms before now," he said.

Mai nodded.

"You are a smart, successful businesswoman, Mai. Why didn't you see a doctor as soon as the symptoms appeared?"

Mai wouldn't meet his eyes.

"What is it?" he asked.

Mai sighed. There was no reason not to tell him. "You know I came here from Vietnam. Back then, during the war, I had to support my son any way I could. I became a prostitute for about two years. I am sure that is how it started, and I was ashamed."

He was quiet for a moment. Then: "We don't know where cancer comes from. It is far from certain your—your activities were the cause. What about Agent Orange? Did you ever come into contact with that in Vietnam?"

"Yes. The Americans sprayed our land with it. Often."

"That is more likely to have something to do with cancer than prostitution. Plus all the years you spent in the nail salons. You know how toxic those chemicals are."

"What?" She searched his eyes, horrified.

"The toluene in nail polish is quite hazardous if you've been exposed to it over a long period. Formaldehyde, too. And acetone as well, which is in nail polish remover."

"I did not know this."

The doctor must have realized he'd said the wrong thing, because his expression changed, and his tone became gentler. "But, as I said, we don't yet know the cause of cancer."

Mai looked away again. "How much time do I have?"

"Probably six months or thereabouts. The end will not be pleasant. I suggest you come here when you know it is time. We will deal with it together."

"My people will want a *học viên y tá*, a nurse practitioner, to take care of me. And I have a sister."

"Mai, I respect your culture. And your customs. But I can assure you, when it's time, we can make you more comfortable here. You will not feel any pain." He rubbed his nose with his hand. "For your son, at least—please take my advice."

Đêm Nguyệt! When he was little he'd played at the salons. He still worked at the one in Rogers Park. Was he going to get cancer too? What had she done? Her chest tightened, and she had trouble breathing. Everything she had done, said, and accomplished since his birth was for him. Everything. If she had poisoned her son—even unintentionally—she would carry the shame and guilt of it forever. How could she make it up to him? The answer was she couldn't. And the worst part of it was that neither she nor Đêm Nguyệt would know if she had planted a time bomb in her son that would kill him before his time.

She looked back at the doctor. "I need to go home."

The next afternoon Mai took a long walk over to Lake Michigan. In the middle of autumn, the trees were dressed in their finest: blazing reds, oranges, and yellows. The deep blue sky matched Đêm Nguyệt's eyes, and the puffy white clouds looked playful. She sat on a bench with a view of the curving Chicago skyline.

The city was a good fit for her. There was a unique energy in Chicago, a sense that anyone could make it there no matter where they came from. The key was to have goals and work hard. That was Mai. Even though she had arrived with a misdirected dream of reuniting with Sandy, she never confused her feelings with ambition. She'd succeeded on her own. But what was it all worth if Đêm Nguyệt would pay the price?

Why? Why did the Buddha or God or whatever they called him give and then take it all away? She was only twenty-six. Tears streamed down her face and she railed against the unfairness of it all. Why, after all the sacrifices she'd made? The perfect son she'd brought into the world? He had so much life ahead of him. A wonderful life in a new world. If he survived. Why were the spirits so fickle?

The modern-day Mai knew there was no answer. Life—and death

—was random. Look how many Vietnamese had lost their lives. How many children had died during the war. She'd been spared; she didn't know why. But she was afraid. "Dirty Rabbit" had not been powerful enough to keep her safe.

Birds swooped and soared in the distance. Behind her cars sped by on Lake Shore Drive, drivers in their own world with their own worries. No one cared about a young Vietnamese refugee now dying of cancer. But she didn't care about them either.

Eventually her thoughts turned to the practical, as usual. There was much to do. She needed to ensure that Đêm Nguyệt was in good hands. He had only asked about his birth father once. She'd told him his father was an American, and he was her gift from their newly adopted country. He would want to know more and it would be soon. He'd heard her speech at the Vietnamese Refugee Center, but she would write him a letter explaining it all. She would trust that Tâm would give it to him when the time was right.

Vinh had been more of a father to him than any man. A sad smile poked through her tears. She still thought about him. The sweetest, most loving man she had known. A caring, and, as it turned out, loyal husband trapped in a loveless marriage. She still had the emerald necklace Anh Vinh had given her back in Saigon. It was now in her safe-deposit box, and it was worth a lot of money. She would have it appraised, sell it, and use the proceeds to set up an account for Đêm Nguyệt's college education. What did they call them here? Trust funds. Combined with the sale of the salons, which she had decided to put on the market right away, those funds would give him options. If he did get sick, he could be able to afford the best care.

Also in her safe-deposit box was Freddy's purple heart, along with Joe Hunter's address in Munster, Indiana. She would send the ribbon back along with a letter telling him that she would love him to meet her son. Assuming he wanted to. What was the word the Americans used? Role model. Perhaps, if it worked out, he could be the American man Đêm Nguyệt—Joe would call him Witt, of course—looked up to.

And, of course, there was Chị Tâm. It was time to forget about risks and dangers and close ranks. They needed to be a family again. For Đêm Nguyệt's sake, if no one else. Mai dried her tears. She had to make sure the circle was complete. Somehow, somewhere, Tâm had lost her footing and, along with it, her confidence. But that was beginning to change. Mai had to make sure it continued before she died.

Chapter 87

By the time the Chicago snow fell, Mai was no longer able to work and was at home. She was weak, thin, and pale, but the doctor had prescribed strong pills that took most of the pain away. She tried to get up, at least for a few hours a day to watch the snow, but she mostly lay on her sofa in the living room. She was dozing when Đêm Nguyệt and Joe Hunter returned late one afternoon.

Joe had called her as soon as he got her letter and the Purple Heart. He told her how happy he was to hear from her. "I would love to meet Witt," he said. He no longer lived with his mother and had rented an apartment off Irving Park Road, not far from Mai's apartment. Within a week he was taking him to basketball practice after school and showing him tricks so he'd never miss a layup.

Witt went to his room to start his homework. She and Joe were alone. "You don't know how many times I waited for your call or letter," he began. "I never stopped thinking about you. I was devastated to hear your sad news." His eyes turned glassy, as if he was holding back tears. Mai sat up awkwardly and patted the seat cushion next to her.

"I wish you had called me when you arrived," he went on. "You know I wanted to, well ... I wanted—"

She leaned toward him and stroked the hair on his forehead. She gave him a sad smile. "The Buddha had another path for us. Maybe in the next world ..."

His tears spilled over, but rather than comforting him, Mai scolded him. "No, Joe. You must be strong. Witt needs you to be. I hope you will play a huge part in his life."

He wiped his eyes with the arm of his shirt. "You can bet on it. What about your sister?"

"She will be his primary guardian. But he needs a strong man to lean on."

He nodded. "I'm honored you chose me."

She took him into her arms then, and they embraced, neither of them in a hurry to break away.

A key rattled the lock, and Chị Tâm came in, her cheeks red, snowflakes on her coat. "Tell me, Mai," she said in English, "what evil spirit has cursed Chicago with this snow?"

Both Joe and Mai laughed. Tâm went into the kitchen to brew tea. Joe said he had to get home but would pick Witt up again tomorrow. Mai shot him a grateful glance. He went in to say goodbye to Witt, shrugged into his coat, and left.

"We'll have to make him a key, you know," Mai said.

"I'll do that tomorrow."

"Thanks."

Tâm brought the tea out. "How are you feeling?" She plumped some cushions so Mai could rest against them and handed her the tea.

Mai took a sip and set it down on an end table. "I am so glad you and Đêm Nguyệt are getting to know each other."

"He's a whirlwind of energy and curiosity. He has your determination."

Mai smiled. "But, Chị Tâm, you must remember he is only ten. He still needs a mother." She blinked. "Are you ready for that?"

"Does he know?"

Mai shook her head. "I haven't been able to tell him. Yet."

"He may sense something," Tâm said. "Children can feel seismic changes in their lives well before adults."

"Did we?" Mai asked. "You had all those conversations about the war with Papa. Did you feel our world was about to explode?"

Tâm raised her eyebrows. "I must have. On some level. Perhaps that's why . . ." She let her voice trail off.

Mai changed the subject. "I'd like you to teach him about flowers and trees . . . and fishing." Mai raised her wrist.

Tâm gave her a wry smile. "Better me than you."

"I never pretended to be a fisherman," Mai shot back. But she lightened the retort with a giggle. Then she grew serious. "Chị Tâm, you already know I want you to raise him when I'm gone. You are his aunt. But you will also be his legal guardian. My lawyer has drawn up the papers."

"I would be honored, Mai." Tâm paused. "But I would hate my— my situation to cause trouble for your son. It may be too risky."

"Life is full of risks. Look at me. Three months ago, who would have thought I would get sick?"

"But as you said then," Tâm said, "actions have consequences. And sometimes there are years between one and the other."

"I know what I said," Mai said. "But we—you—can't live in fear. I never did before Đêm Nguyệt was born. I was sure I could solve any problem. Overcome any obstacle. I was arrogant. Certain I would survive. Even prosper. After Đêm Nguyệt came into my life, though, I had something to lose. The stakes were higher. And I knew fear." She pulled an afghan draped over the back of the sofa close around her. "Most of it was the war. Its uncertainty, chaos, and terror. Now the war is over, and it's time to put fear behind us. Neither of us can control the future. If trouble comes, it will. But if you love Đêm Nguyệt half as much as I, you'll know the right thing to do if danger knocks on the door."

"You have grown into a brave woman, Linh Mai. I wish I had your courage. Are you sure about this?"

"You will find the courage. You are my sister. My family. Who else is there?"

"We have wasted so many years."

Mai shrugged. "You were doing what you thought was right. So was I." She cleared her throat but could not stop coughing. "I am tired. I should lie down. But there is one other matter we need to discuss."

Tâm, inclining her head, reached for a glass of water and handed it to Mai.

"I have a buyer for the nail salons. I am going to sell them."

Tâm almost dropped her glass. "What?"

"I want you to buy a flower store with the proceeds."

"How can you say that? The salons are your life."

"The doctor thinks the cancer is probably because of the poisonous chemicals at the salons. I don't want you or Đêm Nguyệt exposed to them. And you know so much about flowers."

"I—I don't know what to say."

"I will leave the flower store to Đêm Nguyệt in my will. But you will run it. When he is old enough, he can decide whether to keep it. He may not want it. In that case, it will be yours. If you expand, which I hope you will, they will provide you with a good income. But—" She coughed again. "You will need to learn how American bookkeeping works."

At that moment, Đêm Nguyệt bounded into the room. "Do you need a cough drop, Mama?" He reached into his pocket and pulled out a package of cherry-flavored lozenges. "Here."

Mai tousled his hair and took the cough drop. "Luckily I know exactly the right person to teach you."

"Teach what?" Đêm Nguyệt said.

"Will you and Joe teach Auntie Tâm about American bookkeeping? And arithmetic? How we count. Add and subtract. Multiply."

"Me? I will teach her?"

"You will. She is going to work at a flower shop soon. Is that all right with you, Chị Tâm?"

"Only if Đêm Nguyệt teaches me." She grinned at him.

Witt's chest billowed with pride. "I will. I will be the best teacher."

"I know you will," Tâm said.

"You know, Tâm," Mai cut in. "I think many women would love to buy beautiful flowers to hold in their beautiful hands."

"Perhaps," Tâm murmured. Her own flower shop. She was afraid to let herself dream of something so full of joy. She couldn't bear to be disappointed. Then again, she was in America. Free to do whatever she chose. She had her sister's example to inspire her.

Tâm looked over at Witt, who had brought a book with him. "What is your book about, Đêm Nguyệt?"

"It is a book of stories."

He gave it to Tâm, who opened it up. "It's in Vietnamese."

"Uncle Vinh gave it to me."

Tâm shot Mai an inquiring look. Mai replied with a small smile and shook her head. "Not now."

"Why not, Mama?"

"No, not you, Witt. Something else. Of course Auntie Tâm will read you a story, won't you?"

Đêm Nguyệt smiled and settled himself on the floor. Tâm opened the book.

She read. "Once there was a young, beautiful fairy who lived high in the mountains. Her name was Âu Cơ. She was very skilled in medicine and had a compassionate heart. So she traveled the world to help those who were sick."

"People like Mama . . ." Đêm Nguyệt said.

"Yes," Tâm said. "Like your mother."

"One day, a monster suddenly appeared beside her. It frightened her so much that she tried to escape by turning herself into a crane. Lạc Long Quân, the dragon king from the sea, passed by, but what he saw was a beautiful lady in danger, so he grabbed a rock and killed the monster.

"Âu Cơ turned back into a fairy and instantly fell in love with her benefactor. And he with her. Soon she laid one hundred eggs, from which hatched a hundred children.

"Soon, though, despite their love for each other, Âu Cơ wanted to live in the mountains but Lạc Long Quân yearned to be near the sea. So they separated, each taking fifty children. Âu Cơ settled in mountainous northern Vietnam, where she raised fifty young, intelligent, strong leaders, who later became Hùng kings, the fathers of Vietnam."

Đêm Nguyệt clapped his hands.

Tâm smiled. "Now, why don't you look at the pictures?" She turned to Mai, who had closed her eyes. Tâm moved her chair closer and took Mai's hand. It was dark outside, but a silver blue half-moon angled into the windows of the room, spilling a ghostly light onto Mai's face.

"Âu Cơ wanted to live in the mountains, but Lạc Long Quân yearned for the sea," Tâm whispered. "But they would love each other forever, and their children would grow up and do splendid things."

The flicker of a smile crossed Mai's face.

Tâm held her sister's hand until she fell asleep.

AUTHOR'S NOTE

While I was watching last summer's demonstrations after George Floyd's murder, a young woman waved a sign that read, "I understand that I will never understand." That young woman recognized that human circumstances vary widely and often depend on factors we cannot control. And she's right. It's virtually impossible to step into someone else's shoes, particularly when decades and centuries of history have institutionalized patterns of thought and behavior.

As storytellers, however, it's our job to imagine the effect of those circumstances and patterns on an individual. Or a family. Or a neighborhood, city, even a country. We write about the full range of human emotions, trying to illustrate how conflict, oppression, war, and abuse have marked people. We try to frame the story in a way that readers will understand and identify with. Whatever we choose to write about, we succeed only when we elicit an emotional response, a fundamental realization that no matter the time, setting, or situation, our readers "get it."

That's one of the reasons I wrote my first historical non-mystery, set during the Vietnam War or, if you're Vietnamese, the American War. Why Vietnam fifty years later? Mostly because Americans still see the war through a strictly American lens: the draft, the anti-war movement, hippies, Agent Orange, Kent State, Nixon's election, the Chicago Seven. But what about the Vietnamese people? What were the consequences of a decade of war on them? How did they deal with the loss of family members, homes, villages, their very way of life? After the Communists took control, what did they think of reeducation camps (if they remained in Vietnam) and possible execution? How did families on different sides of the conflict reunite? How do they feel about America today?

I tried to find out. I visited Vietnam. I researched the war before, during, and after. I interviewed a former North Vietnamese colonel in Hanoi and sought out former refugees and boat people in the U.S. I also worked with a Vietnamese editor to make sure the story rings true. And while I understand that I will never completely understand, the same holds true for every author who writes about another culture or time. We try to unearth and share the emotional truth of the characters' journey, no matter who they are or what their struggles.

I hope you will indulge this writer's attempt to do just that.

Glossary

Word	Pronunciation	Translation
Anh	ang - as in "rang"	Honorific term that is used for one's older brother or for men who are slightly older than they are. It is also used in romantic heterosexual relationships - the man is called Anh and the is called woman Em ("younger sibling")
áo bà ba	ow (upward pitch); ba (dropping pitch); ba (even pitch)	The literal translation of áo is "shirt"; this is a type of silk button-down shirt with long sleeves, often paired with loose silk pants
áo dài	ow (upward pitch); zai (dropping pitch)	Literal translation is "long shirt." This is a tight-fitting tunic with a slit on the sides over loose pants
ARVN	-	Army Republic Viet Nam (South Vietnamese army)
Bà	ba (dropping pitch)	Literal translation: grandma or great-aunt. This honorific term can be used to address a woman who is elderly or around the same age as one's grandmother
Bác	bach (upward pitch)	Literal translation: uncle or great-uncle/aunt or great-Aunt. This honorific term can be used for to address a person who is slightly older than one's parents.
bánh xèo	bang (upward pitch); seow (dropping pitch)	Vietnamese crepe, filled with pork, shrimp, and beansprouts.
bảo mẫu	bow (dropping pitch); moe (mid-low dropping pitch)	Nanny

bún cá	boon (upward pitch); kah (upward pitch)	A noodle soup dish that consists of vermicelli rice noodle, fish, tomato, dill, and other herbs.
Cao Đài	kow (even pitch); dai (as in dial, with a dropping pitch)	A new religious movement founded in Vietnam. It mixes ideas from other religions. Cao Đài is a syncretic, monotheistic religion officially established in the city of Tây Ninh, southern Vietnam in 1926. The religion combines Buddhism, Christianity, Taoism, Confucianism, and Islam.
Chào	chow (dropping pitch)	Greeting that is used for both "hello" and "good bye"
Cháu	chow (upward pitch)	The term for niece/nephew; something an older person might call a younger person who might be the age of their own child or grandchild.
Chị	chee (dropping pitch)	Literal translation: older sister. This honorific term can also be used to address a woman who is slightly older than you. In this novel, Mai refers to Tam as Chị Tam
Chú	choo (upward pitch)	Literal translation: uncle. This honorific term can be used to address a man who is about the age of one's father or slightly younger (but not as close in age to you as someone who might be your older brother).
Cô	a hard "c" that sounds like a combination of "go" and "koh" (even pitch)	Literal translation: aunt. It is an honorific for a woman who is about the age of one's mother or slightly younger (but not as close in age to you as someone who might be your older sister).

Con điếm	a hard "c" that sounds like a combination of "gon" and "kohn" (even pitch); deem (upward pitch)	whore
đấu tranh	dow (upward pitch); cheng (even pitch)	struggle
đồng	doh-ng (dropping pitch)	Vietnamese currency
đồng tính nữ	doh-ng (dropping pitch); ting (upward pitch); n	lesbian
Đường Trường Sơn	duh-ng (dropping pitch); choong (dropping pitch); suh-n (even pitch)	Vietnamese name for the Ho Chi Minh Trail.
Em	-	A term used to address someone a few years younger; can be used for "younger brother" or "younger sister." It is also used in romantic heterosexual relationships - the man is called Anh and the is called woman Em ("younger sibling")
giải phóng	zai (mid-low dropping pitch); fow-ng (upward pitch)	liberation
gook	-	Derogatory term used predominantly by US Americans, common during military conflicts in Korea, Phillippines, and Vietnam
khăn rằn	gan; run (dropping pitch)	A traditional checkered black and white scarf that was often worn by Viet Cong soldiers to identify themselves
ma cô	mah; go (even pitch)	Pimp

NLF	-	National Liberation Front (Southern militia, Viet Cong) - a more political part of the Viet Cong. Answered to the People's Revolution Party, overseen by the Central Office for South Vietnam under the direction of the government in Hanoi, North Vietnam.
nón lá	non (upward pitch); lah (upward pitch)	Conical straw hat. The literal translation is "leaf hat."
NVA	-	North Vietnam Army
PAVN/VPA	-	People's Army of Vietnam or Vietnamese Peoples Army. Army of Socialist Vietnam (North); during French era, they were known as the Viet Minh.
phở	fuh (mid-low dropping pitch)	beef or chicken rice noodle soup
PLAF	-	People's Liberation Armed Forces - the military part of the Viet Cong. Answered to the People's Revolution Party, overseen by the Central Office for South Vietnam under the direction of the government in Hanoi, North Vietnam.
PRG	-	Provisional Revolutionary Government. The Việt Cộng created an urban front in 1968 called the Alliance of National, Democratic, and Peace Forces. The group's manifesto called for an independent, non-aligned South Vietnam and stated that "national reunification cannot be achieved overnight." In June 1969, the alliance merged with the NLF to form a "Provisional Revolutionary Government."

Rose Silk Thread God -		A god responsible for blessing marriages.
sampan	sahm-pahn	A sampan is a relatively flat-bottomed Chinese and Malay wooden boat. Some sampans include a small shelter on board and may be used as a permanent habitation on inland waters. Sampans are generally used for transportation in coastal areas or rivers and are often used as traditional fishing boats.
Tết	tay-et (upward pitch)	Vietnamese Lunar New Year.
trà đắng	cha (downward pitch); dah-ng (upward pitch)	bitter green tea
Tự Do	tuh (downward pitch); zoah	Literal meaning: independence. During the American War, this was a street in Saigon with bars and hangouts for American GIs
Việt Cộng	-	Also known as the National Liberation Front of South Vietnam or FNL (from the French Front National de Libération), was a mass political organization in South Vietnam and Cambodia with its own army – the Liberation Army of South Vietnam (LASV) – that fought against the United States and South Vietnamese governments during the Vietnam War, eventually emerging on the winning side. Considered a branch of the VPA by the North Vietnamese; the military arm of the NLF.

BIBLIOGRAPHY

Following are some of the books I read and referenced while researching and writing *A Bend in the River*. I also read many online articles and reports.

Bowden, Mark. *Hue 1968: A Turning Point of the American War in Vietnam*. New York: Atlantic Monthly Press, 2017.

Butler, Robert Olen. *A Good Scent from a Strange Mountain*. New York: Grove Press, 1992.

Duffy, Michael. *From Chicago to Vietnam: A Memoir of War*. Tigard, OR: Inkwater Press, 2016.

Karnow, Stanley. *Vietnam: A History*. 2nd ed. New York: Penguin Books, 1997.

Nguyễn, Phan Que Mai. *The Mountains Sing*. Chapel Hill, NC: Algonquin Books, 2020.

Nguyễn, Viet Thanh. *The Sympathizer*. New York: Grove Press, 2015.

Sachs, Dana. *The House on Dream Street*. Chapel Hill, NC: Algonquin Books, 2000.

Soli, Tatjana. *The Lotus Eaters*. New York: St. Martin's Griffin, 2010.

Thi, Kim Ohuc Phan, and Ashley Wiersma. *Fire Road*. Carol Stream, IL: Tyndale House, 2017.

Vuong, Ocean. *On Earth We're Briefly Gorgeous*. New York: Penguin Press, 2019.

ACKNOWLEDGMENTS

I am exceedingly grateful to Thảo Tran, who edited this manuscript. Her input was invaluable. She corrected and supplied proper salutations and honorifics for the Vietnamese characters in the story. Furthermore, her knowledge of Vietnamese history, customs, and proper nomenclature helped me avoid errors. Any that remain are on me. She also created the glossary. I could not have published this novel without her.

My gratitude extends also to Chi Nguyen Bach, whom I met through my water aerobics instructor (one of those "small world" stories), Susan Brierton. With Susan's help, I interviewed Chi, who escaped Vietnam with her family in 1975 and eventually settled in Chicago. Mai's journey in the novel has similarities to Chi's. Michael Duffy, author of *From Chicago to Vietnam: A Memoir of War*, graciously allowed me to use a scene from his memoir. Jason Fischer, a student of Buddhism, helped ensure the references to Buddha and his teachings were accurate. Again, any remaining errors are mine alone. Thanks also to Philip Krasny, whose enthusiasm and ideas helped enormously.

My early readers included Reba Meshulam, Philip Krasny, Angela Baldree, Eric Arnall, Tim Chapman, Billie Fischer, Kent Krueger,

Cara Black, and Emily Victorson. Thank you for your feedback. You helped make this a better book.

I also want to acknowledge graphics designer Miguel Ortuno, whose cover designs always speak to me (and, hopefully, you), and Sue Trowbridge, whose interior design is professional and meticulous, as is her management of my website and other digital entities. Once again, Eileen Chetti was my copy editor and helped me avoid embarrassment with her astute editing.

Gratitude also goes to Teresa Ellet Russ, Pam Stack, and Wiley Saichek, whose support, aid, and comfort are irreplaceable.

Thank you so much for reading *A Bend In The River*. I hope you enjoyed it. If so, would you consider leaving a review on your favorite platform? Reviews are the lifeblood for an author, and we appreciate them more than you know. And if you're in a Book Club, I hope you'll consider choosing *Bend* for one of your group reads. Let me know if you do. Perhaps we could set up a Zoom event.

libbyhellmann.com

Facebook: authorLibbyFischerHellmann
Twitter: libbyhellmann
Instagram: msthrillerauthor

Made in United States
Troutdale, OR
03/08/2024

18318107R00257